PRAISE FOR JEFF NOON

"A heady psychedelic mix, packed with literary allusions, which brilliantly explores notions of self-identity, personal awareness and how we fit into our own stories."
The Guardian

"This is a beguiling introduction to a strange new world, and a trip worth taking… Rich, inventive and recommended."
Sci-Fi Now

"Style has always been Noon's strongest suit, and in creating the varied cityscapes of *A Man of Shadows*, his talent for hallucinatory imagery has found a perfect match. This book is absolutely drenched in arresting visuals."
Barnes & Noble Sci-Fi & Fantasy Blog

"By … the … creat a … story that sticks in the mind long after the novel itself is read."
British Fantasy Society

"*The Body Library* is a brilliant piece of writing that does a satisfying job of merging noir, magical realism, and a love of all things literary."
SF Revu

"Wonderful and uniquely absorbing."
Starburst

BY THE SAME AUTHOR

THE NYQUIST MYSTERIES
A Man of Shadows
The Body Library

Slow Motion Ghosts
Mappalujo (with Steve Beard)
Channel SK1N
Falling Out of Cars
Cobralingus
Needle in the Groove
Pixel Juice
Nymphomation
Automated Alice
Pollen
Vurt

JEFF NOON

CREEPING JENNY

A Nyquist Mystery

ANGRY ROBOT

ANGRY ROBOT
An imprint of Watkins Media Ltd

Unit 11, Shepperton House
89 Shepperton Road
London N1 3DF
UK

angryrobotbooks.com
twitter.com/angryrobotbooks
All Saints Day

An Angry Robot paperback original, 2020

Edited by Paul Simpson and Claire Rushbrook
Cover by Kieryn Tyler
Set in Meridien

ISBN 978 0 85766 840 0
Ebook ISBN 978 0 85766 851 6

Printed and bound in the United Kingdom by TJ International.

9 8 7 6 5 4 3 2 1

For Bridget, Paul and Harriet

A guinea for her Ladyship
Two bob for Creeping Jenny.
Mr Brown likes half a crown,
But the devil takes a penny.

18ᵀᴴ CENTURY RHYME
(MEANING UNKNOWN)

PART ONE
A BIRD IN A CAGE

FOOL'S CHARM

Nyquist wiped his mouth and pulled his coat and scarf tighter around him and tilted his trilby further down over his brow, giving himself a shadow to hide within. It wasn't enough, and so he closed his eyes, adding darkness. It still wasn't enough. He couldn't shut down all his senses. Birdsong, the constant play of the wind. The great outdoors. He felt sick. And Christ, what was that smell, some kind of animal dung? Or rotting plants, or dead flesh? He tried looking round again and felt just as faint. He needed something to focus on, one thing, and all he could choose was the hedge lining one side of the road. He stared at the twigs and the thorns and the remains of a spider's web, and he kept them all in view for as long as possible, until his heart settled.

He turned at the sound of a voice. Two other passengers had alighted from the bus and they were looking at him now. He gave them a nod and his best attempt at a smile, but they continued to gaze at him, their expressions unreadable, and then without a word they moved to the door of a roadside cottage.

Nyquist took in his surroundings. There was a signpost that pointed in three directions: up and down the country road to Lockhampton and Bligh, and across a field towards Hoxley.

And everywhere he looked, on all sides, the moors stretched away. His mind reeled. There was too much open space, too much sky. Perhaps his business would be finished quickly and he'd soon be standing here again, waiting for the bus to take him back to the train station.

Perhaps the whole thing had been a mistake. Or a joke. A terrible joke.

Battered suitcase in hand, he set off across the field, following a pathway. The clouds were mottled gray and black, threatening rain. He kept his head down and walked on, hoping the village wouldn't be too far, and at last he reached a stretch of woodland. He breathed a little easier here, in the shadowed interior. Fallen leaves had turned to mulch underfoot. Branches creaked, twigs rustled against each other. A lone bird chattered. It sounded like a tiny engine winding up and winding back down. The pathway merged into the undergrowth and he was soon entirely surrounded by trees. He really didn't know where he was going.

He stepped into a clearing, and he stood where he was, unmoving.

The sky was visible above the circle of trees, even cloudier now, heavier.

A moment of silence took him over. No, not quite silence. He could hear a fluttering sound. He listened closely and then peered into the knotted branches, where he spied a small white object. It was a card, a plain white card, dangling at the end of a length of thread. The thread was tied at the other end around a twig. He peered into the tangle of the trees and saw that two words were written on the card, on one side only. The words were visible and then not, as the card turned and turned in the breeze.

Broken Bone...
Broken Bone...
Broken Bone...

And now that he'd seen one card others became apparent to him, hanging from other branches of this tree, and from the branches and twigs of all the trees around. Nyquist could only imagine they had been placed here by children from the village, a game or spell of some kind. Each card held a word or phrase of its own: *Scatter Seed, Witch's Knot, Waving Hands, Aerial, Silver Shiver, Pretty Pattern, Long to Depart, Spider's Home.* Hundreds of the cards were visible. *Wormwood, Motionless, Shape of Wings...*

He moved on at random, hoping to locate the path once more, but had taken only a few steps when he heard another sound, a human sound. A single cry of anguish. He spun round, in time to see something moving, low down among the branches. Nyquist approached and a figure darted aside in a snap and clatter of twigs.

"Who's there?"

There was no answer, only the sound of the wood settling back into a slow trembling state. And then the figure announced, "I'm alone here."

Nyquist replied quickly. "So am I."

A moment passed and then the voice announced, "We can't both be alone, otherwise we wouldn't be alone."

Nyquist considered in turn: "We were alone, but now we're not."

It was enough of an answer, for now the figure stood upright and stepped forward. It was a woman of singular aspect, entirely at home in the evening shade. She had wild and ragged hair and her hands were tipped with fingernails which were long, sharp, and dirty with shreds of bark. It was impossible to tell how old she was. The woods stirred, stirred again, and there she was, standing in front of him, using the branches around her as a set of levers by which she propelled herself forward. Nyquist was fascinated. She might easily be mistaken for a creature of myth, until she came close enough to show her eyes, which were a quite startling blue, and entirely human.

"Good evening, sir. My name is Sylvia."

She was dressed in black rags and her hair was woven with twigs and stems and leaves and husks and burrs, either caught there in her travels or threaded on purpose.

"I'm guessing you're lost," she said.

"That might be the case."

The woman shuffled forward, causing the branches to groan and rasp. "You're my first guest this evening. But that's usually the case, on this particular day. I used to be a midwife, you know?"

"Is that a fact?"

Nyquist found it difficult to follow her logic.

"It is a fact." Sylvia danced from foot to foot. "But then I lost one brother to sickness, and another to the war. Only my sister remains to me."

"And this stopped you from being a midwife, because…?"

"Careful now. Please don't disturb the names."

It took him a moment to understand her warning – one of the name tags had snagged on his scarf and was being pulled away from the branch, the thread almost breaking. He stepped forward, relieving the pressure. Sylvia came to him to unhook the card from his clothing.

"It takes me a long time to make them up."

She carried a small bag slung across her shoulder. She dipped into this and pulled out another card and a wax crayon. She chose a nearby branch seemingly at random, thought for a moment and then prepared to write on the card. "*Forked Tongue*? No, *Oberon's Favorite*? No. Let me think… *The One who Talks With the Sky*? Argh, no. Too much, far too much, who do you think you are, Wordsworth?! No. Come on, Sylvia. Think, woman!"

"What are you doing?"

She looked at Nyquist sideways on. "Deciding on a name, what else?"

"You're naming the tree?"

"No, a name for the branch, of course, the branch! Every branch has a different name."

"Why?"

"Because every branch is different, why else? A unique object in the universe." Her arms spread out wide. "The tree has a name, a central name, and the trunk has a name, each visible root has a name. And each and every branch will have a name, once I've finished. And I've already made a start on the twigs, one by one. Hopefully I'll be done by springtime, and then I'll start on the leaves and the buds, one by one by one, naming each in turn. Oh, I am so looking forward to the spring!"

Nyquist started to ask for the way to the village, but Sylvia held up a hand, urging him to silence.

"Ah, I have it." Now she wrote, pressing hard with the crayon to darken the mark as much as possible. "There it is. Perfect. What do you think?" She held the card out for him to look at: *Tangled Hair*.

He nodded. "It's a good name."

"Oh, but wait, what about *Sun Pointer*? Isn't that better?"

"Maybe…"

Sylvia frowned. "Well, I've made the card out now, so I'll stick with it." She tied the thread around the branch, allowing the card to dangle down. It spun and spun and then settled. "Actually, now it's in place, I like it. *Tangled Hair.* Yes, I am pleased with that one."

They both looked on as the naming card moved in the breeze.

"Now then." She turned to Nyquist. "Where are you heading? Perhaps I can help."

"Hoxley-on-the-Hale."

"Good choice." She smiled. "Take the middle path."

Nyquist stared into the trees of the clearing.

"Can't you see it?"

"Not quite."

Sylvia danced again. "Come, I'll show you. Step lightly. And don't disturb my cards!"

He followed her through a gap between the trees and soon a clear path could be made out. He thanked Sylvia and was about to tell her his name when she stopped him with a finger to his lips

"Hush! Now just hush. I don't need to know your name."

"Why's that?"

"I have already given you a name. A new name. A proper name. Here, let me write it down for you." She wrote with her crayon on a fresh card and presented it to him, face-down. "Don't look at it now. Later, later, give it one hour to act upon itself, and upon your person. And then gaze at it for fully ten minutes. Go on, hide it away, put it in your pocket. Here, let me." She slipped the card into an inside pocket of his overcoat.

Nyquist went on his way. The branches waved their tags at him: *Perfect Perch, Twig For Sale, Lady Anna's Fan, Not Quite an Oak, Billy Splinters, Birds Come Hither*. Nyquist recited each name to himself, whispering: the poem of the woods.

Soon he came to a stile in a fence, with open land beyond. Night was slowly falling. He climbed over. A field sloped down into a valley and for a good few moments he stood where he was, staring into the dim air. A carrier pigeon was sitting on a fence post nearby, a tiny metal tube attached to its leg.

The distant *crack* of a shotgun sent the bird flapping away.

The gun sounded another two times. Far off, muffled. In the city the noise would make him duck for cover, but here it was probably hunters taking advantage of the last of the light, some poor hare or rabbit or grouse their target. Country life. Blood and guts and tooth and claw. Nyquist swore to himself. This wasn't his kind of place, not at all. He was a child of the city, of narrow streets and neon signs and people who came alive at night, or in the fierce heat of day, stalkers, hawkers, crooks and hookers, crazy-eyed teenagers scrawling their names on the walls, the fierce hustle and bustle of life pressed up close. And specimens like himself – investigators, seekers after clues, grubbing around in the dark in hope of a sparkle. Still, there was no choice in the matter. He had to see this through.

Below, cradled in the vale, lay the village of Hoxley.

The first drops of rain fell as he picked up his case and set off down the slope.

THE BATTLE OF THE TEACUP

It was a tiny place. A high street, a dozen or so houses on each side, a pub and a corner shop, a few other streets and lanes leading off the first but all in one direction only, and that was about it. A church at one end, a school at the other. Two street lamps. Nyquist stood at the head of the road, under one of the lamps, and he took an envelope from his suitcase. He drew out a set of photographs, and found one depicting the street. The edges of the image were faded and details were lost here and there, blurred over, but yes, it was the same location. In fact, the photograph had been taken from somewhere near this exact spot. And he was sure then, for the first time, that he had come to the right place: Hoxley-on-the-Hale.

He was nervous. What would he find here?

The rain had come and gone: a short but violent downpour, enough to soak him through and to drive people indoors. The street was deserted. He walked along, passing the shop and the pub, both closed, and the expanse of a village green with a circular pond and an oak tree that looked as old as the village itself. A maypole stood at the center of the green, its revelries long passed. The clock on the church tower crept towards six The cold set in deep and his breath silvered the air.

He crossed over a stone bridge. The waters of the river Hale passed beneath, and the church and its graveyard waited for him on the other side. He walked around the building, left to right. It was a small church. The tombstones were laid out without pattern, many of them cracked or fallen over, pushed up by the roots of trees. The newest addition seemed to be *Gladys Coombes*. She'd died in the spring of this year, aged 38. A fresh bunch of flowers lay at her graveside. The doors to the church were locked. Beyond the church the woods took up again; no more houses. He walked back over the bridge onto the high street. The pub was called The Swan With Two Necks. It would probably open up soon and he could see if they had a room available. And a drink. He sat down on a bench. He was tired and dirty, having traveled all day to get here. What could he do next? Perhaps one of the customers in the pub would help him? Yes, that was it, he'd ask everyone about the person he had to find. But then he thought again: would such a move be wise? Maybe it was best to play it tight.

Across the way a light came on in the downstairs room of a house.

Nyquist examined the photographs by the glow of the street lamp. Each was dark in places, or spotted with white dots, or blurred.

A village street.

A church.

A corner shop.

A field with a tower visible in the distance.

Two people standing outside a house. Male, female. Talking to each other, their faces turned from the camera.

Another man, older, mid-fifties. The face as subject matter:

a portrait of sorts. But his features were slightly distorted in parts, smeared across the surface.

Six images, each one taken through the same damaged lens.

The church was the same church he had walked round, and the shop across the street was identical to the one in the photo. *Featherstonehaugh's Store*. The letters were squashed and tiny, in order to fit on the board.

A pair of winter moths fluttered above his head: his thoughts taking flight.

Nyquist slid the photographs back into their envelope, all except for one, the image of the couple standing outside a house. Perhaps if he found this residence, it would give him a way forward. He stood up and walked from end of the high street to the other, checking each house in turn against the one in the image, but none of them matched.

He took the first of the side streets, nearest the school. It was called Hodgepodge Lane: just six houses and then open country, the meagre light of the village waning quickly into a gray landscape. None of the houses corresponded to the one in the photograph. He moved on, exploring each side street in turn. One of them, Pyke Road, was much longer than the others, allowing the village to continue up the gentle slopes of the valley. He walked up, looking into one tiny side street after another. He was about to give up and head back down to the village center, when at last he found the cottage he was looking for. He'd already passed it once. He held the photograph up to his eye line, to match each feature and decoration in turn. The house was called *Yew Tree Cottage*. Nyquist rapped the crow's head knocker against the door.

It took a while. It took a long while. Until at last he heard someone moving around inside and a voice calling out, "Go away. No visitors today."

Nyquist rapped again, louder this time. "Hello. I need to talk to you. It's important."

Minutes passed. He was tempted to knock a third time, but then the door opened and a man peered out at him through a gap. One eye was visible.

"Yes, what do you want?"

"I'm trying to find someone."

"There's no one here to find."

"You might be able to help. I was given this address." It wasn't quite true, but Nyquist needed to act.

The visible eye blinked a few times. "Who are you?"

"Can I come in, please? It's freezing out here, and I got caught in the rain."

"Quickly then, before someone sees you!"

The door opened wider and the man grabbed Nyquist by the arm and pulled him inside, dragging him roughly into the hallway. The door closed immediately. The man's face loomed close. "What were you doing out there? You shouldn't be outside, not today." He gestured to an inner doorway. "Well then, make yourself at home. I'll be with you in a minute."

The householder walked off towards the kitchen at the back of the house, where the kettle was already whistling. Nyquist entered the living room. It was softly lit by a standard lamp, and it took him a few moments to realize he wasn't alone. A woman was sitting in an armchair, facing the radio. He nodded to her. She remained as she was, perfectly still, staring at the radio's grille with eyes that never seemed to move. But the apparatus was silent: no voices, no music.

Nyquist coughed and looked around the room, taking

in the sideboard complete with a set of decorative plates, a birdcage on a tall stand, a painting showing a dismal seascape. He went over to the fireplace and warmed his hands.

The woman sat in silence.

The clock on the mantel ticked gently.

He turned to the birdcage, peering through the bars at a blue and yellow budgerigar. He made a chirruping noise, but the bird was too busy examining itself in a small oval mirror.

He looked again at the woman: she was as still as before, staring, staring, staring.

The man who had let him in came into the room, carrying a teapot and cups on a tray. He put these down on a side table and poured Nyquist a cup of tea. Biscuits were offered. The woman in the chair was ignored. The two men sat adjacent to each other at a table and drank their tea and ate their custard creams.

Introductions were made: "We are the Bainbridges. Ian, and Hilda." He nodded to the woman in the armchair, but she didn't turn to look his way. "My wife." He said it with a heavy heart.

Nyquist gave his name in turn. Then he said, "I need your help." He knew of no other opening.

Bainbridge looked nervous and he spoke in a sudden rush, "As you might ascertain I am a man of some intelligence, but really, this is beyond my comprehension, that such a thing might happen on today of all days." He was in his forties, yet he seemed older in his speech patterns, his mannerisms, and the way he dressed: a brown jumper over a check shirt, cavalry twill trousers and polished brogues. His hair was shiny with brilliantine, a lot of it. He was healthy looking, well-bred, yet his eyes were the oldest part of him: all the pains of his life had collected here. He rubbed at them now, spreading tears on his cheeks, and he repeated: "Today of all days!"

"It's a Thursday," Nyquist said. "I don't understand."

"Not any old Thursday. It's Saint Switten's Day."

The very mention of the saint was enough to cause Bainbridge's head to bow down so low that his chin was tucked into his chest. He was mumbling a prayer, the words unheard until the final amen. The budgerigar sang sweetly in its cage.

Bainbridge looked up, a calmness on his face as he explained: "We're not supposed to go outside on Switten's Day, not until midnight."

"That's when the curfew ends?"

"It's not a curfew. It is time put aside for silent contemplation. Of course, not everyone follows this to the letter, darting from house to pub and back, thinking a few minutes here and there don't count. Or else they cover their heads with an umbrella, so the sunrays or the moonlight doesn't touch them." He tutted. "Ridiculous."

"What's the punishment?"

The man showed a set of yellowing teeth. "This is not a day for flippancy."

Nyquist was scrutinized. The table was cleared of crumbs. More tea was poured. The Queen's face smiled demurely from the curve of the cup, a souvenir of the coronation.

"Tell me about Saint Switten's Day."

"We have our traditions. Our ritual observances. This one goes back to when Switten himself walked these fields around, centuries past." Bainbridge tapped on the birdcage, causing the occupant to flap its wings uselessly. "Abel Switten was punished terribly for his beliefs, stripped bare and staked out in the dirt." He made a blessing, his hands descending from brow to stomach, tapping at five points in between in a serpentine curve. "We are beholden to our benefactors."

Nyquist felt the day was getting the better of him. He said, "I've been traveling by train since eight this morning. I haven't eaten, not properly. And then a long wait for a bus, and a ride across country. Another hour of that. And then I had to walk through the fields, through a wood! A goddamn wood! In the rain."

Bainbridge shook his head in wonder.

Nyquist cursed. "I've never stood in a field before, not one so large."

"Never?"

"The sky hurts me."

The budgerigar started pecking at the bars of its cage repeatedly, making a racket. Mr Bainbridge tried to calm the bird, rubbing fingers and thumb together and speaking softly: "Here, Bertie. Here, Bertie, Bertie." And so on. It had a suitable effect and the creature was quiet once more.

Nyquist placed the photograph of the house on the table. Bainbridge looked surprised. "That is my house. Yew Tree Cottage. Why do you have a picture of my house?"

"And this is you?" Nyquist tapped at one of the two people depicted. "It looks like you. And the other person looks very like your wife."

Bainbridge picked up the photograph and studied it more closely.

"I'm sorry, Mr Nyquist. I'm afraid I don't understand what you're asking–"

The radio crackled suddenly. Hilda Bainbridge bent forward slightly in response to the single burst of static.

Her husband held his breath.

Nyquist looked from one person to the other, expecting a deeper reaction or a speech. But none came.

The budgerigar sang the same few notes over and over, like a broken recording.

Nyquist decided to tell the truth. He took the other five photographs from the envelope and laid them out on the tablecloth so that each image was visible.

"I received these in the post a few days ago. There was no accompanying letter. So I don't know who sent them. Or why." He paused. "But I intend to find out."

Bainbridge looked at the photographs without speaking.

Nyquist carried on: "All of them show scenes from this village. Look." He showed the postmark on the envelope: "Hoxley. There are a number of villages called that, so I had to do a little detective work. The name of the church, and the shop, and this delivery van, here." He pointed to the photograph of the high street, to a parked van. "*Sutton's*. A bakers. You can make out the address painted on the side. I needed a magnifying glass to read it."

"The Suttons are well known around these parts," Mr Bainbridge said. He pointed out the brand name on the one remaining custard cream. "They're a local firm."

"Exactly. A *local* firm." Nyquist's eye passed over each photograph. "So I did a bit of digging, and I put it all together."

"I'm impressed."

"It's my job. How I make my living."

Bainbridge looked at him in a new way. "You're a police officer?"

"A private investigator."

"I see. So, this a case you're working on, for a client?"

Nyquist took a moment to answer. "This is for me. Entirely for me."

Bainbridge turned his attention to another image, the one showing the tower in a field. He said, "I've never seen this building before. I don't think it's from around here."

"It's not very clear in the shot."

"Still, I don't recognize it."

Nyquist turned one of the photographs over. "What about this? The photographer's mark. It's on all six pictures." It was small pale blue-inked rectangle, somewhat faded, the stamp damaged. "But I can't see the name properly. Nor the address."

Bainbridge squinted. "No. It's too faint."

"There aren't any photographers in the village, professional ones, I mean?"

"Oh, maybe, yes, but I don't believe they live here anymore. I think they left the village a little while ago."

"What were they called?"

"I really can't remember. I don't like having my photograph taken, neither does Hilda. We're very private people."

"But somebody took this picture of you and your wife."

Bainbridge looked puzzled. "As you can see, it was taken without our knowledge. Why would anyone do that? It scares me, to think of it."

"You've no idea?"

"Hilda and I, we lead ordinary lives. It sounds ridiculous to say it, but there is nothing to *spy* upon. Nothing at all."

There was an awkward moment. Neither man spoke. Nyquist glanced at the clock on the mantel: ten past seven.

"What I don't understand," Bainbridge said, "is why you've come all this way? I mean to say, why is this so important to you?"

Nyquist gathered up the photographs until only one was left on the table, the portrait of the middle-aged man.

"Tell me, do you know this person?"

Bainbridge glanced at the image and shook his head. "No."

"Take a closer look."

"I've told you. I don't know him."

There was a noise from the corner of the room and Nyquist looked that way, hoping the woman was alert now, that she might have something to offer. But she was sitting there as before, gazing intently at the now silent radio set. Perhaps her eyes moved slightly, perhaps they flickered?

Bainbridge picked up the photograph. "I can see a family resemblance."

"Yes. It's my father."

Nyquist could feel his heart being wound up tight, a fragile half-broken machine. "I haven't seen him since I was a child. A boy. Twenty-four years have passed. I thought he was dead. And now…" He looked at the photograph. "And now this."

Ian Bainbridge stared at his guest. This stranger, a wanderer, someone who didn't know the rules, a lost soul. He said, "I swear. I swear on Saint Switten's unmarked grave, in all my years I have never seen this man."

Nyquist frowned. He gazed at his father's face. Then he swallowed the last gulp of tea and said, "There's something in my cup."

"There is?"

"Christ. It's moving about."

Bainbridge was puzzled. "You know my mother used to read the shapes in tea leaves. She could view a person's future through them."

Nyquist was irritated. "What would she make of this?"

Bainbridge looked into the offered receptacle. "I cannot say." But his eyes widened, as Nyquist reached into the cup and made to pull out the worm or insect or whatever it was. The creature's squirming body stretched out, one end of it still clinging to the cup's interior.

"What the hell are you feeding me?"

"I'm really sorry about this," Bainbridge answered. "I don't know what to say."

The worm or whatever it was, was still clinging on, lengthening as Nyquist tried to pull it loose. He leaned forward to examine the foreign body.

"I don't think it's a worm. It's the wrong color. Unless you have green worms around here?"

"No, of course not. Green? No. Nothing like that. Just normal worms, nothing special."

"I think this is more like a plant."

"A plant? Really?"

"It's a tendril, or a piece of root." Nyquist turned the teacup this way and that under the light. He said, "But the way it moves, it's more like a living creature."

Bainbridge looked worried, terrified almost. His voice rose in pitch. "We only bring the coronation tea set out when we have guests, which is very rarely these days. And anyway, I keep a clean house!"

Now the two men were both looking at the strange fibrous substance held between cup, and Nyquist's forefinger and thumb. It had stretched to about a foot in length and was still clinging onto the china by its suckered end. Queen Elizabeth II continued to smile gracefully from the cup's outer surface.

"I can feel it pulling back at me," Nyquist said. He felt

lightheaded. His eyes couldn't quite stay in focus. His tongue was thick in his mouth.

"I don't feel well."

The dark green fiber was wet and sticky. Tiny burrs hooked at his skin. He gave it a sharp tug, but instead of the sucker coming loose from the cup, the tendril extended itself even further and wrapped itself around his fingers.

"It's got you!"

"The thing's digging in." It was beginning to hurt. "It's tightening." Nyquist pulled with all his strength, watching in a kind of horrified fascination as the tendril stretched out, further and further.

"I think it likes you," Bainbridge whispered. The fear had left him. Now he had a look of wonder in his eyes. "It doesn't like me. And it doesn't like Hilda. It likes you."

"Hold the cup!"

Bainbridge did so, as Nyquist backed away from the table, until he reached the limits of the creature's physical hold. There was a bureau in the corner of the room, and his free hand scrabbled around until it closed on the handle of a paper knife. Bainbridge gasped, and he whispered, "Don't hurt it." Nyquist swore at him. Or tried to. Nothing made sense, not a single thought or word. Had he been poisoned? Was he hallucinating? Only one thing mattered now. He placed the blade against the tendril and started to slice into it. It was awkward using his left hand, and the thing was resilient, but eventually the knife did its work and the tendril snapped in two. Bainbridge groaned aloud. His wife looked on, her eyes turned at last to the scene before her, a lone silent member of the audience at an absurdist drama.

One section of the tendril was still wrapped around Nyquist's fingers, but it was weaker now. He pulled it loose and threw it to the floor.

"I felt that." He could speak again, after a fashion.

"What? You're mumbling. I can't hear you."

Nyquist rubbed at the fingers of his hand. "When I cut into it, it really dug in. Holding on for dear life." He grabbed the cup from Bainbridge's hands, and examined the remaining half of the tendril. There was a green ooze seeping from the severed end.

"Is that blood?" Bainbridge asked.

"It's green. Like sap."

"So it is a plant then." Bainbridge's mood had changed again. He now looked like a man in a puzzle palace, trying to find his way out.

Nyquist put the cup down on the table. "I killed one half of it. But this section's still alive. It's like a worm that's been cut in two."

"You said it wasn't a worm."

"Well then, I don't know…" Nyquist couldn't finish the sentence. He tried to gather up the photographs, but his hands wouldn't quite do what he asked of them.

"I'm sorry I can't help you further," Bainbridge said.

"I can taste it."

"What?"

"That thing you put in my tea." He steadied himself against the table's edge.

"I didn't put–"

"It's nasty. Bitter. It tastes like…"

"Like what?"

"Like biting into a moth. Not that I've ever…"

Bainbridge grinned. "Oh, I'm sure the effects are temporary."

"I don't feel too good."

"You see, I'm just trying to…"

"Yes?"

"To live my life. And to look after Hilda, that's all."

Nyquist felt sick in his stomach. "All I need is… all is need is information… relating to my father." His body was slowing down.

"I've told you everything I know."

He looked into Bainbridge's face. "I've interviewed lots of men." He had put on an act, forcing the words out. "Tougher guys than you."

"You have?"

One last effort: "I know when someone's lying."

Hilda Bainbridge clapped her hands together, just the once.

The sound was shocking.

It set the budgerigar fluttering and chirping madly. It took Nyquist's every last ounce of strength, just to stay upright. He looked at the woman in the armchair. She was staring at him intently, without a flicker of her eyelids. The room trembled.

One shiver, a second shiver.

He placed a hand against the wall, holding on.

Like so. Concentrate. You can…

The third shiver.

The budgie started to ring its little silver bell, over and over and over.

THE MAYPOLE DANCE

He looked up and saw the moon and the overarching swathe of stars, more than he had ever seen in his life, and for a moment he felt unsteady. Drops of rain fell on his face, refreshing him. A drink from the gods. Nyquist stayed like this for a while, until he felt steady on his feet and able to move on. He walked towards Pyke Road and then turned to head back down the hill. By his watch it was past eight o'clock. The streets were deserted, not a soul was seen, no cars drove by. He remembered what Ian Bainbridge had told him, that nobody was supposed to be outside on Saint Switten's Day. He passed lighted and darkened windows, curtained and uncurtained, and on occasion he glanced in and saw families in living rooms, gathered around the radio or playing board games, or old men and women alone, or young couples sitting together on the settee. One life after another, so many doors to be knocked upon, so many questions to be asked. *Have you seen this man, he's called George, he's my father, do you know where he his?* But Nyquist walked on. He could not intrude, not yet.

Ahead he saw the village green. He was approaching it from a new direction: the oak tree, the pond, the maypole, they all seemed in a different relationship to each other. But he was relieved and he stopped to take in the scene. The public house was visible from here, its windows glowing with a welcoming light. He realized the significance of the pub's name. In the city of his birth, people used different names for the night sky constellations, and one of the most famous was the Swan With Two Necks. Surely, this was a good omen. He could remember standing in the back yard and his father pointing out the visible stars to him, and calling out the names of the patterns one by one.

The Hooded Man
Dove with Broken Wing and Olive Branch
The Music Box
Maiden in Waiting
The Swan With Two Necks

Nyquist set off across the remains of a cricket field, the white markings barely seen in the browning grass. A circle of burnt earth marked the remains of a bonfire. There were no lights on the green, and he could hardly see where to step.

The bright ribbons, wrapped around the maypole for the winter months, had come loose and were flapping in the wind.

The rain fell softly, a caress on his skin.

The water in the pond looked like black ink. The branches of the oak tree creaked and rustled and he thought again of Sylvia of the Woods and her naming tags. His hand reached into his pocket to pull out the card she had placed there: his new name. He stopped to read it but it was too dark to see clearly, and the wording seemed to be out of focus.

Nyquist placed his suitcase on the ground.

A large bird had landed on the top of the maypole, a raven. It flapped and hopped and settled, and made its raucous croak, the notes loud enough to call out the dead. In response, two nebulous shapes now danced around the pole: shadows, nothing more. Another joined them, and one more. Children. Boys and girls. One by one until six were gathered together, each clothed in moonlight. He could hear their voices singing from afar. Their bodies had traveled a great distance to get here, months, or years even, to appear as phantoms of spring in the wintertime. Hazy figures. Was he seeing things? Was this another effect of the poison in the teacup?

Nyquist stood his ground. He remembered Bainbridge's final words to him, at the door of the cottage; "Whatever you do, don't talk to anyone. If they're out tonight, they're up to no good. Or ghosts." Still, something had to be done. He spoke softly.

"Who are you?"

The shadows danced on. The ribbons slapped and hissed, winding and unwinding. A strange clattering sound was heard, perhaps an effect of the wind on the pole.

Nyquist stepped closer and tried to peer into the gloom.

The dancers circled around each other, and around the pole. Their song continued, its words audible now, or nearly so, floating in the dark air.

Sing along a Sally, O
The moon is in the valley, O

He couldn't help but be drawn forth by the sight and the sound, close enough to feel the shadow children as they passed by, close enough almost to be a dancer himself, caught in a game. And even this close he was still unsure: were the children real, or imagined? The music, the slap of the ribbons and the shrieks of joy or terror, the motion of the wind writing its own story across the surface of the pond, he saw it all, and saw nothing, and reached out, steady now, steady, and he brushed against one child, a young boy, and felt hardly anything from the contact other than a breath. Their song had more substance than their bodies.

Come to grief or come what may,
Tolly Man, Tolly Man, come out to play!

And then they were gone, in an instant. He heard only the cries of the children as they raced across the green, he saw only their white tunics in the dark night. Now all was silent, and pure. The drug from the plant in the teacup in the cottage in the village in the landscape: all these things were in his mind.

Nyquist felt dizzy. He reached out with both hands, holding the naming card aloft.

This world… this world is waiting for you…

He gathered moonlight in his eyes.

He gathered life from the pond's black depths, from whatever stirred there, and from the oak tree, the branches, the roots.

He gathered the silent song from the maypole where a night bird was perched.

He gathered time from the cricketers who played here in the summer months, the *chock* of ball on bat and the cheers of the crowd and the sound of lemonade poured into glasses, here, in the cold early days of December, 1959.

He gathered the night and the blood and the breath and the games. Nyquist felt it all, all in that place, all in that one moment collected together.

And his father's face appeared before him, dark and clouded, floating as a mist, blown hither and fro by the wind but always buffeted back to where it appeared. Almost pulled apart by a sudden gust, but returning, returning to its shapes, its form of dust and shadow.

Voices echoed across the green.

Tolly Man, O Tolly Man...

Nyquist could not move.

Come to grief or come what may...

The ghost of his father whispered, catching the last of the children's cries.

Come out to play...

The apparition was drifting away, scattering. Nyquist moved at last, only to be attacked by the raven as it flew down from its perch, circling around him, cawing, flashing its wings, mocking him, pecking at his clothes and the skin of his hands.

He batted it away. The wind cut through him.

And then he was alone once more.

The children had gone, his father also.

The maypole was silent, its ribbons tightly bound.

He shivered to his soul. The back of his hand was bleeding.

The bird sat atop the pole, as before. Something was held in its beak, a white object. Nyquist squinted into the moonlight. He could see that the raven had stolen his naming card. It brought a sadness to him. He reached up, but the pole was too high. He called out in some ridiculous fashion, making noises.

The bird flew off, over to the trees that lined the far end of the green.

A SEWING LESSON

He woke up and looked around drowsily from the bed, his eyes drawn to the only lighted object in the room, an illuminated figure on a shelf. Nyquist put his mind back together one thought at a time. He wondered how he'd slept at all, but the day's travels had exhausted him. Add to which the effects of whatever had been in that tea. He remembered how the landlord of the pub had explained to him that Saint Switten would look over him: "I always put his icon out for our guests. They find it calming." And yes, surprisingly, it did seem to have a hypnotic effect.

Nyquist sat up. He was still fully clothed, lost at the edges of himself, half blinded by memories good and bad. He rubbed at his stubbled face with his hands and thought about food, and getting clean. He looked to the shelf where the figure of the saint stood, its golden hair surmounted by a lighted halo.

He swung his feet to the carpeted floor, stumbled to the sink on the wall, and he washed his face. A leaf fell from his hair. He found his wristwatch at the bedside: ten to midnight. So, he'd only caught an hour or so of sleep, dream-laden as it was.

He could hear noises from downstairs, talking, laughter.

Customers were still here, still drinking in the bar. It must be a lock-in. He'd gone straight up to his room, after he'd checked in, not able to face anybody after the strange incident on the green. But maybe he should spruce himself up and wander downstairs, get to know the people of Hoxley. Hoxleyites? Hoxlians? Hoxans, Hoxeni, Hoxagonals? Hoxes? He could pass around the photograph of his father, see what response he got.

He turned on the light and immediately Saint Switten lost his enchantment. It was just a cheaply modelled religious icon on a dusty shelf. He lifted his suitcase onto the bed and clicked it open. Held within the layers of his one change of clothes was a handkerchief. He took this out and unfolded it carefully, one quarter at a time. Inside was another photograph, number seven in his collection. He kept it separate from the others. Of similar size and shape, its imagery held a different kind of fascination. It was overexposed, completely so – entirely white, but within its blank whiteness a slightly darker shape seemed to glow. A shimmer, a shiver. Nothing more. But the eye was always drawn to it. The back of this photograph was also a little different from the others, bearing the legend *St Leander's Day 1958*. He placed the photograph face up on the eiderdown. His fingers moved over the surface, feeling for dust particles, a lost image, hidden faults, a code, as a blind person might read a series of raised dots. The skin of his fingertips seemed to spark on each moment of contact. All the build-up of the years of friction, this against that, life against death, love against hate against loneliness against darkness, against light: he had felt it all and paid it no mind, indeed making his living from it – so much in payment for so much taken in pain, and damn the consequences. But now,

now the sparks flew and he felt the pain of loss, and he did something odd, something he never expected to do.

He prayed.

He wasn't one for prayer, not usually. He had known a number of gods in the two cities he had lived in: gods of gas lamps and neon signs, of fog and words, and magic and masks, and had learned or half learned a number of prayers and spells along the way. But tonight, he had no god other than the one found inside his heart on a dark and lonely night. He prayed that he might find his father here, in this place, this village. He prayed to the photograph, the single blank image, the missing subject. He prayed with his eyes closed and his eyes open, with silent lips, and with lips that mouthed each word.

I have journeyed north and walked through woodland and met with a strange woman and been given a new name, and nothing is happening, I am no clearer, no closer, I am lost in the woods and the pathway is dark and overgrown and twisted, and my name has been stolen, there is no light ahead...

The incantation tasted bitter in his mouth.

I thought you were dead!

He prayed for a figure to appear on the photograph's surface, as it had once before, on the day he'd received the photographs through the post. The ghost or whatever it might be had appeared to him then, a figure in the half light of the image, briefly glimpsed – a few seconds of life that quickly faded, features unknown, gender unknown. A blur. He saw it now as a kind of precursor of his journey, although he couldn't see the connection. Still, he hoped that something might be uncovered. But for now, the figure remained trapped in the image, hiding away.

Nyquist stood up and rubbed at the back of his neck. He tucked the blank photograph into the safety of the handkerchief and returned it to the suitcase.

The church clock chimed loudly twelve times.

He went to the window and peered out. People were leaving the pub, walking onto the village green. Perhaps the landlord was finally kicking them out? Yet they all seemed to be moving with a purpose. And he remembered the words of Mr Bainbridge, that Saint Switten lost his power over the village at midnight.

The green was now crowded. The lights of a pathway had been switched on, pushing the dark to the edges of the grass. He could imagine that everyone of adult age was out there, celebrating the end of a full day indoors. In fact, he saw a number of children darting in play or clinging to their parents' hands. Some of the revellers carried lanterns. They were chatting to each other, seemingly overjoyed at the end of the privation. A young couple danced.

Nyquist pulled on his jacket and overcoat. He donned his hat and his scarf. He walked downstairs, through the empty bar and out onto the street. Moonlight glimmered. Cold air. A slight mist above the village pond. The people were milling about, carrying glasses of beer and wine from the pub. Teenagers chatted at the maypole. Thursday night in the village of the true believers. He walked among them, receiving a few glances, a couple of words cast his way, but in the main they let him be. Over by the oak tree a band of revellers held court. They looked drunk, heady, composed equally of joy and desire. One of them raised a pint glass high above his head and shouted out at the top of his lungs, "Blessings upon Saint Switten! May he rest in peace for another year." Those nearby echoed the cry of liberation. Nyquist felt his heart beat faster at the sight and sound of such communion among people; he couldn't help but be caught up in the shared excitement.

"I say, old boy. Is it your innings?"

The woman's voice was deep and clear, and her breath was visible in the cold air. Her hair was puffed up and frosted with lacquer, as silvery as the backing of a mirror. She was dressed in a tweed jacket and matching skirt above woollen stocking and sturdy shoes. Her nose had been broken at some point. Her only adornment was an oval brooch with a gemstone at its center. Nyquist asked her what she meant.

"Your innings, sir?"

The woman gestured to the ground. Nyquist looked down and saw the faint marks left over from the cricket season. His feet were squarely placed in the batsman's crease, the three holes to receive the stumps still visible but now darkened, pasted with dead grass and dry soil.

"I've never played," he answered.

"Never?" She took a sip of ale from a tankard. "Dearie me, that's a disgrace. Surely at school?"

"I spent my time daydreaming."

"Is that Applied Daydreaming, or Pure?"

"Both, as needed." He offered her a cigarette.

His new companion shook her head. "I'm a pipe woman, myself. Virginia Flaked. Black cherry flavor. Trouble is, Fanshaw's doesn't stock my blend and have to send off for supplies, and it can take weeks to arrive, especially in the winter."

"Fanshaw's?"

"The corner shop."

"I thought it was called Featherstonehaugh's."

"It is. An old, old name. But these days we call it Fanshaw's."

"Why?"

"To make more time for saying other things, why else?"

"Doesn't the shopkeeper mind?"

"Oh she does, she does. After all, she's paid all that money to have the sign painted, so much per letter. Sad, really."

Nyquist looked around the green. "So what's happening here?"

"A period of respite before bedtime, now that Saint Switten has been put aside for the year, thank heavens." She studied the stranger's face, noting each scar and furrow. "You'll be Mr Nyquist, then, our man of mystery?"

"As far as I know, that's me."

"A stranger in the midst."

"So word gets around? Even when no one's allowed outside."

She laughed. "Don't worry. You'll find us an amiable lot, once you've got to know our little idiosyncrasies."

"I'm sure."

"I live at number 17, on the high street. The one over there, with the gables? Drop in anytime for a chat and a bowlful."

"I might just do that, thank you."

"I'm Doctor Higgs, by the way. Sawbones. So then, any ailments I need to know about?"

"Does existential doubt count?"

She laughed again. "So, you're a pupil of Sartre and that crowd, are you?"

"In practice, not theory."

"Now I'm intrigued. Here, hold this, will you?"

She handed him the tankard of ale and reached into her pocket, pulling out a briar pipe, ready loaded with tobacco. "Take a sip, if you like," she said, indicating the beer. Nyquist did so. He watched intrigued as the doctor lit the pipe with a Swan Vesta, first skimming the lighted match around the top of the bowl in a circular motion, to get the contents charring. Once happy with the result, she sucked mightily on the hard-bitten stem and the tobacco was soon burning fully. It glowed with a warm red light, and the smoke reached his nostrils. His eyes blinked rapidly.

"What's wrong? Have you never seen a spinster smoke a pipe before?"

"Not with such pleasure and expertise."

Now she looked at him sideways through a wreathe of tobacco smoke. "I like you, Mr Nyquist. You're a man of the world."

"I'm a man of *a* world. I lived all my life in one city alone, and never traveled beyond it until half a year ago."

"You did better than me. Hoxley born and bred. And no doubt I'll pop my clogs here."

Directly on cue, her enjoyment of the pipe was cut short by a series of harsh coughs. He could practically hear her lungs rattling.

"Are you alright, doctor?"

"Oh cruel life, that pleasure must always turn into its opposite." She emptied her pipe out onto the ground. "So, what brings you here?" Her voice was strained.

"On the lookout."

"A place to live?"

"A person."

"Well, if they're in the village, there's a good chance they'll be on the green tonight. The end of Saint Switten's Day always brings them out."

"I'll take a wander."

He handed back the tankard to Doctor Higgs, only to hear her call out, "Watch out for the Tolly Man."

"And who would that be?"

"It's a greeting, that's all." Her eyes sparkled. "A friendly greeting."

She was soon lost in the crowd. Nyquist found himself at the maypole amid a gang of teenagers. They were village kids, their faces set in a universal expression of surliness. One of them cocked her head at Nyquist and called him a name. He didn't catch it, and didn't care to, but her loyal companions laughed on cue. He moved on, nodding at Mr Bainbridge in passing. Mrs Bainbridge was with him, her hand in his, her eyes void of all feeling. The couple stood apart from the others, the occupants of a lonely circle. The landlord was also there, with his daughter Mavis, who helped out in the pub. The landlord looked like a six-foot pile of house bricks wrapped in thick skin. His daughter was dressed in black, a shadow of a girl. Both of them had an air of melancholy that Nyquist could not yet fathom.

He was suddenly whacked on the shoulder, and a loud jovial voice greeted him: "You'll be the strange cove that everyone's chatting about." The owner of the voice was a heavyset man, sporting a ruddy face above waxed platinum whiskers. "Gerald Sutton." He shook Nyquist's hand until the bones ached. "Baker. Factory owner. Major employer around these parts. You'll have eaten our produce, no doubt?" Nyquist shook his head. "What? You're staying at the Swan, aren't you? They serve Sutton's rolls and cakes every breakfast, dinner and tea. Come on, let me make the introductions." He manhandled Nyquist over to a group of people, local dignitaries, a whirl of names and faces: the vicar, the keeper of the corner shop (pronounced Fanshaw, as predicted), a former magistrate, and a local councilor who looked like he'd been drinking for most of the day. A young police constable stood close by. Sutton steered Nyquist quickly on. "The landlord you'll have met. Nigel Coombes. Poor chap. A terrible tragedy. And his girl. Terrible, terrible. Ah, now then, the pearl in my crown, here she is. My good wife, Mrs Jane Sutton. Or, my sweet Lady Jane, as I like to call her. Ha ha." His laughter shook through him, fold upon fold of flesh. "We were born too low for such titles, but my God, by all the saints, I'll raise myself up one day and spit in the eye of my so-called betters, you wait and see!"

Jane Sutton was opposite in shape and manner to her husband – svelte and tall and very well-dressed, with lovingly coiffured hair. Nyquist learned that she was the headmistress of the local school. Sutton described Nyquist to his wife as, "A man from afar, a private enquiry agent, no less." He chuckled. "Perhaps he's come all this way to investigate us." Cue laughter from the gathered circle of friends. Where Sutton got this information from, Nyquist couldn't guess: he had said nothing of his purpose on booking his room. Perhaps Ian Bainbridge had been gossiping. There were no secrets here. A series of well-mannered jokes ensued, none of which Nyquist understood, even if he suspected they were at his expense. Twice, he tried a witticism himself and failed miserably both times. He smiled dutifully. At one point he found himself alone with Jane Sutton – alone on purpose as he found out when a manicured hand slipped into the crook of his elbow and she whispered close in his ear, "I do hope you won't cause us any trouble, Mr Nyquist." He examined her face for signs to match the slight threat in her voice, but the smile was fixed, and her eyes the same, all charm and *bonhomie*.

Now the crowd thinned out as people started to make their way home. Nyquist moved among them, searching each face in turn, hoping for a glimpse of his father. He thought of shouting his father's name aloud. But he kept quiet and he moved on. No sign, no shape, no remembered expression, no one calling out to his son in the cold night air. Nyquist shivered and pulled his overcoat tighter around him. He didn't want to be left out here alone, so he made his way back to The Swan With Two Necks. The publican locked the door behind him and bid him *goodnight*. One word, no more. Nyquist remembered Gerald Sutton's remarks about a tragedy for the Coombes, but refrained from asking any questions. He climbed the stairs. He wasn't tired anymore, he was excited. He wanted to explore the village, to knock on every door. Tomorrow, he would do just that. Yes. He made a bargain with himself. He would spend a full day searching and if nothing came up by sunset then he would walk back through the woods and across the field and catch the evening bus. He'd leave this place and tear up the photographs, or better yet, burn them. A ceremony of his own.

Nyquist stopped at the door to his room.

It was slightly ajar, less than an inch. There was no lock and key, and he'd made sure to pull it to, when he'd left. Cautiously, he opened the door. Everything looked the same as it was, but he knew that his things had been searched through. His suitcase was on the bed, but in a different position. He opened it up and checked the contents. The photograph was still wrapped in the handkerchief. To be honest, he had nothing to steal, nothing of monetary value – he had traveled light and his wallet was in his jacket pocket. But a tremor went through him. He reached for the envelope and drew out the six photographs. All were present, but the one of his father had been damaged, or rather augmented.

George Nyquist's mouth had been closed up with thread, the stitches woven through the paper, from lip to lip and back again, five times, and then tied in a knot.

VILLAGE MUTE

He woke up late on Friday morning to find that someone, the landlord most probably, had been in the room early on and replaced Saint Switten. This new saint was female, her body formed from fired clay. Drapes of hair hung down on each side of her face; it looked like real hair – human or animal. A metal band was wrapped around the lower part of her face, hiding the mouth. Probably a scold's bridle, or some other instrument of torture. It was a crude figurine, far more primitive looking than yesterday's illuminated icon.

Nyquist washed himself at the sink, and then shaved. He had a feeling the people of Hoxley would appreciate a well-groomed specimen, and he needed to get them on his side. He combed a dab of brilliantine through his hair.

The Swan was quiet at this hour, with only the daughter of the house working in the bar, wiping the tables down with a cloth. She looked up at him. He found the dining room, where he was served eggs, bacon and mushrooms. It looked like he was the only guest, which is how he liked it: no forced conversations. And the food was good. He hadn't eaten since the custard creams and the poisoned tea of yesterday evening. The daughter, Mavis, also acted as waitress, and cook. It seemed that she did most of the work around the place. She brought him extra slices of toast without being asked, and left again without a word spoken. Nyquist's thoughts were elsewhere throughout the meal. All he could see was his father's face with the lips sewn together. It was a horrible image.

As the plates were being cleared away, he felt the need to ask a few questions. He said, "Mavis, someone came in my room last night, when I was out. They went through my property. Do you know anything about this?"

The girl shook her head vigorously, her face filled with worry.

Nyquist took her at her word, or lack of words. He placed the defaced photograph of his father on the tabletop, saying, "One more thing. Have you ever seen this man?"

Mavis barely glanced at the image before again shaking her head. Her hands moved in a series of elaborate gestures.

"You've never seen him, anywhere around the village? Mavis, I really need to know."

His anger upset her. She brought her hand up to her mouth, covering her lips.

"Where's your dad? Perhaps he knows more?"

There was no response. Mavis simply stood there in silence, her hand still in place over her mouth, her eyes staring coldly at him. And then, at the merest sign that he was going to ask another question, she turned and hurried into the kitchen. Nyquist was dumbfounded. He placed some coins on the table as a tip and then left the dining room. He looked into the bar, and in the office next to the stairs, but there was no sign of the publican.

Outside the sunlight was soft, the air crisp and clear, a perfect winter's day. People were going about their business, walking along the high street, popping in and out of the corner shop. Nyquist walked by the school. It was playtime, and the kids were running around madly, skipping along a hopscotch pattern chalked on the ground, dancing and leaping, pretending to shoot each other with Tommy guns, but all in deathly silence. No shrieks of joy, no howls of made-up pain. He moved on. A man and woman waved at each other from opposite sides of the street, a dog trotted by pulling an elderly man on a lead. The dog's jaws were covered in a leather muzzle. Two women bumped into each other outside the shop. They stopped to chat but Nyquist could hear no words exchanged between them. Their hands moved rapidly, forming shapes. Was it a kind of sign language?

"Excuse me."

His voice froze them, mid gesture.

"Would you mind taking a look at this picture?"

They looked at him in abject horror, there was no other way to describe it. Their eyes told a story, shared between them, a story with a bad ending. One of the women took a few halting steps away from Nyquist, while the other stood her ground. Both of them raised their hands to their faces to cover their mouths, just as Mavis had done in the dining room of the pub. He tried again to speak, but a single word from his lips caused both women to take off down the street in a hurry.

He walked along the edge of the village green. A few people were gathered around the old oak tree, two of them reaching up to touch the trunk. A Sutton's delivery van drove down the high street and turned onto a side road. As the last rumbles of the engine died away, Nyquist was suddenly aware of the intense silence that followed. He was trapped at the center of it, this great silence, as though captured inside a bubble. People nodded at him in passing, or they made hand gestures in his direction. But that was all. And it came to him then – not a single person was speaking, or even making a noise of any kind, and he started to wonder if an order had gone out, a warning not to speak to the stranger. He couldn't think why, and he started to feel uncomfortable. One word! One word was all he desired. A single sentence at the most. It would be a message from the heart of the village, to tell him that all was good, that he was welcome here.

But the silence followed him down the street.

He was about to turn onto Pyke Road when he spotted a woman waving at him from the open doorway of a house. He recognised her from last night. It was Doctor Higgs. A smiling face. She welcomed him into her house with a sweep of her hand. But she too was silent, and they stood together in her living room with the carriage clock on the mantel ticking away the seconds.

He knew better than to speak. And so he waited.

The air smelled of furniture polish and carbolic, and some other medicinal scents added on top. A portrait in oils looked down from above the fireplace, a severe-looking husband and wife dressed in dour, restrictive clothing. Perhaps the doctor's parents? A scratching sound made him turn. The doctor was scribbling on a prescription pad with a fountain pen. She tore off this top sheet and handed it to him. He read the words to himself.

Don't say anything. I won't be able to answer. Not today.

He made an open gesture with his hands, as though to say,

Why not? The doctor wrote another note.

> *Today is Saint Meade's Day. She was struck dumb in the*
> *sight of the Lord. And so we follow her example.*

He read this one while she quickly wrote another. Luckily, she was making an effort not to use a family doctor's traditional unreadable scrawl. This third note said:

> *Don't worry. It is a short day. We can all speak again at 8*
> *o'clock tonight.*

Nyquist cursed aloud, he couldn't help himself. Higgs grew agitated, and she quickly covered her mouth with her hand. He was used to the gesture by now, and he took it to mean *Be quiet,* or even *Shut up!* But what could he do? He had set this day aside for his search through the village, asking everyone he met about his father, showing them the photograph, asking questions, many questions.

But none of that could happen now.

He took the pen from Higgs and wrote a note on the back of the current message.

> *Is there a new saint every day?*

She answered:

> *Almost always. They run from one spring equinox to the next, in*
> *a random cycle. But we do have a No Saint's Day every so often.*

Higgs kept writing, using one leaf of paper after another,

handing each one to Nyquist as she finished it, and then moving onto a new sheet. Altogether it read:

I hate No Saint's Day! There are five of them scattered throughout the year, and six in a leap year. I never know what to do. It's horrible. How am I supposed to behave? You see, each saint has a different way of behaving. It gives us control, all of us in the village. We are always governed by the same limitations, a different set for each day. It's a perfect system. But when a No Saint's Day comes around, well then, confusion reigns!

Nyquist thought about this. Higgs handed him a pen of his own, and a new notepad. He responded with a simple message.

That sounds like a perfectly normal day, for me.

The doctor's response was:

Ha ha. That's a good joke. I am laughing.

Nyquist replied with a shrug:

It's true. No rules. Only here. In the mind.

He tapped at the side of his head.

Now they both looked at each other, and for a moment neither of them communicated. Nyquist broke the silence of the page by writing:

What will tomorrow's saint bring?

And the doctor answered:

I don't know.

This puzzled Nyquist.

Why not?

And the answer came back:

I told you. They're chosen at random. But it will probably be worse than today's. For you anyway. Maybe you should leave?

He wrote quickly:

I can't do that. I'm looking for my father. George Nyquist. I believe he's in the village somewhere.

He handed her the photograph and asked:

Have you seen him anywhere?

The doctor's fingers, stained from years of mixing herbs and medicines, touched gently at the black cotton threads around the lips. A conversation followed, back and forth on paper:

Sorry, no. He's not one of my patients, that's for sure. And I look after all the people who live here.

Perhaps he's never been ill?

He looks ill.
Yes. He does.

Very ill.

OK. Don't go on. There's no need.

Nyquist's words stopped on the page. There was nothing more to be said, nothing to be written out aloud in thickly etched lines, nor in a whisper of faintly brushed words.

Doctor Higgs taught him the basics of the sign language, moving his hands as she moved hers, getting him to follow the patterns. She taught him *Hello* and *Goodbye*. And *Please* and *Thank you*. His fingers were stiff and not used to the shapes, which seemed strange and ill-suited to human digits. And when he tried to sign the phrase *My name is John* he felt he was speaking to himself in a foreign language. He asked via the notepad:

Is this the same as sign language for the deaf?

Higgs shook her head.

Not really, although there are some common shapes. But most of them are unique to the village of Hoxley, and have been passed down from one generation to the next by word of mouth, and of course by word of hand.

She smiled at her own turn of phrase, and he did the same,

and his hands practiced the movements over and over until gradually they settled into a more comfortable rhythm. He made the sign for *Thank you*, and she answered with what he took to be the gesture for *You're welcome*, and she urged him to keep the pad and pen for his own use during the day.

He wrote a message on the back of the photograph of his father and then set off once more, leaving the good doctor to attend to her duties.

The village had a different feel now. He was growing accustomed to its ways, peculiar as they were, and he walked down the high street with renewed vigor. Prescription pad in hand, he was ready. He would still ask his questions, and still pursue his father – ghost or otherwise. The first person he talked to was the postman, who had finished his round and was making his way back to his van. What better person was there to ask? Nyquist was nervous as he made the welcoming hand signal, his fingers catching on each other, but the postman smiled and nodded and made the same gesture back at him. All was well. Nyquist showed him the back of the photograph with its handwritten message: *Could you help me please. I'm trying to find this man. Do you know where he is?* Then he turned the photo over, bringing his father's face uppermost. The postman stared at it and then took it from Nyquist's grip. His eyes opened a little wider, enough to give hope. But then the postman shook his head, handed back the image, and made a series of highly complex hand movements.

Nyquist was blind and deaf to their meaning. But he could see the negative in every twist of every finger. He stumbled through *Thank you, Goodbye* and moved on. He showed the photograph to everyone he met, and he let them read the message, and got the same result every time. He didn't knock on any doors, not yet, but he walked along each of the side streets in turn, looking out for people to ask. He passed Yew Tree Cottage and imagined the occupants at their play: Mr Bainbridge sitting as silent as Mrs Bainbridge, both for once joined in their afflictions. He looked at the window, where an icon sat on the inside ledge, gazing back at him: Saint Meade, with her bridled mouth and her long black hair. It made him think of the threads sewn into the photograph, sealing his father's mouth. Was Nyquist being warned off? *Keep your mouth shut, don't ask questions.*

He walked far from the village center and saw that it was a larger place than he'd first suspected. There was a community hall advertizing a lecture and slide show that evening: "Old Hoxley, Pastimes and Customs", but the door was locked for now. He climbed a road that sloped upwards, following the curve of the valley, asking his silent questions to every one he saw, receiving silent answers in return: no, no and no. There were newer houses up here, evidence of expansion, and places of work, small workshops and garages in the main. He noted a much larger building, a factory, marked with the *Sutton's Bakery* sign. The air smelled temptingly sweet around the open doors. And then on: more cottages, garden sheds, allotments, a rubbish dump. Soon he came to the upper slopes of the hill and the village's furthest limit. Beyond were only fields and more hills and the lonely, lonely sky. He sat on a bench and looked down into the valley, taking in the irregular sprawl of houses, the streets that petered out into open fields, the church spire, the bridge over the river, the Hale itself as it wound through the built-up area, vanishing for a while and then reappearing on the other side of Hoxley, flowing on. A line of electric pylons. A few remote cottages or farmhouses. Otherwise, the fields around were empty of human habitation. The hills stretched away into the distance, veiled at their summits with snow. It really was a sight to behold. Within this isolated world, the village of Hoxley looked peaceful, sleepy even, a realm of calm and repose. And yet already he had found a strange growth in a teacup, had his name stolen by a raven, danced with youthful apparitions around the maypole, and had his property damaged – and on top of all that, he'd broken the rules of not one but two saints!

He looked down at the photograph in his hands. It could almost be himself, twenty or so years from now, the future that awaited him. There was a deep sense of loss in his father's eyes: life still beat there amid the wrinkles and the thinning hair, but only just.

It was a painful mirror.

With trembling fingers, Nyquist unpicked the cotton threads, releasing his father's lips from their bindings.

A light dusting of snow started to fall, ash on the daylight.

A hare moved close by, its silvered fur shining, and its nose low to the ground as it snuffled through a patch of dry weeds. Nyquist shifted on the bench, enough to make the hare look up at him. Then it took off at speed, climbing further up the hill. Nyquist turned to follow its progress. He felt a sudden desire to follow the creature, to rise up into the clouds at the summit where sunlight washed the sky clean. He imagined himself disappearing into the haze to never be seen again, not even by himself. It was a comforting thought.

But he turned back to face the valley and he sat there a moment longer and watched as a lone figure trudged up the hill towards him. It was a man, getting on a bit, walking with the aid of a stick. Nyquist sat forward, expectant. He almost looked down at the photographic image to remind himself what his father now looked like, but that was a ridiculous thing to do: he would know, he would just know! They both would. And so he waited until the figure came close enough for his face to come into focus through the snow and the cold air.

It was just an old man. A stranger. He sat down on the bench, keeping a good distance between himself and Nyquist. For a while the two men sat there, until the snow had finished. Nyquist wiped the photograph on the sleeve of his overcoat, to brush away the melting flakes. The old man took a cigarette from a packet and set it aflame, his silver lighter trembling in reddened fingers. He smoked contentedly, staring ahead. Nyquist fought down the urge to speak. The old man took exactly six drags of the cigarette and then carefully stubbed it out on the bench and replaced it back in the packet. A poor man then, or frugal. Ex-soldier, probably. But then his hands started to talk, moving quickly for one so old, his fingerless mittens dancing up and down and then circling back on themselves. Nyquist felt he was being told a story, and a good one at that, a tale from yesteryear; yet every word was unknown to him.

The hands came to rest. The old man took the photograph from Nyquist's hand and he gazed at it intently. Then he made a signal, of writing in space. Nyquist gave him his pen. The old man wrote on the back of the image. Satisfied, he placed it on the bench, stood up, and started off down the hill, back to whichever cottage he came from, to whatever family he might have left in this world.

Nyquist picked up the photograph and read the message.

A name, an occupation, an address.
Thomas Dunne, photographer.
At last: a clue.

OLD OAK

Nyquist took a shortcut across the village green and stopped at the pond. It was half frozen over and yet goldfish were seen beneath the frosting of ice, swimming around slowly. Life going on. He was fixated on the flashes of color and so it took him a moment to realize that he was hearing voices, human voices. He was surprised by this and he looked over see a group of young people standing around the oak tree, three of them, and they were speaking to each other. He moved close and listened as they chatted of this and that, mostly of personal tales of family life gone wrong, and the latest singing sensations. They were entirely bound up in their conversation, so Nyquist could watch them easily. Two women and a man, late teens, early twenties, their fashionable outfits constructed from whatever they could find: second-hand clothes and hand-me-downs. The man was especially peacockish, with a velvet jacket over a purple shirt, and a bootlace tie. He was dressed for his own pleasure rather than the weather, and every so often a shiver ran through his body and his hands dug into his trouser pockets for warmth. And then one of the teens noticed Nyquist standing there and she turned to stare at him. The others followed suit. He took a step closer and dared to speak. The young man raised his hand to his mouth in the traditional sign for *be quiet*, but he did this in a studied, almost ironic manner. He was an expert at ironic or cynical sign language. Now the two girls raised their hands in the same manner to cover their mouths, and they looked at him with mischief in their eyes; he imagined that every hand hid a smile. But he had to know: how could they speak, when everyone else was silent? He took another step, trying out a few of the gestures the doctor had taught him. But he felt helpless, a castaway seeking a kind word from a native. The teenage girl who had first spotted him lowered her hand from her face and started to talk to him in a rapid display of signs. Her hands were a blur. She must have seen the helpless look on his face, because she came forward and took his hand in hers and pulled him gently towards the oak. She pressed his hand against the rough bark and held her own hand there as well, a few inches from his. And then she spoke aloud.

"Blade of Moon allows your presence."

Nyquist didn't have a clue what she meant.

"Blade of Moon is the root of the village, planted as a seed when Hoxley itself was born, as a ford across the river Hale."

The teenager looked at him with wide open eyes, as though expecting a response. He made none.

"You may speak," she said. "As long as your hand is held to the bark, Blade of Moon allows you words."

He spoke. Or tried to. Nothing would come easily. He was nervous.

The girl smiled. "Only by this touch may we speak on the day of Saint Meade."

Nyquist took a breath and pressed his hand more firmly against the bark of the tree. He tried again to speak. The girl helped him along. "My name is Becca. I'm helping out at the school. I don't know, maybe I'll be a teacher one day."

She had a milder accent than the older people he had met. Her hair was protected from the wind by a colorful headscarf tied in a knot under her chin, and her coat was lilac in color, with a dash of yellow at the collar and cuffs. Her lipstick glowed bright and pink. It would be easy to imagine her posing on the cover of a long-playing record: *Rock Around the Mulberry Bush*. Something like that.

He told her his name, a single word. "Nyquist."

Becca drew with a finger the shape of a letter N on the bark, saying sweetly, "Oh yes, we've heard all about you. Watch."

She moved her hand off the tree trunk and used it as part of a series of gestures.

"What does that mean?" Nyquist asked.

Becca reconnected with the bark. "Your name," she said. "John Nyquist in shapes, such and such." She made the hand movement a second time, at a much faster speed. "It was invented this morning by Miss Godley. She's one of the teachers at the school. By now everyone knows it."

He shook his head. Somewhere in the movement she had shown him, his own name existed, a tangled web.

Becca's two friends were standing to the side, sharing a cigarette. Neither of them spoke, but they were both listening to him, evidently fascinated by this newcomer. An older couple were walking by and they glanced sideways at the group around the tree and made sly, dismissive gestures with their hands.

Becca waved at them. She leaned into Nyquist and said in a low voice, "Not everyone likes us talking out loud, they think it defiles the memory of Saint Meade and the sacrifices she made for the good of the parish."

She smiled at the madness of her own words.

"But this tree is where she lost her voice, poor thing. Or rather, where she had it stolen from her by a vision of the Lord. Or the devil. Whichever story you like to hear. Anyway..." She brightened once more. "Welcome, good sir, to Hoxley-on-the-Hale. It's a bit of a dead end, I'm afraid. A blot upon this fair isle."

"Blade of Moon is the oak tree?" Nyquist asked. "You've given it a name?"

"Sylvia gave it the name. Sylvia Keepsake. She lives in a hut in Morden Wood."

Nyquist nodded. "I think I met her on my way to the village."

"Did she name you?" It was said with a smile, but Nyquist could sense the seriousness behind her question.

"She did. She wrote it on a card, but a raven swooped down and stole it from me."

The young man laughed at this. Becca looked at him, a certain look that held meaning between them, and he shut his mouth instantly and went back to staring across the green.

She turned back to Nyquist.

"You didn't see it, your new name? You don't know what it is, then?"

Nyquist shook his head. "Is it important?"

"Sylvia doesn't name many people. Usually, she sticks to trees and stones and birds and the like, not people."

"What does it mean, having a new name?"

Any answer was interrupted by the other girl, who stepped up to the tree and reached to it, placing her hand close to Nyquist's. "Becca, pet," she said. "I'm frozen. Come on, let's eat at my house. I'll play you the new June Holler single." She pushed in front of her friend and stared at Nyquist with a mocking look on her face. "This one's a bit too humdrum for my liking. Too square by half. And that's half a square too far, see, and it doesn't add up, nowhere near. Sorry, my love, no offence."

Nyquist kept his silence.

"Aye, alright then, Val," Becca said. "I'll catch you up."

She watched as her two friends walked away across the grass. And then her looks changed, darkened, and Nyquist saw the traces of fear hidden there. She spoke softly: "I'm worried about Teddy."

"The young man?"

"He's my brother." She looked down at the roots of the tree. "There's not much to do round here, and it's easy to get caught up in your own head."

Nyquist read between the lines. "What happened to him?"

"Sylvia named him."

"You mean she gave Teddy a new name?"

A quick nod. "Baptized him. The silly bugger asked her to do it. I think he must've been crazy or something, angry at life. He gets that way. Anyway, I've warned him about saying the name out loud."

"What would happen if he did?"

Her breath curled away in the cold air, and her eyes were glittery.

"Now listen to me, kind sir, no one knows about this. Not even Valerie. I think she kind of loves him, or fancies him at least, but she's a bit of a flighty girl, see, and I'm sure she'd be off like a lark in the morning, if she knew the truth."

"It's a secret?"

"Aye, that it is. And I'm only telling you because you're a stranger, and I reckon you'll be gone soon."

"I will. You'll never see me again."

"Good, good…" Her voice trailed off and her hand rose from the bark of the tree.

Nyquist thought she might be done, that their conversation was over. But he needed to know more.

"Becca, tell me. What's so bad about getting a new name?"

A single index finger touched the bark. "Whatever Sylvia Keepsake names you, that's what you become. That's the rule."

"So if she calls you a poet?'

"You become a poet. You start rhyming."

Nyquist couldn't help smiling.

"Laugh away, mister. But what if she names you a murderer, what then?"

"I'll fight the impulse."

Becca nodded. "I wish you luck." And she added, "Now listen here, I didn't believe any of this myself, not until the story of Gladys Coombes was told."

"A relative of the landlord?"

"Yes, Nigel's wife. She was a darling, she really was, but she went a bit doolally. You know, the cuckoos came calling? Anyway, Gladys received a new name from Sylvia and ever afterwards she went gadding about the village, telling everyone she met, insisting that she be known by this new name, and that her old name was never to be used, not ever, not by her husband, not even by her daughter."

"What was the name?"

"*Lady of the Lake.* But the trouble was, everyone kept forgetting this new moniker, and using her old name, her proper name, or else they did it on purpose, you know, just to save her, because after all, Gladys was the name given her by the Lord, when the vicar dabbed her little forehead with holy water."

"What happened to her?"

"I really think she would've ended up being taken away, you know, to the mental home? But she beat them to it." Becca breathed in heavily. "Her body was found at the edge of the pond. The poor dear. Earlier this year, this was. A death in springtime."

"She drowned?"

"Not quite. She cut her wrists... and then... and then she lowered her hands into the water." Becca shivered, visited by a ghost. "She held them there for minutes on end, her blood flowing away into the pond."

Nyquist remembered the gravestone he had seen in the churchyard. Now he understood the sadness in the air of the public house. Beyond that, he didn't know what to say.

They both stood in silence.

Becca looked at him, her expression suddenly tense. "I swear, I'll go loopy myself, if anything should happen to Teddy." Her voice lowered, a secret being told: "He's hurt himself before." Before Nyquist could respond she looked away, over to where her friends were waving from the edge of the green. "Look, I have to go, right? Just... Just be careful. Don't let the Tolly Man catch you."

"I won't. Whatever it means."

Becca's hand lifted from the oak and she hurried away over the grass, holding her scarf to her head against the wind's clutches.

Nyquist broke contact with the tree. He set off towards the high street. It was past noon and the street was busier than he'd seen it before. He stopped outside the corner shop. The window held a curious display of items: a crystal decanter, a piggy bank, assorted tinplate toys, a packet of Sutton's rich tea biscuits, icons of five different saints, cobwebs galore, an empty cake stand, a model of *Sputnik* made from matchsticks, a tin of Bisto gravy browning, and a single book – a study of dream interpretation by "Madame Fontaine, Gypsy fortune teller". There were many other goods on sale, all crammed up next to one another. One object of interest was a small white packet marked, "The Hair of Creeping Jenny", whatever that might be. The figurines of the saints made a bizarre collection: one had antlers growing from his temples, another the carved head of a crow on a human body. More curious still was a small bottle made of blue glass. The label bore the legend *Penny Blood*. It looked Victorian in design. The flask had a card propped up next to it: *Genuine blood of Saint Belvedere.*

Nyquist reminded himself: no speech, no speech. A bell tinkled above the door as he went inside and the two customers and the shopkeeper all looked at him as he entered, their hands frozen mid-gesture. He made his best shot at the *Hello* symbol. Despite the grubby state of the window, the shop itself was clean and well laid out. Shelving units held goods of every kind, from ironware to groceries to rolls of cloth, magazines and jars of boiled sweets. The customers and the shopkeeper – a lady of advancing years – resumed their conversation, and Nyquist could see their hands sometimes working together, thirty fingers and thumbs intermingling to construct complex ideas and sentences. Were they talking about him? Probably.

He selected a local atlas from a stand and placed it on the counter along with the exact money: one shilling. No change necessary. He was hoping to keep interaction to a minimum. He needn't have bothered, for Mrs Featherstonehaugh was in no mood to chat. The lower part of her face was bound with a roll of cotton decorated with flowers, her mouth completely hidden. She took his coins and rang up the price on the till. Nyquist gestured the hand sign for *Thank you*, hoping he hadn't said something rude by mistake. Outside he breathed clean air and was glad of it. Dust had settled on him.

He walked across the street to the pub and ordered a plate of egg and chips. Mavis nodded, a slight smile across her lips. While he waited for his meal, he opened the atlas and looked up Beadle Street in the gazetteer. This was the address the old man had written on the back of his father's photograph, the location of Mr Thomas Dunne, Photographer. He was directed to page 19, an area called Lower Hoxley. He would have to walk along the river to get there. He glanced through the other pages. The outlying areas were mainly devoid of features, just blank white space representing the fields and hills around the village, with only the occasional name denoting a ridge or crest or river crossing. Strangest of all was a symbol on one of these fields, a single red exclamation mark. Perhaps it marked a site of historic interest, or an area of danger?

Mavis returned to the room and placed his meal down in front of him. Nyquist tapped at the atlas with his pen and then inscribed a question mark next to the exclamation on the map. She looked at this with unblinking eyes and then wrote on his napkin.

Stay away.

He wrote: *Why?*

The answer was a single word.

Ghosts.

She would say no more.

PEEPER

He crossed over the bridge and walked along the bank, away from the village. The Hale widened into a pool where a flotilla of swans was swimming, perfectly content in the waters of winter. A sign advised against feeding the birds. The river ran on over a weir, and the land started to dip, following the valley floor to a slightly lower level. A small lane and a few old cottages marked the way. And then open country. A little later he saw the foundations of a new set of houses visible in the ground, next to a pile of tools and machinery covered in tarpaulin. He followed the river around a curve of land and there before him was Lower Hoxley. Only twenty minutes' walk separated the two built-up areas but he could see straight away that the lower-lying village was a different prospect than its older cousin. He imagined that most of this village had been built in the last fifty years or so. For a moment, Nyquist imagined that they might ignore the calls of the saints in this place, but no, he saw that people were using the Hoxlian sign language. Following the directions of his atlas, he came to the village's center. He turned onto Beadle Street and found house number 11. It was a large two-story building, the door marked *Closed Until Further Notice*. The painted sign above the

window read *Thomas Dunne, Photographer and Picture Framer*.
He ventured down a side alley and found a window with a
missing panel of glass. Nobody could see him. He reached in,
lifted the latch and climbed over the ledge into a kitchen. The
place stank of neglect. He walked along a corridor lined with
portraits, all depicting the same woman. She was dark haired
and fair skinned with eyes that often looked away from the
camera. Each photograph was marked with a name and date:
Agnes, February 1956; *Agnes, September 1957* and so on. A first
door led to a small living room, another to photographic
darkroom, and a third to the front of the shop: a counter, a
battered filing cabinet, a cash register with its empty drawer
open. There was nothing here of interest, so he tried the living
room, but it showed only the usual furniture and attributes
of lower middle-class life. He walked into the darkroom. Bare
walls, cupboards, metal trays on a worktop, each containing
a layer of murky liquid. A single photographic sheet floated
in one of the trays, its image completely blackened, lost
forever. A pigeon's feather and a collection of dead flies and
bugs dotted the surface of the liquid, which was a strange
color, a bluish tinge with tiny glints of silver floating within
it. Nyquist looked around the room. It was easy to imagine
voices whispering in this airless space. It was a place where
memories had been solidified, the moment captured. The
thought was clear: the photographs he'd been sent through
the post had been processed here, on this worktop. He tried
the light switch, and the room was flooded with a deep red
light. A moth was roused from slumber. It started to bat
against the bulb over and over again in an angry, compulsive
manner. Nyquist knew the feeling.

He took the staircase to a landing: a bedroom in the front, a bathroom and toilet, and a large storage room in the rear filled with empty picture frames and cardboard boxes. He looked through one of the boxes, finding a vast depository of images: bucolic family scenes, brave-faced young men dressed in uniform, woman in summer dresses and high-necked gowns, children sitting stiffly under the lights, local landscapes, the village in sepia tones. One image was marked: *Hoxley High Street, 1891*. Nearly seventy years ago. It didn't look that much different from today. He wondered if he should look inside some of the other boxes. But did he really think he'd find more pictures of his father? No. Nyquist shivered. This place was getting to him, making him uneasy.

On one side of the room a row of large objects was hidden under sheets of white linen. He uncovered the first one and saw it was a peep-show machine, the kind he'd seen in penny arcades when he was a boy. The Mutoscope. That was the official name of the device, but his father always called them "What the Butler Saw" machines, as they were meant for adult viewing only. This one advertised the wicked delights of "Lady Anna's Boudoir". Mr Dunne must have supplied images for them, or else he collected them for his own pleasure. Nyquist pulled the sheets off the other machines. Two of them offered the usual erotic titillations, but the last peep show in the line held a very different kind of promise.

Dance of the Tolly Man.

And below that a date: *St Algreave's Day 1939*.

He took a penny from his pocket and dropped it in the slot. A handle was released from the side of the machine. Nyquist placed his eyes against the viewing aperture and started to crank the handle, around and around.

It was a flickering world.

Black, white, black, white, black, white.

The cards clattered as they turned on the drum, each one holding a new image, moving on the story one frame at a time. His eyes were painted with motion.

The village green in the summer, people gathering in jerky motion, captured so many years ago, preserved and brought back to life.

A faraway song was heard, seemingly arriving from somewhere in his head.

Sing along a Sally, O
The moon is in the valley, O

The children appeared. They were dressed in white gowns, with flowers woven in their hair. They danced around the pole, the ribbons they held knotting and unknotting in elaborate patterns, back and forth, weaving in and out, in and out.

Around and around, turning, turning.

Black, white, flickerings of day and night.

Insert: a raven flying across in a slow blur of wings.

Stutter. A jump in time.

The moon suddenly overhead, waxing gibbous.

The dance continuing.

Come to grief or come what may,
Tolly Man, Tolly Man, come out to play!

A figure shambled into view, called from the depths, from the past, from the heart of the village and whatever secrets might be held there.

Insert: drops of blood, black smudges.

The Tolly Man once more, closer to the dancing circle.

Nyquist looked on, his eyes pressed tightly against the aperture, his hand turning and turning the handle as the children turned and turned again, around and around the pole, the ribbons fluttering and the Tolly Man turning, turning, turning towards the camera's view, a shambling man whose face was covered entirely in woven twigs stripped of their leaves, the mask bound together with two strands of wire, top and bottom. Flickering, flickering, gray and white and black and sepia toned. It looked monstrous, something out of a nightmare.

Insert: a spinning top.

Flecks of spittle. Scratches.

A cradle rocking.

The Tolly Man.

Closer, closer, swaying back and forth. The masked figure was staring at the camera. His face filled the screen entirely, close enough for Nyquist to see through the gaps in the twigs. He viewed the face beneath, glimpses of flesh, a mouth, a licking tongue, and those dark wet black eyes that never left his, peering from the knotted branches, from the darkness, from the gloom of that long-ago night, across the years and the days, turning, turning, around and around.

The mask touched the screen.

Thorns pressing at skin.

THE GO-BETWEEN

flicker

flicker
flicker

blank

flicker
flicker
blank
flicker

flicker

flicker
blank

Nyquist thought at first that his eyes were blinking, the room appearing to him intermittently, but even when he opened his eyes wide and kept them so, the flickering stayed on, lingering, as though the cards of the Mutoscope were still clicking past one by one inside his head, one blank image at a time. Low level after-effects.

Flicker, blank, flicker…

He was lying on the floor of the storage room. He groaned and tried to move and felt he was climbing upwards from a dream that held onto him, that wrapped around his wrists and ankles and chest, trying its best to drag him back.

He broke loose. He broke loose by banging his fist down on the bare floorboards, again and again until the skin cracked on his knuckles and the pain woke him completely from the spell, and he sat up and rubbed at his eyes and massaged his head at the temples and dragged his tongue across his teeth feeling the dirt and the dust.

Flicker, blank, blank, blank…

He got to his feet and looked around. The room was dark. Or darker than before. And when he looked out of the window, he saw that dusk had fallen. He'd been out for a long time, far too long. Hours had passed. What the hell had happened? He stared at the Tolly Man machine. It looked entirely innocent, a relic from another age.

He heard a noise from downstairs and he moved to the stairhead, peering down. All was silent. He placed a foot on the top stair. There it was again, a banging sound, louder this time. His skin prickled. Had someone else broken in? Or was it the Dunnes, returning home?

One stair, another. Listening, stepping as quietly as he could.

The noise sounded like someone trying to escape a wooden box, a tiny confined space of some kind.

Now he hurried downstairs, his fear banished by action.

The sound was continuous, coming from the rear of the building, from the kitchen.

Nyquist stopped at the open doorway and looked within.

It was a pigeon. That's all. His heart settled.

The bird was sitting on the kitchen table, casting a wary eye on Nyquist. And when he approached, it took off, flying around the room in a panic, its wings beating against the walls every so often. This was the noise he'd heard while upstairs. It suddenly flew at his head and then away, fluttering madly. For a moment it headed for the open window but then changed its mind, landing on the table once more.

Nyquist stood where he was. There was a small metal tube attached to the creature's leg. It was a carrier pigeon, like the one that had greeted him on first arriving in the valley. It might even be the same bird, for all he knew; gray mottled with brown, a ring of white around its neck. He reached out a hand and made what he hoped was a pigeon-like call. The bird shook its head and hopped away, leaving tiny claw-prints in the dust of the tabletop.

Gray feathers floated down in the dimly lit room.

Nyquist moved gently, slowly. He expected the bird to leap away again, or even to peck at him. But instead it made a surprise action, melting into his hands, surrendering, its warm body perfectly lodged in his curved palms.

A tiny heart beating, and his own pulse matching it exactly.

They both fell into calm at the same moment, and the bird allowed itself to be picked up. It made a cooing sound. Nyquist pulled the metal tube free of its leg and placed the bird back on the table. Immediately it took off and flew away through the open window.

Message delivered.

The tube was easily opened. Inside was a rolled-up piece of

paper, which, flattened out, revealed a few lines of neat italic script.

My dear Agnes. I can't stop thinking about you. Please meet me at the Mocking Gate, tomorrow morning at nine o'clock. I shall wait there for you.
   Your loving friend, Leonard.

Nyquist felt cheap, like he'd walked in on a scene of intimate lovemaking. *What the Private Eye Saw.* This whole affair was turning into a series of puzzles or riddles, but the questions were never asked correctly, which meant that the solutions could never be worked out.

He remembered that he'd left the red light on in the darkroom. He went to turn it off, and saw that the moth was still fluttering about. Its flightpath always brought it back to the lamp and then away, and back: like an obsession. But then it landed on the wall and settled and he had a chance to gaze upon its colors, its wings marked with two ovals of red, the eyes of a demon. The eyes opened and closed as the moth flexed its wings, before it took off once more. But this time it made a mistake, burning itself on the lamp. A wing sizzled, and the poor insect fell into one of the metal trays on the worktop. This was the tray that held the submerged photograph, the black image. Nyquist went over to see if he could help the moth. Something odd was happening: the silver particles in the fluid sparkled as though activated. The moth tried to stay afloat, but its wings were drenched. It was dying. But the process of development had already begun, the chemicals released from slumber. The photographic image lightened, just slightly, and then more so, the black ground fading to patches of gray, and then to areas of almost white. Slowly, slowly, one detail at a time, an image was forming. It showed a road, a house at the end of a row, and a view of open land beyond that, all a little blurred as yet. But Nyquist could not look away. He waited, hoping the image would develop further. For he could only believe that this was another photograph meant for him. He shook the tray gently with his hands, helping the process along.

There it was, clearly seen: a street sign.

EXCHANGE OF GOODS

Dovecote Lane was on the far edge of Lower Hoxley, a poor area compared to the rest of the village. Number 23 was the end terrace. It had the look of a final outpost before the moors took over from humankind. For the second time in two days, Nyquist compared a house with its image in a photograph. Everything looked the same; the red door and window frames, the overgrown garden. There was even a van parked on the open ground nearby, as there was in the image. A dog started to bark as Nyquist approached. The beast's entire body strained at the leash that held it to a post. He ignored the animal and knocked on the front door. There was no answer, so he decided to check out the rear of the property. The parked van was marked with a business name: *Sadler's Household Repairs & Removals*. The side wall of the house was pockmarked and crumbling into dust in many places, injuries from decades of wind, rain and hail. A pair of wooden buttresses had been erected against the wall to reinforce it, or to keep the house from sliding away. The dusk was heavy in the sky and the fields beyond were already dark. The wind blasted across the open land right into his face.

Demons in every gust, he could hear them.

There was a back yard with three outbuildings. One was a large shed – through the open door, Nyquist saw a workbench with tools set out, and a half-built rocking horse sitting on the floor. A number of painted wooden figures stood on the ground beyond the yard; they looked like fairground icons, or the figureheads of galleons. The other two buildings were cages. Inside each one a great number of pigeons were sitting on perches, or hopping from one resting place to another, vying for space. The air reeked of bird shit. Hundreds of cooing sounds merged into dissonance. The hunched figure of a man was standing at the open door of one of the cages. He was dressed in blue overalls and had a cloth cap pulled down low on his brow. His overalls were spotted with a mixture of paint daubs and pigeon poo: there was no way to tell which was which. The man's face wasn't yet visible. He was attending to the birds, scattering seed in the feeding trays. Some of the pigeons alighted on his shoulders. He had a workman's hands, scarred and shredded, but he stroked at the birds with a gentle touch. Some of them, Nyquist saw, had metal carrier tubes attached to their legs.

The two men looked at each other through the hexagonal mesh. Nyquist felt he was being scrutinized, as the other man's eyes moved from one feature to the next. But too much was at stake; despite the day's ruling he could no longer stay quiet. "I need to talk to you," he began. But the pigeon fancier shushed him with a single finger raised to his lips, a gesture of more gentle persuasion than the covering hand of the other villagers, but an order nonetheless. Nyquist kept quiet. Close up, he could see the lines of stress written on the man's face: he had lived a life of struggles. His cheeks were as pockmarked as the exposed wall of his house and his eyes were narrowed into slits pressed between pulps of blue skin.

Nyquist watched as the man came out of the cage and led the way through a back door of the house, into a warm kitchen. Every single space was occupied by some object or other. A wood-fired stove was roaring, and a pot of stew bubbled on a gas stove. Around this the crates, gadgets, utensils and bric-a-brac crowded in: this was the house of a hoarder. The hall corridor and the other rooms were the same, all packed to the walls and ceilings, with only narrow channels to give access. Nyquist had to turn sideways to squeeze through. Many of the items had a handmade look to them. Sadler was a craftsman.

Nyquist was surprised by the titles of the books on a set of shelves: *Mrs Dalloway*, *A Shropshire Lad*, *The Decline and Fall of the Roman Empire*, *The Waste Land*, and many other such classics. He had to adjust his thoughts about the man who led the way through the crowded rooms. They took a flight of steps down into a cellar. It was dark, no windows, a smell of damp. Nyquist banged his knee on a box and held back from cursing out loud.

Stay silent, follow the rules: gather what you can.

His mind pressed forward, even as his hands groped blindly. A light was clicked on, a single bulb that hung low over a table placed in the center of the floor. A multitude of objects were crammed in around this central area: suitcases, stuffed animals, a ragged Union Jack flag, the top half of a human skeleton, African masks, a set of congas, a tailor's dummy, a miniature garden under a glass dome. Nyquist had to negotiate his way carefully, but at last he reached the table. The other man gestured for him to sit. He did so, and now they faced each other in the semi-dark and the silence.

Not quite silence: something skittered among the hoarded

goods. Nyquist didn't like to think about what it might be.

The branch of a tree was laid across the tabletop. It was a dead branch, years dead, the bark powdery and gray, devoid of sap. No leaf would ever grow from this surface. And yet the owner of the house placed one hand on this branch and made a sign with the other that Nyquist should copy his lead. It only took the barest touch.

"Len Sadler's the name. How do you do?"

It was a thick working-class accent, deeply burred. Sadler was in his mid-forties, with sparse reddish hair visible now the flat cap had been removed.

Nyquist responded, "We can speak?"

"We can, but always keep a hand on the branch."

"So this is a branch from the special oak tree, from the Blade of Night?"

Sadler smiled. "Blade of Moon. Also, we never use the definite article."

"Right. I was speaking with some teenagers earlier, on the green."

"Now don't go thinking that I've stolen this myself, that I took a hacksaw to the sacred oak. I would never do such a thing."

"I understand."

"I found this in the household of an old woman who died last year. The saints alone know how she got hold of it."

"But how do you know it's the real thing? It might be any…"

"Any old piece of wood, is that what you're saying?"

"Well, yes."

"In which case, we'd just be two daft blokes sitting here in silence. Is that what you want? No, I didn't think so." Sadler settled in his chair. "So then, what would you like to buy?"

Nyquist leaned forward. "You think that's why I'm here?"

"It's the only reason anyone comes to visit me. As you can see, I have many things on offer, all very reasonably priced. Although I should warn you..."

"Yes?"

"Not everything's for sale." This was said with a sly grin which gave the statement a philosophical twist.

Nyquist placed the photograph on the table. "I found this today. It shows your house."

Sadler didn't even glance down. "Does it?"

A finger pointed to the various areas: "The street sign: Dovecote Lane. The number of the house: 23. The parked van–"

"Yes, yes. I believe you. Where did you find this?"

"In a photographer's studio, belonging to Thomas Dunne."

Now Sadler looked at Nyquist. His brow creased into lines as he ran a hand nervously through what was left of his hair. A few strands came free and he looked at them in an absent way and muttered, "There'll be none left soon." He gave a nervous laugh.

Nyquist cut right to it: "I've come here in search of my father."

"I see. I see, yes. Interesting. And your name is?"

"John Nyquist."

The answer startled Sadler.

"So you know who I'm talking about?"

"I do. Or at least, I did. But I haven't..."

Nyquist felt a breath catch in his throat. "What are you saying?"

"I haven't seen him in a while."

Nyquist didn't know whether to believe him, or not. His old street knowledge, built up over years of city living, meant next to nothing out here in the wilderness. But he had to know more! He had to check.

"What can you tell me about him? Don't you know where he is?"

Sadler held up his free hand, calling for silence. He looked again at the visitor's face, this time studying it in even more detail than he had in the pigeon coop. And then he said something that almost made Nyquist weep with joy, or fear.

"Yes, you do look like him."

The dust settled in the cellar. Even the skittering behind the boxes had stopped.

"I thought there was something familiar about you."

"You knew… you knew my father?"

"Oh briefly, briefly."

"I need to know, the whole story. If you're lying…"

"There's little to tell."

The words jabbed deep like a needle. Nyquist's hand rose from the branch in his anger. "I need to know everything!"

Sadler leaned back and raised his hand to his mouth, not a single finger as before, but the full hand covering the lips.

Nyquist groaned.

Sadler kept his mouth covered. He wouldn't even look at the rule breaker. Not until Nyquist's hand had returned to the branch.

"Saint Meade bids you be silent, unless Blade of Moon allows otherwise."

Nyquist was calm now. He had to be, he had to let the story be told as it may, in the right manner. He said quietly, "I saw one of your pigeons, at the photographer's."

"Oh yes? Which one?"

"The gray one."

"They're all very different, you do know that?"

"There was a canister attached to its leg. I unscrewed it." He had Sadler's full attention. "I have the message here."

He placed the unrolled piece of paper on the table. Sadler hesitated and then reached out. He read the message quickly to himself, his lips moving, his eyes crinkling in pain.

"Leonard? I take it that's you?"

"Everyone calls me Len. Everyone that is, except for Agnes." He smiled a little at a memory. "She always insisted on using my full and proper name. Perhaps it made what we were doing together more, well... proper." He read the message a second time. "But I haven't seen her, not for weeks now."

"So, Agnes is Thomas Dunne's wife?"

Sadler grimaced. "That's right. I was certain I could persuade her to leave him, for me. But she... well, she never made it to the Mocking Gate." Tears were staining his face. He looked at Nyquist through their glitter and took a deep breath. "What happened to the pigeon, do you know?"

"It flew away, through the window."

Sadler smiled a little. "Sweet Kira. She is the most talented of all my birds. She will never give up."

"You mean..."

"She's been flying around ever since, searching for Agnes, to hand over the message."

"Perhaps Kira will find her one day."

"Yes, maybe. And then we'll all be together."

The scratching sound had started up again from a pile of boxes. Sadler cocked his head at the noise and a muscle twitched on his unshaven cheek. He took a moment to shake off his sadness – the act of pure will was visible on his face, and in the tightness with which he clung to Blade of Moon. "Everything you see here," he said, "and in the other rooms, they've all come from houses in the village. My target is to have one item at least from every house in the area. Lower, Upper, and all surrounding environs, farmhouses, remote cottages. If it's on the Hoxley map, I will have been there, I will have collected something." He raised one hand in protest. "But never stolen, mind, well, unless the place was deserted, but that doesn't count. No, the majority were given freely as gifts or swapped in fair exchange for work undertaken, painting, household repairs and so on."

"Will you tell me how you know my father?"

Sadler hesitated, as though worried by what he was about to say.

"What's wrong, Len? Do you need payment? Is that it?"

"Payment?"

"I don't have a lot." Nyquist took out his wallet.

"All the saints alive! What kind of man do you take me for?"

Nyquist didn't know how to answer, especially when Sadler held up the message taken from Kira's metal canister.

"This! Bringing *this* back to me. Payment enough, believe me."

"I'm sorry. I understand. I think I do..." Nyquist looked away.

Sadler made to speak, to continue the argument, but then stopped himself. He found other words instead, saying, "You tell me, sir. You tell *me* about your father. Because I'll bet you know more than I do."

Nyquist turned back. "I haven't seen him in more than twenty years. I thought he was dead. So there isn't much to say. Only memories."

"Tell me one good thing."

The choice came easily. "He was like you, Len. He liked to build things. But nothing useful. Just bizarre objects made out of junk and whatever he found on his travels. But he thought they had a purpose, he really did. I liked that side of him. As a kid, it was magical, even if these machines never actually contacted Mars, or captured the voices of the dead." Nyquist frowned. "Looking back, I used to think he was entertaining me. But nowadays, I really think he was crazy. His mind was elsewhere."

Sadler nodded.

Nyquist continued, "A few days ago I received news that he might be alive. It was a shock. But I don't know. I'm just trying to find out, yes or no. Alive or dead?"

Sadler lifted his hands off the branch. He kept them raised an inch or so above Blade of Moon. They hovered there. His eyes never left Nyquist. And then the hands lowered again, and he told a story.

"Earlier this year I was called out to a house in Ouslemere, a village further down the Hale valley. It was a decorating job. The first day's work took a while and it was dark by the time I set off back home. There are no street lights out that way, so it was pitch black. But I saw a light in King's Grave field. There's an old cottage there, but it's stood empty for a long time, for years. No one will buy it. I was curious, so I took the off-road and drove up to the house. It's not an easy drive, because the access road is in a sorry state, but my van managed it. I had to drive across a field."

Sadler paused and listened with half an ear to the noise in the boxes.

"The light in the window had gone out by the time I got there. I don't mind telling you, I was pretty scared. But I felt it my duty to investigate. I had my torch with me."

Nyquist asked, "What did you find?"

Sadler continued, "The door of the house was unlocked. Inside, it looked empty. But there was evidence of someone living there. A bed, a little stove, a few tin cans. I had the impression that I was being watched, by a pair of eyes in the shadows."

Nyquist whispered, "Who was it?"

"I didn't know, not at that time. But the following night, I was once again driving back and I saw the same light on, glowing yellow across the field. I made my way to the cottage and went inside, and I waited in the room, where the bed and the stove were, and I waited and waited, until at last a man stepped forward."

Nyquist could hardly breathe. He didn't dare to speak.

Sadler went on, "There was a hell of a look about him. Like he'd traveled a long, long way to get here, and paid a heavy price for it. I mean, his face... the way he stared at me. It was unnerving. But a great yearning lay in those eyes of his, a need to connect."

"You talked to him?"

"I did. I gave him my name, and I asked for his. And he told me: *George*."

Nyquist's hand tightened on Blade of Moon. "That's right. My father's name."

Sadler nodded. *"George Oliver Nyquist.* He pronounced all three names, like they had equal importance."

"Yes, he liked to do that."

But Nyquist had to make sure. He took the photograph of his father from his pocket and placed it on the table and said, "Is this the man you spoke to?"

There was the slightest pause from Sadler. And then: "That's him. That's him, in every detail."

It was enough, recognition. This wasn't a game, it wasn't a joke. It was real! His father had been here, he was alive… he'd been alive all this time, while Nyquist had thought him dead. *Twenty years*. His eyes closed as the idea took hold, the very promise of it!

He looked again at Sadler and said, "I need to know what you talked about, everything, please, every word."

"I'm not sure–"

"Just talk to me, will you?"

"I can't remember–"

The table shook as Nyquist brought his fist down on it.

"Do you hear me! Every bloody word!"

Sadler nodded, his tongue licking nonstop at his lips, his face screwed up against the sudden noise and the cloud of dust that lifted from the tabletop and the dead branch of the oldest tree. And he said, "I'll… I'll try."

"Good."

"He… well, here's the thing, he didn't say that much. I'm telling the truth, mister, I swear. You have to believe me."

"Keep going."

Sadler gathered himself. "We met a few times, three altogether. That's all. But I was only there for an hour or so each time, and then he would dismiss me. Always at night, this was. He seemed to like that for some reason. Maybe the sunlight disagreed with him? He always kept to the shadows."

Nyquist gestured: carry on.

"He said very little. I wouldn't call him lonely, because I think he was used to such a state. But he liked to listen to me talking, he liked to hear the news, about things that were happening in the village, just gossip really, the little things that ordinary people get up to. Who was arguing with whom, who was having an affair, who was losing their wits, that kind of thing. Ordinary life, as he called it, one time. *Ordinary life…*"

Sadler's voice trailed off.

"What's wrong?"

"I need a drink. My mouth's dry."

Nyquist nodded consent and Sadler got up from the table and walked over to a sink set in the wall between a rusting bed frame and a crumbling garden statue. A mechanical figure of Punch looked on, as tall as a grown man, its yellow painted eyes staring from the shadows. Sadler poured himself a tumbler of water and returned to the table. Now the two men sat facing each other again and Sadler's hand returned to Blade of Moon.

"At other times he wanted to hear about the wider world, about politics and culture and things like that, and from events of the last few decades. He was fascinated by that. I got the impression… how can I put this… that he'd been away for a time, a very long time."

"Where had he been, did he tell you?"

Sadler shook his head. "No. I did ask one time, but he wouldn't answer."

"He must've said something to you. He can't just have listened."

"There was one thing…"

"Let me hear it."

"He talked about his wife."

"His wife? You mean…"

"Darla."

Nyquist had to smile at this. "It was a term of endearment. Darla. Her real name was Dorothy."

"Yes, well… he told me how he missed Darla… Dorothy… how he missed her still, even after all this time."

"My mother died in a road accident. When I was young, a boy."

Sadler puffed out his cheeks. "You've had a life and a half, I'm gathering."

"Go on. What did he say about her?"

"Just that. That he missed her."

Nyquist collected his thoughts. "What happened after the third night?"

"I went back a fourth time. In truth, I liked the man. I'm alone most days, and your old man was good company, a good listener. I told him all my problems, and he nodded his head and gave me little encouraging smiles, things like that. Sometimes, even, words of advice."

"What happened this last time?"

"He was gone. The cottage was deserted. The bed was still there, the stove, his books."

"Books?"

"Didn't I mention that? He liked to read. There was one particular subject. Right from the start he asked me if I had any suitable guidebooks I could lend him. So I plucked one off my shelves and brought that along, on my second visit. It was a book about ornithology. Birdwatching, you know. Chiffchaffs, dunnocks, the lesser spotted woodpecker."

"My father had an interest in such things?"

"Very much so. In fact, that was the subject that drew us together, once he found out about my pigeon colony. He wanted to know all the details of how my birds were getting on: Little Tess and Lord Montague, and dear sweet Broodie, and Old Mrs McIntyre–"

Nyquist stopped him in mid-flight. "When did all this take place?"

"Late summer. September. A few months back."

"Why did he leave the cottage?"

"I can't tell you that. But he seemed very agitated on that last visit. He argued with me. He didn't like me mentioning Agnes, I really don't know why."

Nyquist thought about this. Because of the photographs, he knew that his father and Thomas Dunne were connected in some way, as was Agnes Dunne. But he couldn't work it out, not yet.

"He asked me to leave," Sadler continued. "Demanded it of me, actually. Which pissed me off, no end, let me tell you. His face shivered strangely in the dim light. I thought he was having a breakdown, or something. And that was the last time I saw him."

Nyquist tried to stay calm. He touched at the photograph of his father and asked, "Did you send this picture to me?"

"Of course not. Why would I do that? I've only just met you."

"He didn't tell you to get in touch with me?"

"I swear! Absolutely not."

Nyquist pulled another photograph from his pocket. "What about this one, of the black tower? Do you recognize that place?"

Sadler shook his head. "No. I've never seen it before."

"But why would it be sent to me, if it's in a different village, or a faraway field? It doesn't make sense."

"How much of anything makes sense?"

Nyquist ignored the comment. He pushed his village atlas forward and said, "I'd like you to mark where the cottage is, where you met with my father."

Sadler turned the pages. His pen hovered over an empty space well outside the built-up areas. "It's not on the map," he said. "Like I said, it's abandoned–"

"Mark it."

The pen nib came down and made a small cross in the middle of a field. "King's Grave. There's a turning off Ousle Road, but I'm warning you, it peters out in a dirt track."

"Don't worry about that. I'll get there."

Nyquist studied the map. A simple question needed to be asked, and it took him a moment to get up the courage.

"Did my father mention me?"

"What?"

"Did he mention my name? Or did he talk about me, his son, his only child? Well?"

Len Sadler looked nervous. "No. I can't recall such a thing. Not directly."

"What do you mean, not directly?"

"There was one time…"

"Go on."

"When he talked about the book of birds. He mentioned that it would make a nice gift for someone, a young boy."

"That's it?"

"That's all. Isn't that… isn't that enough?"

Nyquist took his hand off the branch. His head bowed down. The scratching sound filled the silence. Some kind of animal was living here, amid the junk: the noise of it probed at his brain.

"What's wrong?" asked Sadler.

No reply was given.

"I know, you're frustrated, Mr Nyquist. You're lost. You must feel that way. We all do, we all feel lost from time to time."

Nyquist's head remained downturned. He didn't speak. But then his hand moved. It came to rest on the branch and his fingers wrapped around it tightly. He wasn't thinking, his mind was a blank. But the branch felt good in his grip. He had the feeling he might lift it up, raise it high and do some damage with it. He imagined Sadler's brow splitting open. And even before the miserable thought had ended, the very action had taken him over. He was standing over the table, both hands gripping the branch now, ready to swing it down.

Sadler didn't call out. Carefully, slowly, both of his hands came up to his mouth, to seal his lips shut. He was doing the only thing he could: to follow the saint's ruling.

The gesture had an effect. Nyquist fought to get his anger under control. And at last he lowered the branch back to the table. His hand was still touching it, which allowed him to speak. "I just need to find my father." It was a simple desire. And with the saying of it, Nyquist was a boy again, a boy of six or seven, a running boy, a crying boy, a boy with dirt on his hands and knees and the streaks of tears down his grubby cheeks, he was a boy leaping over walls and balancing on the lip of a shed's roof, he was the soldier at war, he was the fighter plane, the Spitfire, arms outstretched, making the noise of the engines and the guns, he was the cowboy, the lone jungle explorer, the first astronaut to ever walk on the moon. And his father was there for every mission, urging him on and fighting and patrolling with him, and then gone, gone, no longer a companion, no longer at his side, and the young boy played on alone, alone on the streets of light and dark, a game with no ending, no known outcome, not until the final shadows closed in.

He sat down once more and spoke again, quietly this time.

"I need to find him."

Sadler didn't respond. His eyes darted to one side. The creature was at play again, moving around, shuffling. Scratching. It was a quiet sound, but in the silence it was heard clearly.

"Do you hear that?" Sadler was whispering.

Nyquist nodded.

"Well… I think it's calling to you."

"I don't… I don't know what you mean." Whispering also.

The noise continued, louder now.

Sadler stood up. He walked over to a shelving unit and pushed aside a carriage clock. He pulled out an object from the dark of the shelf and he brought it back to the table. It was a wooden box, the kind of souvenir people brought back from their travels abroad. A jungle cat was carved in the lid.

The noise was coming from inside.

Sadler explained, "I found this in the house of a man who died earlier this year. He was called Mr Holroyd."

"I've never heard of him."

"I don't think that matters. Please, take a look…"

Nyquist clicked open a brass catch and lifted the lid.

Immediately, the noise stopped.

He peered aside, at the object that lay within, fitted snugly in a green baize bed. For a long moment he could not comprehend what he was seeing. He looked to Sadler for an answer, but the other man stayed silent.

Turning his attention back to the object, he said, "It's a service revolver. Enfield make. Double action. Looks like Army issue. Point 38 caliber."

"You know about guns, then?"

"A little. I owned one for a while, but it was taken from me."

"Maybe this is meant to be a replacement?"

"I'm not sure I want it."

"Well then, neither do I. Not now."

Nyquist pulled the revolver from the box and examined it in more detail. Straightaway he saw that the gun was still attached to the baize by a green cord. It was identical in every aspect to the tendril he'd found in the teacup at the Bainbridge household. He pulled the handgun further away from the box and the fibrous material stretched out and then detached itself from the baize with a quiet *pop* and sprung back towards the revolver, wrapping itself around the barrel.

Both Nyquist and Sadler were staring at the gun and its strange occupant.

The only moving object in sight was the tendril as it tightened and loosened its hold on the revolver.

"This is the creature that was making the noise?"

Sadler nodded. "Yes. It's been quiet ever since I took the box home. But now, as soon as you arrive, it starts to call out. Here, take a look." He handed a magnifying glass to his visitor. Using this, Nyquist could see that the parasite, or whatever it might be, was attached to the outside of the trigger guard: it actually seemed to be fused with the metal. The other end of the tendril waved in the air, tipped by a collection of hair-like fibers. They trembled as an insect's antennae might, seeking a new surface to cling to. It was alive. Nyquist lowered the glass. He had never seen anything like this, not in all his years.

"Be careful. It's moving!"

Sadler's voice startled him. The tendril unravelled from the barrel at speed. Nyquist couldn't help himself, he dropped the revolver and it clattered on the tabletop. The creature was writhing around, almost whipping from side to side at speed.

"Jesus."

"Indeed, and all the saints." Sadler's brow was covered in sweat.

At last the creature settled once more, stirring slightly, its body undulating.

Nyquist asked, "Do you know what this is?"

"I've seen it before, yes. Once before."

"You need to start talking."

"I am talking. Can't you hear me–"

"Louder, more clearly. To the bloody point!"

Sadler wiped the sweat from his upper lip. Then he pointed to the tendril and said, "This is a prime example of what people around here call Creeping Jenny. Or at least, a small part of her."

"I'll need more than that."

"The gun is linked to you in some way. And nothing, nothing at all, is going to sever that connection. Not ever! Don't you see?" There was an excited look in Sadler's eyes. "The Creeping Jenny tendril connects the gun to your story. That's why it came alive, when you entered the room." He moaned with pleasure. "Oh my, it's so rare, and such a beautiful thing to witness."

Nyquist felt his grip on reality weakening.

"You've handled a few of these?"

"Just the one. I sold a hunting knife some years ago, to a man not that dissimilar to yourself. The handle of the hunting knife had the same thing attached to it. Other than that, I've heard stories. We all have."

"Tell me about them."

"I'm not sure that would be helpful."

Nyquist said, "The thing is, I've already seen this creature before, on another object."

"Really?"

"Not a gun. But on a teacup. That's all. Just a normal teacup."

Sadler's eyes lit up. "Oh, but this is incredible! I've never heard of this before. Two objects! Two objects joined to the same person, to the same story! And you know what the old songs say?" He supplied his own answer: "Once Creeping Jenny calls you, there's no escaping her." He started to sing. The tune was suitable for a childhood chant, but Sadler's raspy tenor gave it a poignant melancholic air.

By weed and by hook
By candle and book
By wood and by weir
Creeping Jenny is near.

As the song continued, Nyquist checked the revolver's cylinder: five empty chambers, and a single cartridge loaded and ready to fire. He closed it up again and heard the satisfying sound of the parts clicking back together: it was well-made and well looked after. But the tendril was disturbed. It seemed to be reaching out for Nyquist. He let it happen, allowing the fibers to move across the back of his hand. It tickled, but nothing more. It wrapped itself lightly around his index finger. He was now joined to the gun by this living, organic material. It gave him the strangest sensation: he thought of a story unfolding, a pathway branching in two, and two again, and again, and so on, ever onwards, and then twining together with other pathways, other stories, from now until the moment when the trigger was pulled and the hammer met the firing pin causing the powder to explode and the cartridge to shoot forth and to meet with flesh or whatever the target might be.

A cry of pain and shock, a spray of blood...

It felt real in his mind, like the gunshot was actually happening there and then. So real. Until the song ended, and then the tendril moved away from his finger to float back to the revolver's barrel, and the vision faded as quickly as it had come.

"I think the gun belongs to you," Sadler said. "I don't want it in my house anymore."

"Tell me about the other item you sold, the hunting knife?"

Sadler hesitated.

"What is it? Did the owner hurt someone with it?"

"You could say that. He killed himself."

THE FARAWAY MAN

The moorlands were a great weight, a beast pressing down on the earth. Nyquist kept to the pathway, almost stumbling a few times, and was grateful to hear the river moving in its brook, the water lit with silvery aspects like a disturbed mirror in a blacked-out room. He used it as a guide, keeping the sound to his right, but even then, he thought he might be lost. All land was the same land, all darkness the same darkness, himself a darkened figure in the dark landscape – and the inside of his head held the same darkness. But he kept on, until he could make out a pattern of yellow dots far ahead: lamps and lighted windows. Now a firefly buzzed in his mind and flitted over the things he had learned from Sadler and his hoard of curious objects. He ranged over the mysteries: the threads of cotton woven into a photograph, the missing name that Sylvia Keepsake had given him, the reason for his father's appearance in this village after so many years, and so away far from his home. Most of all he saw again the image of Sadler's house emerging on the sheet of paper in the developing tray. Somebody was sending him clues, that was all he could think. But why?

One step, another, in the dark, the pattering of the stream, a night bird calling lonesome in the moors, the moon almost full but hidden by clouds. The swan pool. The stone bridge across the river. He was back in Hoxley-on-the-Hale. It was a Friday night and the high street was busy with people enjoying the start of the weekend. The windows of The Swan With Two Necks glowed with a cheery light. But of course, nobody spoke, nobody made a sound. The revolver weighed heavy in Nyquist's jacket pocket and he was shamefully aware that he was carrying a loaded firearm through this supposedly peaceful little village: he felt more out of place than ever. Couples walked by, some of them hand in hand, their bodies wrapped in wool and fur to keep out the cold. He peeked in at the door of the public house and saw the drinkers at the tables and the bar, all in silence, each person making their hand signals, telling jokes, spreading gossip, arguing and flirting, but all in gestures only. Nigel Coombes didn't join in with the merriment, but he served everyone efficiently, with a professional landlord's smile in place. Nyquist was tempted by the atmosphere, but he wasn't ready to settle down just yet. His hands were empty of words. And he had one more job to do that night.

He walked along Pyke Road until he reached the Bainbridge household. His plan was simple; he would wait until eight o'clock, when Saint Meade lost her control over the village, and then he would knock loudly on the door of Yew Tree Cottage and demand to know why the Bainbridges possessed that particular teacup, the one with the tendril attached. If Len Sadler was to be believed, then cup and gun were linked. A chain looped around in his mind: *myself, the cup, the gun, the cup, the gun, myself, the gun, the cup, the gun, myself...*

Damn it to hell and back! The Bainbridges *had* to know something.

He waited until twenty to the hour, and grew restless. He walked on a little way and came to the community center, where the night's lecture was in progress. He paid a shilling at the door and stood in the semi-dark watching images flicker on a screen set up on a small stage. The place was only a quarter full. Nyquist ignored the empty seats and walked over to the tea and refreshments table, but only a pair of stale-looking pink wafers were left on the plate, surrounded by the crumbs of finer biscuits. He ate what was on offer, and stood with his back to the wall watching the lecture. A young man was working a magic lantern from the center aisle and an older woman was standing on the stage, indicating various details with a pointer. Not a word was uttered, not a sound was heard, only the clicking of the lantern as one photographic slide after another was slotted into place, and a new picture appeared on the screen. Even when one image was shown upside down, nobody made a comment, not even through laughter. Shadows danced on the viewers' rapt faces. Nyquist saw birds in flight and children playing with hoops and the moon above a forest and the high street strung with bunting and a lone black tower and a smiling man and white-clad cricketers on the green and the wave of a hand from a soldier marching off to war and a young woman arranging flowers on a grave and the church of Hoxley decked out for the harvest festival. But he couldn't for the life of him work out what the sequence meant or why people would sit here and look at such things. It was hardly *Bride of Blood*, or *The Moonstruck Corpse* starring Jack Hawkins.

Five minutes of random images was enough. He left the hall and made his back to the Bainbridges' cottage. Only a short time remained until the day's silence came to an end.

The atmosphere seemed heavy, drained of all noise. Not a single animal cry or bird call disturbed the purity of that moment; even the wind had died down. Nyquist could hardly dare breathe in case he ruined the effect. And he wondered if everyone would suddenly make a loud noise and all start talking at once, when the clock struck eight, in recompense for all the hours of being mute.

He thought of the wordless lecture he'd just witnessed and was certain that he'd missed something in the flicker of images, something he needed to focus on.

Was that the same dark tower as...

The noise came too soon.

He wasn't prepared. It scared him. His heart leapt.

The noise, the scream. It came too soon, three minutes too soon.

The night was cut open by it.

He imagined blood pouring from silence, from wounded silence.

The scream continued. A woman's high voice in pain, in terrible pain.

At last Nyquist was able to move. He ran to the door of Yew Tree Cottage and banged on it with his fist.

"Bainbridge! Bainbridge, open up!"

But there was no response. He looked through the window, through a gap in the curtain where the illuminated Saint Meade icon was standing, but the living room was empty.

Other people were appearing at their doors along the street, their faces in shock.

What could this be, this noise? What can it mean?

But there was still a minute left, and even now they did not speak.

Nyquist ran down the pathway at the side of the cottage. The back door was on the latch. He pushed it open. What he saw froze him to the spot.

Hilda Bainbridge was standing pressed against the kitchen wall, her hands clenched at her sides, her upper body rocking back and forth: on each backward stroke the rear of her head knocked against the plaster. The noise of contact grew louder with each hit.

And she was still screaming.

Screaming, on this long night of silence.

Nyquist called out her name. "Hilda." But it did no good. Now he really feared for her, so he reached out and grabbed her with both hands and he pulled her forward. At last she fell silent. Nyquist saw the small patch of blood on the wall where she'd been hitting her head repeatedly. She looked at him with wild red-rimmed eyes, her entire face covered in tears. Her mouth was still open, trying to draw in one breath after another, each of them labored.

The aftermath of the scream rang like an echo, heard and unheard at the same time.

Hilda's eyes darted about feverishly. She would rather do anything other than to look at the figure sitting at the kitchen table. Nyquist left her for a moment and went over to place a hand against the man's neck. No pulse, no signal from within.

Ian Bainbridge had found his own way out of the troubles of life, the lonely exit door of suicide. He was still sitting upright, bizarrely, his hands still outstretched, calmly resting on the tabletop near to a glass of sherry. But nothing had been disturbed, there had been no last-minute regrets, no struggle. His body had quite simply given up. There were a number of fresh scratches all over his face. And his lips were

darkly colored with the juice of a berry. His fingertips were
stained with the same ruby color. The remains of the berries
lay in a bowl on the tabletop, their off-white skins broken
open to reveal the dark red pulp and juice within. Beside the
bowl lay a thorned twig cut from a tree. Flakes of bark were
scattered across the white cloth.

Bainbridge's eyes stared ahead, seeing vistas beyond the
stone wall of the kitchen, the utensils arranged in neat rows,
the copy of *Mrs Beeton's Cookbook* and the tea towel with its
flowered pattern. He was looking beyond these walls, faraway,
out into the fields, and then the moors and the sky where all
worldly cares faded into mist.

Hilda had slumped into a chair near the stove. She sat
there with her hands in her lap, her shoulders bent forward,
her face hidden. For the first time Nyquist noticed that her
hair was wet, and that she smelled of soap. She was wearing
a flannelette gown. Obviously, she'd had a bath and then
come back downstairs to find her husband like this. But such
thoughts only took him so far. He was at a loss: what could
he do to help her?

There was a noise at the door. It was one of the neighbors.
He took a step into the kitchen and then stopped, gazing in
horror at the paralyzed man at the table. Nyquist said, "Fetch
a policeman. Can you do that?" The neighbor stared at him.
"Now!" At last the frightened man stepped back through the
door and was gone. Nyquist looked around. He had a few
minutes before more people arrived, including the local
officer. Probably he'd be asked to leave, and most likely be
questioned. He was ready for all that, whatever may come,
but he still needed to search the household, as far as he could.

He kept to the kitchen, hoping to find the teacup. It wasn't on the table or in the sink. He opened one cupboard after another, until he found the crockery neatly laid out on shelves. But the teacup wasn't there, nor any of the matching set. He kept searching, moving into the hallway. A glass-fronted cabinet held a few special items, family treasures such as brooches, fancy ornaments, and the coronation tea service: cups, saucers, teapot, milk jug, each item carrying the Queen's portrait. But only five cups – one saucer was empty. Despite this, he checked inside each cup, hoping to see the strange growth within, the remains of the tendril. But all the cups were clean.

A clattering sound came from the living room. He entered warily, expecting to find a person in there. But the room was empty. And quiet now, except for the carriage clock on the mantel and the low crackling of the fire in the grate. Everything looked in place, normal, comforting. Saint Meade stood on the window ledge, looking out at the street.

Her reign was over.

The noise came again. Nyquist turned. He walked over to the birdcage on its stand. It was covered in a purple cloth. He lifted this off and peered through the bars. The brightly colored budgerigar was no longer in residence. Instead a raven was standing on the perch, its body and wingspan far too large for the cage. Like a creature from a nightmare it beaded him with one yellow eye, its head turned to the side. A single diamond of white marked its forehead, like the symbol of a caste, or an assassin's guild.

The raven's huge wings flapped madly, rattling the cage so that it might almost topple over to the carpet. At the same time, it let out a mighty cawing sound, which turned the quaint living room into a wild realm, just for a second or two. And then the bird settled back onto the perch, looking pleased with itself.

Nyquist looked down at the floor of the cage. He knew instantly that he'd seen this bird before, on his first night in the village. This horrible specimen had stolen his naming card from him, the one given freely by Sylvia in the Woods – the same card that now lay scattered about the sawdust and droppings on the floor of the cage, torn into many pieces. He saw the letters OD written on one piece, and on another the single letter W. One fragment contained the word IN, or was it only part of a word?

All the other pieces were turned upside down: message unknown.

The raven guarded them all, its beak ready for action.

PART 2
CONNECTIVE TISSUE

ALICE AND EDMUND WELCOME YOU

Nyquist woke late again to find himself tightly wound within the bed sheets. He could hardly move, evidence of a night of bad dreams. The air was dense and smoky. He managed to free himself, and sat there on the edge of the bed, holding his heads in his hands. A bottle of whiskey rested on his bedside table, a good three quarters empty. Next to it was an ashtray overflowing with butts. Hence the bad air of the room, and the way his mouth felt. He unstuck his tongue from his upper palate. He wasn't used to alcohol, not these days. A sharp needle prodded at his left temple. It took him a while to remember – he'd bought the whiskey off the landlord late last night, when he'd returned. Yes, it had been a difficult time, with the questioning and the waiting around and the comings and goings, and the police constable's suspicions and Doctor Higgs examining the body and Hilda Bainbridge weeping silently in the corner of the living room and then being led away to spend the night elsewhere. And even now, after the death of her husband and the scream she had made, still, not a single word had issued from her lips, not even under all the pressure of the officer's enquiries: not one.

He stood up and splashed water on his face and cleaned his

teeth, all the time keeping his eyes averted from the mirror, scared of what he might find there. He would have to wear the same shirt today, and hopefully make some arrangement to get his laundry done. Otherwise he would spend the evening scrubbing his clothes in the sink in his room, the glamorous life.

There was a new icon standing on the cabinet. He moved his head slightly and tried to focus his eyes and wondered if he was seeing double. No, his vision was fine. A second icon was standing next to the first. Two saints. This did not bode well. They each looked identical, or nearly so, brother and sister from the look of it, and fairly sophisticated compared to previous icons, being made of molded plastic and clothed in modern apparel, a perfectly tailored blue suit for the man, and a plain but well-cut blue dress for the woman. Their faces were soft and hardly delineated: no wrinkles, no lines, and no expression.

Nyquist went downstairs. There was a new waitress in the dining room, a girl who looked aside when he greeted her and did the same when she served him his breakfast, a little later. She looked oddly familiar. But in truth everything was still a little blurred and fuzzy at the edges. He was hoping to cure his hangover with greasy food, lots of it, but the noise in his head continued, and his mouth felt clogged with mush or feathers, and the food on top of it made it worse, not better. He couldn't finish his meal. He felt sick. The waitress came back. This time he asked for her name and got a reply so quiet he could barely hear it.

"What was that again?"

"Alice, sir."

Again he tried to look at her, but she kept turning away from his stare.

"Where's Mavis?" he asked. "Isn't she working today?"

"I don't know anyone called Mavis."

And before he could ask another question, she turned on her heels, and hurried away towards the kitchen door, carrying his plate and his empty teacup.

Nyquist made his way outside. It was a Saturday morning, one of those special days winter sometimes gives you, when the world seems at rest and the air is bright and silvered, like the insides of an unstruck bell. A banner had been strung across the street, from one house to another. In stitched-on letters it read: *ALICE AND EDMUND WELCOME YOU TO THEIR VILLAGE.* Nyquist set off for the doctor's surgery. On the way a middle-aged couple stared at him with open animosity in their eyes. He had the feeling he'd seen them both before, somewhere. But where, and when, he just couldn't work out. Other people shook their heads and whispered to each other. He was a figure of curiosity, or hatred. And then, as he walked along, the high street came more clearly into focus and he saw that each face was the same, or at least very similar. Everyone seemed to be wearing a mask, which covered their faces entirely, giving them a new expression. One for men, and another face for women, the two faces repeated in each person that he met. The same faces as the two icons in his room.

He took a guess. Were they perhaps Saint Edmund and Saint Alice? And the people had adopted their faces for the day.

Something hit him on the back of his neck.

Nyquist turned.

Three people were staring at him, all of them young by the look of it, and all wearing their own masks, two Edmunds and an Alice.

One of the young men scooped up another stone from the gutter.

"Don't try it, kid."

Nyquist's threat had little effect. The other young man came forward until he was but a few inches away and spoke through the moving lips of his mask. "Who are you, sir? You are no one. Leave this place. We don't want you here." It was coldly said, with utter disgust in each phrase.

Nyquist stared back at him, unwilling to give any ground.

The mask was plainly fashioned, of thin almost transparent plastic, and the man's real features could be glimpsed underneath. It was an exact copy of the male icon's mask. The young woman came to join her friend, and her mask was a similar design, but made to replicated the features of Saint Alice.

"Who are you? What's your name? What are you doing here?"

It was then he realised it was one of the teenage girls he'd met by the oak tree, Blade of Moon. Through his addled brain, he searched for her name.

"Val, isn't it? Why are you–?"

"Do not call me that. My name is Alice."

He was about to argue with her, when a stone hit him on the chest, thrown by the third young man, who was hanging back from the group, rocking back and forth on his feet as though getting ready to pounce.

"You do that again…"

The youth stared at Nyquist. He bent down for another stone.

Valerie took charge: "Come on, Edmund, let's go." And all three of them moved off down the road.

Nyquist walked on, past the village green where a

decorative tent was being set up. A notice board next to the tent read, *Madame Fontaine, Fortune Teller Extraordinaire*. A man was standing by the board, putting the finishing touches in place. He too wore the day's mask. He was covering up the name *Fontaine* with a piece of white card bearing a new name: *Grey*. An odd thing to do, unless Madame Fontaine had been taken ill.

Nyquist rang the bell at the doctor's house and was let in by the maid. He was getting used to the effect of seeing people with their faces changed, and he actually said without thinking, "Hello Alice, is the doctor free?"

The maid led him to the study. Doctor Higgs was sitting at her desk, reading a report. She greeted her visitor with a smile.

"Can I help you, sir? Are you ailing?"

"It's me, doc. You know damn well who it is."

"I am sorry, I don't think we've met before–"

"Higgs, come on, take that mask off."

The maid gasped. She was still standing in the doorway, awaiting instruction.

The doctor's mask quivered, mirroring her facial expression changing underneath. Nyquist couldn't make out what she was really feeling, it was well hidden, despite the semi-transparent nature of the covering.

And then Doctor Higgs composed herself. She said to the maid in a cheerful voice, "Alice, dear, get our friend a cup of coffee will you?"

The maid left the room. Nyquist remained where he was, standing by the sideboard. A pair of goldfish swam around aimlessly in their tank. The two saintly icons stood guard to the left and right of the aquarium.

The doctor was concerned. "Sit down, won't you, Edmund?

You look ill." He could see her eyes blinking within their apertures, pale and blue.

He remained on his feet, swaying slightly, the room moving with him.

"Edmund, have you been overindulging?"

"You can drop the pretence."

"I'm afraid I don't know what you mean."

He'd come to rely on Higgs for her commonsense, and her guidance, and not least her friendship. But now he looked on her with confusion in his mind.

"My name is not Edmund. It's John. John Nyquist."

"I really don't think that's true–"

"That's my name!"

She let his outburst fade away into silence. Then she said quietly, and politely, "For today, however, I shall call you Edmund. I hope you don't mind? It makes everything so much easier."

Nyquist stepped towards the desk. He wanted to do two opposite things at the same time: leave the doctor in peace… and pull the mask from her face.

"Please, Edmund. Please."

"I can't talk to you, not when you're wearing that."

For a moment she looked at him as though he were a madman. Anger pitted every word. "You wouldn't be able to remove it, even if I let you get anywhere near."

The door opened and the maid entered. Immediately, Nyquist stepped away, his hands falling to his side. The maid placed a coffee pot and two cups on the sideboard.

The maid looked from him to the doctor. "Is everything alright, ma'am?"

"Yes, thank you, Alice. You may go." Higgs got up from her

chair and walked over to the sideboard. "I'll be mother, shall I?" She poured her visitor a cup of coffee. Nyquist took a long drink. It was hot and strong, and it worked like a charm on his hangover.

Higgs opened a drawer in the sideboard and took out a rolled-up piece of plastic. "Take this. It will do you the power of good."

The mask was clammy to the touch, and when he unrolled it, he saw the two eyeholes and the mouth-hole, and the cold skin of the flesh.

"It clings on its own volition," she explained. "Things have certainly improved since my childhood, when we used string, or even glue!"

"Higgs!"

"I'm sorry, I truly am. But my name is Alice. Alice Grey. And you are Edmund, my only brother. For you see, on this day of all days, every man is Edmund Grey, and every woman is Alice. Doesn't that make sense to you? It's perfectly simple."

Nyquist groaned. He sat down in a chair, the plastic mask in his lap.

The doctor stood in front of him. "I can't stand to see you this way, Edmund."

He looked at her. He felt suddenly compliant. "Alice…"

"Yes. It's me. Doctor Alice. Oh, but your hands, you've damaged them!"

He gazed in surprise at his own palms, holding them both out for inspection. Each was crisscrossed with cuts, many of them, the blood dried over. The doctor's fingers touched gently at the scabs.

"How did this happen?"

"Last night…"

"Yes? I can give you some ointment, if you like."

"I can't… I can't remember…"

She fussed over him. "Finding a dead man, such a terrible thing for you to witness."

Nyquist pulled himself free of her ministrations. "How is Hilda? I need to see her; I need to talk to her."

"Hilda? Oh, you mean Alice?"

"Yes, if you say so."

"She stayed the night here, in my guestroom, and left early this morning."

"Where did she go? Back home?"

"Most probably. Her husband will be at the funeral home in Bligh by now. Oh, that poor woman! She must be out of her mind with grief."

Nyquist started to pace. "What about the victim, Ian Bainbridge?"

The doctor looked confused. "I'm afraid I don't know who Mr Bainbridge is. Do you mean Edmund Grey, the man who died last night?"

Nyquist felt his mind starting to reel. "Yes, yes. Edmund Grey. When did he die, do you know? The exact time?"

"Not long before you got there, I think."

"The cause of death?"

She hesitated.

"In your considered opinion?"

The doctor took up her pipe. She started to fill it with tobacco. "Paralysis of the heart muscles due to ingestion of moonsilver."

"Tell me about that."

"Moonsilver is what we call the berries of the myre tree. They are very poisonous, and even three or four of them can slow the body's system down, to a standstill. We teach our children from day one to never eat them, or even touch them. Sadly, some do not learn."

"So, you do think it was suicide?"

"Yes, of course. He made a choice."

"Why would he kill himself?"

Higgs thought for a moment. And then she said, "The Tolly Man came to visit him."

"What do you mean?"

"The Tolly Man appears once a year, on Saint Algreave's Day. A villager dresses up in the twigs and branches of the myre tree. It's a tradition."

Nyquist remembered the strange figure he'd seen in the peep show machine.

"Isn't that dangerous?"

"Oh, don't worry. We remove the berries before making the mask."

"But why… why would the Tolly Man lead to suicide?"

"It doesn't. But thoughts of the Tolly Man can easily scare us. He is a figure of evil repute, some call him a demon. And so, if a villager kills themselves in this way, using the myre berries, then we say that the Tolly Man has come to visit. That's all."

Nyquist took a breath. He tried to keep his mind clear. He asked, "And what about the raven in the cage? Is that another of your traditions?"

"No. That's just a puzzle."

"And I need to solve it." He frowned. "One thing's for certain: we're not dealing with an everyday suicide. Something crazy went on in that house last night."

"Is something worrying you, Edmund?"

"You know why I'm here, in the village."

"And you think this… this death is connected to your missing father?"

"Higgs, I know it is."

"Please, please, please, please, please, please, please don't call me that! Don't call me that name. I hate and detest that name, and everything it stands for. My name is Alice. Doctor Alice Grey!"

The saints had taken her over completely. Nyquist watched her mask as she struggled to bring herself back under control: the emotions half hidden, half on display. But at last she managed it, and she said, "I'm very sorry for my outburst. But you have to know, Edmund, this is one of our most important days. Brother and sister died to save the village from intruders, only sixty years ago, in 1899. It's a date that every schoolchild learns in their first history lesson." She added calmly, "The Greys are our most recent martyrs."

Nyquist nodded. "Of course, I understand."

Higgs pushed the stem of her pipe through the mask, into her mouth. It looked absurd. But she seemed happy enough with the effect, and puffed contently, all upset forgotten.

"What's the story with Hilda?" he asked. "With Alice, I mean. When did she fall silent?"

"Three years ago. Saint Meade's Day, 1956. She gave up speaking for the day, as she must, and never opened her mouth again. Nobody knows why."

"Do the saints often have that kind of effect?"

"No, not often. Our rules give us sustenance. They protect us."

"But sometimes it goes wrong, people take it too far? Is that it?"

She didn't answer.

Nyquist watched the goldfish at their play, seeking the exit door of the bowl. He said, "I might pay Yew Tree Cottage a visit."

"Why?"

"I left something behind, in the birdcage." He looked at his hands as he said this, at the cuts on them.

The doctor looked at him in surprise. "You were fighting the raven?"

"I was trying to retrieve stolen property, but the blighter kept pecking at me. It wouldn't let me anywhere near."

"They do like to hoard. What was it, that was so important?"

"It's personal."

Higgs looked at him through a drift of blue smoke from her pipe. For a moment she frowned, and her mask crinkled slightly. Then she shook her head at the whole affair.

"One more thing," Nyquist said, "I have to go to King's Grave today. It's a field, out beyond–"

"I know where it is."

"There's a house out there, that I need to visit."

"I can take you there in the afternoon. I have to drive out that way, to see a patient."

"Thank you."

Doctor Higgs knocked out the remains of her pipe in an ashtray. "There's one condition though. Well, two actually."

"Go on."

"You have to call me Alice, and nothing but Alice. Alice Grey. And I'll call you Edmund, and you'll damn well respond."

"Granted."

"And one more thing; wear the mask."

"That's three conditions."

"Wear the bloody mask. Because if you don't…"

"I know. I'll get attacked. I've already had stones thrown at me."

"Believe me, Mr Grey. People have died over this, in the past." She let this sink in and then added with a grin, "And if that happened, we might have to beatify *you*. Can you imagine?" And she laughed at loud, the mouth of the mask splitting apart as far as it could go. "Now go on, leave me be."

Nyquist made his way outside. A mother and child were coming his way and the kid was already pointing at him and screaming blue murder. "Don't be rude, Edmund," the mother said to her boy, but she too was giving Nyquist the evil eye. So, he pressed the mask against his face, and immediately he received smiles from the mother, and giddy laughter from the child.

The mask settled and closed on his face. It felt cold to begin with, but soon a pleasant warmth took over. The mask tightened and slithered, finding the optimum bonding points. And then it tightened further, and sank into the flesh. And he was the mask, and the mask was him, and they lived as one being.

John Edmund Nyquist Grey walked up Pyke Road. Strangely, it felt perfectly natural to be viewing the world through two holes pierced in plastic. Each step, each breath he took, each movement, each smile and nod he was given by strangers… the more pleasant it felt. In fact, it was comforting. He couldn't help but celebrate his new identity.

Edmund. Edmund Grey, Esquire.

Sir Edmund Grey of Hoxley-on-the-Hale. At your service.

He was giving himself up to the goodly whims of the daily saints, yes, it was starting to make sense, the comfort, to surrender the will in these areas, to give oneself over to some other, higher purpose…

Nyquist stopped where he was on the street and looked around. He could hear the rattle and snap of sticks knocking against each other. It was two men, fencing with their walking sticks, each with the spirit of youth in their limbs. They looked like geriatric Morris dancers. Were they fighting, or dancing? Both wore the mask of Edmund Grey. One spat at the other, a meagre amount of liquid from parched lips, squeezed through the mask's aperture. The other cursed back and called his friend a stain upon the earth, for wearing the mask of Saint Edmund in such an uncouth fashion. The sticks clattered and parried. He could still hear them as he walked away up the hill.

There was no answer when he knocked on the door of Yew Tree Cottage, and all was quiet within. He peered through the window, seeing only an empty living room. He moved onto his second destination, the community hall. Here he studied the posters on the notice board until he found an advertisement for last night's lecture.

Professor Bryars
presents a local history
told through icons, follies, bric-a-brac
and other miscellanea
Tea and biscuits
Entrance 1s

At the bottom of the poster a warning notice read, *Spectators are advised that certain images may cause distress*. He couldn't remember anything disturbing in the portion of the slide show he'd viewed, or maybe he'd missed the best bit? But he remembered the image of the black tower that he'd seen, and how similar it looked to the building in the photograph. A fleeting glimpse, one slide among many. He needed to make sure. He entered the hall and asked Alice at the reception desk for the whereabouts of Professor Bryars.

"You mean Alice Grey, last night's lecturer?"

"I'm sorry. Yes. My mistake."

"Not that she deserves such a name of course." The receptionist's mask froze and unfroze as her anger seethed beneath.

"Why, did she do something wrong?"

"She did, Edmund. She did. It's the same every year."

"Where do I find her?"

"Take the first left up the hill and then second right onto Fallow Lane. And then just follow the hullabaloo. You can't miss it."

And she was right. He saw the crowds gathered around the house as soon as he turned onto the lane. There were about thirty people, all masked as Edmund and Alice, of all ages of Edmund and Alice, with perhaps more Alices than Edmunds. He saw the two older Morris men in attendance, their differences put aside for the moment as they used their sticks to knock on the windows and door of number 9, where Professor Bryars lived. Everyone was shouting, their voices slightly muffled and restricted by the masks, but loud nonetheless, loud enough surely to stir the woman within the house. But nobody came to the door, nobody answered their call. And the shouts continued, the cries, the calls of abuse. Each protestor emboldened the one next to them, and the anger spread in this manner, person to person, until at last everybody there was crying out as one body. Nyquist watched from down the street. The noise and the emotions on display had momentarily drawn him back to his own sense of self, and he was concerned and distressed by what he saw, this sudden display of mob behavior from the villagers. His hands came up to his mask, to prize it from his face, but there seemed to be no purchase. The plastic covering slithered like jelly under his fingers and the edges were sealed.

Flesh and mask had merged completely together.

He stepped forward into the crowd. Straightaway the mask grew hot on his face and tightened even further, and he felt his features drawing in upon themselves. He was having trouble breathing, and his hands came up to the mask again, but not to pull it this time, but to press it more firmly into place, to become a Grey once more, purely Grey, to the core and proud of it, proud of the name and the power it gave him. There were fellows on every side and it felt good to be held within the mass, as one, one person with one name and one face and one voice, rising up in a chant of fear and aggression, growing ever louder. Edmund found himself entirely without control or choice, joining in with the chant.

Cover yourself. Harlot, cover yourself. Cover yourself!

He surged forward with the others, even closer to the house. A struggle ensued. He braced his hands against the garden fence. Something tapped him on the back of the head, a walking stick perhaps.

And then the door of the house opened.

Professor Bryars stood there, her face on full view for all to see.

No mask, no Alice.

The sight of it was dreadful enough to freeze the heart. Edmund himself was shocked by the naked flesh, the eyes, the line of the nose and the redness of the lips, the color in the cheeks, the wrinkles at the woman's brow. How could such things be visible!

Bryars stood in the doorway, glowering at her visitors.

Nobody spoke, nobody moved.

From the tension in the air, it seemed that a fight was about to break out. But instead the professor raised her hand, showing the mask that she held. She placed this on her face and now Alice Grey looked out from the doorway. Of Professor Bryars, there was no sign. The crowd murmured as one, in peace, smiling as their masks smiled, and nodding as their masks nodded. The group broke apart and scattered until only one man was left on the pavement outside the house.

Edmund looked at Alice and Alice looked back.

"You'd better come in," she said.

Ten minutes later they were sitting at a table in the living room, Edmund with a cup of tea in front of him, and a plate of Sutton's bourbons, and the professor sipping at a glass of wine. He had the feeling it wasn't her first of the day. Her mask was stained red around the lips, while biscuit crumbs and sugar granules clung to his. Edmund wondered if he might take another biscuit. Alice saw his need and pushed the plate forward, and Edmund took up the offer gladly. They had spoken only a few words until now, about the weather, the latest radio play, and the prospects of the Hoxley cricket team come the summer season. But when tea and wine were done Alice said to her guest, "I think we should remove our masks, what do you say?"

"Is that wise?" Edmund replied. "I've quite taken to mine."

"Trust me." Professor Grey smiled. "And then we can talk. Properly. Face to face."

She left the room. Edmund looked around, taking in the furniture and fittings. Lots of brass ornaments, doilies, willow pattern plates, a souvenir ashtray of a seaside visit, and a set of *Encyclopædia Britannica* with a gap on the shelf where volume seven was missing.

The professor returned after a few minutes, carrying a large bowl of water, which she placed on the table in front of her guest.

"We wash it off, is that all it takes?"

"Not quite."

"The water looks dirty."

She smiled. "Just a few special ingredients of my own procurement. Don't worry. I've done this many times before."

Edmund's mask creased with worry. There was something moving around in the water, something alive. "Is that a beetle?" he asked.

Alice explained brightly, "The masks, by their saintly nature, fall off quite naturally at six o'clock tonight. All I'm doing is speeding up the process."

Edmund peered into the bowl. There were a number of the beetles, half a dozen or so – he couldn't count them all for they kept moving about. And there was a silvery tinge to the water, which reminded him of something, something he had seen recently. He couldn't quite place it.

Now the insects were emitting a kind of black ink from their rear glands.

"You're not asking me to drink this, are you?"

"Edmund, that would be ridiculous. Simply lower your face into the bowl, that's all."

"Lower my face?"

"That's it. Quite simple. And hold it there for a minute. A minute and a half, at the most. Just hold your breath and don't open your mouth."

"It's not poisonous, is it?"

The professor grinned. She was holding a bath towel. "Come on. I'll do the same. And then I'll tell you the story of the black tower."

Yes, that's all he wanted. Edmund lowered his face into the filthy water. He felt his mask submerging and growing slightly colder. And then darkness covered him as the towel was placed over his head and shoulders, blocking out the light.

The beetles slithered across his lips.

A SPELL FOR THE WICKED

The first thing he felt was a jab of pain against his skin, a sharp pain and then another, and one more, and he thought that the mask had fallen away and that his skin was bare and being attacked, but it wasn't that, his face and head were still covered, still in darkness, and he felt a sudden panic as though he couldn't breathe, his mouth was closed and his eyes were screwed tight as he felt further stabs against his cheeks and brow, one, two, three stabs, and the panic came again, stronger than before. I am what I become, a villager, a true resident of this place and the rightful and trueborn occupant of this mask, and it will never leave me, and that is that. His mind wandered. The thorns pressed into his skin, jabbing again and again until his face was wet with blood. He could feel it spreading all over his mask and filling his eyes and his mouth, the thorns pricking at his temples and his brow and when he forced his eyes open he knew where he was, he could see through the gaps in the woven twigs and branches and the barbed wire that bound it all together around his head, bound and tied, he was the Tolly Man, hearing the chant of the children as they danced. *Sing along a Sally, O, the moon is in the valley, O*. Now he was dancing too, slow and heavy on his feet, one and two and three and four, around and around the green we go. He was looking out at the village through the mask of the Tolly Man and the villagers pranced before him and laid their sacrifices of blood and flesh and feathers at his feet. *Come to grief or come what may, Tolly Man, Tolly Man, come out to play.* Their song was a prayer in the moonlight.

FAMILY HISTORIES

Half an hour later Nyquist was sitting on a chair in a darkened room as one slide after another passed through the beam of a lantern, sending its image to the screen that rested against the wall. Professor Bryars was feeding her collection of slides into the slot one at a time, causing the light to wax and wane, as the moon did the same, the moon on the screen that Nyquist viewed in various places and phases – now a crescent, now full, now a slither at the edge of a black globe. The moon as it appeared over Hoxley, over the woods, over the fields beyond the village.

"This is my night-time selection," Bryars explained. "I have views for every season and every time of day and weather condition. All taken from the archives." Her voice trembled with passion. "The village never fails to delight me; its people, its history, the way it interacts with land and sky."

One slide, another, image after image. Nyquist was completely spellbound, his face lit, then dark, lit, then dark, his eyes sparkling then eclipsed. He couldn't turn his head away.

"I wish all my viewers were so entranced," Bryars said.

The single member of the audience didn't reply, for a single word would destroy the atmosphere. It was quite simple: he felt he was watching his own life, but in secret. Some other version of himself had lived here in the village, he was sure of it, had lived and died here and been born again, and died again and lived again, and so it went on down the years and the centuries. He was looking at a well of images drawn from deep within, never before seen until this moment, but each one sounding a toll of bells in his mind.

From the darkness they rose, these glades and bowers, the children's games, the tree struck by lightning, the old house that was no longer standing, *Miss Ida Pearson's Depiction of Her Perplexing Dream in Watercolor (Framed)*, a looking glass with the photographer shown in reflection. The sights of the village and its residents moved back and forth in time, from sepia to monochrome to color and back again, the years mixed up: some of the images with a distinct hand-tinted look, others barely seen through a haze of distortion – the flowers that won first prize at the fair, the ladies in their Sunday best, the Whitsun marches, the sun glinting on the instruments of a brass band, the Morris troupe in full costume sitting outside the pub drinking pints of ale, the young girl who seemed to live again in the room, animated by light and shade and chemicals on film. Other images were more unreadable: a spider in a shoebox, a patch of earth, a bloodied knife, the silhouette of an airplane above the woods, the shadow of the Tolly Man on the village green.

And then the black tower came into view. Professor Bryars paused the mechanism, leaving the image on screen.

"This is somewhere near?" Nyquist asked.

"It is. Not too far from the village, but hidden by Morden Wood."

He stood up, taking his own photograph from his pocket, the one showing the tower, and he compared the two.

"It's the same place. But everyone I've asked in the village… nobody seems to know where it is, or if it even exists."

"It does exist, and it's easy to find. Just walk through the woods and take the left-hand path at Sylvia's Glade. And then keep on walking."

Nyquist turned to his host: "So why does nobody want to talk about it?"

Bryars didn't reply at first.

"Professor?"

"Oh please, call me Maude. On a day such as this, don't you think we've earned our real names?"

He nodded. Bryars switched on the overhead light. In its sudden glare her unmasked face looked pallid, almost colorless, with a pasty look to it. To offset this, her wispy hair had a tinge of blue from a dye. Broken veins were visible on her nose, further evidence of a liking for drink. He reckoned she was in her fifties only, but life had taken an early toll.

Her eyes flickered away from Nyquist's stare.

They were standing in an upstairs room which served as both viewing room and storage area. The shelves lining two of the walls were filled with books and alphabetized binders. The place was spotless; it was easy to imagine it being cleaned and dusted every single day.

Bryars said, "First you have to tell me what you saw, what you experienced?"

"When?"

"As the Edmund mask was being removed."

This time Nyquist didn't answer. The professor pushed him a little: "I know you saw something that disturbed you. Your body was reacting quite badly. Your shoulders were heaving and your hands were trembling on the table, each side of the bowl."

"I was thinking back on my past, on my youth, that's all. And I fell into a reverie."

"I think you're lying."

"Perhaps. But why are you so interested?"

"I'm a historian. The people of Hoxley see me as their chronicler, and you, sir, are a figure of much curiosity. I'd like to know your story." Her eyes gleamed. "I'd like to place you in the archive, in the most appropriate category."

"Under what? M for Mysterious Stranger?"

She sighed. "You do know that this is my only pleasure, collecting facts? So please won't you tell me what you saw, as the mask came loose? It would give me such joy."

Nyquist kept up his gentle lie. "As I said, childhood memories."

In truth, he didn't want to talk about the nightmarish vision he'd had; he could still feel the prickles and thorns of the Tolly mask pressing into the skin of his face.

The professor nodded her head a few times. And then she clicked off the magic lantern and moved over to one of the shelves.

"The tower is known as Clud Tower."

She opened a file and pulled out a number of engraved prints, each one showing the building in question. She placed them on the table for Nyquist to look at. "Back in the mid-eighteenth century, when the tower was built, the Cluds were a well-known, indeed infamous family. Most if not all the good people of Hoxley loathed and feared them."

"Why? What did they do?"

Bryars spoke enthusiastically. "The stories begin with one Wilhelmina Clud. She ruled the roost at the start of the seventeenth century, and was known for her dabbling in the occult arts. Her eldest daughter, Hildegard, was condemned as a witch, but failed to die on the gallows. They tried three times. She was banished from the village and took to living in the fields, eating weeds and fruit and sleeping among the sheep in their pen for warmth. She died alone out on the moor." Bryars drew breath. "Wilhelmina's fourth son, Peter Clud, was married to a barren wife, and in recompense took to stealing children from the neighboring villages. He killed himself by the eating of moonsilver, the berries of the myre tree, as poor Mr Bainbridge did." The professor turned the pages of a book as she spoke, her fingers tracing arcane symbols. "I could go on, but you get the picture, I'm sure. They were a family to be avoided. And their tower, Clud Tower, was notorious as a site of evil practice. Oh, the stories abound! Animal sacrifices, the murder of innocents, words scrawled on the walls, offensive words. You know, for parts of the human body…"

"So, this is why nobody wants to talk about the place?"

"Exactly. To even speak the tower's name is thought to bring ruin on a person, and that person's family."

Nyquist looked at the professor. "And yet you speak the name out loud, and you show pictures of it in your lecture."

She nodded. "I believe that many traditions are good, and worthy of preservation, for they bind the tribe together in a necessary way. But others are more problematic. Such as the wearing of identical masks on Saint Edmund's and Saint Alice's Day. It has stopped being a useful belief, and become a habit, and an excuse for bad behavior."

"Do the Cluds still live in the village?"

"Oh yes. A few. But they changed their name first to Clough. And many, many years back they added *Fair* on the front of that, and now the Faircloughs are as fair as fair can be." Her face took on a pinched look. "And by these methods, such and such, they hope the past will fade away." Bryars's eyes sparkled. "You'll have met Rebecca and Edward, I presume?"

It took Nyquist a moment to work out the names. "You mean Becca and Teddy? The young folk. Yes, I've spoken with them."

"Aye, well, they're Faircloughs. Oh, Becca's a sweet enough kid. She's like a pot that's had too much glaze put on it. But him, Teddy…" A shake of the head in dismay. "He's a troubled soul. I feel sorry for him."

"How do you mean?"

In answer, or in a kind of answer, Bryars placed her hand on a lump of twisted metal on a nearby shelf. It was in use as a bookend.

"Teddy gave me this. It's from a crashed airplane. You saw the slide, of the plane flying low over Morden Wood?"

"I did."

"It crashed, out on the edge of the moors, a few years back now. Engine failure, we think. Teddy Fairclough found the crash site. He witnessed the pilot's final moments." She sighed heavily. "The poor kid was ten years old at the time."

"That's not an easy thing to see."

Bryars nodded in agreement. "Teddy and I have always shared a disdain for tradition. We are, the both of us, looking for a way to escape this village… without actually leaving. Myself through history, and Teddy through, well, through his dreams. Dreams of flight."

"It sounds like you're persuading yourself to stay here, forever."

"The thing is, Teddy's got the Clud gene, I'm certain of it. You know, their mum's a drunkard, most of the day and night. And their father's rotten to the core. Dishonorable discharge from the Army. He's in prison right now. Embezzlement. Threatening behavior. Disturbance of the peace. Intoxicated in charge of a–"

"You know all the village secrets?"

She took this as a compliment. "That I do. Past, present, and with a little extrapolation of the known facts… the future. All is revealed."

And counted up, and noted, thought Nyquist. *Entered in a ledger, cross-referenced.*

"The thing is," she added, "some people find it difficult to escape their families, and their family's influence. It's a gravitational pull far greater than the moon's on the sea."

Nyquist thought of his own father, and his arrival in this village.

"What I need to know," he said, "is why someone would send me this picture, of this particular tower?"

"Perhaps your family is related in some way, to the Cluds?"

"I don't know, maybe."

Bryars nodded at this. At first, she looked doubtful, and then a little smile took over her lips. "Your surname is worthy of note," she said. "*Nyquist.*"

"I've never looked into it."

"It comes from a Viking forebear, an invader of this land. A pillager, and then a settler. He must've taken an Anglo Saxon woman for his bride."

"You've got one hell of mind on you, professor."

"How do you mean?"

"The tales you're weaving."

"Parables grown from isolation, nothing more."

"Still, that's quite the story. Viking warriors, Saxon brides."

Bryars preened herself, pleased with the conjuring. "In Swedish, Nyquist means *new branch*, or *new twig*. The new branch of a family perhaps, most probably a bastard line. The old bend sinister."

"That would explain a lot."

"Many people have similar lineages. It's all written in our blood, every last word, every story. You'll have heard of Watson and Crick, I take it."

"They're a double act?"

"Why yes, I suppose they are."

"Comedians?"

"Scientists, actually. Molecular biologists. They've uncovered a double spiral structure to the genetic code. It really is a most beautiful object. So elegant, and simple in its power." Her voice took on a softness, a dreamlike timbre. "And we are in there, in the twists and turns, ourselves, our very meaning, passed on from parent to child. But fragmented, broken, stitched back together, and each tiny mistake adding to our own unique personality."

Nyquist didn't want to think about this too much. Mothers, fathers, and what was given, and what was taken away.

"Look at this." Bryars took a small green bottle down from a shelf. "It's a penny blood."

"Yeah, I saw one in the shop window."

"Oh, but that was a fake, a toy for the children. This one is real. Dated 1807, do you see?"

He read the label out loud: *"Genuine blood of Saint Cristobel.* Really?"

"Drawn from a martyr's wound."

Nyquist watched the professor as she expressed her passion.

"They were very popular at one time, the penny bloods. All three hundred and sixty of our saints are represented. They were carried on the person to repel evil. Many of the bloods exist as unique specimens. Others, like this one of Cristobel, have multiple copies. How can I put it…? She lost a lot of blood in her martyrdom."

Nyquist held the flask up to the light. Whatever liquid was in there was now dark and sluggish. "But they can't all contain real blood, can they?"

"Who knows? But as a symbol, they have a profound meaning, don't you think? Genuine or fake, in the end it matters little, as long as people believe. In this way, the book of flesh is *seen* to be written, page by page by page."

She took the flask from him and replaced it on the shelf.

Nyquist asked, "What about the Tolly Man? What does he stand for?"

In answer she said, "Let me show you something. It might be of interest."

Bryars drew down an old ledger from a shelf, its cover marred with damp and mildew. The pages were yellowed and torn here and there. She said, "This is a list of all the people who have played the Tolly Man, over the centuries. You see here…" She had turned to the first page. "*Adam Clud, 1666.* Yes, to the village's eternal chagrin, the Clud name is the first to be registered. And of course, great store is set by the date containing the number 666, as detailed in the Book of Revelation."

"The Number of the Beast? Yes, I can see how that might upset the villagers."

"Adam was the grandson of Wilhelmina Clud. It is my personal belief that Adam Clud himself invented the mask of twigs, but no one will ever admit that, these days. And then the second wearer, you see, here…" Her finger moved to the next entry in the list of names. "*Jack Tollyman, 1667.* Now, for reasons long lost, Mr Tollyman gave his name to all who followed him down the centuries. Not Clud. *Tollyman.*"

"Is he always played by men?"

"Be careful, please! The pages are fragile." She gently pushed his hands away from the book, before continuing with her explanation. "It was an exclusively male role until the early part of this century. In 1902, Molly Metcalfe became the first ever Tolly Woman. Oh, I wish I had some photographs of her. Alas, she has vanished into dust. Only her name remains. But after that it became quite common for women to take the role. Young and old, rich or poor: all are welcome to take their chance. Although, why anyone would want to, I really can't say! It must be dreadfully painful inside that mask. And their faces and necks look horrible at day's end. Tiny cuts, the rash, welts already forming. Doctor Higgs is always on hand, with her calamine lotion and her sticking plasters."

Nyquist raised a hand to rub at his cheeks, feeling for blood and scars. But he suddenly realised what he was doing, and stopped.

"You know, if you're really keen on the history of our village, we have a little museum of curios." The professor touched a hand to her heart. "I am the curator."

"I haven't seen that yet."

"No, well, it's closed up at the moment, due to lack of funds." She frowned. "I really think the village council need to get their priorities right. But anyway, neither here nor there, neither here nor there…" She worried at a set of beads around her neck. "If you like, I can take you on a tour? There are some very interesting exhibits."

"I'm not on holiday," he answered.

"No, no, I understand that. You're seeking the whereabouts of your father. Of course you are."

"So you know why I'm here?"

"Gossipmongering is rife." She smiled. "And after all, you have been asking a lot of questions, of a lot of people."

"True." Nyquist pushed on. "So it still happens, the Tolly Man?"

"Oh yes, every year on Saint Algreave's Day. Names are put forward, and the wearer of the mask is decided by the elders. Afterwards, the mask is usually burned."

"Why?"

"John, I'm sure you know the answer to that, already."

"To replace setting fire to people, you mean? In sacrifice?"

"Exactly. Civilization, I think, is all about replacing reality with symbols."

"Nice theory. People still get killed, though."

"Yes, they do. Because they become *symbols*, themselves. In someone else's eyes."

Nyquist thought for a moment. "Has Saint Algreave's Day taken place this year?"

"It has. In the spring. Early in the cycle. I thought Mr Dunne acquitted himself well in the role. Of course, I never saw the final moments."

"This is Thomas Dunne, the photographer?"

"It is. Do you know him?"

"No. I went to his studio, but it looked empty, abandoned almost."

"Yes, that makes sense. Thomas was seen around Lower Hoxley for a few weeks after Saint Algreave's Day, but then the Dunnes became reclusive. They hardly ventured out of their home. And then..." Professor Bryars shook her head with concern. "It's believed they left the village one night. Nobody knows why."

Nyquist thought about his place in all this. "There's something going on here, isn't there? In this village? Something strange. Even beyond the madness of the saints."

Bryars shrugged. "I've certainly had my suspicions, over the years."

"I was drawn here on purpose, I know it. But for what end?"

"I can't answer that for you. But this I know: there is a faction in Hoxley who would gladly allow the old Clud spirit to be conjured back to life." Her eyes narrowed. "I don't necessarily mean those bearing that name or its derivations... but those few who worship the dark. And the creatures who live in darkness."

Her fingers idly turned the pages of her book of records.

Nyquist was halfway to asking a question when Bryars's face suddenly lit up, and she announced, "Now then, this is what I wanted to show you. More of the Tolly Men players." She pointed to a group of names in the middle of a page. "Do you see?"

Edwin of Lumbe – 1855
Robert Keepsake – 1856
Unknown – 1857
Mr Charles Holroyd – 1858
William Nyquist – 1859

The last name in the list blurred slightly. The room darkened all around as the shadows moved into living shapes, and every stray noise became a voice in the air, barely heard, muffled, the whispers of the children as they danced around the green. The mask of thorns was pressing once again at his face, obscuring his vision and cutting into his skin, as Maude Bryars told him to read on, one more page...

Jud Wykes – 1899
Young Simon Dale – 1901
Molly Metcalfe – 1902
Mr Alfred Beck – 1903
Owen Nyquist – 1904

INVISIBLE RAVEN

Nyquist walked back down Fallow Lane, his mind filled with the things he had learned from the professor's lecture. The family name was uppermost in his thoughts, and its place on the Tolly Man list: coincidence, or a connection to his father reaching back through the centuries? He'd always thought of his father's line as belonging exclusively to the city of his birth, Dayzone, but now he wondered: did the Nyquists move there at some point, from the north of the country? A deep emotion took him over, the like of which he had never felt before – through the times and the streams of the river and the passing of the years and the clouds that drift away and the blood that flows endlessly on from adult to child, he found himself part of a history untold until this moment.

His mood was broken by cries of derision aimed his way. He turned to see a group of children across the way pointing at his face in fear or mock fear. Their cries grew louder. So he pressed his Edmund Grey mask back in place and felt the flesh taking it up, drawing it in. But he was still himself: some bond had been severed by the ritual of the bowl and the beetles, and he could now live safely behind the mask and yet know his true name clearly.

John Nyquist. John Henry Nyquist.

A black wreath had been placed on the door of Yew Tree Cottage. It was unlocked. He walked into the hallway and stood in a square of cold sunlight, listening. He looked into the living room and saw a number of people staring back at him, a dozen or so of them, all wearing the masks of Alice and Edmund. One of them slowly raised a glass of wine to her lips: this Alice Grey sipped her drink, her eyes peering over the rim of the glass, through the holes in her mask. Nyquist entered the room, squeezing in to find a space. He was pressed up against the woman with the glass of wine, who said to him, "Edmund, I'm so glad you've joined us. Poor Alice needs all our help at the moment."

Nyquist nodded. "Yes. I agree. We all have to show support."

Slowly, he made his way over to the birdcage in the corner of the room. The budgerigar was perched there happily, eating seeds from a tray. The bottom of the cage was empty, with no sign of the torn-up pieces of the naming card.

A voice at his back said, "How's little Bertram doing?"

Nyquist turned to face yet another Edmund Grey, one of the visitors.

"Bertram?"

"Bertie the budgie. By rights, I'd call him Edmund, but he never responds. Anyway, how's the fellow doing? Bearing up I hope, in the face of such grief. You know he was found at the window, yesterday, tap, tap, tapping. Desperate to get back inside, he was, the poor little thing."

"Right. Look, is Hilda here? I mean Alice."

"Alice? Yes, she's around, upstairs, I think. But I don't know anyone called Hilda, I'm afraid."

Nyquist found her in the front bedroom of the house. The

widow Alice. She was sitting at a dressing table, staring at her face in the mirror. In tiny circles she moved a powder puff against the cheeks of her mask.

He called her name gently, "Alice, can we speak?"

She didn't move her eyes from her task.

"Alice?"

He came closer and now she looked at him in the mirror. For a moment they stared at each other in reflection, before she turned towards him fully and he saw that she had already applied lipstick to the lips of the mask, and blue eyeshadow around the eyeholes.

Nyquist pulled up a chair and sat in front of her. He said, "Alice, I know you don't want to speak, or that you can't speak… but I need your help."

She didn't say a word. Grief had given the widow another layer of silence, on top of her muteness. And her face was half hidden behind the mask, adding even further to her self-imposed exile.

"Can you write words down?"

No response, not even a shake of her head, or a nod. Her eyes looked directly at him through the twin apertures. He could see they were red from crying.

"Hilda?"

The sound of her real name spoken aloud caused her to shift back in her seat. In fear. Her whole being trembled from some untold effort.

"Alice. Alice, I'm sorry, I wasn't thinking. I know you're not Hilda. I know Hilda is away from home for the day. Please, look at me. Will you?"

She did, slowly turning back in her seat.

Her held her attention as best he could. "Alice, I have a

few questions for you, that's all. One or two questions." She stared at him without moving. "First of all, I'm interested in your tea set." It sounded absurd, as soon as he'd said it, but he pressed on. "The coronation service. Do you know the one I mean?"

There was no response.

"There's a teacup missing. Alice, do you know where that cup is?"

He searched the mask for any sign at all of a reaction beneath, in the flesh. But there was none. He tried another tack: "What happened to the raven in the cage?"

She continued to stare at him.

"What about the cage itself? The budgie's cage. Was it cleaned out? Alice? Did you clean it out, or did the policeman do it?"

Her eyes returned to the mirror, to her mask reflected there.

"Alice, don't look away." He drew her gently round in her seat, and he held her by the hand. "There were some pieces of card in the cage, in the bottom of the cage, torn pieces. I'm trying to find them. You see…" He paused, not knowing what to say. It seemed hopeless. "You see, they belonged to me, the pieces. I need to read what's on them. It was my naming card."

Her hand tightened in his grip.

He moved closer. "Sylvia Keepsake gave it to me, in the woods. She gave me a new name. And I think it contained a clue, or a message of some kind. Because someone told me that the name Sylvia gives you, whatever it might be, that's what you become. Do you think that's true?"

Was there a movement, the tiniest nod of her head?

He couldn't tell for sure.

"You see… Alice… I'm trying to find my father. I haven't seen him in a long time, since I was a child." He paused again, and then added, "Do you understand? A very long time."

But Alice Grey had settled back into her enclosed world.

The door of the mask had fully closed.

"It's all tied together, I'm sure it is. The name, my father, this village, the saints. I just can't work out the connections."

Her eyes closed.

Nyquist took a breath.

Was there any point in going on?

He let go of her hand, and immediately Hilda turned again to stare continually at her own reflection. Once again Alice was addicted to the looking glass. He watched her for a moment and then shifted in his seat. He looked at his own face in the mirror, or rather his own face beneath the face of Edmund Grey. There were four people at the dressing table, and they all sat in silence, thinking their own thoughts.

A voice disturbed them, although it was directed at Nyquist alone.

"How dare you vex the poor widow so!"

He turned to the door, where a woman stood, her face masked. She said nothing more, so Nyquist stood and went to her. Her Alice Grey mask was different from the others he had seen that day, more elegant and refined, and ever so slightly more transparent, as though the wearer desired her real face to be seen, and her status to be acknowledged.

It was Mrs Jane Sutton.

She glared at him. Her eyes were plainly seen. And she said, "Can't you see that Alice is grieving? She wishes to be alone."

"Is that her own choice?"

"Yes, it is! The saints damn you, sir, for coming here to our lovely village."

"Are you saying that I'm to blame?"

"Of course you are. Do you really think her husband would have killed himself, without your influence?"

"That's hardly–"

"You visited him on your first night here. And the very next day he was dead. You must've have said something to him, something untoward, and unwelcome."

Nyquist didn't know how to answer, because in his heart he suspected her words to be true, or at least partially true. But he didn't know the real trigger for the suicide, whether a word or a gesture on his part, or something else entirely. Certainly, Mrs Sutton had made it plain from the first night that she didn't want him here.

She said now, "I will ask you again to leave my friend alone."

"Why? Are you scared, Mrs Sutton–"

"That is not my name! Kindly–"

"Are you scared that Hilda knows the truth about this village?"

"There is no *truth* here. Only the many different truths of all the villagers."

"I'm starting to think you might be involved."

She drew herself up to her full height, only a bare inch under Nyquist's, and she spoke with every polished vowel that she could muster: "I am Mrs Alice Grey, headmistress. I will *not* be spoken to in this way."

Nyquist held her stare. For a moment he really thought that she was going to grab hold of him and attempt to drag him away. He could see anger in her mask, and in the face beneath it. His presence disturbed her greatly.

"I will have my driver dispel you, if needed."

"Sure. He might end up in hospital."

Now she was exasperated. "What on earth do you want from us?"

He was all set to tell her the story, the simple story of the search for his father, when the sound of breaking glass caused him to stutter.

Jane Sutton gasped.

Nyquist turned.

Hilda Bainbridge had picked up a heavy bottle of perfume and used it to smash the mirror on her dressing table. The fragments of glass lay around her, and on the carpet at her feet. The bottle was still clenched in her hand.

Mrs Sutton made a move towards her but received only a rebuke in return, as Hilda spun on her seat and raised the bottle as though to throw it at the other woman. Jane stopped where she was. Her mask trembled as she realised the truth, that she was the unwanted one. And without another word she made her way to the door, pushed past Nyquist, and left.

He waited until the sound of her footsteps had faded down the stairs. Then he went over to the dressing table and he sat down, as he had before. With a kind hand, he urged Hilda to put down the perfume bottle. She did so. And then he spoke the words he should've said at the very beginning.

"I'm sorry for your loss. I'm sorry that Edmund passed away."

Her mask nodded.

"I'm sorry that your husband, that Ian..."

Her husband's real name caused her to shudder.

"I'm sorry that he did that terrible thing."

Now she controlled herself and kept her body still, and not a word issued from her lips.

Nyquist leaned back in the chair, and felt the muscles in his back tighten. His head ached, and his body was tired. Everything was very quiet in the room. The mourners below could not be heard, and Hilda gathered the silence around her like a shroud, and he rested within the silence, and he felt himself sinking into it. He was lost, it was that simple. His eyes closed of their own accord.

Hssssss

He felt only a breath of air moving, a draft on the skin of his forearm, that was all. It was enough to make him open his eyes.

Hilda was moving her hands. She had locked her hands together using her thumbs, and her outstretched fingers moved up and down on both sides. She lifted her hands to shoulder height, her arms bending and then stretching outwards and upwards, as her fingers repeated their flapping motion.

The wings of a bird.

A game, a children's mime. The movement continued. Hilda's head tilted as her eyes followed the conjured bird in its flight back and forth, back and forth.

Nyquist sat up in his chair.

"A bird? You're making a bird?"

Her only reply was the continued movement of the imagined wings.

"The raven. You mean the raven flew away? Is that what you're saying?"

The hands dipped in response and then soared higher.

"It flew away, through the window? Or the door?"

Yes. The bird flew away through the imagined door. Her movements told him the story. And then she stood and followed the story across the room, her hands outstretched before her, still moving, still a pair of wings. Nyquist came after her, onto the landing and down the stairs, and round into the hallway. The crowd of masks gazed on them from the living room, but Hilda kept on her way, her own flight, on towards the kitchen. Here, the bird was trapped inside, and fluttered madly against the paneling of the back door. Nyquist opened it for her, and Hilda stepped outside and lifted her hands and separated them, allowing the bird to vanish from her fingertips into the clean cold air of winter.

Her hands were now empty.

Nyquist thought she might come back inside, out of the chill, but she remained where she was, looking out at the frosted grass, the hard ground, and the bare trees. He stood with her. The sky was slated over from top to bottom, gray and pitiless. Hilda walked a little way into the garden and stopped, pointing at a patch of earth that had recently been dug over. Nyquist bent down. There was a trowel nearby. He used this to dig into the soil. A little way down he uncovered a bundle of newspaper. The package was damp, smelly, stained with dirt and grease, but he unwrapped it there and then, carefully unfolding the sheets of *The Bligh, Lockhampton & Hoxley Reporter*. The missing coronation tea cup was nestled within, with a tiny crack down one side, and a small piece chipped from the rim. It had fallen to the floor at some point, or been thrown away in disgust or anger. He peered inside and saw the green tendril curled in place at the bottom of the cup, and scattered around it several pieces of torn paper – the remains of his naming card.

He thanked Mrs Bainbridge loudly and keenly and went on his way, taking cup and contents with him. Through lanes narrow and weed-strewn and unpaved and deserted, through well-maintained streets packed with people going about their Saturday business. He walked across the green where the tent belonging to Madame Grey (née Fontaine) was now open, a line of customers queueing up outside to have their fortunes read. He headed towards to The Swan With Two Necks, hardly aware of all the masks around him, Alice and Edmund, Edmund and Alice, Alice with Alice and Edmund alone and then with Alice and another Edmund, each person a blur, of no importance. For only one thing mattered now. He went up to his little room above the pub and emptied the contents of the tea cup onto the eiderdown of his bed. The tendril had stirred awake at his presence, but for now Nyquist put the cup aside and turned all the pieces of card the right way up. There were fourteen of them altogether. He spent a few minutes putting them in order, completing the jigsaw. And now the card lay before him, the torn sections in place and the three words revealed, the name given to him on his very first day here in the village: *Written in Blood*. He remembered Sylvia Keepsake's instructions, that he should stare at the card for ten minutes or more. He did so now. Quite simply, he couldn't look away.

STRANDED IN LIFE

They drove north from Hoxley on a narrow road set between dry-stone walls. Nyquist kept glancing at the doctor's face, at the new mask she was wearing. "It's significant in its effects, don't you think?" Higgs said. "Half the day as a woman, and half as a man. Can there be a sweeter prospect?"

"Don't you get confused?"

"I do. Which is the whole point. And by the way, you have to call me Edmund from now on."

"I've just got used to calling you Alice."

"Times change."

As they left the last house of the village behind, Higgs pointed out the mocking gate. He glimpsed it in passing, a farm gate with four holes cut in it, two at the top and two at the bottom. "That's where we locked up miscreants, in the old days. People liked to throw things at them, attack them even."

Nyquist imagined Len Sadler waiting by the gate for hours, hoping that his love, Agnes Dunne, would show up.

"I say old days. The last person was locked up there in 1943."

Higgs steered the car across a ford. Water splashed away from the sides of the vehicle. Now the road stretched away over the moors. A light mist covered the land, so there wasn't much to see. A damaged fence, the dirty puffball of a sheep, and a crow or two for company. No people, not this far out, not on a day like this. The doctor's Morris Minor trundled on.

"There's one thing I need to know," Nyquist said.

"What's that?"

"How did you remove the Alice mask?"

"Oh, it's quite simple."

"So you put your face in a bowl of water, and let those beetles eat at you?"

"No, I did not. I took a tablet."

"You took a tablet?"

"You sound surprised, Edmund. Oh, don't tell me you visited the professor?" Higgs started to laugh. The little car filled with the sound of her tobacco-assisted throat rattle. It sounded like a magpie claiming its territory.

"I did."

"And she told you all that guff about the beetles?"

He chose not to reply. So Higgs explained, "I used a simple muscle relaxant. It loosens the mask enough for it to be peeled off. I need it for my patients, in case of emergencies, facial injuries, difficulties in breathing and so on."

"So the bowl of water doesn't work then?"

"Oh, it works. It's the traditional method, but only old sticklers like the prof still abide by it. Tell me, did she do it herself?"

"She did."

"And did you see her do it, with your own two eyes?"

"No, my face was covered with a towel."

This set the doctor off again, laughing madly. It quickly turned into a racking cough, which she apologised for.

"This bloody cold, I can't get rid of it, sorry."

She pressed on the car's horn to make a rook take off from the road ahead. Then she said, "The professor took a tablet, I'll bet she did. So typical!"

"Alright, doc. You win. I'm the village idiot."

"Oh, you're more than that, much more. But you do have plenty to learn."

"I've learned some things today, actually. About my family, for one."

"Tell me more."

"There used to be Nyquists in the village, way back when."

"Is that so? How interesting."

"We played the Tolly Man twice. But for some reason the family left the area, and moved down south." He turned to Higgs. "This was back at the turn of the century, according to the prof."

"New era, new prospects. Perhaps they were seeking their fortunes elsewhere?"

"Yes, perhaps."

But the thought of his family set Nyquist into reverie, and the passing countryside had a lulling effect on him. The doctor let him be, and concentrated on her driving.

He felt he'd been in the village for longer than three days. He could barely recall how scared he'd been, at his first sight of open land, and the never-ending sky. Now he felt the landscape mirrored him perfectly, and he felt more at home here. The news of a family connection made him want to dig deeper: it was like finding a puddle of precious water at the bottom of an ancient well.

The doctor was speaking, and he had to tune in to catch her words.

"… and so we had a little fling, the two of us."

"Sorry, who?"

"Myself and the professor. Back when the world was young and full of glee. And she was quite the catch, back then, believe me. Of course, we had to keep it hidden."

"You were Edmund to her Alice?"

"Don't be disgusting. Edmund and Alice are siblings." She smiled. "What do you think I am, a pervert?"

"And what about now?"

"Now? Alone. All alone. Except of course for my beloved saints."

The car bumped over something in the road.

"What was that?" Nyquist asked.

"A dead dog. Actually, just a pothole. Anyway, we're here now. King's Grave, as requested."

She brought the car to a halt. The land seemed to close in around the vehicle. A stone wall on one side of the road, a field on the other, which vanished into a haze of drizzle and mist after only a few yards. It was a lonely place, and cold, and for a few moments both driver and passenger sat in silence.

Higgs spoke first. "We don't know for sure which king is supposed to be buried here. Some old Saxon warlord or other, I suppose. Aelfric Bloodaxe. Something like that."

Nyquist took out his pocket atlas and turned to the page where Len Sadler had marked the location of the farmhouse. He would have to cross open land to get there. A lone magpie hopped along the stone wall, unperturbed by human presence.

The doctor asked, "What are you doing out here, Edmund?"

"I'm not sure. But there's a house somewhere near, an old farmhouse, or a cottage, and I think my father lived there for a while."

Higgs shivered. "Rather you than me. How will you get back?"

"I don't know."

"Well, I'll be driving back this way in a couple of hours, once I've seen to my patient. I'll park here and wait for a quarter hour or so. After that…"

"Yes, I know."

"You're on your own."

"Thank you." But he was reluctant to leave.

"What is it?" she asked. "What's wrong?"

"I've told you about the photographs?"

"I don't think so."

"I showed you the one of my father."

"Oh yes."

"Well there are seven of them altogether. Seven photographs. Somebody sent them to me, and I don't know who it was. But they brought me here, to the village."

"They're a kind of lure, do you mean?"

He looked at her. "There was a game I used to play with my dad. We'd cut a random set of images from a book, and from newspapers and magazines, arrange them in a circle, and then tell a story backwards, using the pictures as prompts, or clues."

"No wonder you ended up a detective!"

"Maybe."

"So how did you win?"

"By making up the funniest or the wackiest story."

"You invented this game?"

"No. My father did. He called it Widdershins."

"Which means counterclockwise. To go against. Or to move in an opposite direction."

"Really? I thought he'd just made the word up."

Higgs smiled at this. "We were taught the word at school, and instructed never to walk widdershins around the church, or else we'd bump into the devil."

"I think I took the left-hand path around the church, on my first day here."

"Oh? Who did you meet?"

"Just your common or garden ghosts. But they were inside my head."

"The worst kind, I always think."

"The point is, my father always beat me at widdershins. He had a fierce imagination."

"So you think the photographs you were sent connect to this game, in some way?"

He shrugged.

"But that means your father sent them to you, doesn't it? Isn't that what you want?"

"Maybe. Look, if I don't see you later, doc, I tell you how I got on tomorrow." He opened the door and stepped out into the road. The magpie flew off. Likewise, the car drove away and was soon lost from sight and hearing.

Nyquist was alone in the wilderness, more now than ever. The sky was low enough that he felt he could reach up and touch the dark clouds. The air was heavy with humidity. It wasn't exactly raining, but he was soaked by the time he'd taken the half-cobbled path that led across the field: his skin and clothes collected moisture. But he kept going, bowing his head whenever the wind came up. And with each step he felt the mask was taking him over once again; perhaps the beetle's effect was wearing off? He did his best to fight against the impulse, to keep his mind clear. He had to find this house, he had to see if his father was still there. The slightest chance took a hold of him and would not let go. He stepped off the pathway, onto grass. He could only trust he was going in the right direction. He passed the remains of an animal, half eaten, the wool a matted bloody mess around a wound. A lost sheep, most probably. Or a sacrificial lamb.

Now his feet were sinking into the soft muddy ground. Each step was a struggle. He imagined that his progress was churning up the bones of the Saxon king, long dead, probably more peat than calcium. A blast of wind attacked him; his overcoat whipped at his sides like the wings of a demented crow. Droplets of rain found their way inside his mask giving him the feeling of being underwater, like he was drowning. He tried to shake off the fear. And then, conjured from his thoughts almost, a dark mass appeared in the distance, a structure of some kind. He had to hope it was the cottage and he started to walk faster.

Now the rain hit hard, driven sideways by the wind.

He battled on, head down, body bent over. He had no sense of time passing, only the placing of one foot in front of the other, counting the steps taken for no reason other than to keep himself distracted. *52, 53, 54, 55, 56…* And when he next glanced up, he was already standing in front of the cottage. It was shrouded in mist, the one window boarded up. It was a small place, single story, made of local stone, with holes in the roof slates and the walls crumbling at every edge and surface that had met the wind and the rain over the years. But it wasn't quite the ruin he'd expected from Len Sadler's description.

The door was locked. A tour of the building yielded no easy entrance: no back door, a single window at the rear, also boarded up. A number of metal sculptures or totems occupied the garden area, made out of rusting engine parts. They reminded him of the sort of thing his father used to make in his workshop, devices for strange operations, or machines to record shapes in the mist.

The door of a wooden outbuilding was banging in the wind. There was a toilet inside, actually just a hole in the ground, probably with a cesspit below. He leaned over and dared to look down. Only darkness. Not even a smell to indicate it had been used recently. But when he turned back to the house, he took note of a bicycle propped against the wall. It looked new, well-cared for. It must belong to someone. He walked back to the front door. Nyquist stood there helpless as the rain fell on him, and ran down his collar. What a pitiless scene this was! And then he saw the upturned flowerpot next to the step. He lifted it up to reveal a key. Quickly he unlocked the door and stepped inside, grateful to be out of the elements. His entire body was shivering from the cold. He felt that he'd walked a good five miles or more, not the few hundred yards from the road.

It was one single room, quiet but not silent. The wooden beams creaked and the wind whistled mournfully at every tiny crevice. The stones of the walls were slowly and softly grinding against each other. There was a sink in one corner, but no taps, no running water: there must be a well somewhere close by. But the cottage was tidy; it was being looked after by someone, that was evident. The sheets on the bed in the corner were neat and tucked in, a woollen blanket folded on top. Even the fireplace was spotlessly clean, free of ash and soot. It wasn't a paradise, by any means – patches of moss grew on the walls and rain dripped in through a hole in the ceiling. A metal bucket had been placed beneath the drip. It beat an out-of-time tattoo.

plink
plink

plink

It was easy to imagine a person ending up here, as a hideout, someone on the run, in hope of disappearance from the crowded life. Which begged the question: what the hell had brought his father to this place?

Nyquist made a closer examination of the room's contents. A small stash of tin cans: garden peas, baked beans, luncheon meat. A camping stove. A row of books on a shelf. An oil painting on the wall, an amateur work by the looks of it, depicting green fields and hills bathed in sunlight. There was something odd about the image. He moved closer. In tiny lettering across the bottom edge someone had written a message in red: *Creeping Jenny is calling.* Nyquist thought of the name Sylvia had given him: "Written in Blood." Was it a coincidence, the red color? Did it mean something? Was this a warning from his father? The painting held his eye. And without knowing why, Nyquist mumbled a little phrase to himself: *Written in blood. One penny's worth.* And he thought about the penny blood bottle Professor Bryars had shown him. Was that the correct amount of money to be spent, for a relic? For evidence? Evidence of what? Paternity? *One penny is all it takes, kind sir, lay your money down, absolute bargain. A splash of your father's blood, guaranteed genuine.* He shook the thoughts away. It was the goddamn cottage, it was getting to him, making him nervous. The shadows, the ghosts in the walls, and the creaking timbers and the rain dripping down.

Nyquist drew his coat tighter, against the cold and the mood.

It was difficult to connect the proud, fine, upstanding man he remembered from his early childhood with the possible resident of this room. And yet he *had* run away, leaving his son to fend for himself. Had this impulse to wander always been there, a part of his father's nature, waiting to be activated, perhaps by his wife's death, by Darla's passing? She'd died when Nyquist was just seven years old. Everything changed after that, everything. But what had made his father want to disappear into the fog one day, and then reappear here, in the village of his ancestors, so many years later? And then, why choose to live here, in isolation, rather than in the village? None of it made sense.

plink
plink, plink

plink

A strange mathematical equation took Nyquist over: from the rate of the drips, and the diameter of the hole in the ceiling, and the precise amount of rainwater in the tin bucket, he might be able to work out the date when his father had left this place. All he would need is a record of the rainfall over the last few weeks, or months…

Of course, it was madness.

He walked over to the bookshelf and ran a finger along the spines. *Forgotten Moon, Gunshots from Hell, Viper's Kiss, The Devil's*

Mistress, Night Prowler. It was certainly typical of his father's reading habits, as remembered from youthful days. But the last book on the shelf was very different. Nyquist took it down. It was a guide to birdspotting entitled *Auberon's Guide to the Birds of Great Britain*. He remembered Len Sadler mentioning this – that his father had asked for such a book, and that Sadler had found one for him. And more than that, much more: now that he saw the cover, Nyquist remembered this book from his youth. It was the most popular of all the bird books, at the time, and his father had given him a copy as a birthday present. He opened it now. The title page told its own story: *To my son, Johnny, on his 7th birthday*. It was his father's handwriting. His father had for some reason written exactly the same inscription in this copy, as he had all those years ago. Nyquist had forgotten all about this. He had forgotten until this moment.

plink
plink

The book trembled in his hands as he turned from one page to another: the colored plates, the different species, the details of song and habitat and migration patterns.

Mute swan... Cygnus olor... waterfowl native to most parts of the islands... resident in all seasons of the year... orange and black beak, graceful curved neck...

It was strange present to give to a boy, for the city they'd lived in wasn't known for its birdlife, or wildlife of any kind, really, beyond the rat, the street dog, and the pigeon. Yet the book had fascinated him, and he would often lie awake at night, gazing at the pictures, and then falling asleep to dream of flight. The skylark!

He turned to another page at random, the pied wagtail, and knew at once that the book was meant for him – now, as it was back in his youth – for a green tendril rose from the page as he opened it. It was much thinner than the other two he'd seen, on cup and gun, but it moved quickly, stretching out and wrapping itself around his finger, seeking a bond with flesh. This time he let the plant-like creature be. He was joined to the paper. Here she was, Creeping Jenny herself, or at least a tiny part of her, as Sadler had explained. The tendril slithered and tied itself around his whole hand, and then the wrist, more of it arising each second from the depths of the book, from the story within, the story of chirrups and squawks, of claws and beaks and feathers, of flight and egg laying, and nest building and fledglings. He was lost in the long glide to earth from the heights, the sudden updraft under the wings, the skimming of the airwaves, the swoop and turn in midair, escaping gravity…

A noise was heard, coming from outside.

Footsteps.

Nyquist panicked. He dropped the book and pressed himself against the wall. It wasn't fear, or at least not fear of a stranger, but fear of his father; that he would now have to face him, man to man – young to old, child to parent after all this time apart. He felt vulnerable. Exposed. And yet he had to move, he had to see, to make sure. Yet still he hesitated.

A few last drops of rain fell into the bucket.

plink
plink, plink

plink

And then silence. Perhaps the two men were as fearful as each other, both unseen, both in hiding. Father and son, could it be? Nyquist put an end to the waiting. He stepped into the doorway and over the threshold into the dim light of the field where a figure was standing, swathed in a large rainproof coat, the hood up, face shadowed. There was no time to act, no time to be startled even, as the figure strode forward, arm raised, something clenched within it, a club, or a branch. Nyquist felt the impact on the side of his head and he plunged into the darkness of day, and he fell to the ground, to the wet ground, his feet and then his right hand slipping in the mud as the hooded figure came in to strike a second time.

No. No more.

It wasn't said aloud. The words were spoken inside, inside – no, not spoken, but cried out. No, not cried… but screamed, screamed out inside, in silence.

NO MORE!

And Nyquist's hand came up to protect himself, to grab at the branch his attacker held, and they struggled momentarily, the two of them, before the other staggered away, dropping the weapon and taking off across the field.

Nyquist rested where he was on the ground. His hand came up to the side of his head, where he felt blood from the cut. His hair was matted, the blood running down inside his mask, across his face. His eyes were covered in a red sheen, the field of King's Grave painted with the same color. Frantically, his hands pulled at the mask, trying to tear it free, but the thing was stuck, glued in place, the spell still working.

He got to his feet, feeling dazed and weak, almost falling again.

But he kept upright, and moved around clumsily, looking out across the moors, into the distance – the sky low down and unrelenting in gray, brooding, the sun already dipping toward the horizon. His eyes blinked away the blood as he searched for his attacker, but the fields were empty. He moved around the cottage, seeking another vantage, and then he saw a shape moving along the line of a hill, running away and disappearing over the crest. Nyquist set off in pursuit, his feet seeking a good purchase on the muddy ground. As he went, he repeated each of his three names to himself, trying to make a choice, to fix himself in one identity. But each name had its own and equal claim on him. *Edmund Grey. John Nyquist. Written in Blood. John Nyquist. Written in Blood. Edmund Grey...*

And so it went on. He was out of breath by the time he made the top of the hill. He looked down into a shallow valley where several pieces of metal lay scattered around.

The rain had stopped completely by now.

Nyquist walked down the slope, past the rusting machinery, the spilled innards of an engine, a broken wing decorated with a scarred ensign: the red, blue and white roundel of the RAF. It was the remains of a small airplane, the fuselage already half buried and covered over with bracken and moss. A large pool of water lay to one side, framed in rocks and earth, its surface dark and motionless beneath the sky. The single blade of a propeller protruded from the center of the tarn; it must've been thrown there in the crash. Nyquist couldn't help thinking of the sword Excalibur returned to Lake Avalon.

The hooded figure stood among the wreckage of the plane. He was no longer trying to run away. Nyquist stopped moving also, not wanting to scare the young man. For he could see now who it was.

"Teddy?"

The name acted as a trigger, causing the man to lower the hood of his coat, bringing his face into view.

"It's me, Nyquist. John Nyquist."

The lad shook his head in disgust. "I know who you are."

"You're not wearing a mask."

"I don't need to." Teddy's voice was petulant, always on the edge of hurt. "No one can make me do it."

"You're braver than I am, then."

This brought a smile to Teddy's lips, and he said, "I hate all the saints equally, and all that they make people do, in the name of belief."

"Why don't you leave then? Leave Hoxley. Move away, find–"

Teddy raised his arms in a sudden movement, flinging them wide, and he shouted at the top of his voice – a primitive, wordless cry. It echoed around the valley causing a grouse to take off in fright from the moor. In the dim light, with the parts of the crashed airplane around him, he looked like a pilot lamenting the breaking of his wings.

Neither man spoke until the cry had faded away completely, and then Teddy said, "What were you doing at the cottage? It's not your place."

"I know that."

Nyquist realised that one wrong word might send the young man running off again, and this time there would be no catching him.

"I was looking for someone. And I thought they might live there."

"Who?"

"My father. George."

He watched for a strong reaction, but the young man only scowled. "I call him Mr Nyquist. Or sir. As befits a man of his standing, and intellect."

"So you've been looking after the place?"

Teddy's face lit up. "Cleaning, tidying. And as soon as the weather clears up, I'll start on the roof, to stop those leaks."

"Why are you doing this?"

"For when he comes back."

"You think he might?"

Now worry took over his features. "I know he will."

"Are you sure, Teddy? Are you positive?"

"He promised me. He promised me!"

Nyquist let the promise ring out, empty or well-meant. He felt shivery inside, an after-effect of the fight and the blow to the head, and the cold.

"Let's go back to the cottage. I'm freezing, and my head aches, and there's blood inside my mask."

"I'm sorry," the young man answered. "I thought you'd come to inspect the cottage, or something. To take away Mr Nyquist's possessions."

"I think you knew exactly who I was, Teddy, right from the start, from day one. And I think you were jealous. Is that it?"

"No."

His face said otherwise. Nyquist started to put it together: "So you're the person who broke into my room, on my first night in the village."

"I didn't break in. The door was open."

"So what were you looking for?"

"I'd already heard about you, we all had. I knew your name."

"That gave you a shock, I imagine."

The young man nodded. "At first I thought it was him – the *real* Mr Nyquist. I thought he'd come back for me. But then I saw you on the green that night, after we all went outside, on Saint Meade's day. And I knew, I just knew, that you were here for no good purpose, that you would take him away, if you could."

"And now? Do you still think that?"

Teddy hesitated. "I think you're as lost as I am, and as sad."

Nyquist felt a sting of remorse. It turned quickly to anger.

"Tell me one thing, kid. Why in the name of hell did you stitch up my father's mouth, on the photograph?"

The question brought a strange reaction. Teddy started to shake, and to sway from side to side. His face was taken over by a series of nervous tics. Seeing this, Nyquist took a step forward. But the action only emboldened the young man. "It's called Birdbeck tarn," he said, gesturing to the pool. There was longing in his voice. And for a moment, it looked as though he might go in, that he might actually step into the water. It couldn't be that deep, if the plane's propeller was lodged in the rocky bed, but it was deep enough to drown in, and cold, cold and dark. The blood would freeze.

Nyquist held out a hand. "It's alright, Teddy. I'm not coming any closer."

"Good. Thank you. Don't do that."

"We should get back. It's going to rain again. Is that your bicycle at the cottage?"

Teddy nodded, but he made no attempt at compliance: he stood his ground.

Nyquist pressed at his mask, forcing the blood to seep down, away from his eyes. He moved his hand onto the wound on the side of his head; it felt pulpy, but not too bad.

"When did you meet Mr Nyquist?" he asked.

"Three months and two days ago."

"Early September?"

"Yes. I was cycling out this way, to visit the crash site. It's my favorite place, when I want to get away from people. But when I got to the crest of Hawley Ridge, I saw a figure moving about down below, gathering bits of metal from the plane wreck. Then he walked down to the cottage. I was curious, because the house had been empty for more than a year. It was pretty much uninhabitable."

"So you went down to meet him?"

"No. Not that day. But half a week later I came back and I lay in the grass and I spied on him. I'd brought a pair of binoculars with me. I saw him working in the back garden, making the first of his machines from the pieces of metal that he'd collected."

"What were you thinking?"

"That he might be a spy, an enemy of the people, or a criminal on the run. That he was building a weapon of some kind."

"What were you going to do, apprehend him?"

"No. Join him."

"And was he any of those things? A spy? A criminal?"

Teddy looked away over the hill, past the wreckage of the plane, out to where the sky met the land, far away, pathless, snow-peaked.

"I don't think you know him," he said, when he'd turned back. "You don't know him, not like I do."

"I'll agree with you there."

The admittance seemed to calm the young man, and he relaxed his arms and his stance, and he actually took a step closer to Nyquist.

"Two days later I plucked up the courage to walk down to the cottage and to speak with him."

"What did you talk about?"

"Everything! Oh, everything. So many things. I'd never met anyone like this before. The people of Hoxley… well, you've met them, you know what they're like."

Nyquist gestured for him to carry on.

"I couldn't stop listening to him, his stories. The places he'd been, his travels."

This was painful to hear, as though this young man had stolen Nyquist's life, in some way. He felt his teeth grinding together, and he tried to relax.

Teddy carried on. "He taught me about the machines he was making in the garden."

"The sculptures?"

"Not sculptures, no. Machines of communication."

"Communicating with whom?"

"People hidden, people lost, the heavens themselves. Messages from beyond. He told me he was looking for a spirit, one in particular."

"Don't tell me, his dead wife?"

The young man nodded in agreement. "He said that she lived on in the air, and all he had to do was gather her scattered atoms together, to make her whole once more."

Nyquist cursed. He had heard all this before, when he was a lad. The madness of his father's various schemes and séances, and how young Johnny would get dragged into the process.

"He killed her, you know? Did he tell you that? No, of course he didn't. He killed her in a car accident."

Teddy looked distraught at this news. "That's not true–"

Nyquist cut him off. "What about Sadler?" he asked. "Len Sadler. Did you see him at the cottage?"

It was a welcome change of subject. "Yes, I saw him hanging around once, but I stayed hidden until he'd gone, the interfering bastard."

"Sadler told me that my father didn't speak much."

Teddy looked positively gleeful at this. "Well there it is, you see! He preferred me. He liked to talk to me."

"You wanted Mr Nyquist all to yourself?"

"I didn't want other people talking to him, not even my sister. Or Val. So I didn't tell anybody in the village about him. And that's how he wanted it. He wished for seclusion."

"Did he tell you where he'd come from?"

"He told me stories of a city of light and dark, of the sky never seen – the sun and the moon, never seen – of streets filled with lamps and lanterns and gas flames, so many of them! It sounded like a dream."

"I was born in that place," Nyquist told him. "It's called Dayzone."

"Yes, of course I've heard of it. One part of it is called Dusk."

"That's right. It's filled with mist, endless mist."

Teddy nodded. "Mr Nyquist talked about the dusklands, and how he'd lived there for a while."

"He ran away into the dusk, when I was a lad. And he never came back."

"Yes, he mentioned… Mr Nyquist mentioned a son… somebody lost…"

Again, the pain struck home, like a needle. One jab, another. Pain, then hope.

"Why did he come here, to Hoxley?" Nyquist asked. "Did he tell you?"

"He was drawn here."

"What does that mean?"

"I can't say. I'm not allowed to."

"Teddy. Speak to me."

Nyquist reached forward and the young man swayed back in response, and the balance point between them shifted.

"I've told you before. Stay away!"

"I'm not… I'm not moving. Look. Teddy. Look at me."

The young man moved toward the pool, his feet sinking in the newly formed mud at the bank. He stared into the depths as he spoke: "One day Mr Nyquist stepped into the water. This is what he did. One step, two steps, right out into the center. I saw this from the ridge, up there, and I shouted down at him, as loud as I could. But he acted as though he couldn't hear me. And then he lowered himself into the pool completely. And he sank down below the surface. I saw it all."

"Why would he do that?"

"To return. To go back, back home."

"What happened? You're not… you're not saying he drowned, are you? Teddy?"

"I ran down and tried to pull him out, but… but he struggled against me and he slipped away, and the water was dark, darker than it should be, and I couldn't find him. I searched, and searched. I held my breath and sank down again and again, and I looked everywhere for him."

"But you saved him, didn't you? You found him, and you dragged him free?"

"Yes. Yes. I saved him. His hand reached out for mine and I held on tightly, I pulled him to the bank. He was sobbing, sobbing. He kept saying…"

"Yes? What did he say? Teddy!"

"That he was stranded. *Stranded in life.* That is what he said."

Teddy was shaking. He took another step and now the water seeped around the soles of his shoes.

"Teddy! Look at me. This way, lad. That's it, that's it." Nyquist had to keep him talking, to keep him from acting on impulse. "When did this happen? When did you last see my father?"

Teddy wiped tears from his face with the back of his hand. "At the end of the month. September 27th. I will always remember. He was worried all the time, see, that was the problem. Mr Nyquist was scared that he'd be found out. That they'd discover where he was."

"Who was looking for him?"

"He didn't say. He wouldn't tell me. But he was fearful, I could see that. And I was worried too, see, that Len Sadler might tell tales."

"I don't think he did, lad, as far as I know."

Teddy bit at his lip. "Whoever it was, they came for him. And he had to run, to find somewhere else to hide out. Or else they took him away." His hands beat at his sides. "I don't know which it was. I don't know. But the next time I came out here… he was gone. Just the empty cottage. A few belongings."

"You haven't seen him since then?"

The young man shook his head. He looked worried.

"He might not return, Teddy. Believe me."

"He will. I think he will. He has to."

It was a simple statement of truth, and Nyquist saw it as such. There was no argument against it. He said in hope of compliance, "Teddy. I'm going to walk back down to the cottage now, and try to get warm. Because I'm suffering out here, I'm freezing, and my head hurts from where you hit me. And I need to get back to the village. Doctor Higgs will be driving back this way sometime soon. I'm going to wait for her on the road. I need her to look at my injuries. And I need to get this mask off." He paused, to give all this a chance to sink in.

And then he asked, "Will you come with me?"

The young man hesitated. He moved away from the pool and turned toward Nyquist. He spoke calmly, as though reciting a speech.

"I stitched up your father's mouth on the photograph so as not to allow him to speak."

"It was an act of magic?"

"Yes. And by these means he wouldn't be able to tell you the secret."

"Which secret?"

"The one he pledged me to keep, to keep hidden, in here." He pressed at his heart. "It will never be revealed, not to anyone."

Nyquist could no longer control himself. He stepped forward. "Teddy… I need to know everything. I have to find my father."

"No, no. He doesn't belong to you."

"What did he say?"

Now they stood together on the edge of the pool. Nyquist held the other man by the upper arms, face to face.

"Tell me!"

Teddy's voice took on a trancelike effect, devoid of emotion. "I was born and raised here in Hoxley-on-the-Hale. I will live and die here." He was creating his place in the world, one fact at a time. "My dad rots in prison. My mum is a drunkard. My sister waits only for marriage. Next week, I will be twenty years old."

There was no struggle in the young man, no attempt to escape.

"My name used to be Edward Patrick Fairclough."

And too late, Nyquist remembered Becca's story of her brother and the new name given to him.

"Sylvia of the Woods has spoken. She has renamed me. I am *Born to Follow*. And by that phrase shall I be known and remembered. I am baptized!"

And with that he twisted out of Nyquist's grasp and plunged into the water of the pool, his legs making awkward, heavy strides. Nyquist was pulled with him, clinging onto the young man's hood in some vain hope of rescue.

Into the depths they fell, one then the other, rolling over and over.

Water soon filled Nyquist's overcoat, dragging him down. His hands hit bottom and his fingers dug into silt and pebbles, gaining purchase.

His eyes opened and saw only the cloud of silt rising through the darkness: the breath of a monster.

All sound was cut off except for a booming noise in the distance.

His own heart, amplified.

Teddy was close by, another object, struggling, struggling for life, for death, whichever proved strongest.

With a great effort Nyquist reached out in the dark and

groped blindly until his hand grabbed hold of something sturdy and sharp and he clung to it for safety, and then he pushed upwards to let his head break through the surface of the pool, where he sucked in a huge gulp of air. He was holding onto the blade of the propeller. Excalibur! He looked around, this way and that, but there was no sign of the other man. "Teddy, Teddy!" Dirt clogged his mouth and throat: dirt and grit and black water, weeds and insects. "Teddy!" He got to his feet and stood up. The water came up to his lower chest. Yet the surface was calm and shiny and as darkly hewn as before, with no sign at all of the recent disturbance.

Nyquist's voice rang out over the hills.

Strangely, the cold had not yet hit him, and yet his body was shivering. Voices were screaming in his head, the loudest of them urging him to return to the bank and to climb out onto dry land. Instead he ducked down under the water again and clung to the stones below, the weeds, the roots of ancient trees, pulling himself along, and this time all was calm and quiet and barely understandable, otherworldly, a dreaming realm. The water was warm and soothing. It had a bluish tinge, with silver particles floating within it. Magic lived here, submerged, waiting. Nyquist felt his mask slip away from his face. He saw coins and animal bones and jewels amid the pebbles and shards of the pool's bed, and the blade of a dagger inscribed with runes, and small machine parts from an airplane, nuts and bolts, and objects wrapped in ribbon, a lost and broken clock showing the correct time of day, his own Edmund Grey mask floating by, gently suspended, and the painted head of a doll, a pair of flying goggles, bones, buttons, a die, a skull, and most enticing of all a mirror framed in wood, its glass surface uppermost, briefly reflecting his movement, his progress, his face, no, not his face, but the face of his father, old and wise and smiling, and by now even the cold was dissipating from Nyquist's body and blood, and he felt completely at peace, the cloud of silt parting before him as he searched, and searched again until he found in the semi-darkness a hand, a hand reaching out for his and taking hold, entwined.

TENDRILS

The saints looked down upon them. Saint Alice and her brother Edmund looked down on the two men and smiled at their struggles, and bade them good progress. The rain stayed away and the skies cleared over King's Grave and the wind dropped to a whisper. They fell into the cottage and gathered their wits and banged their arms around themselves for warmth and comfort. Nyquist pulled the blanket off the bed and wrapped it around Teddy's body. He took a cotton sheet for himself. "I'll make a fire," Teddy said, his teeth chattering. But Nyquist said no, they had to keep moving, to get to the road and to pray they weren't too late. He picked up the birdwatching guide and took one more look at his father's belongings, and then they set off once more. Teddy wanted to take his bicycle. "No. Leave it." Nyquist forced the young man to walk ahead, for he would know the quickest and the surest way. And so it was. They reached the road and waited there for just ten minutes, no more, before a car came into view along the road. Dusk colored the air, and a sudden quiet fell over the land as the Morris Minor pulled up. Doctor Higgs greeted them both happily, until she saw the state they were in. And then her professional nature took over; she bundled Teddy in the back seat, and Nyquist in the front, and she set off without a word being said. Back at the surgery she washed the blood off Nyquist's face and attended to his wound, wrapping a bandage around his head. Both men had to strip themselves of their clothes, which were hung up to dry. Now they sat in front of a roaring fire, wearing dressing gowns, their feet resting in bowls of hot water. Nyquist drank whiskey, Teddy drank tea. The doctor sat at her desk, smoking her pipe and reading this week's copy of *The Lady*. She was still wearing her Edmund Grey mask. Every so often she would look up and mutter something under her breath.

"If you have anything to say, doc, you'd best say it."

She glowered at Nyquist. "I don't suppose you're going to tell me what happened out there?"

"A spot of bother. Nothing more."

She sighed, and then smiled. "What really gets my goat is that I have two men in my house, neither of them wearing masks. People will talk!"

"Let them."

"They'll make up stories about us."

Nyquist shrugged. He said, "I live in a place called Storyville. The streets are littered with last week's tales of woe. People soon move on."

"It wasn't cold."

This was Teddy speaking, the first proper words he'd said since arriving back at the village.

The doctor responded: "And what's that supposed to mean?"

"The tarn wasn't as cold as it should've been. Don't you think?"

Nyquist was noncommittal. "It was cold enough."

"No. No it wasn't! There's something about that whole area, where the plane crashed, something weird. Nothing goes right out there. Nothing grows properly–"

His words were cut short by a loud banging at the door and by angry raised voices from outside. The doctor went to see who it was, while Nyquist made a gesture for Teddy to remain calm. The young man rose to his feet, just as Becca and Val made their entrance, both of them wearing their Alice Grey masks.

"What's going on here?" Val demanded. "Why is he like this? Where are his clothes?"

"Teddy was in an accident, out in the fields," the doctor started.

"An accident?"

"But he's fine, there's nothing that can't be cured with a hot water bottle–"

"We'll see about that."

Val started to pull Teddy's clothes off the dryer, while Becca went to her brother and fussed over him. He was led from the room. At the door Becca turned and faced Nyquist.

"I don't want you anywhere near my brother, do you hear me?"

Nyquist did.

"In fact, mister, I think you should leave. Leave the village!"

She spun on her heel and immediately turned back and shouted at him once more: "And why isn't Teddy wearing a mask?! Is that your doing as well?"

He made to speak, but was cut off.

"You disgust me."

And with that she was gone, and the room settled back into quiet. Nyquist finished his drink in a long swallow. The doctor started to cough badly. She wiped at the mouth of her mask with a handkerchief and examined the folds of linen.

"Are you ill?" Nyquist asked. "Tell me."

She nodded and showed him the handkerchief. It was spotted with red.

"Is it bad?"

This time she didn't answer. Nyquist watched her for a moment and then said, "So what do you think, doc? Should I leave Hoxley? Is that for the best?"

"Who knows?" She touched at her mask; it was coming loose on her face. "Perhaps tomorrow will be Saint Belvedere's Day, when we all have to be nice to each other, dawn till midnight. Oh no, wait… we've already had that day this year. Damn it. Sorry! I shouldn't swear. Bad form."

"What do you know about Teddy?" Nyquist asked. "Or do you want me to keep calling him Edmund?" There was a hard edge to his voice.

"Oh, well… I think we've gone beyond the saint, now."

"So tell me about the lad."

"He worked at the bakery, up to a month ago."

"I can't imagine him hard at work."

"Office job. Actually, he's got the aptitude for that, when he cares to show it. A good head for figures. But then he gets the sack."

"Why?"

"Rumour has it, he badmouthed the Suttons."

"Now that I can believe."

Higgs shrugged her shoulders. "Yes, he's a troubled soul."

"What I can't understand is why he's still here, still in Hoxley? He obviously doesn't like the place."

She didn't answer. But she looked at Nyquist strangely and

said, "John, you do need to be careful. Things may soon come to a head. And whatever it is you hope to find–"

"There's no time for care, none at all."

The doctor stared at him, him at her. And they stayed like that until the clock on the mantel struck six times. Higgs smiled weakly.

"The hour has come."

She pressed at her mask again and this time it came off her face easily, clinging to her fingers. "I am myself once more. Irene Higgs, General Practitioner." There was a sadness in her words.

Nyquist was looking through his clothes. They were almost dry. He found the atlas in the pocket of his overcoat. Its pages were damp and crinkled. He tried to open it, succeeding only in tearing one of the pages. He asked the doctor if she had a copy of her own, and she did, fetching it from a cupboard.

"What do you need it for?"

"To find out where I was today. Teddy called the pool Birdbeck tarn." He searched for the page he needed. "He was right, by the way."

"About what?"

"The tarn wasn't exactly freezing, not as I'd thought it would be."

"The body acts in this way, for its own protection. Shock, adrenaline…"

"Maybe. Or perhaps a hot spring?"

"We did have a spring here, it's true, but much closer to the village. It dried up in the nineteenth century."

Nyquist brought the feeling to mind. "When I sank down below the surface, it was very calm, and warm. I don't know. It was comforting. No, that's the wrong word. It was… yes, consoling. *Consoling*. I felt that I might float there for a long time, at peace with the world. And there were a lot of objects on the bottom of the pool, as though they had been cast there on purpose. Offerings, and the like."

"Offerings? I'm afraid I don't understand."

"You know, like in a wishing well."

His finger traced a vague route on the page of the atlas, across the field of King's Grave and beyond the cottage, over the crest of the hill marked Hawley Ridge and down to the shallow valley. But the tarn wasn't shown: no symbol, no irregular shape of water. The area was represented by an exclamation mark, and he remembered his chat with Mavis Coombes at the pub, when he'd enquired about this, and she'd written a word of warning on his napkin.

Ghosts.

Nyquist told this story to Higgs, and she said in reply, "It's a village pastime, I'm afraid, the weaving of fancy tales."

"But it means something, otherwise why mark it on the map?"

"Yes." The doctor gave in. "There are apparitions seen up there, by the tarn. And all across King's Grave. But like I said, stories–"

"I'll find out the truth."

Nyquist had suffered enough, enough from the day and the rain and the wind, and the masks and the saints. He took up his clothes and put them on in the adjacent room. Then he said goodbye to the doctor and made his way back to the Swan. It was good to see the normal everyday faces of the residents revealed, now that six o'clock had passed. They were smiling happily, chattering, telling each other off, laughing together. A young couple smooched in a doorway.

Life in full, viewed in full. More than once he saw discarded masks lying on the pavements, Alice and Edmund cast aside.

He walked up to his room, turned on the gas fire and hunched over it, warming his hands. He placed the birdwatching book on his bed, and retrieved the handgun and the teacup from their hiding place. His collection of objects was growing. He pictured in his mind a display case of ebony and polished glass.

Item one: for your delectation – a tea cup.

Item two: one Enfield revolver, of notable interest.

Item three: a guidebook of birds, with heartfelt inscription.

One day soon, in ways as yet unknown, he would need them all.

He placed the seven photographs on the eiderdown alongside the fragments of his torn-up naming card. From these various offerings, his task was formed. Idly, he moved them around, placing the gun in the center, then the cup; he arranged the pieces of card in a circle; each photograph was given a different position around the edge, moving one step at a time, widdershins. Yes, he knew more than he did three nights ago, when he'd arrived, but so much remained a mystery. He tested the bandage on his head, making sure it was tight.

He opened *Auberon's Guide to the Birds of Great Britain*. His father had made lots of marks, scribbled notes, marginalia. From page to page the colored illustrations flickered under his fingers, one species after another: color of eggs, length of wingspan, feathers, eating habits, calls and songs.

Raven… Corvus corax… commonly known as a bird of ill omen. A handwritten note in the margin read: *Keeper of secrets.*

Why had his father left this book for him, in the cottage?

For he believed by now that it had been left there deliberately, that his father knew he would arrive in Hoxley one day. It seemed likely that George Nyquist had sent the photographs to him. But why? Why not just write a letter, to make all his intentions plain?

He reached the page where the pied wagtail was described and pictured.

Motacilla alba… gathers at dusk in large flocks… eggs are cream-colored, with a turquoise tint, speckled with reddish brown…

His father had added another note here: *Often seen in dreams.*

The tendril slithered across the paper, as though activated by light or air. This time it didn't reach for Nyquist's hand, but it crawled to the book's edge, reaching out. The matching tendrils on cup and gun also stretched themselves, each one reaching toward the other two, making contact. Connection. Twist and bind. Entangle.

Nyquist felt his body reacting, in a way he couldn't understand, his hands tingling, his skin itching at first and then settling into warmth. He felt strong, that he could keep on with this task, this quest. He saw clearly the dust motes in the air and the mites on the bed sheets. Every nerve was activated and the hairs on his arms rose and trembled like antennae. The moment lasted for a second or two, no more. And then the three objects separated from each other, and became once more a cup, a gun and a book. As Nyquist became once more a human, a simple person, a visitor, a man on his own in a dingy room above a public house. He moved his collection to the bedside table, undressed and climbed in between the sheets and fell asleep without a moment's hesitation. It wasn't yet half past seven. Saturday evening was still in full swing downstairs in the lounge bar and the snug, but the raised voices and the clink of glasses never reached him. He slept on deep into the night.

The hours passed. His room was dark, moonless. Now the pub was silent.

Somewhere in the depths of the house a clock struck the hour softly, once, twice. The door to the room opened and the dark-shaded figure glided in, a woman. She held in her hands a pair of thorned twigs taken from the myre tree. One twig rubbed against another and gave off a small sound. She breathed as wood might breathe, as a forest will breathe in the night, quietly, quietly, one bare branch after another, one berry, one seed. The woman stood next to the bed, looking down at the sleeping man. Now she made a whispering sound, a whisper that held a song that held a rhyme and a threat and a promise and a game. *Sing along a Sally, O, the moon is in the valley, O*. The words lingered. *Come what may, come out to play.* The two twigs – each adorned with a cluster of moonsilver – were lowered towards the victim. The berries glowed with their inner light, pale on the outside, and crimson inside the skin, filled with poison. The thorns were sharp and slightly hooked at the tips. They moved closer to the sleeper's face.

Nyquist shivered. His eyelids flickered.

His eyes opened.

His eyes didn't open.

He was both asleep, and awake. Asleep, awake. Asleep, awake.

The edges of the night were blurred and he was caught there, on the borderland.

Asleep, awake, asleep, awake.

He didn't see the visitor, but he dreamt about her. But he didn't really dream about her, for the visit actually happened.

But it didn't exactly happen, as such, it was more like a haunting. Or rather, something conjured from the sleeper's mind, his darkened mind, a figment of the imagination. Or not so much imagined, more remembered from his past, his childhood, or from a long-ago story. Not so much a story, and not so much a memory, but more an event that took place in another land, or planet. But not some distant planet, more the planet of the room and the village and the sleeper's place within it. And so, in this way, the visitation both happened, and didn't happen, simultaneously. Or perhaps the visit existed somewhere between the two states, happening, not happening, over and over – happening, not happening, happening, not happening, and on and on and on until the sleeper awoke.

Or didn't awake.

PART 3
WIDDERSHINS

THE CALLING BELL

It was strange. Not a sound greeted him, neither from downstairs, nor from outside, but the day was already well begun – he could see sunlight streaming through the part-open curtain. A new saint's icon was resting on the shelf, a plant in a pot, a kind of miniature tree whose twisted trunk and branches grew into a distinctly human shape with arms extended and its hair and hands made of twigs. The face was carved directly in the bark, a crude mouth, nose and eyes. Nyquist imagined the martyr, whoever he or she might be, must have been bound to a tree for their beliefs.

He spent some time in the bathroom, lying in the tub until the water grew cold. After getting ready, he went downstairs. He was starving hungry. But the dining room was empty. He sat at the table and waited for a couple of minutes, but nobody came to take his order. There was no sign of Mavis or her father. He looked into the kitchen; it too was empty. The cooking process had been started, and then abandoned. The gas hob was burning. Nyquist turned it off and searched the rest of the building, top to bottom.

The place was deserted.

The silence was intense, it settled in each room like a darkness.

The front door of the public house had been left wide open. He walked outside into the bright steel of the winter sun. Not a person was in sight on the high street. His footsteps echoed on the cobbles.

Each door was open. Every door of every house as he passed was wide open, inviting him to enter. But instead he kept on, hoping to see another villager, or to hear a call, a greeting; even a shout or a howl of anger would have satisfied him. But there was nothing. He checked his wristwatch and noted without surprise that it was already a quarter to eleven. He had slept for too many hours, far too many.

It was a Sunday. Perhaps that explained it. The day of rest.

At the open doorway of the doctor's surgery he hesitated, and then walked inside, along the hallway into the living room. Only last night this same room had been filled with noise and chatter, human life, a roaring fire, intruders, arguments, accusations. Now silence took charge. He checked the aquarium, but even the goldfish had gone missing. He looked out through the window, at an empty dog kennel and the bare lawn. Every tiny movement that Nyquist made seemed to damage the silence. It was uncanny. And for a good few moments he dared not stir. Nor speak. Nor breathe. Something was waiting for him to make a noise, something or someone, some creature, waiting in the quiet unseen places.

He turned slowly and saw the icon of the day's saint growing from a clay pot on the sideboard. It stared at him from behind its face of bark.

A bird chattered in the garden, a single repeated note song.

The mood broke and Nyquist moved on, checking the upstairs rooms.

Empty, empty.

In the main bedroom he saw an identical icon on the dressing table. This one had a label tied around one the branches: *Saint Leander*. The name surprised him. He took photograph number seven from his pocket and stared at the blank white image. He turned it over and saw again the legend: *St Leander's Day 1958*. So on this day last year, this photograph was taken. No. No, that wasn't right. Because Higgs had told him that the saints were chosen randomly; they didn't follow the normal calendar. Not exactly a year ago then, but whenever Leander had ruled last year. It had to mean something: empty village, empty image.

He took one last look around the room. He noticed the speckles of blood on the pillow case. He was looking at the doctor's secret life, and he felt both ashamed, and worried.

Ten minutes later he was walking along Pyke Road. Again, every single door of every house and building was open. He could hear nothing, nothing at all, not even a child's laugh or a baby's gurgle. And yet all the cars were still in place outside the houses or parked in driveways, and the doors of every vehicle, front and rear and boot, had been left open. If the villagers had journeyed elsewhere, they had traveled on foot. Or else he imagined them peeping out from their hiding places, spying on his solitary progress, quietly laughing to themselves at his predicament.

Nyquist was alone.

He rapped on the open door of Yew Tree Cottage, but there was no answer. He went inside and saw the birdcage in the living room, empty now of any occupant – the songs had flown away, or been taken into storage: song, feathers, bones, claws and beak, all gone. He called out Hilda's name: if she answered, she answered in silence.

A ghost would have a made a louder noise.

He went back outside and continued on his search for another person, for any evidence of life. He passed the community center and Sutton's bakery, and then he doubled back. He crossed the village green, past the pond and Blade of Moon, into the school with its empty classrooms, yes, he checked each one. Echoes in the cold air, chalk dust, a column of sums on the blackboard. And he came back outside and wondered to himself if he would ever see another person in all his life; he felt like Robinson Crusoe newly arrived on his island.

There was only the silence, and the emptiness.

He could only imagine everyone had gathered in the same place, in the woods or in the fields for some obscure ritual of their own invention. And he cursed aloud the good doctor or Coombes the landlord for not telling him where to go.

And then...

And then a noise disturbed him.

He stopped and listened. It was very quiet, barely existent.

It came and went, like a bell swinging back and forth. A small bell held in the hand and rattled to make a sound. Or else it was a whistle of some kind, high pitched, clear and bright. It was impossible to know the precise nature of the sound. It was a young child's dream of a bird, calling, calling on the edge of hearing. It sounded like the bell at the Bainbridge house, the one the budgie liked to tap. What was he called now? Yes, Bertie. That was it. Little Bertie Bainbridge. Ting-a-ling.

Only quieter.

ting-a-ling-a-ling

Slowly Nyquist turned in a circle, trying to locate the sound, to pinpoint it to a house or an alleyway or a shadow.

But the silence had returned.

Silence. Emptiness.

He made his way back to the high street and carried on, taking the bridge over the river. The waters ran softly. He entered the church and stood in the nave, gazing down the aisle towards the altar: silent empty pews, voiceless hymns, the nonexistent incantation. Even today. Even on the Lord's day! He made his way along one side of the church, checking the niches set at different heights in the walls. There were many of them, hundreds, and each held an icon of a different saint. None of the saints were named, so he could only identify the few he had seen up to now, in his room at the pub, and around the village. A small number of the alcoves were empty and this puzzled him greatly until he remembered the doctor's mention of the five No Saint's Days. How blissful that would be! He moved to the opposite wall of the church, where more icons were displayed. Most held the wax deposits of burnt-out candles in front of them; a lesser number had fresh candles standing in their holders. Nyquist worked it out: this was a marking system, to show which saint had been used this year, and which were still in waiting. His theory was proved correct when he found that only one icon, the tree-grown shape of Saint Leander, had a lighted candle in front of it. Today's figure of worship. The flame danced as though someone had blown on it.

He walked back outside. For the first time he noticed that a single myre tree was growing in the churchyard, its branches hung with clusters of the dreadful moonsilver berry, the roots nourished by the rich soil. Deliberately he took the left-hand path around the building, willing the devil to appear. Even that would be company. But no one disturbed him. He pulled back knots of vines and dry weeds from the gravestones. Here were the old names, the names of the dead and of their families still living: *Keepsake, Clud, Clough, Tattersthwaite, Bryars, Wykes, Holroyd, Dunne, Fitten, Higgs, Prudholme, Fairclough, Coombes, Bainbridge, Metcalfe.* One name – *Elizabeth Margaret Featherstonehaugh* – had to be split onto a second line. And well hidden behind a thicket he found a grave with his own family name inscribed: *William Nyquist, 1835-1859.* Twenty-four years old at his death. *Gathered here with his beloved wife, Edwina, and their son, Henry.* Every letter of each name and date was cracked and chipped and filled with dirt and the fibrous roots of plants and bird excrement, and he had to prize the details free with his bare hands.

1859. The date of William Nyquist's death. One hundred years ago.

It seemed important, and he brought to mind the list of Tolly Men that Professor Bryars had shown him. That was it, he remembered now: 1859 was the year when William had taken on the role: he had died sometime after wearing the mask of thorns. Was there a connection? Had the Tolly Man in some way led to his ancestor's death?

He imagined the family's leave-taking of Hoxley-on-the-Hale, perhaps under their own free will, or cast out, and the journey south. Was it one Nyquist alone, or a young couple, maybe with a child in tow? Perhaps they escaped by night, fleeing persecution, or poverty. Yes, he was already romanticizing his family history. And many, many years later, in exile, a child is born, a son: John Henry Nyquist. Himself. A child, now a man. And he felt that his entire body was sinking into the earth, taking up root here, by this river, in these moorlands. He thought back on the name Sylvia Keepsake had given him: perhaps Written in Blood was really about lineage, the family, what is passed on down the generations, and what is lost, or cast aside in disgust. Nyquist had been drawn back here, to the village, the wellspring – but to what end? Or what beginning?

He left the churchyard and took the path along the river, down towards Lower Hoxley. He was glad to see the swans swimming on the pool by the weir; evidence of biological life other than his own. But nobody passed him on the route, and the only sound came from the quiet burbling of the water and the occasional call of a bird from the banks of gorse.

The sun was well past its highest point, and the air grew colder. December brought out the best in the land, making it sparkle with icy brilliance. Nyquist pulled his overcoat around himself and walked on along the pathway.

Lower Hoxley greeted him with silence.

Empty streets, empty houses, each door wide open.

No cats, no dogs. Not even a stir of a shadow of a footstep of a breath of a leaf falling.

I am alone. I am alone here.

He passed the photographer's studio and walked on, up the hill to the outskirts of the village, where Len Sadler lived. The decorator's van was parked by the side of his house, all of its doors open. Nyquist went around the back of the house and saw the empty cages, the vacated perches. The doors were open on each enclosure, and he imagined the pigeons flying away, *en masse*, each with a message attached, a blank piece of paper, which decoded might read: *There's nothing here today. Do not come to Hoxley, there's little point, you will find nothing of use. Walk on.*

And he did, back down the slope of the road. Halfway down he heard again the jingle of the bell, calling to him from one doorway or another, he could not tell which. But this time he walked on, ignoring the chimes. He knew enough by now that only shadows waited for him. He popped in the corner shop – virtually a twin of the one in Upper Hoxley. It was called Cholmondeley's General Store. He picked up twenty Woodbine, a ham and cheese sandwich and a bottle of dandelion and burdock, leaving a tidy stack of shillings and pennies on the counter: more than enough. As he turned back to the door, he saw a stand filled with novelty items, little toys and practical jokes and balloons and the like. One item was the *Hair of Creeping Jenny* that he'd seen in the other shop's window. He bought a packet.

Five minutes later he was sitting on a bench in the village square, eating the sandwich as he stared at the names of the dead on the war memorial. He smoked a cigarette, and felt himself relax. Saint Leander had taken charge of his life. He was at her mercy. *I am alone. Yes.* And for the first time he didn't mind it, not at all. He had spent his entire life on busy streets and narrow alleyways, inside crumbling apartment blocks and one-room offices, in seedy bars and gambling dens, under neon signs and illuminated hoardings, in crowded markets and busy train stations. He had felt the crush and press of other people's flesh against his body, over and over, day in, day out. But did he need that now? Couldn't he stay here for the rest of his days, in Hoxley-on-the-Hale, following the decrees of each saint as they came along, changing his behavior accordingly?

It was an unruly thought, and yet a comforting one.

His meal was finished, Nyquist opened the packet of Creeping Jenny's Hair and pulled out the five strands. They were colored a bright green, each about two feet long when unrolled fully. But unlike the ones that clung to his own objects, these were made of some kind of elastic, with a little plastic hook attached to each end. He read the back of the packet:

> *Use these strands of Creeping Jenny's hair to attach one object to another. They will then be connected in a story. You too can act like Creeping Jenny, joining the strangest things together! Hours of fun guaranteed!*

He reached into his coat pocket for the envelope of photographs. He studied each scene not as a stranger might, but as a long-term resident: the church, the high street, the shop, Clud Tower, the Bainbridges outside their house. His father's face. But it was the seventh image that he concentrated on, staring deep into the blank landscape, and deeper still, and deeper... and then the answer came to him. Of course! It seemed incredibly simple, now that the thought had taken hold. One strand connecting to another.

Nyquist made his way to the photographer's studio. The front door was open. The place was exactly as he'd left it: the bird prints in the dust of the kitchen table, the portraits of Agnes Dunne on the walls, and the stink of old chemicals. He walked into the darkroom and placed the seventh photograph in the developing tray. The remains of the dead moth were still floating on the surface. He recognized the clear blue liquid with its scattering of silver particles: it was the same fluid that filled the hill pool of Birdbeck tarn. Thomas Dunne had collected liquid from there, and was using it in the photographic process. With a shudder, Nyquist recalled his plunge into the pool and the things he'd seen among the rocks and pebbles, submerged, and the feelings that had taken him over.

Magic. Transformation. One thing becoming another.

He gave the tray a gentle shake and he looked inside. Last time this process had formed an image for him – that of Len Sadler's house; now it did the same, but of a very different subject.

The bell chimed in the room behind him, dancing in the air: the dream of the village at play. But he didn't turn around. For he knew that no one would be present, not even a ghost. Instead his entire focus was on the tray and the photograph in the liquid, on the picture that was slowly emerging, a shadow darkening on the white ground, creating a building... no, a room, or some kind of interior space. Nyquist kept his eyes in focus as the image faded into view, one detail at a time – shelves, a glass cabinet of some kind, not yet seen clearly. And a person who stood to one side of the cabinet, now taking on form, color, shape and features, her face now clear, a woman. She was holding aloft a small silver bell, the kind used in handbell ringing.

He stood where he was for a good long while, not knowing how to move, with only his eyes alert and functioning as he took in the image and its various details, all he could gather: foreground and back, her body and stance, her face, her hair. But this was a stranger. Not a villager he had seen before, nor someone from his life, his past.

Someone unknown.

He made his way back to the street and from there to the river, following its winding course towards Hoxley-on-the-Hale. No one welcomed him: all the doors were wide open but no one invited him inside. And by three in the afternoon the sense of loneliness being a good thing had disappeared entirely, leaving only a man walking along, one empty street after another, so many empty houses, empty rooms, his eyes filled with equal emptiness. In one household he sat on the toilet for fifteen minutes, reading a story in a woman's magazine. *Oh Margaret, you should never have gone back to him!* He pulled up his trousers and carried on with his wanderings. Every so often he would glance down at the seventh photograph, and then up again, seeking a connection between image and reality, a certain location: where the cabinet stood, where the woman stood. He made sure that every street was visited, one after another, marking each one in his atlas. And then onwards. He dined alone on fancy food at the house of Doctor Higgs: ox tongue, stilton cheese, and a thick slice of Sutton's fruitcake for dessert. He felt gently bloated, as he sat in the doctor's armchair and read her copy of *The Bligh, Lockhampton & Hoxley Reporter*, cover to cover, the small ads, the local news, the flower show, the long-felt after-effects of last month's Saint Juniper's Day. He was looking for clues more than anything, clues to the village and its true nature, and to the woman who had appeared in the photograph.

Nothing was learned.

He continued on his quest, this time heading for the village green where the fortune teller's tent was still in place. He unknotted the ties and pulled aside the flap and stepped inside.

It was dark within. He fully expected Madame Fontaine to be absent, but a figure was sitting at a table, her face hidden in shadow.

Nyquist held himself still, against his reason.

His fingers twitched nervously.

To be in the presence of another being after such a day, such wanderings, it was too much to take! And yet the woman at the table also kept her silence. She did not move, not even when he managed to call out to her.

There were two large candles on the table. He struck a match and lit both of them, and by their light he saw the face of the Gypsy woman, her features entirely still, dead to any reaction. She was carved from wood. It was expertly done, the lines and planes of her nose and cheekbones and brow all lovingly made and textured. Her lips were painted red. She wore a gown of outlandish colors that covered her body from head to foot. Her two hands lay on the tabletop, emerging from the long sleeves of the gown. They too were carved from wood, and jointed with metal at each knuckle and at the wrist. But it was her face that captivated, for he had seen it before somewhere. Recognition hovered in his mind, and then slipped away. A mechanical raven was sitting on a perch nearby. A white diamond shape was painted on its brow.

Nyquist found a tanner in his pocket and dropped it into the slot on the table. Madame Fontaine came to life. Slowly at first, her arms creaking, her head bobbing slightly on her neck. The raven raised its wings and made a screeching noise; it sounded like two rough metal plates rubbing against each other. The fortune teller's right hand rose from the tabletop and moved over to a box containing a pack of playing cards. The fingers reached down and grabbed a card, seemingly at random. This was carried over to the center of the table where it was placed clumsily on the surface. It was a card from the Tarot. Nyquist knew very little of such things, but he watched in fascination as the operation was repeated twice more, giving three cards in total. *The Ten of Wands, The World (Reversed), The High Priestess*. The raven screeched again. Madame Fontaine chose another card, this time from a different box. This one spelled out his fortune. Nyquist picked it up and read the text.

Follow a pathway through the woods. Ask your question of the fire.

All coherent thought left his mind, only a puzzle remained, endless puzzles, fragments of meaning. Nyquist reached out to inspect some of the other fortune cards that might have been picked: *You will receive good news.* Or, *A relative from abroad will send you a gift.* Or even, *You will meet a tall handsome stranger.* It was absurd, and he had to laugh; there was no other proper response. It was a laugh in the face of all the collected saints, and whoever it was who spun out stories and meaning in this village built on craziness. Creeping Jenny herself.

He took one last look at Madame Fontaine, and this time he recognised her likeness. It looked very much like Agnes Dunne. He'd seen her image at the photographer's studio. This surprised him, until he explored the mechanical Gypsy and the table she was sitting at, and he found the maker's name on a brass plaque. *Leonard Sadler.* So then, Sadler had made the figure as a tribute to the woman he loved.

Nyquist left the tent and moved on across the green, hoping to find a street he hadn't seen before, a hidden entranceway

or alley. Every nook and cranny was explored, every room of
every house.

Meeting no one.

Seeing no one, not even in the distance, not even the
shadow of a person.

Hearing no one.

Even the calling bell was silent now.

Soon enough dusk would fall. He was getting tired, from
so much walking. In the dimming light the village seemed
abandoned, rather than deserted. And he feared that even
when this day ended and a new one began, still the streets
would be empty. He would live here forever, unable to
leave, only following the ever-dwindling traces of ghosts.
But he knew that he had to find the woman depicted in the
photograph on this very day, Saint Leander's Day, and no
other: that even tomorrow would be too late.

Nyquist continued on his journey, moving at random now,
turning corners as he came to them, the road atlas forgotten.
The vacated houses depressed him. Missing people: unheard
chatter, children's rhymes hushed to the point of nothingness,
all domestic arguments too quiet to be heard.

And then he saw something that brought him to a standstill,
that genuinely shocked him, that scared him almost.

A closed door.

One single door that was closed.

It was the first such thing he'd seen since leaving the pub
that morning. He approached the house warily. It was a larger
property than most others in the village, mock Tudor style,
with an adjoining garage. The garage door was open, showing
the bonnet of a Bentley parked within, but the house itself was
locked up. A sign in the front garden told him the house was

called *White Flower Lodge*. Nyquist pressed at the doorbell. It rang and rang inside, echoing along empty corridors without answer. He peered through the windows into a living room. There was no one at home. But Saint Leander was growing from her pot on a table… so why was the door locked, it didn't make sense. What set this house apart from all the others? He walked around into the back garden and tried the kitchen door; it too was locked. He felt like banging his head repeatedly against the door until blood seeped from his brow, and the bone started to splinter. He was sorely tempted. Such pain, such release. But instead he gathered his resolve and walked on, back down the hill towards the center of the village.

And then he stopped. He could go no further.

He cried.

He cried out. He screamed. A wordless noise.

Hoping for an answer, a response from the village, from a single person.

None came. None at all.

Alone, alone, alone.

He screamed again, and heard himself screaming again down the empty street.

echo, echo
echo

He was standing outside the community center. After a long day's wandering around so many domestic interiors, this building seemed to be the true center of the village, a neutral place. No attachments, no memories. He went inside, for warmth and comfort more than anything else, for he had already explored it earlier in the day. There was a small foyer with the receptionist's desk and the notice board, and an open door leading to the administrator's office. Nyquist looked around. Here was the hall where he had watched Professor Bryars's slide show: the screen was still in place. And here was the table where he had enjoyed tea and biscuits. He climbed onto the stage. There was a handwritten notice pinned to the screen, reading, "Tonight's lecture on basket weaving has been cancelled due to non-attendance." He tore this down and then turned to look out at the rows of empty chairs, at the invisible audience. He took a breath.

"Good afternoon, ladies and gentlemen. My name is John Nyquist. The elders of the village have kindly asked me to say a few words about myself, and my purpose here."

No one listened to him. He felt lightheaded as though a part of his mind had become displaced from the rest.

"I have also been known as Edmund Grey. And also as Mr Written in Blood."

He knew he wasn't supposed to say the new name out loud, but nobody seemed to mind, not one member of the audience.

"I was born in a city called Dayzone, a place of intense light and heat, of loud noise and teeming crowds. And of a region called Dusk, where mist reigns over all who venture there." He took a moment, to let his message sink in. "I have come to your village seeking the whereabouts of my father, who ran off into the dusklands when I was but a boy, eight years old. Here are some slides." And he gestured to the empty screen. "The house where I was born, under a glow of neon signs. My mother, Dorothy, who died when I was young. My father, George. I will pause here." The invisible image flickered on the screen. "Please, good people of Hoxley-on-the-Hale, please study this man's face. Has anybody seen him?"

No one answered.

"Please look carefully. I believe he came to the village in September of this year, but he may have been reclusive. I am trying to find his current whereabouts."

Silence, from all the seats.

He stared out at them, all the missing people.

"Please, I beg of you. Will you not give help to a stranger in need?"

They would not.

Nyquist's eyes scanned the empty hall and then finally settled on one particular chair, slightly off-center on the left, three rows from the front. This he knew was the seat his father would choose, if he ever came to a public event. He spoke to this chair alone.

"Eschewing modesty for the moment, I would like to think that I have made something of my life. I am a private eye. I have witnessed events so strange they have brought me to the edge of madness, and yet I have survived these hardships, often by accident more than skill. I have made my way to this point in time, despite all. I am alive!"

Anger broke free of his words.

But his audience made not a murmur: they really didn't care. He brought himself under control and carried on with his speech in a calmer tone, speaking once more to his father's empty chair.

"Father, whatever you think you have done wrong... I have done the same, or worse."

He paused, suddenly unable to formulate his words.

"And yet... and yet..."

His audience waited, or didn't wait. He imagined a chair scraping; someone at the back was leaving. Another person followed.

"And yet, in recompense, through my work, I have... I would like to believe... that I have helped... that I have eased a few troubles here and there... and that I have, almost by chance, discovered..."

One by one the invisible audience was leaving.

"... That I have uncovered hidden mysteries."

Now the empty chairs were doubly empty. The hall was deserted, twice over. Or not quite, for Nyquist saw that one seat was still invisibly occupied, his father's chair. And seeing this, he felt possessed, taken over by the twin spirits of seeking, and finding. Those twin spirits who really, secretly, hated each other.

"I know that you killed your wife, Dorothy... my mother... I know it was an accident... I know that you were drunk at the time."

His thoughts could never quite complete themselves.

"In consequence of which... speaking freely... if I ever did find you... father... I don't know if I would love you madly... or kill you."

Here he paused again, for there seemed little more to say. And he had a sudden insight, that he was talking to an empty room, and that he might as well talk to an empty mirror, for all the response he would get: an empty broken mirror.

And yet he had one last thing to say: "Are there any... are there any questions?"

Silence, utter silence.

Until at last...

Until at last someone got up the courage to speak.

There was a question from the floor.

Nyquist stood very still, all his soul fixed on the act of listening.

But it wasn't asked in words, this question, more in sound, in the sound of a small bell chiming. A shiver of silver in the air. He tried to locate the source, but every turn of his head seemed to move the bell away from his direct hearing. And then he bent down on his hands and knees and lowered the side of his face to the wooden floor. Yes, it was coming from there, from beneath the stage!

He searched in vain for a trap door. He walked down the steps and saw the little door in the side of the stage. It was ajar by half an inch. Nyquist ducked down low and entered a dark space filled with theatrical properties, costumes, hats, make-up kits, and rolled-up backdrops. Bent over double at the waist he made his way to a set of stairs, leading downwards.

The bell called him on.

It was getting louder, just slightly. He was closing in.

He was now in a cellar area. Here he could stand upright, although the top of his head brushed the plaster ceiling and a cloud of dust gathered about his hair. The space was tiny, with a single door offering progress. It too was partway open. A painted sign announced in a decorative script, *HOXLEY MUSEUM & ART GALLERY*. Below that a printed notice said, "Closed for refurbishment." It was doubtful that any repairs had been done in a while, and he remembered Professor Bryars's comments about the museum, and its lack of funds.

Nyquist pulled the door fully open. Immediately the sound of the bell was hushed.

He stood where he was, not daring to move.

He breathed deeply, preparing himself. And the bell took up

again, even louder now, in response to his body's expression. Spurred on by this, he stepped into a wide corridor lined on both sides with display cases. His hand found a light switch but it only turned on a single nearby bulb, leaving the further reaches in darkness. The cases were the same style as the one shown in the photograph. The woman must've stood in this place, somewhere, posing herself, or being posed. The photographer would have used a flashbulb.

Nyquist moved forward cautiously. His first step set the cobwebs trembling around his head; his second caused a small creature to scurry away into the shadows.

Each display case held a dusty item. Stuffed hares and weasels posed in panoramas of rocks and dried heather; a single white glove decorated with pearls; the face of an old clock, one yard across; a book of spells open at a certain page, the text and diagrams on view; the empty flattened skin of an adder positioned next to the bones of its jaw. A turn in the corridor led to an area given over to painted portraits and landscapes. He read a few of the labels: the paintings depicted local people, and local scenes, some of which he recognized. There was also a portrait of King Edward VII in pasty oils, all the royal colors dulled to brown and cream. Another turning led to more display cases. Contained within were early examples of the saintly icons, carved by hand, sculpted from mud and leaves, cast in tin or copper, glued or strung together, chiseled, broken, partway repaired, with hands and faces missing, iron figures wearing gowns of rust, the mummified head of a chicken stuck on a child's doll. One horrible face was pasted over with insect wings, hundreds of them.

A notice informed the visitor that the first saint to be

revered by the people of Hoxley was Saint Algreave, in the year 1666. There was that date again, with its trio of sixes. So the first saint and the first wearing of the Tolly mask both happened in the same year: perhaps one was a result of the other, the saints as holy protection against the devil? And almost three centuries later, the cycle was still being played out.

The next room housed a collection of human blood, held in storage, all three hundred and sixty examples displayed on shelves in cabinets. Arranged by date, the containers varied through time: thick colored glass, clear glass, test-tubes, Petri dishes and so on. Each was labeled with the saint's name. A few from the Victorian and Edwardian periods had their prices marked on them: a farthing, a halfpenny, one penny, a shilling, and so on. And despite the differing prices, the one name had stuck. Penny bloods. A handwritten card, very old and crinkly, displayed a poem or spell.

A guinea for her Ladyship
Two bob for Creeping Jenny.
Mr Brown likes half a crown,
But the devil takes a penny.

It was the kind of rhyme whose meaning, and characters, had been lost over time. And although it was described as an "18th Century charm to ward off evil", it could easily mean the opposite. Nyquist didn't know what to make of it all. The corridor was dark, lit by a few hidden bulbs, giving the bottles, flasks and tubes an eerie half-shadowed glow. Were they genuine blood relics, drawn from wounds in holy flesh? And if the people believed it so, then didn't that make it true, as Professor Bryars had insisted? Symbols held just as much power as reality.

One last turning led to an enclosed room. He no longer knew which direction he was facing, or where he was in relation to the community hall above. Perhaps he was under a different building by now? Time and distance slithered against each other. He felt sick inside, and dizzy. Only the sound of the bell drew him forward.

The Tolly Man stared out at him from a cabinet.

Another step; another mask, arriving out of the gloom. Six of them altogether. Each was dated – *1799, 1824, 1859, 1899, 1912, 1937.* The earliest looked more like a pile of dead twigs bound together with rotten vines. Nyquist studied each mask in turn. Branches of the myre tree, and wires and string or rope or fishing twine if no wire was available, and thorns and the ragged holes where once a person's eyes would have peered out, and the tiny stalks where the moonsilver berries had been torn off, and the tangle of darkness at each mask's center. He paused at the exhibit marked *1859*, and shivered inside, knowing that one of his ancestors had worn this very mask. And he remembered for the first time the event in the night – dream, or otherwise – of the Tolly Man or Woman standing over his bed, and touching his face with sharp prickly fingers. He broke away from the troubling thought and moved on and then paused once more at the final display cabinet. There should have been a seventh mask held here, constructed in 1947 according to its card, but the cabinet had been broken into. Shards of glass lay on the floor. The mask had been stolen. A hollow inside a hollow. It made him uneasy. He was hardly aware that the bell had fallen silent.

The silence pooled in the room, mixing with the shadows.

He could make out another door on the far side of the room. It was labeled *Exhibit 149*. It was open, of course, but only darkness could be seen within, a rich tempting darkness. But instead of exploring this next chamber, he stood where he was, unmoving, suddenly fearful.

He wasn't alone.

For every breath that he took, another person took a breath. And when he held his breath, the other person did the same, in tandem.

The room was deathly quiet.

Nyquist turned.

And there in the shadows, her face half in darkness, a woman was waiting for him. She raised her arm to show him what she held in her fingers. It was a silver bell. And in that one precise moment, every single detail of the seventh photograph was brought to life.

Slowly, quietly, softly lulling, hardly heard – the bell started to ring.

THE FLOOD

The light shifted, or else the woman moved, and now her face was fully encased in shadow. Yet even in the dark, her presence was palpable, a weight to the air that pressed on his skin: the room was a drugged space. The hand bell sounded again. It made a far quieter noise than it should, given its size. It appeared to be muffled, or to be ringing from a distance. The chimes merged with silence… and then found silence.

"Who are you?" Without realizing, he was speaking quietly.

He could hear her breathing, nothing more.

He thought of repeating his question.

But then she spoke, saying, "I've been watching you."

Her voice was steady, almost too much so, as though she were holding the words in place, carefully, one by one as they were uttered. "I have been watching you, off and on, whenever by chance our pathways crossed, and whenever I took a break from my work."

"Today?"

"Yes. Only today. Didn't you hear my bell, calling to you?"

"I did. But you didn't show yourself."

"I couldn't." There was a hint of regret. "I had to wait… and you had to find me. As the rulings decree."

Nyquist thought carefully on what to say, for he knew that this woman held secrets that were important to him, and he also knew, or rather he sensed, that she would fall silent, or even hide herself away, if pushed too far. So, he kept his voice as level as hers: "Haven't I seen you before, around the village?"

"No. That isn't possible, I'm afraid. It brings me sadness. But there it is."

"Why not? Why can I only see you today?"

"Because…"

"I'm listening."

He could hear her clothing rustle. "They won't let me out, except for Saint Leander's Day."

"I see. And what's your name?"

"I know only the name given to me by the villagers. They had a competition, and a vote was made for the best entry."

"And which name won?"

"Madelyn. Madelyn Arkwright."

"There can't be much cause for those, around here."

"I'm sorry?"

"Arks. And the building of them."

She took his remark entirely seriously. "Your assumption is correct."

"Unless it rains for forty days and nights."

"That has never happened, not for that precise duration, not in my lifetime."

It was a bizarre undertaking, to engage with her in this way. There wasn't a trace of guile, or humor, in her tone and subject matter. It was a kind of innocence, and yet not one born of inexperience or even ignorance, but rather one arriving fully formed in life, and remaining so forever. What

kind of person was she? How had she come to this position in
her society? Why on earth wouldn't the villagers let her out
on other days?

Now she said, "But you do know that the name Madelyn
means *woman from the high tower*? And why on earth would
a woman in a high tower need an ark? It doesn't make any
kind of sense. Let it rain and rain, she is safe in her tower
from all fear of flooding."

Nyquist nodded at this, in the hope that she could see him.

And she added, "And yet I have to live with the
contradictions. Happily, over the years I have come to terms
with all such ambiguities."

"Madelyn, won't you let me see your face?"

She answered with a small step forward. The bell was still
in her hand, but lowered to her waist. With her other hand
she reached out for a wall switch and turned on the light. It
was a dull and dusty bulb, enough to give her face a glow,
nothing more, but under its light she smiled at him. Or at
least tried to; emotion was a curse on her face, something to
be struggled with.

"How do I look?"

It was a difficult question to answer, for she held no
distinguishing features. Or rather, too many features at once.
It was, for instance, almost impossible to guess her age: at
first glance he would have said his own age or thereabouts,
mid-thirties, perhaps; but a second and a third look caused
him to doubt that. She might be anywhere from twenty-one
to forty-five, depending on how the light hit her face, and
her mood. Even as he watched, her face seemed to age for
a moment, to crease up, to wither, and then to settle back
into a clearer, younger expression. And now that he saw

her clearly for the first time, her gender was not quite so obviously stated. Despite the name given to her, Madelyn was an androgynous figure, from her cat-like eyes – one blue, one green – to her short-tufted hair, and her slim, shapeless body draped by a simple gray tunic, and trousers. Not a speck of color or adornment was seen. Her hair was halfway between blonde and brown, and even showed flecks of gray at the temples. Her voice shifted from guttural to singsong halfway through a sentence. Looking at her, Nyquist got an inkling of why some of the staid residents of Hoxley might not like her too much.

He asked. "Where do you live when it's not Saint Leander's Day?"

"In the dark."

"Are they keeping you prisoner?"

The question worried her, bringing her older expression into view once more.

"I shouldn't really be talking to you," she said. "It's dangerous. If the villagers return, and if they find us together…"

"What can they do?"

Madelyn shook her head at this, dismissing the notion. "I will keep us safe," she said, "for as long as I can."

For a moment the two of them stood there, staring at each other. And then Madelyn said, "You haven't answered my question."

"Which one? You'll have to remind me."

"How do I look?"

Nyquist gave it some thought. "I don't know, in all honesty. Your face…"

"Yes?" She looked hopeful.

"You have a striking face." It was the best he could find.

"Striking? Like a match, you mean? Like a matchstick catching fire." Her eyes took on more light than the room could give them, far more. She was excited, and her fingers danced in the air. "Like a flicker. Like a flame?"

"Yes, if you like."

"Oh, I do like that! Such a notion… I have a flickering, fiery face! It has never come to me before, not in all my long years."

And within an older face, Madelyn's features grew young, then old once more, and then young. Nyquist watched as her gaze turned to the seventh cabinet with its broken glass and its missing exhibit. "Who do you think stole this mask?" she asked.

"I don't know."

"It's a crying shame. Somebody must really hate the village, and all that it stands for. Someone from outside, I think." And then she coughed politely and said, "You will have to excuse me, I'm afraid."

"Why's that?"

"I am not used to having such a conversation."

"You're doing fine."

"I am learning, one sentence at a time."

"Look, I'm the same. I hardly know what to say to people…"

"The thing is, you see, John… you don't mind me using your first name?"

He shrugged in reply. "So, you know who I am?"

"Of course, of course." She carried on freely: "The thing is, I don't get many people to talk to. I had a nice chat some years ago, to a woman called Norma. Norma Spence. Oh that was a lovely conversation! We talked for one hour and thirteen minutes and twenty-two seconds. In fact, she was a visitor, like yourself. She came here from New Zealand. John, do you know of that country?"

"Down under, next to Australia."

"Yes, that's correct. Miss Spence was a robust individual, a woman of fierce pride and of excellent constitution. A pioneer. She was passing through the area on a holiday of the north of England and she happened to stay here for the night, in Hoxley, in the local pub, and it just so happened that the next day was Saint Leander's Day, and so we got to meet each other. That was the last time I spoke freely with anyone, answering back and forth as you and I are doing now, back and forth, nattering away. Oh, repartee, repartee! It's such a delight!" And then she hushed herself. "Oh dear, look at me, rambling on and on–"

"What about the villagers who keep you prisoner? Don't they talk to you?"

"They speak to me, but I cannot speak back. For on all other days but this, my voice is silent, as I am bound, by the covenant of the village."

Nyquist worried about Madelyn's state of mind. How much of what she was saying was true? And how much a delusion of some kind? His hope of uncovering secrets was fading away. The old anger nudged at him, a loyal friend, or enemy.

He asked, "So how long ago was it, when you met with Miss Spence?"

"Nine years ago."

"Nine?"

"So you see, if I'm a little out of practice."

"You're saying that you haven't spoken to anyone for nine years?"

"I have not. Correct. And in truth I think I scared Norma off, for she ran away as fast as her sturdy legs would carry her. You're not going to do that, are you, John? Promise me?"

The answer came quickly, without thought: "I promise."

"Norma found out my true nature. I scared her dreadfully."

"And what is your true nature?"

She reveled in her answer, in the word itself: "Multitudinous."

Her face gathered all of its younger elements and displayed them at once. "What do you think of that, John? Here I stand before you, Madelyn the Multitudinous. The one and only, in all her lovely otherness. Madelyn the Multitudinous!"

She had turned it into a song, a brief song for it faded out after one verse, and Nyquist was able to ask, "Will you tell me who took your photograph?"

"I don't know what you mean. I've never had my picture taken."

He took out the photograph and handed it to her. She stared at it for a good while, her face showing only the hints of a puzzle.

"This is me?"

"It is?"

"I don't often look in mirrors. I find it too confusing."

"I can assure you, Madelyn, it's you. So you can't remember it being taken?"

"No, I swear."

"But it's taken here, in the museum, right where you're standing now. And you're looking directly at the camera, do you see that?"

She nodded.

"It was taken last year, on Saint Leander's Day."

Now Madelyn looked up from her own image. "It's true that I did visit the Museum of Curios, last time. It's part of my annual itinerary. Every place, every doorway. But I was alone, of that I'm certain."

"You don't remember a flash going off?"

"What do you mean?"

"A flashbulb. To allow enough light to enter the lens."

A shake of the head. But then she glanced at the photograph and said, "I have the bell in my hand?"

"You do."

"I would be calling for companions."

Madelyn raised the bell and rang it once more. It was louder now, high and clear in its tone, and it worked as a magic charm, sending out a wave of bright air that Nyquist felt on the skin of his face.

She posed herself, replicating perfectly the image.

The bell rang on, and then slowed, and stopped.

Echoes dusted the air.

Nyquist took the photograph from her. He said, "Madelyn, do you know of a man named George Nyquist?"

Her eyes closed momentarily, the lids flickering as though in a dream.

"You do know him?"

She brought herself in focus and spoke slowly, "I have heard him spoken of, yes, and I have heard him speak, yes, inside, in here, in my head. I hear them all speak, I can hear them now, all of them at once."

"My father? What is he saying?"

"Saying, not saying, all at once unsaying, everything being said all at once, forever."

"Madelyn?"

It was no good, she was lost in another world.

"Who's speaking to you, the villagers?"

"Yes, all of them, they are talking to me."

"They speak to you, but you can't answer?"

"That is correct, yes."

"And what are they saying?"

"Oh, they're angry, John. They are growing angry with me." Her face aged instantly, as the fear took over. "They are coming back, they are coming close, I can hear them. So many of them. Voices, voices! Some of them are shouting, they're shouting at me, John! It hurts. It is hurtful, the things they are saying! John, help me, help me." By now she was crying out in panic. "Keep them away." She backed against a cabinet and put her free hand up to her face for protection against some unseen force. Her bell rang out madly. "Stay away! Get away from me!" Now she screamed out loud.

Only two people stood in the room.

The six masks of the Tolly Man looked on in silence.

Madelyn's face slithered with expressions, one after the other, all different, all vying for dominance. Nyquist went to her, but this only caused her further distress and she twisted away before he could even reach her, and slipped under his arms. "Don't touch me. Do not touch me!" And with that she was gone, running from the room.

He followed her along the corridors, one after another, one turning and a second and a third, past the various cabinets and their contents, through unlit rooms, in darkness and shadow, through tiny patches of light, of dust. Madelyn still carried in her hand the bell, and as she ran along the bell sounded, and it was this that Nyquist followed, a spun-silver thread through the labyrinth. He took a flight of stairs to a door and rushed though into a yard at the rear of the hall. Here he stood to get his breath, and to listen. The bell sounded quietly, from many miles away. An alleyway stretched away in both directions, but there was no one in sight, no one at all.

And the bell was silent.

He chose a direction and walked along until he reached a narrow lane and from there made his way back to Pyke Road. It was a quarter to six. The air was dark, with night falling rapidly, and there was still no sign of any other villagers. He felt even lonelier than before. The thought of leaving Hoxley for good took him over, but only for a moment or two, because he suddenly realized where Madelyn might be.

The doors were still closed up and locked on the large well-appointed Tudor house on Stickleback Avenue: *White Flower Lodge*. Nyquist worked the brass knocker, and waited. He stepped back along the garden path and looked up at the bedroom windows. One of the curtains moved and he knew he was being watched. He didn't do anything, except to move back to the front door. It took a while, but eventually he heard someone on the other side of the paneling. The lock clicked and a woman spoke. It was Madelyn. The door remained closed.

"I'll leave it on the latch," she said.

"That's fine."

"Don't come in straightaway."

"I won't. I'll wait here."

He did so, counting three minutes on his watch, and then he pushed the door open and entered the hallway. He checked the downstairs rooms, all empty, and then made his way up to the first floor. He could smell turpentine and oil paint and he knew he was nearing an artist's studio. It was located in a room at the back of the house, a converted bedroom. Two large windows looked out onto a gray-white sky and the tops of trees in a small copse. Various paintings, both oils and watercolors, were propped up against the walls or arranged on easels. But a vast tapestry dominated the room, taking up almost an entire wall. It showed an image of Noah's Ark with a long line of paired animals queueing to come aboard and the storm clouds brewing in the distance over jagged cliff tops. The work was halfway complete, or a little more, and a stretch of empty cloth still awaited the needle and the colored threads.

Madelyn was sitting on a tall stool, working on a section of the tapestry, her fingers moving swiftly and deftly, her entire concentration fixed on the small portion in her sight. He watched her for a while. Neither of them spoke, or acknowledged the other. And then without looking up she told him, "This is the house of Mr and Mrs Sutton. They're quite well to do."

"I've met them briefly. The good Lady Sutton warned me off. Twice."

"She's very protective of the village, it's true. But their bread and pasties are adored up and down the county, and beyond. They own five separate bakeries." She smiled with delight. "You'll have noticed the pun, I'm thinking? In the house name?"

He had to think about it for a moment. "I get it. So the Suttons let you stay here?"

"They gave me this room and set it up as a studio for me." She pointed over to a side table. "Mrs Sutton always bakes me a cake. It's a Victoria sponge this year. Have a slice, please, John. It's as light as a dandelion clock on a summer's day."

Nyquist declined the offer. "Are you free to go wherever you choose?"

"On this day, yes. Let loose to prowl where I may." Her fingers worked at the needle, pulling on a thread, adding details to the fur of a leopard. "Everyone is very kind, they always leave their doors open for me." She added another stitch and them looked at Nyquist for the first time, saying, "I've done less work this year, because of you. Because of your presence, John. Far fewer stitches."

"How long have you been working on this?"

"Since 1902. But I only have one day a year to add to it, so I don't think I've done so badly, not really."

"Madelyn, how old are you?"

She looked at him with an inquisitive eye. "How do you want to measure that? By the single days of life, one per year, or by all the years combined, even when I'm trapped in the dark?"

"The second."

"It was in 1724 when Saint Leander was first introduced to the calendar, so why don't you work it out for yourself?"

He did so, but didn't say anything.

"You're looking at me in a funny way. I can't imagine why. Oh, I suppose you think that's very old? Yes, I am an ancient being. But in myself, I still feel young. I am not wearied by life, not at all. Come closer, please. Examine my work."

He stepped up to the tapestry and took in the fine detail, the claws of the beasts, the wings of the insects, the moss growing on a rock, each feather on each bird, all expertly rendered. Noah stood at the brow of his ship, with his family arranged behind him.

"You see," Madelyn said, "I have a fine pair of eyes, and my hands are steady. I will set my ark afloat before the darkness takes me completely, if it ever does."

Nyquist wanted to ask her again about his father, about his whereabouts, but knew that the wrong word could easily push her away, or trouble her too much.

He said, "It's a great work."

This pleased her. She put down her needle and thread and stood up. "Let me show you some of my other pieces." She led him over to an easel where an oil painting rested, a portrait of Professor Bryars. Other portraits of villagers were hung on the walls. They were all very good likenesses, highly skilled, realistic. "I wonder sometimes," she said, "whether I should dabble in a more modernistic style. I understand it's all the rage in cosmopolitan areas?"

"Sure. Why not? I can see Doctor Higgs with a Cubist face. One staring eye, her ear on backwards..."

Madelyn stared at him, not a smile touching her lips. Instead, she explained her method: "I work from photographs." She nodded to a shelf which held a collection of framed images of people from the village. "I use these as models for my portraits. I hope to paint everyone in the village, eventually, as they live and die and I carry on, year by year."

Nyquist thought about her answer: she was creating her own population.

"What about this?"

He touched at the edge of a white cloth draped over an object on a plinth. Madelyn removed the cloth for him, revealing the sculpture underneath. It was a Tolly Man mask, a work in progress, more than three-quarters complete.

"I made this myself," she said proudly. "Every knot, every twist and turn."

He believed her. The disembodied head was closely woven from twigs and dry leaves, with one or two black feathers among them, the whole thing wrapped in wire. The barbs of the wire and the thorns together gave the mask a sinister, painful aspect. Evidently, the mask had been a few years in the making, for the lower twigs and branches were drier than the uppermost, with far less color to them. The jagged outline made it an angry god or demon, whichever it was, and it was easy to imagine the intense feelings generated in the wearer, once their head and shoulders were encased. Nyquist noted a single a cluster of berries among the newer tangles at the brow.

"I left the moonsilver attached," she said. "Although I'm not supposed to, really."

"Artistic license?"

"Yes. To represent the poison in the human soul." It was said in a flat tone of voice, a simple stating of a fact. "This is why I like to go to the museum, to study the old examples. Oh, but they had such craftsmanship in those days!" Around the base of the effigy were a number of woodworking and gardening tools, among them a pair of shears and a pruning knife. Madelyn continued, "I would like my mask to be used one year, if the committee approves, and if Saint Algreave allows it. That would be an honor."

"I suppose you've never seen the Tolly Man, in real life?"

"No never. I'm always locked away on that day." She sounded wistful, a little lost within herself. "You know the mask is burned every year, after being used."

"I was told that, yes."

"Only those few exhibits in the museum have survived up to now."

"Why is that?"

"When Saint Algreave's Day falls on a full moon, the mask is sacrosanct. The full moon turns it into an object of great beauty and devotion, something to be revered, and not a mask of the devil, as is usually assumed."

Nyquist drew his gaze away from the Tolly Man.

"Look at me. Madelyn. Turn this way."

At first her eyes wouldn't meet his, but then they did, and she held herself in place by sheer power of the will. "You must promise not to touch me," she said. "Not even in the slightest. Not a breath must fall on me. Even your shadow across mine would cause problems for us both. You would be drawn in."

"As you say."

"I do say. This is why poor Norma Spence took such a fright."

"You're wearing a mask yourself, isn't that true? Right now?"

"Not a mask, John. No. But everyone all together contained within me."

"Everyone?"

"Everyone in the village, yes."

"You believe that everyone in Hoxley village lives inside you, and they're all talking to you, is that it?"

She stared at him, her eyes quite dark for once. "It's not a belief. It is a fact."

"So you can see everything, through their eyes?"

"Whatever is seen through all eyes available to me, yes. All things that are pleasant to look upon, and all that are fearful, and wicked. I witness them all."

"So you know of my father's whereabouts? You can see him?"

"I don't know. Oh John, it's so frustrating! There are areas of shadow, where I cannot see. Here and there, in the many rooms of my head. Shadows. It is horrible–"

This was too much to take. "Madelyn, you have to tell me!"

"I would like to…"

"Well then?"

"Alas, I am not allowed. The shadows will not speak to me."

And with that, she walked away, across the room. Nyquist thought of pushing it further, but he knew it was hopeless.

"How do you like this one, John?" she said.

He went to her. She was standing in front of a portrait of Ian Bainbridge. It was a fine work, and the man's despair had been perfectly captured, especially around the eyes. He told her that he liked it, very much so, and she replied, "He is dead now. I can no longer hear him speak. One less, one less." Her voice sounded wistful.

Nyquist saw something in her face, a fleeting expression of pain. He said, "What is it, Madelyn? Do you know something about his death?"

"I do. And it puzzles me."

"Tell me."

She breathed in. "There was someone with him, some other person."

"Someone was with him, when he died? You mean his wife, Hilda?"

"No, no. Someone else. They are keeping their face hidden from me. And I don't know why they are doing that."

"Ian Bainbridge was murdered? Is this what you're saying? The berries were forced into his mouth?"

"I don't know. But it happened because of…"

"Yes? Come on. Madelyn! Tell me what you know."

"I am trying to speak. I am trying to find out for you. But the shadows won't let me."

"Please, if you can…"

It took a great physical effort, and her body seemed to fold in upon itself, but then she said in a rush, "Mr Bainbridge died because of your father."

Nyquist froze. A shock ran through him. Despite all his doubts about Madelyn's mental state, he felt he was nearing the truth.

"Why? What does it have to do with my father?"

"I first noticed him, his voice, George Nyquist's voice, and his presence in the village… on Saint Algreave's Day this year."

"The day of the Tolly Man? That's when he came here?"

She spoke in a rush. "Yes, and that's when all the trouble started, with your father's arrival. Strand by strand the story begins on that day, and months later Mr Bainbridge is caught up in those strands, and they tighten, oh, Miss Creeping Jenny has hold of him, and he's scared, oh, so scared, how he cried out, how he screamed!"

Madelyn's face twisted up with sudden pain and she started to shudder. She looked to be a person of fifty years or so. Nyquist took a step towards her.

"No! No, you mustn't! Not too close!"

He stopped and looked at her, his whole being held at the point of knowing and not knowing. And he said, "Show me." Cold and clear.

"I can't control it that easily–"

"Show me!"

There was a moment's hesitation and then Madelyn's face

flickered and her features shifted as though pushed to one side a fraction, allowing Nyquist to catch a glimpse of another face within hers, a woman's face, older, far older, one of the elderly ladies of Hoxley, he had seen her once or twice on the streets, tottering along with her walking cane and with her gray hair bound in a net. And then the face was gone, and another took its place, a man this time, a man of distinctive features, one of the young men of the village, the man's arrogance playing on Madelyn's face for a second, no more, and then gone. And another took its place, and then one more, face after face, and Nyquist saw them all as he looked upon her, one person after another, all the villagers. He saw Doctor Higgs stricken with illness, and he saw Maude Bryars with her serious demeanor. He saw the woman who ran the corner shop, and the postman, and the vicar and the part-time police constable, and he saw strangers also, the residents of Hoxley he had not yet seen or talked to on his travels, he saw the young and the old, man and woman and child, one and all, he saw a flash of blue and yellow feathers as a budgerigar flew within Madelyn's features, and he saw the yellow eyes of cats and the wet nose and long fangs of a dog and its slavering pink tongue, he saw the goldfish swimming as though in the bowl of the face, he saw Becca Fairclough and her friend Val and Nigel the landlord and his daughter Mavis and so many others, one by one by one or superimposed upon each other: all the residents of the village of Hoxley, Upper and Lower. He saw them all in the face of the woman called Madelyn Arkwright, builder of the ark, contained within he saw them all, hiding there, living there, some of them ashamed to be seen, others proud, some of the laughing madly, others frowning, or grinning or crying in pain, and he heard their voices, a chaos of words without meaning, chopped and changed. Nyquist could not draw himself away and he felt weak in their sight, and dizzy, privileged, scared half to death, staring into a whirlpool, into a deep mirror that held all its reflections prisoner, until such a day as the glass might break. Nyquist teetered on the edge of falling. And still they came on, the faces, repeating now, Higgs again, then Val, now Len Sadler, now Hilda, the aging Morris men still arguing, but never in the same sequence, each time a different face in a different order, over and over, ever-changing without end, a parade of eyes and mouths and noses and brows and cheekbones and blemishes and wrinkles, flesh upon flesh, skin tone fading one onto the other, from dark to light and all shades between, and all the time he was only waiting for one face among them all, his father's face, yes, despite the fact that Madelyn had said he was hidden away, still he waited in hope, his eyes fixed, set tight, focused, willing the face to be shown, his father's face, George Oliver Nyquist, whether old or young he did not care, only to be proved right, this is all he desired, only to know that a chance still existed, yes, and that this story might come to an end in the light rather than the dark, in sunlight rather than night, and that he might yet reach forward and…

He touched her.

His hand brushed at the shoulder of Madelyn.

The merest contact, that was all it took.

Her eyes expressed one moment of shock.

And then Nyquist was gone, gone, falling at last. Over the rim.

Darkness at first, with the many voices calling to him, and then light and a clear sweet silence. And he was still falling.

Falling on and on into the mirror's pool until the glass parted like a warm slow moon-heavy motionless dream-silver liquid and he was gathered together, taken up in a crowd, a flood of people.

One among many.

Many among one.

Held in place, bound in the flesh.

A villager at last, lost in the push and pull.

Doctor Higgs was suddenly at his side, her hands extended, her face filled with worry. He called out to her, or tried to, *Doctor, help me! What's happening?* But her face was drawn away, back into the crowd.

Nyquist tried to work out where he was.

An enclosed area. Somewhere indoors. Everybody was here, all the known residents of Hoxley, far too many people for the size of the space. Bodies pushed at him from all sides: arms, legs, elbows jabbing. Faces loomed close and then away, moving on. So many people squeezed together, swaying as one at times, acting as one multifarious creature, one body of flesh, and then breaking apart into separate entities, and struggling with each other for space, for air, for one good breath of air, one stray beam of light.

But there was only darkness, and flesh.

Even his thoughts started to merge with theirs, to become blurred.

His name slipped away.

His sense of time slipped away.

His self, his mind, all the stories that woven together made him what he was, or what he used to be, all were now jumbled together with theirs, and he felt the rage of the people, the rage, the love, and the hatred and the pettiness, the need, the boredom, impatience, kindness, the broken hearts and the scattered hopes, collected from years and years of longing, all as one, as one person, one villager.

My name is John Henry Belinda Thomas Claybourne Johanna Edward Keepsake Fitten Potten Postlethwaite Maude Jack Sutton Lumbe Lumley Lambert Becca Cholmondeley Edwina Higgs Gladys Fairclough Underwood Gough Dunne Dunnock Jud Lillian Hoxton Geoffrey Myrethorpe Nigel Joan Patricia Clegg Featherstonehaugh Prudholme Lillian Emma Jim Dorothy Sadler Iris Ollerenshaw Deidre Hilda Alice Patrick George Oliver Bainbridge Nyquist George Jack Oliver Nyquist Oliver George Nyquist Oliver George George Oliver George Oliver Nyquist…

And out of the darkness came the face of his father, formed before him in a haze, and then clear, yes, clearly seen.

Time was suspended.

The crowd stood in silence all around.

Father and son staring at each other. One reaching out for the other, son for father, fingers almost touching in the vast close-up distance.

One moment in the darkness of time of slowness of dreaming…

Almost, almost. And then lost, one face among many, too many faces, hundreds of faces. Nyquist pushed through the crowd, searching, searching. But it was no good. He was suddenly in pain, stumbling, almost falling. Only the crowd kept him upright. *Listen to me, you need to leave the village.* One voice. A whisper, up close. *Go home, why don't you? Go on, piss off!* At first, he couldn't tell whose voice it was, male or female, old or young, but it was said with vehemence, with spite in every word. And then he saw the face, and the voice formed itself properly: Jane Sutton. She spat at him. She raised her hands and he saw the knife that she held. Nyquist staggered back a few steps and felt the moment letting him go, the crowd letting him go, falling, falling away into the depths of skin and bone and blood once more, and he opened his eyes.

He was standing in the studio, before the mask of the Tolly Man on its plinth.

In a daze he saw Madelyn Arkwright close by. They were alone, just the two of them.

"What happened?" he asked. "I was in a crowd…" He lifted a hand to his head. He felt weak, dizzy.

"Yes, I'm sorry, John. I think I've…"

He saw that she held one the woodworking tools in her hand, a knife of some kind. The blade was red.

"I believe I've hurt you." She was talking rapidly. "It wasn't my fault, it wasn't! It was Mrs Sutton, I think. She took me over, she forced my hand."

Nyquist looked down and saw the blood on his shirt, over his midriff.

The room tilted sideways a little, and he followed in the same direction, called to the edge by a faraway sound he couldn't place, that he could never quite hear.

JOLLY GOOD SHOW

At first he thought he was standing near the weir pool on the River Hale, but then he saw the wings and fuselage of the airplane embedded in the soil. Birdbeck tarn lay before him. It was night. A pale half-moon gave its glow to the scene. The mist hung over the water, and the banks of the tarn were softened by it, hardly seen. Only the water existed, its surface shining black, unreadable. The long blade of the propeller rose from the center of the pool, its metal polished, seemingly new. It drew him closer to the bank.

Not a sound could be heard.

The water lapped gently at his feet.

Nyquist bent down and looked into the black mirror. He saw himself, but not as he was now, but older, the years taking their toll, lining his face and thinning his hair. It was his father's face looking back at him from the depths. He put a hand into the water, to gather an object into his grasp, but his fingers merely caused the face to drift away, and now the surface was perfectly blank once more, with no reflection seen, none at all.

He stood up and looked out across the tarn. Something was disturbing the water out there, causing tiny ripples to appear. It took a while for the creature to emerge from the mist, moving along at a stately pace.

It was a swan, a mute swan. *Cygnus olor.*

Its white plumage and folded wings glistened under the moonlight. Moving gracefully, it swam around the propeller blade and then came to a halt. Nyquist gazed with wonder at the two necks that grew from the bird's breast; with wonder, and with complete acceptance, for it seemed not so much a creature of fantasy, more a natural offspring of the village and its various rules. Each of the necks ended not with a bird's head, not in feathers: but with a hand, a human hand, the left and the right. One of these hands mimed itself into a beak-like shape, fingers and thumb joined in a point. The bird ducked this temporary head into the water as though to feed, and then brought it back up again, into the air, shaking droplets off its fingers. It swam closer to the bank where Nyquist stood. The bird held both palms up for inspection, and he saw the lines of life, heart and mind written there, he saw old scars and abrasions. It was showing off, its long life, the battles won and lost.

And then the swan brought the two hands together in a slow clapping motion, over and over again. It was a cruel and mocking sound.

Well done, sir. Absolutely spiffing. Jolly good show and all that, old bean. Splendid effort. Hip hip.

The sound of the applause echoed away over the moors, into the lands of mist.

THE WELL-KNOWN STRANGER

He imagined he had brought a little of the mist with him, from the shallows of his dream, for upon waking fully he could see only a short distance ahead of him, a couple of feet or so – beyond that limit the world faded into a thick gray haze. Slowly and awkwardly he raised his arm from the bed cover and watched in a kind of stupor as his hand vanished into the haze, first the fingertips, then the fingers whole, and the palm, the wrist. The haze tingled around his skin and gave off a not unpleasant warmth. He stopped the forward motion and pulled his hand from the mist, bringing it back into view.

How strange.

Nyquist witnessed the event as a child might, watching a magic show.

He made the same movement again, again a witness to his own hand disappearing and then reappearing. He lay back on the bed and closed his eyes tightly and imagined that all was well, and that when he opened them again the world would be as it was, fully in sight.

Now take a look. Dare yourself to…

The mist hung above the bed and on all sides, a gray cocoon.

Or a shroud.

The thought disturbed him. He had to act, and so he sat up in the sheets and felt a dull ache in his side. He was bandaged there, and a tiny spot of red blossomed.

A pattern.

He couldn't quite work it out. And where the hell was he? This wasn't his usual bed at the public house with its over-washed linen and the scratchy eiderdown. The sheets were softer, whiter, and they smelled of flowers.

How had he got here?

So many questions, piling up one by one in his head.

Now he tried to get up from the bed, one hand on the bedstead for balance, the other pressed firmly to the mattress. He pushed up and saw to his dismay that the gray haze moved with him, wherever he went, always around him, always a couple of feet or a yard away, always hiding the faraway reaches of the room from his sight.

And he sat back down.

And waited. And hoped for clarity, for his eyes to be clear.

Nyquist felt no pain. But he was aware of it as a possibility, somewhere close by. A drug held his body softly in its grasp. He thought of Higgs. Yes, of course, the good doctor must've taken charge of him. That was it. And from this one fact his memory took over, and he recalled piece by piece his meeting with Madelyn and all or most of what had happened afterwards, in her studio.

The stabbing.

His hand felt at the bandages around his waist, at the wet spot of blood. Somehow in his sleep, in the movements of his dream, he had pulled a stitch loose. He thought of calling out for help, for the doctor to attend to him, but the blind haze made him fearful of what might lie beyond it, good or evil. He had to make sure. And so he got to his feet once more and this time took a step or two, always surrounded by the mist no matter where he moved. Objects came and went from his sight as his point of view moved, and from this limited vantage he made out the walls and floor of the bedroom, one section at a time. Yes, he recognized it as a back bedroom at Higgs's house; he had searched here yesterday, seeking a friendly face in the empty village. But there was still nobody here, not as far as he could see. He turned in a slow circle and then moved forward, his hands outstretched before him like a blind person, and in this manner he found his clothes neatly folded over a chair. He got dressed as quickly as he could, and set off once more on his journey around the room. This is what it felt like, that he was exploring a land he had never visited before, somewhere faraway and strange. Groping at the limits of his eyesight he made it to the dressing table, where a new icon sat waiting for him. A male figure this time, made of rough clay, naked but for a loincloth. The saint's hands were held behind his back, and his face was entirely covered in white gauze, several inches of it wrapped around his head and tied off in a tiny knot. There was no label, no name given. But he knew now that a day had passed. He had slept the night here. But what day was it? He tried to work it out.

Thursday, arrival. No one allowed outside.

Friday. No talking.

Saturday. Masks, masks, masks.

Sunday. All doors open. Village deserted. Crazy Madelyn with the knife.

So it was Monday.

Nyquist turned again and felt a little unsteady in doing so. A step at a time, that was the rule. One step. Let the mist move with you, settle. Another step. Keep moving, keep looking, allow the world around you to be become clear in your eyes. Then memorize what you see. And move on. By this method he found a door, but it opened before he could get there and someone entered the room.

Nyquist stepped back, he couldn't help himself. His vision blurred at the edges and the door and the intruder vanished from his sight, But this was worse! Much worse. There was another person in the room, it could be anyone. He lurched forward again, almost falling, hoping to catch sight of the intruder, to know for sure if he was in danger.

The voice called to him. "Nyquist? Are you there?"

It was the doctor. He felt a sudden rush of joy and turned in her direction, following the voice as it moved around him, and they met in the circle of the haze like two wanderers in the night. He wanted to embrace her, but resisted the impulse. He couldn't trust what he was seeing.

"What are you doing out of bed?" she said in exasperation. "Look at you. I will need to redress your wound. Come on, back to bed. Come on."

He pushed her away in panic, and watched in dismay as she vanished from sight. He could feel his heart pounding, and sweat broke out on his skin, all over. He was expecting an attack at any moment. Higgs was calling for him, unseen, asking him to calm down, to find his way to the bed. But he'd turned around so many times that all sense of direction had been lost. He rushed forward, knocking over a table. A lamp crashed to the floor. He kept on, moving this way and that until he banged into the wall. He paced along it, his arms clinging to the surface like a man climbing a sheer cliff face. By chance he reached the open doorway and he hurried through it in relief, and then almost fell down the stairs. His fingers gripped at the banister, and he tried to stay calm, to settle his breath. *I am going blind. I'm going blind!* He crept downstairs, one step at a time, towards the haze that always moved with him, all the time, always keeping itself at the same distance all around. Doctor Higgs called from the landing above but he was already at the front door of the house. He yanked it open and staggered outside, hoping to see the street stretching away on each side, how blissful that would be!

But the haze enclosed him, totally.

He could see the pavement below his feet. Looking up he saw only the haze.

No sun, no sky.

He moved forward carefully, into the road… but then he hesitated. Not a step could be taken.

What if a car hits me?

A woman entered his circle.

It shocked him.

The woman nodded and smiled and moved on into the dark of the mist, vanishing.

He was alone once more.

Somewhere, somewhere there had to be an end to this, to these limits he was trapped inside. He stepped forward, without knowing which way he was going, with no knowledge beyond the short distance he could see around him. Other people met him and moved on, appearing and disappearing. One of them knocked into him and cursed, telling him to look where he was going! But Nyquist could not do that. It was impossible.

He stopped where he was, waiting, waiting…

By some means he had walked across the road. The corner shop was visible, just about. Nyquist moved towards it and sat down on a bench. He let a few minutes pass by, and his breathing eased at last, and his heart slowed.

The haze lay before him, and all around, its surface a constantly shifting swirl of black and gray and lilac. Living smoke. That was the phrase that came to him. He had experienced something similar in his journey into the dusklands, back in the city of his birth; but that had been a vast landscape filled with silvery fog. This was different. This wasn't fog or mist or any kind of vapor, it was localized, concerned with his body, or his mind. Yes, it could be an illusion, a trick of the eyes brought on in some way by the power of suggestion. It billowed like a cloud. Tiny lights flickered in its depths, blue and red and yellow. He hadn't noticed these before. They lasted only a moment, these sparkles, before others took their place: orange, green, blue once more. He noticed that the lights flickered mostly around the part where his hand had penetrated. Had he disturbed the haze, causing it to react to his presence?

The haze was linked to him, it was part of his body, emanating from him.

Aura. That was the word.

The thought made him feel sick. He got to his feet, taking careful steps this time, with one hand keeping contact with the wall, the other stretched out before him as a guide and a warning. Voices. Footsteps. Laughter. Other people were moving along. Occasionally they entered his circle of view and then moved on. They too had their hands out before them, or else used raised walking sticks as a guide. And he thought: they are the same as I am, encased as I am. *Every person in the village has this same condition, is that it?* Was this the ruling of the day, that all should be held within their own little worlds?

A young child surprised Nyquist, running along the pavement at speed, a stick banging on the ground repeatedly. He was screaming with joy. The kid's mum followed, shouting for him, "Brian! Brian, come back here!" The boy ran on into the haze, the mother also. They were far more adept at this than he was, the haze wasn't a hindrance to them, but just another delight, another saintly effect, something to revel in.

Nyquist was steadier now, more confident. He wouldn't fall over, he wouldn't bump into people, as long as he stayed calm and in control. And then he stopped again, and he closed his eyes and wondered just how far he had come, how close he was to being crazy, that he was accepting such a thing as this. It was true, he had seen other wonders in his life, and experienced strangeness and the irresistible bounty of the hidden world. But never before had he thought of himself as mad – only as a wanderer, a fighter, a struggler against doubt and pain and the unknown.

He looked around and saw that he'd reached by chance The Swan With Two Necks. The pub's sign loomed out of the surrounding mist. He made his way inside and took the stairs up to his room. Nigel and Mavis were getting ready for the dinner time opening: he could hear their voices. His little room was a haven, and the haze both followed him and led him onwards. They were bound together, man and cloud. And so it was that they both sat on the bed together, and when Nyquist bowed his head down, the haze bowed with him. And when his head rose once more, the haze rose with him, and when he got to his feet, the haze stood with him. Always, it surrounded him. He was a prisoner. And this would be true for all of this terrible day.

His side ached and he lifted his shirt to examine the bandage; it was deep red where the blood was seeping through. He needed another dose of painkillers, urgently. Damn it! He should've let Higgs take care of him. The haze was to blame; he thought he could outrun it, but no, it stayed with him, it clung on. He thought of cutting it loose in some way, finding a magical knife, a rusty old kitchen-drawer vorpal blade: locating the points of contact between flesh and smoke. And then… a quick *slice*. Slicing it clean!

Instead he turned in a slow circle, navigating the clouded world of his room. A new icon sat on the cabinet, the clay man with the wrapped head. There was a naming card: *Saint Athelstan*. He noticed that the saint's arms were not only held behind his back, they were caught there, the wrists bound together by wire.

He moved to the sink. The mirror.

His own face emerged through the haze as he approached the glass.

He hadn't had a shave in days, and his clothes were dirty. And he could smell himself, the unwashed flesh, the dirt, the sweat, the stink of the antiseptic that Higgs had put on his wound. He clung to the edge of the sink with both hands, confronting the well-known stranger in the glass. The eyes that asked so many questions of their reflected selves, riddles without end or answer. Behind his head in the mirror he could see the reflected image of the haze, billowing softly, slowly, waiting patiently for Nyquist's next move. But he didn't know what that might be. He wanted only to stay here, frozen before himself, or perhaps to climb into bed and sleep until the day had passed and the world had opened up once more in all directions. That was his only desire.

It was not to be. He was in danger. He'd been stabbed. And he thought of the things he had seen yesterday, inside Madelyn Arkwright's head: all the villagers contained there, and his own father among them, hidden away, and the knife in the hands of Mrs Sutton. And then the knife in the hands of Madelyn.

Two knives, two worlds. Both operating at the same time, one guiding the other. Jane Sutton acting as a kind of inner force, compelling Madelyn to make the attack. Or else Madelyn herself had simply played out her madness to the ultimate degree, seeing him as the intruder, the unwanted guest, attacking him. He had no way of knowing which it was; Hoxley-on-the-Hale had taken away all sense of reason.

He moved from the mirror, over to the bed. He lifted the mattress, to bring out the revolver. If it was true, that this gun would have to be used one day, well then he would have it ready. Protection, if nothing else. His hand groped further under the mattress, searching for the weapon. There was nothing there. He raised the mattress with both hands and shoved it onto the floor. The sprung base of the bed was bare. And there was nothing on the floor beneath. The handgun had been stolen, taken away. He went over to the bedside cabinet and searched the bottom shelf. The teacup and the book of birds were also missing. All three, all three of the magical objects with their tendrils. But who would take them, and why? His mind ached with doubt.

Nyquist made his way out of the room, hand over hand along the wall, downstairs again. He called out for the landlord and received a swift response from the bar. But

Nigel Coombes could not be seen, not yet. The room was obscured.

He called out, "Where are you?"

"I'm right here, at the bar. Where are you, Mr Nyquist?"

"I'm here."

And by their voices they found each other, two circles of haze merging, coinciding. Nigel had a mop and bucket in his hands.

"Someone's been in my room," Nyquist said. "Things have been stolen."

The landlord looked worried. "Are you sure? What is missing?"

Nyquist couldn't answer. He couldn't mention the gun, without it seeming crazy, or a threat. He said instead, "I need to find the culprit."

"Are you… are you blaming me? Or my daughter for this?"

Nyquist looked at him fiercely. He saw the landlord's hands tighten on the handle of the mop, as though it might be used as a weapon. But the moment passed. Coombes sighed and placed the mop and bucket on the floor and he tapped Nyquist on the shoulder and said, "Let's have a look together. You might have mislaid it, that's all."

Yes, yes, it was possible. In the current mood, with his restricted vision, Nyquist felt it might be true. He let himself be led towards the stairs but they both came to a halt as Becca Fairclough appeared in the corridor. Nyquist heard her first, and then saw her as she shared his circle of haze. She looked terrible, fearful, her eyes wide open, and at first she couldn't speak. She was in shock.

"What is it?" Coombes asked her. "What's wrong?"

At last she found her voice. "Something's happened at the school, an accident."

"What kind of accident?"

"I don't know, I don't know." Becca was stricken. "It's Mrs Sutton... I think she's... I need to find Doctor Higgs. Where is she?"

The landlord shook his head in answer. Nyquist said, "She was at her surgery. I saw her there, not long ago."

"She's not there now."

Becca ran off. Nyquist followed her, out of the door. But only the haze existed now, she was no longer seen. He moved along the street, hurrying his pace, hands groping ahead for fear of meeting obstruction. He simply moved in what he thought was the right direction, trusting to the saint's power and grace, and soon enough came to the end of the street where the school resided. He saw the metal fence, and then heard the children playing in the yard, running and laughing together. Two girls were just about visible on the other side of the fence, skipping and chanting inside their twin circles of haze. It was song about a familiar subject.

> *Two steps forward, one step back,*
> *Widdershins, widdershins, turn and clap.*
> *Call for Jimmy and call for Jack,*
> *Creeping Jenny is at my back!*

With this final line, the two girls screamed in merry shock, and the game was repeated, each taking turns to play the monster.

Nyquist reached the school gate. He walked across the yard. He could hear children all around him, unseen, and then suddenly appearing, running at great speed across his field of vision. He reached out and caught one boy by the shoulder. The kid – he was seven or eight – looked up at him in shock at first, and then anger, and tried to run away. Nyquist hung on tight. "I need to see your headmistress. Do you know where she is?"

The kid tried to escape.

"Mrs Sutton. Take me to her! Come on, there's a tanner in it for you."

"One shilling, please."

"If you like. But hurry."

That was incentive enough. The boy led him safely through the murk of the playground over to the main entrance of the school. At one point Teddy Fairclough appeared, his eyes wild and his face set in a fierce expression. He looked like a crazed beast, completely at home in this half-hidden world, in this cloud that once more engulfed him.

Nyquist and the boy went inside the building and straight away the atmosphere changed. Murmurs were heard, whispers, a hissing sound. The kid was worried now. He said, "I'm scared. My fret doesn't feel right. It's the wrong color."

"What do you mean by that?"

"The fret. It's what we call Saint Athelstan's mist." The boy stopped moving. He looked up at Nyquist and said, "Has something bad happened?"

"What's your name?"

"Harry Clegg."

"I'll look after you, Harry, don't worry. I just need to speak with Mrs Sutton."

The boy blinked a few times. Then he took Nyquist's hand and together they walked the length of the corridor until they reached a small group of teachers clustered at a doorway. They looked at Nyquist as he arrived, this stranger in the mist, in the *fret*, his face unshaven, his suit dirty and creased, and with a slight edge in his voice due to the increasing pain in his midriff.

"Where's Mrs Sutton? What's happened to her?"

Nobody answered at first. Their faces were either pained or dulled with shock.

Nyquist fished a silver coin from his pocket and threw it to the boy, and then urged him to run back outside. Harry did so, with obvious relief.

One of the teachers said, "Are you Mr Nyquist?"

"That's right. I'm a friend of Doctor Higgs. She's on her way."

"We're waiting for Joe Ferneyhough."

"The police constable?"

"Yes. I don't think we should disturb the..." The teacher couldn't finish the sentence.

Nyquist asked, "Is she dead?"

Nobody answered. So many people, so many eyes, all looking at him. He pushed his way through, and entered the classroom. He could see very little at first, for his fret had closed in, and darkened itself, almost in fear. But he kept moving until he came to a row of school desks and chairs, and then a second row. All the chairs were empty. The room was deathly quiet. He moved on. More desks, more chairs. Exercise books set out, pencils and rulers in neat rows. Following the direction the chairs were facing, he walked to the front of the classroom. He called out and the fret took his voice; there was no answer. And then Jane Sutton appeared in the cloud of the fret: her hands, her upper body, her face.

The headmistress was sitting at her desk, perfectly still. Nyquist moved closer, until he could see the blackboard behind her. Chalked here were the same words he'd seen in his father's cottage, out at King's Grave. Was this a final message from the victim, or a warning from a killer? Or just a line from the day's lesson?

Creeping Jenny is calling.

Mrs Sutton was sitting crooked at the desk, with one hand resting on the tabletop and the other hanging down at her side. Her chest and upper body were twisted to the side and her face was thrust forward, almost savagely. She was dressed and presented as well as ever, in a blue cardigan and a tweed skirt, but the buttons were popped and torn on the cardigan, and one was missing. Many strands of hair had escaped the knot of her bun. Her eyes stared ahead, and for a moment Nyquist thought they moved to look at him. It was a startling effect and it made him reach out to touch her neck, searching for a pulse. But all was silent within, all unmoving.

He stepped back a little, catching his breath.

The skins and scarce remains of crushed myre berries were piled high in a bowl on the desk. The fruit had been eaten. The headmistress's lips and chin were darkly colored with ruby. Her face was marked here and there with many tiny scratches. The blood was already drying on them.

She had died as Ian Bainbridge had died. But whereas his eyes had looked out over miles and miles of distance, over emptiness, Jane Sutton had a very different point of focus: her eyes were filled with yearning. Nyquist could only think that – at the very end, when the final struggle was over – she had welcomed death.

CONVERSATIONS WITH FIREFLIES

That afternoon an inquest took place, originally planned to look into Ian Bainbridge's death, and now to investigate Jane Sutton's as well. A local magistrate acted as coroner for the day, and the community hall served as a makeshift court. Nyquist was sitting near the back of the packed hall. He could see only the people in front and to his side, nothing of the stage. The collected frets of the villagers obscured the undertakings. But he heard the witnesses' voices, and the coroner's questions. On occasion a person would pass through his tiny circle of sighted objects, on their way to the stage. Mr Gerald Sutton sounded stoical. He answered in a controlled monotone. But every so often his voice betrayed him as a word cracked: anger was brewing. Hilda Bainbridge was the opposite, refusing to answer any of the coroner's questions. Her silence persisted, even now. Nyquist stared at the shifting contours of the fret and imagined Hilda's expressions and gestures, her fluttering hands, the sense of loss in her eyes, the shudder every time her husband's name was spoken aloud.

In her turn, Rebecca Fairclough described finding the body of the headmistress. "I help out at the school whenever I can," she said. "Mrs Sutton was taking an English class that morning, for the older children."

"I see. And you found the body during the morning break?"

"That's right. The children were in the playground. I went into the classroom to clean the blackboard, and give the place a tidy. At first, I thought I was alone, but then I went to tidy up the teacher's desk and that's when I found Mrs Sutton, just... just sitting there, staring ahead."

"You didn't see anyone else in the classroom, or anyone leaving? Or in the corridor?"

"No."

"But your vision must have been limited, because of today's saintly effect – the fret?"

"It was. But, as you know, our other senses come into play, in compensation. I was alone, definitely."

Nyquist listened to this with interest, thinking of how he'd seen Becca's brother Teddy in the playground. Was she hiding something?

Doctor Higgs took the stage and wasted no time in describing the effects of the myre berry on the human nervous system: "If sufficient are taken, paralysis sets in quickly after ingestion. Death follows in five to ten minutes."

The coroner asked her, "There is no question of foul play, in your opinion?"

"No. None at all."

"In both cases?"

"That's correct."

"What about the scratches on Mrs Sutton's face? You mentioned this..." There was the sound of paper rustling. "In your report. *Many small cuts on the face*. There was a similar effect on Mr Bainbridge's face. Can you explain this?"

Nyquist waited to hear the doctor's response. It took a while: "I believe they did this themselves, sir, when they collected the berries."

Nyquist doubted this, for he'd seen that the cuts had been recently made. The coroner shared his doubts.

"That doesn't sit well with me, Doctor Higgs."

She spoke firmly in reply. "The expected symptoms of myre poisoning were evident on both Mr Bainbridge and Mrs Sutton: broken capillaries, crooked fingers, a slight discoloring at each temple. Without a doubt they both died from the same cause."

The coroner sneezed, and excused himself. Then he asked, "People don't often die from eating the berries, isn't that true?"

"It is. The last death in Hoxley was seven years ago. But I have treated cases of mild poisoning since then. Two or three berries will cause the body and the senses to slow down. But they taste very bitter. For that many to be swallowed, it takes an act of pure will."

"You're saying they chose to take this action?"

"I am. Both victims desired death."

There was a gasp from the audience. Nyquist couldn't see the person responsible, but he could guess. Hilda. A gasp, and then a wracking sob.

The doctor carried on regardless. "They took the berries one by one, or in handfuls, and they kept taking them until the ultimate effect had taken place."

"That is your professional opinion, doctor?"

"It is."

"Thank you. You may sit down."

After a few more witnesses were called, Nyquist himself

gave evidence. He made his way to the stage, helped along by a hand here and there to keep him on course. People were being kind, or perhaps they were simply agog to hear what he had to say. The fret followed him faithfully. By now he had grown used to it, as a dog will to a collar and lead. He was freshly shaved, with new stitches in his side, and a clean bandage. The painkillers that Higgs had given him were working their magic. He spoke the truth as he knew it, first telling the story of Friday night, when he'd heard a scream coming from Yew Tree Cottage, and his finding of the body of Mr Bainbridge, and his wife cowering against the kitchen wall. He described the bowl of berries on the kitchen table, and the corresponding bowl he'd seen in front of Jane Sutton in the classroom, and the stains he'd seen around the mouths of both victims. There were no more questions asked, and Nyquist returned to his seat.

Finally, the coroner called out to the room for any further witnesses to step forward, if they had anything of import to add. A quivering voice rose out of the cloud: "I have, sir." The coroner asked the witness to come forward. Nyquist saw him as he walked down the aisle: it was the old man who'd sat on the bench next to him, days ago, the one who had told him the name and address of the photographer. What could this old person have to say? Nyquist leaned forward in his seat, to better hear the man's voice as it floated in along the swirls of murky air. "I was walking my dog, sir, the summer of this year this would be, in the woods, sir, out by Tatterly Edge, when I spied a couple at their business, sir." The coroner asked him what he meant by this. The old man resorted to Latin; "*In flagrante delicto*, sir." Gasps of surprise and horror went through the hall. But the old man ploughed on. "Among the trees, this was. As Adam knew his wife, Eve, sir." The coroner interrupted him, to prevent further elaboration, and asked why this was relevant. The witness replied, "The man and woman in question sir, were Mr Bainbridge, sir, and Mrs Sutton. Hard at it–" Now the place erupted. Among the cries and moans, Nyquist could hear the bellow of Gerald Sutton and the long drawn out wail of Hilda Bainbridge. The coroner banged his gavel repeatedly on the tabletop and called out for order. Once the din had quietened, he quickly brought the proceedings to an end, announcing a verdict in both cases of "death by their own hands", adding, "Possibly – *possibly*, I say – brought on by matters of a personal nature." He finished by calling the whole affair a "very sad and cautionary tale."

After the inquest Nyquist went back to Doctor Higgs's house, and they ate a meal together: beef and vegetables in red wine. Their individual frets settled one into the other at the table's edge. Neither of them spoke much. The food was good. Nyquist had a glass of wine. The alcohol set off purple sparks of light that played in the mist. They acted more like insects than dots of light, these sparkles, flittering about at tangents to each other, and sometimes leaving colored trails in their wake.

Fireflies, glowbugs. Thoughts made real in the air, possibilities colliding.

Eventually he had to broach the subject, he could hold off no longer.

"Perhaps it wasn't suicide? For either of them."

"Nyquist, you heard about the affair they were having. Isn't it obvious, now?"

"Listen, doc. What if somebody made them eat the berries, under duress. Or maybe some other force was at play."

"You'll need to explain that."

He thought back on what Madelyn Arkwright had told him, of somebody else being present at Ian Bainbridge's death. "I mean a psychological force of some kind. It's affecting people in the village."

"A shared depression?"

"Or a spell of some kind. A jinx. Could such a thing take place?"

"In Hoxley? Anything can happen, for good and for ill. Anything at all. The saints see to that."

"The thing is, what if this is just the start? What if more people eat the berries?"

Higgs didn't answer him directly. Instead she made an after-dinner pipe for herself and started to speak of the village's history, as she'd learned it at school. The Tolly Man, the witch trials of the 17th Century, the varied saints as a protective device against evil.

"But the thing is, there's another way of looking at it."

Nyquist lit a cigarette. "Go on."

"Saints have been added over the years, to make up the current three hundred and sixty examples. What if they're acting as a sort of computation device?"

He smiled. "You mean like an abacus?"

She shook her head. "More like a way of forcing us to experience many different kinds of behavior, a lot of it extreme in nature, on a regular basis, year after year. There are patterns in the chaos, but they never coincide, not exactly, due to the random choosing of the saints. Everything is set up to create this vast *engine*… I can't think of any other word. And the villagers are the moving parts."

Nyquist thought about what she was saying. It was a surprising idea. "And where does all this lead?"

"Who can tell? The engine of the saints has been running now for centuries. There must be an outcome at some point, and perhaps quite soon."

"I'm not sure I want to be around when that happens."

"Some might actively seek it."

"You know, Professor Bryars said something similar."

The doctor's eyes perked up. "Did she?"

"She claimed that a number of the villagers are seeking to bring back the spirit of the Clud family. The dark spirit."

"Oh, she'll have us sacrificing animals soon enough, that one! Honestly, her mind takes such a fancy, it really does."

Nyquist left it there. He asked, "How are they chosen?"

"I'm sorry?"

"How are the saints chosen for each day?"

"I can't tell you, truly. Perhaps they draw lots? Or a pebble is chosen from a bowl."

"You really don't know?"

The doctor shook her head. "It is a private ceremony, performed each morning."

"Can it be manipulated? So that a certain saint–"

"No! No, no." Her face grew quite livid. "That isn't possible, not at all. Why, our entire way of life would be at risk! How could you even suggest such a thing?"

Nyquist nodded. He gestured to the two frets that lingered around the table, asking, "How does this work?"

Higgs lingered over her pipe and then answered, "All living bodies are surrounded by the fret, and are a natural part of it. Just as the fret is part of them, inseparable. But only in this village, on this day, is it visible. Glory be to Saint Athelstan in his wisdom."

He studied her face for signs of humor, or craziness.

"What's wrong? Don't you believe me?"

He smiled. "You know, I have seen a few strange things in my life."

"Yes, John, I believe that is true. For, despite the many years of your family's exile, you are a true Hoxleyite at heart. You have carried the saints with you, inside here, wherever you have traveled." She was touching at her heart.

He tried to think of an offering in return, but she hushed him with a raised hand and said, "Watch!" Her hand continued outwards, into the fret. The stars within the gathered mist sparkled around her fingers. She guided them this way and that, making them dance and flicker in different colors: blue, green, yellow, red. At one point she actually grabbed a few of them in her fist and the light glowed between her fingers. Then she let them go and they fluttered away, joining their partners.

"You see? They are joined to me. Try it."

He did so. But his hand caused only a few sparkles to rise. There was no dancing.

"You'll get it," Higgs said. "Keep practicing."

But he'd had enough. He leaned back in his chair. "What time does the fret disappear?"

"Midnight. Which is good, because it really comes alive after dark. You should join us, out on the green after nightfall. It's quite spectacular. You will understand the true beauty of the saints."

He nodded. But he had a different subject on his mind.

"Who is Creeping Jenny?"

"I'm sorry?"

"Creeping Jenny. It was written on the blackboard in Jane Sutton's class."

It took the doctor a while to answer, as though she were gathering information from the mist around here.

"She's a mythological figure. Traditionally, the wife of the Tolly Man. But that idea has changed over the last few decades, giving her a more independent existence. Whereas the Tolly represents death... Creeping Jenny is the spirit of the plants, the woods, the flowers, the earth in springtime. The Green Woman. Regeneration."

"She has something to do with storytelling, is that right?"

"It's another of her attributes, the ability to join objects together into a narrative."

"Why was the name written on the board?"

"John, the headmistress was teaching the children–"

"*Creeping Jenny is calling you.*"

"Yes, but–"

"And Jane Sutton responded. She moved towards the spirit."

Higgs grimaced. "Now you're worrying me."

"I *saw* it! I saw it in her eyes."

The doctor looked away. But Nyquist said to her, "Let me show you something." He cleared the plates and glasses to the side, and then laid out the seven photographs that had first drawn him to this place. "You've seen the one of my father," he said. "But these others were also sent to me, anonymously. They are all of Hoxley, or round about, as you can see."

The doctor glanced at each image in turn as Nyquist spoke.

"This is Ian and Hilda Bainbridge, at Yew Tree Cottage. And here..." He pointed to another photograph. "Here is the corner shop. But you see the van parked outside? Sutton's Bakery."

"What are you saying, John?"

"I'm not sure. But something has to connect the two deaths. And I believe my father lies at the center of it. These..." He swept his hand along the photographs. "These are clues. All I have to do is work out their true meaning."

"You really won't give up, will you?"

"No. It's written in the blood: never stop searching."

She looked at him in a curious manner, but he knew that she understood perfectly what he was saying. And then he picked up the seventh photograph, the one showing Madelyn Arkwright in the museum. "Do you know who this is?" he asked.

"I do. It's Madelyn. A villager."

"She lives here?"

"Yes. But she's very reclusive. In fact..."

"Don't tell me. She only comes outside one day a year. Saint Leander's Day."

"That's right."

"And where does everybody else go on that day?"

There was no immediate answer, so he asked a more direct question. "Doctor Higgs, where did you vanish to yesterday?"

"You know where."

"Do I?"

"We met. We almost met. In the room, the crowded room. I saw you."

"I don't think so. I was alone all day, and then I met Madelyn, and we talked in her studio at the Sutton house. And then I had some kind of blackout, and I imagined that I saw you, and everybody else. And then Madelyn attacked me, with a knife."

"Are you sure it was her who stabbed you? You didn't see anyone else, holding the knife?"

Nyquist hesitated.

Higgs persisted. "I need to know, John. It's very important."

"Yes. I saw Mrs Sutton."

"So it was Jane who stabbed you? Jane Sutton? Is that what you're saying?"

"I... I don't know. I'm not sure." His mind was clouded with shadows. He remembered the threats that Mrs Sutton had made against him, right from his first night here.

He asked, "Where was I found?"

"On the green. At ten o'clock. After we'd all come home."

"I must've been taken there then, from the Suttons' house."

"Yes, perhaps. The family have power. And of course, a bakery van to carry you in."

Nyquist rubbed at his eyes, willing the memories to come clean.

"Would you like me to give you something, John?" The doctor's voice was soothing, overly so. "Another tablet, perhaps? Do you have a headache?"

He didn't answer.

Her voice lowered to a whisper. It sounded very close in his ear, saying, "For one day of the year, we live inside Madelyn, and for the rest of the year, she lives inside us. As the village permits. It's a pleasant arrangement–"

"Pleasant!"

Nyquist's fist banged down on the table, causing the cutlery and the plates to rattle. The noise and the action broke him out of a spell.

"John. What is wrong? Have I upset you?"

He turned on her. "It's one secret after another."

"I thought we were friends."

"I've been here for... for what, four days?"

"Five."

"You know nothing about me. How can you?"

She nodded. "I understand. But let me tell you one thing. Of all the visitors that have come to us… you, above all, have partaken of our spirit."

He stood up, and gathered together his photographs, one to seven.

"John, please. Sit down. Don't be angry."

It was too late. Nyquist was already walking away. He took his coat off the stand in the hallway and made his way outside. It was dusk. And although the fret stayed with him, he could see that it was changing as the air darkened. His body was warm, as though wrapped in a cocoon. It was more like a spring day, rather than the dead of winter. The mist glowed with its own light, a dusting of the moon: pale, translucent. Even more of the flickering dots of color were seen within the swirls. He tried to brush them aside, but they clung to their places, and regrouped, and shivered freely.

He felt different. It was a sudden effect. The anger was drifting away.

And now he was sure of every step, avoiding the other pedestrians easily. He didn't even have to think about it; the fret was part of his body, it did exactly as he bid. Protecting, observing, showing him within its limits the nature of his own vision.

He was following in his father's footsteps. But where did they lead? He recalled the one useful piece of information that Madelyn had told him, that George Nyquist had first arrived in the village on Saint Algreave's Day. Was that a coincidence, or was his father connected in some way with the Tolly Man ritual? He felt this was the most vital question: once answered, everything else would fall into place.

The village green filled with people, adults and children. Nyquist joined them. By now, his fret was luminous, and comforting. It was no longer fully opaque. Through its shifting veil he saw the faces of people he knew. He saw the tree named Blade of Moon, and he saw the ducking pond where Gladys Coombes had met her end. He saw the village as though for the first time. He saw that many of the villagers had decorated their frets with flowing ever-shifting bands of black hue, in mourning for Ian Bainbridge, and for Jane Sutton. The sparkles of his own fret danced before his eyes. His hand reached out to touch them, to set them trembling. He felt their heat on his palm. With a simple gesture, a mere thought even, he could make the sparks change color, from red to gold to green and back again. They were the fireflies of his own body, set loose, given flight. He was engaging with them, beyond words. And he was astonished by it, and by all that he saw.

He walked in light and smoke and stars and heat.

The moon bathed him.

The night held him.

The fret caressed him.

Nyquist felt that his dreaming self had escaped his body, and was now enveloping him: his own dreaming self, and the village's... and where the two dreams met, this is where he moved and breathed.

He saw Professor Bryars approaching. But he could not face her just now, preferring to be alone with his own thoughts translated, as they were, into colors in the air. He would study them, seeking hidden connections, and find a new pathway through the maze. The idea excited him. He moved away, leaving the village green. With a simple click of his fingers he turned his fret jet black, opaque. He could no longer see ahead, but at least no one could follow him now. He would find a place of his own. He walked on, feeling the world at the fret's limits, seeing with the mist where it touched at objects: the walls of the houses, a street lamp, and then the corner shop. He stopped here. A noise was coming from the alley at the side of the shop. It sounded like a person in distress.

He brightened his fret once more, so he could see partway down the alleyway.

It looked like someone was being attacked.

A number of frets billowed together in the narrow space, two of them shuddering with anger, the third trembling in pain. The colors danced with each blow. Nyquist walked down towards the fight, which was taking place in a tiny back yard. His presence stopped the next blow from falling. The two assailants stared at him, suddenly uncertain. They were both young, and tough looking. And their victim was younger still, and weak. It was Teddy Fairclough. His fret was a poor, thin, trembling affair, little more than a wisp, pale cream in color, and splashed with red to match the wounds on his face and hands. The punch landed. And the fret burst into fresh crimson, like a flower. Teddy whimpered, and curled up, folding his hands around his head.

Nyquist said, "This doesn't look like a fair fight."

One of the men came forward, his arm already flexed for a hit. He lunged forward clumsily. Stars cascaded around the young man's bunched hand.

Time seemed to slow down.

Nyquist's fret billowed around the approaching fist. He countered it easily, and then took a fast aim for his assailant's stomach. The blow made contact, first with the other man's fret, and then with flesh. The man staggered back and almost fell. He banged against the wall. Seeing this, his comrade left Teddy alone and made his way into the fray. But a voice stopped his progress.

"No more of this. Not now."

The speaker stepped forward, pushing his two minions aside. It was Gerald Sutton. His fret was brimming with many different colors, a magnificent creation, He'd probably paid a fair packet to have the thing improved, souped up. The man's pride, and his grief and anger, played in the haze as twists and strands of dark blue, crimson and puce. The sparkles shone like newly born stars, and then fell away into darkness.

"This is private business, Mr Nyquist."

"No longer."

The two men stared at each other. Where their frets met, the air roiled and fizzed.

"I'm sorry for your loss. Your wife was—"

"Do not speak of my wife!"

Sutton's anger burned golden. It clouded, and spun apart, and merged once more. The sparks collided, shooting off from each other at wild tangents. One of his ruffians moved forward, but Sutton held him back with a raised hand. He never let his eyes leave Nyquist.

"Do not speak of my wife, sir. It offends me."

Nyquist kept his silence, letting Sutton's frustration play out.

"It offends me that a... that a stranger should take on such airs, as though he knew her. As though he knew of Jane's beauty, and refinement, and her intellect." Every line on his face was deeply etched. "And don't dare speak to me of what that old man said at the inquest!"

"I wasn't going to."

"Lies, damn lies! My Jane would not sully herself. Certainly, not for a man like Ian Bainbridge. She had far better taste than that."

The anger burned away, and Sutton's fret settled a little,

awash now with grief. Nyquist could read the man through the colors that he showed, whether voluntarily or otherwise. It gave him a way of proceeding.

"I know you want to blame me, Mr Sutton. And that's fair enough. Things have taken a turn since my arrival."

"We are a community. We have our ways."

"Granted. But why are you punishing the lad?"

Sutton looked back at Fairclough. "The bugger was seen, at the school this morning. He was talking to my wife, just before she…" The man's face creased into pain. He spat to clear his throat. "One of the kids told me."

"And what, you think Teddy's at fault? He's afraid of his own shadow."

Black ink spread across Sutton's fret, and his voice softened. "Someone made her do it. I know that to be the case. I know it, sir. She was a strong woman, my Jane." His mood closed in. "She would not take her own life."

"We're in agreement, then."

Sutton moved closer. Nyquist was now enclosed fully by the other man's fret. He felt how powerful a force it was, how all-encompassing.

"What do you mean? Speak plainly."

"I mean that other forces are at play here, in Hoxley." Nyquist held the man's stare, before adding, "And I think you know what they are. But you wish to hide them from yourself. And so…"

"The saints damn you!"

"And so you take it out on Teddy."

Sutton rose up to his full five foot nine, and his voice and his fret combined, speaking in deep blood and fury.

"God preserve me for saying it, but I wish that Jane had finished you off!"

And Nyquist knew the truth then, of what had happened yesterday evening. It *was* Jane Sutton who had attacked him with the knife, using Madelyn Arkwright only as a vehicle.

"You should've taken my wife's advice, old chap."

"What? And leave Hoxley?"

Gerald Sutton smiled and leaned in close. "I have a different option for you. In fact, I dearly hope you do find what you're looking for." He paused here, using a well-practiced effect, before finishing: "And I hope it kills you."

For a good long moment, the anger was fixed in place. It made a fierce show. But the pain of loss was hiding beneath, and now it showed. His fret crumbled and shivered. Sutton groaned. It was a strange sound to make, like a wounded, cornered animal. And then he turned and called for his two underlings. They scurried after him, along an alleyway that ran behind the row of houses. Nyquist went over to Edward Fairclough and bent down to help him. The young man revealed his face, each wound on show. Nyquist used a handkerchief to clean Teddy's face. It didn't look too bad, once the blood was wiped off. He drew him to his feet.

"Come on, we'll find the doctor."

"No!"

"Higgs will take a look at you."

"No. No, not her. She's involved."

"How do you mean?"

"Her and Jane Sutton, making their plans. I saw them together more than once, out by Birdbeck tarn."

"What were they doing there?"

"I don't know. Testing the waters. Preparing a spell."

"This was before you saw my father at the old cottage?"

"Yes, before that, a few weeks before."

Nyquist looked at him. They were standing in the yard behind the shop. It was quiet here, with no direct lights, only the moon's glow and the spilled light from the bedroom window of a neighboring house. It was enough to give their frets a lovely shine, a blue gold shimmer. Their mingled clouds trembled, and the sparkles in each flickered and danced like insects talking one to one, many to many, in the ever-changing colors of love and hate, and Nyquist felt all the things that Teddy Fairclough was feeling, as though they were his own emotions on offer. It was cold fear, and contempt for those around him, and alarm, a constant sense of foreboding. And yet a kindness was there, hidden away; it showed as a faint pastel wash across the fret. The lad was a fragile creature, no doubt about it. Fragile and frightened.

Nyquist kept his voice low. "If you don't want the doctor, we can find your sister, Becca. Is that better for you?"

Teddy nodded. He let himself be led a little way along the side alley, back toward the high street. He said in a low voice, "Have you found your father yet?"

"No. I'm still looking."

"He's around here somewhere, I'm sure of it. He hasn't left the village."

"Maybe."

"I know it. But... but listen... it's you he waits for, not me."

"Come on, kid–"

"Not me, not me!"

"Don't beat yourself up. Not when there are other people to do it for you."

Nyquist tried for a laugh. It didn't work. The lad's face was deadly serious as he spoke. "Your father told me of his journey."

They had come to a stop halfway down the passage. Nyquist looked at him. "How do you mean?"

"Mr Nyquist, he told me that…"

"Go on."

"That he had traveled the long passage of death to be here, and seen monsters along the way. And he…" Teddy paused. His eyes darted this way and that, on the lookout for enemies, "… and he urged me to run away from the village. Otherwise they might come for me as well. Creeping Jenny and her children, the one thousand tendrils. For there was no escape, once hooked. But he said I had to keep this to myself. A secret."

"Don't worry, we'll fight them, Teddy. You and me together."

"I wish… I wish that could be."

"It will be." Nyquist put a hand round the lad's shoulder. "And listen, full Marquess of Queensberry rules. No cheating, not on our part. Agreed?"

Teddy nodded at this, seemingly happy. His eyes engaged with Nyquist. In the enclosed world of their conjoined frets, they looked at each other and Nyquist felt for a moment that all was good, that nothing more needed to be said. He had a friend here, a true friend. And he felt that he had to help the young man, in some practical way. Nyquist took a five pound note from his wallet and handed it over. Teddy looked at this in surprise, but he was happy to take it as a gift. Nyquist said, "Treat yourself, lad, whatever you fancy. Or else buy your girl, Val, something nice with it."

"She's not… she's not my girl."

Teddy carefully folded the money into his pocket. But then a different look came to his face. He was having trouble breathing, and whatever peace there had been upon him, was fleeting. He now looked petrified.

"What is it?" Nyquist asked. "What's wrong?"

"You're too kind." It almost looked as though he might start crying.

"Forget about that. Just–"

"Sir, I've seen too much."

"Yes, you've been through it, I know."

"I saw the killer's face." Teddy's voice lowered. He was whispering. "At the school. I was going to find Becca. We'd argued at breakfast, and I wanted to apologize to her."

"Go on."

Teddy made a visible effort to concentrate. "But I got lost in all the school kids' frets, so many of them. It was like a fog bank." He paused for breath, and then said, "I walked along the corridor. I was alone. Or I thought I was, until I heard a noise in the mist."

"What kind of noise?"

"A twig. A twig cracking! Right there in the corridor."

He made a noise, in imitation of what he'd heard. *Krickk!*

Nyquist urged him on. "And then what?"

"Someone came out of the classroom, the one where they found the headmistress. Right there in the daytime, undercover of the fret's darkness."

"You mean…?"

"It looked like the Tolly Man at first, walking right past me. This close. Like you are now." His hand tightened on Nyquist's sleeve. "I was scared. Shivering all over. The fret was clouding the figure, thick and billowing, monstrous. Opaque. Like fog. Like the fog in the trees in the morning. Only the mask was seen. The mask of twigs. Only…"

"Teddy, tell me true. What did you see?"

"The twigs were moved aside. It wasn't a mask, I saw that

now. The woman was only holding them up, you see, like this..." His hands came up, to cover his face. "Two branches, one in each hand, and the berries bright upon them. And then her hands moved aside. Like this." His face was revealed.

"It was a woman, you say?"

Teddy nodded.

"Who was it?"

"Madame Fontaine. The fortune teller. She killed Mrs Sutton."

And with that the young man pulled free of Nyquist and took off at a staggering run back down the alleyway. He scrambled up onto a dustbin and climbed from there to the top of the wall, where he vanished from sight, dropping down on the other side. The pale blue, star-speckled glow of his fret lingered at the top of the wall for a moment, and then that too was whisked away.

MANY TIMES AROUND

Nyquist returned to the village green. He moved from one group to another, seeking one person only, hoping that this person was here, among the revelers. He asked for advice, for sightings, and was directed to the edge of the pond, where he found his quarry.

Len Sadler was chatting with Nigel Coombes. Sadler was laughing heartily, Coombes was nodding his head, obviously not seeing the joke. The glow of their cigarettes was intensified by the frets, transformed into miniature suns. Nyquist interrupted their talk, and asked to speak with Sadler alone. Coombes left them to it, already calling out to his daughter.

Sadler was drunk. He said. "Nyquist, my friend from afar, I hope you haven't shot anyone yet?"

"Sorry?"

"That revolver I gave you, do you still have it?"

"No. It was stolen."

"Stolen? Oh, that's bad news. It was meant for you, and you alone."

"No doubt it will turn up again."

Nyquist pulled a piece of card from his pocket. He said, "I had my fortune read today."

Sadler looked excited. "Madame Fontaine spoke to you?"

"She did."

"A nice piece of craftsmanship, that was, though I say so myself."

"You gave Fontaine the face of Agnes Dunne."

Sadler was mildly irritated. "So? So what? Is it wrong to be in love?"

Nyquist ignored the remark, asking instead, "Who put the fortune cards in the box?"

"I did. But Agnes wrote them out for me." He was slurring his words. "I just loaded the cards in the box."

"All of them?"

"Yes, yes. As far as I know. What's this about?"

By the fret's glow Nyquist read aloud the card's message: *"Follow a pathway through the woods, ask your question of the fire."* He looked at Sadler, and received no response. "What do you think that means, Len?"

"How would I know. I've never been very good at riddles."

"Where is she now?"

"Agnes? Maybe she's left the village. That's what people are saying–"

"No. I think she's still here."

Sadler looked anxious. He opened his mouth to speak, and then thought against it. He started to move off across the green. Nyquist grabbed hold of him by the arm, but Sadler was strong and turned back to curse in Nyquist's face.

"Piss off! Go on, get away from here. We've had enough of you."

Nyquist wiped spittle off his face with his sleeve.

Their frets were buffeted by a sudden gust of wind, but within their confines, the two men felt only a gentle wave of air, and a sense of warmth. They were cut off from the wide world, and would in most circumstances be comforted in isolation. But comfort wasn't on offer.

"I think you know where she's hiding," Nyquist said.

"I don't. I really don't! Why would I lie to you?" Sadler's voice cracked.

"To protect her."

"From what? I don't know what you're talking about."

Nyquist thought the emotions were genuine, but still, something was amiss.

"She was seen, Len. Today. At the school."

"Agnes was?"

"At the time of Jane Sutton's death."

It took a moment: various new colors bled across Sadler's fret, each one mirroring the trouble on his face, the changing expressions. Finally, the colors burst into words.

"She's not to blame!"

"For what?"

"She didn't kill anyone. Not Bainbridge. Nor Sutton."

"So who did then?"

"I don't know. But Agnes wouldn't do something like that."

Nyquist looked around. Beyond the limits of his fret, the night was dark, the moon veiled. He could see people not too far away, on the far side of the pond, their own frets aglow: yellow, green, orange. He turned back to Sadler. The other man looked a wreck, his face covered in sweat and his eyes red raw. His beer glass was empty and it slipped through his fingers and fell to the grass. Nyquist knew the exact feelings Sadler was going through, having experienced them all himself, when drunk, and the darkness was closing in.

"I'm sorry for messing you about. But if you think Agnes is involved, then you need to tell the truth."

"I can't... I can't tell the truth."

"It's too painful?"

Sadler managed to find a speck to focus on, one tiny speck of red light in his fret. And then he turned his eyes on Nyquist and made an attempt to control his speech.

"Ah, I've fucked up. I should never have..."

"What? Fallen for her?"

"It was all a mistake, and now I'm paying for it."

Nyquist knew he was close, that Sadler was on the edge of confession. "What form does the payment take?" he asked.

"Oh... so much, so much! Blood and tears, so much per pound, weighed out. Look, look at my hands..."

He showed his palms to Nyquist. They were crisscrossed with scars and nicks, old and new, made by chisels and hammers.

"You've worked hard, Len. All your life. That's what you are."

"Yes, yes." Sadler's head nodded. He seemed to have lost most of his inner strength, and his body was ready to drop. "But where has it got me? I'll be working till I die."

Nyquist took hold of him and led him over to a bench at the edge of the green. For a good long moment, they both sat there in silence. But then Sadler sobbed out loud. His fret trembled.

Nyquist kept his voice low. "Do you know where she is?"

Sadler shook his head. "No. I swear. But she came to me." He took a deep breath. "I thought she'd left Hoxley, along with her husband. I really did. But then, one night, she came to see me."

"When was this?"

"A couple of weeks ago. Saint Pepper's Day, when everybody looks the other way, and walks sideways instead of going forward. Agnes took advantage of this, to always be out of people's sight… until she walked into mine."

Nyquist thought about the days when the two deaths had occurred: Bainbridge had died when nobody could make a sound, and Jane Sutton when the mists of the fret clouded the village. The killer was taking advantage of the rulings, to move in secret.

"Go on. What did she want of you?"

Sadler's eyes told the whole story even before he spoke. "I thought she wanted to be with me. That she'd left her husband." He blinked sadly. "It wasn't to be."

Nyquist persisted, keeping Sadler on course: "What *did* she want?"

"To tell me the truth, of what she'd done. Or rather, what she was about to do." He paused, and licked his lips. "I need a drink."

"Not yet. Keep going."

"God damn you, Nyquist. Can't you leave a man be?"

"No."

Sadler moaned. He said, "Agnes wanted to punish the villagers who had harmed her husband, Thomas Dunne. But I don't think she meant to kill them."

Nyquist had to feel for the man: his love for Agnes had blinded him to the truth, or at least a possible truth.

"And what had happened to her husband, what was the harm done?"

Sadler looked away. "She wouldn't tell me that. And pretty soon afterwards, she went on her way. I tried to make her stay, but it was no good. We kissed in the doorway. That was it. And I realized…" His face seemed to crumple, and his fret followed suit, shuddering in blue and black. "I knew then that she loved her husband far more than she did me." He clenched his jaw tight. "I've been a fool."

Nyquist thought the conversation was over, that Sadler would have nothing more to say – but after a moment he looked up and said, "There is one place. We used to go there, the two of us, when we were teenagers. But I can't tell you where it is."

"Sadler. Come on. It's time."

"Listen to me." He spoke slowly and deliberately. "I *cannot* tell you where it is. I would come to great harm, if I did so."

The conversation ended abruptly as Sadler stood up and walked off, his colors fading into the night. Nyquist made his way back to the high street. There was only one thing on his mind now, one destination. The idea came to him from deep down. But as he set off, he saw another fret merging with his. It was the doctor. She looked agitated.

"Nyquist, what are you playing at?"

"I was wondering when you'd admit to it."

"I'm not admitting anything. I just need you to be careful–"

"You keep saying that."

"Haven't I been your friend here, your confidant?"

"You've been checking up on me, that's true, every step of the way. Keeping close."

Now Higgs looked irritated. She shouted at him, "Maybe I'm protecting you, John, have you thought about that?" But her outburst only brought on a coughing fit. She put a hand over her mouth. Her face turned red, her fret also, and the coughs made their way as waves of disturbance through the mist.

Nyquist said, "I'm not here to fight you. You do know that?"

Higgs stared at him. For a moment it seemed she might have some kind of rejoinder. But her body gave in, and then her mind, and she told him for the first time of her fears, of the sickness, and how little time she had left.

"Maude Bryars will help you," Nyquist said. "She will care for you, I'm sure."

"That's not enough."

Nyquist thought about what she was saying. "Irene. Please tell me you haven't made some kind of deal, a deal with the devil? You know that never goes right."

"I need to get better."

"And this is the way, is it?"

"It's the only way."

Nyquist shook his head in despair. "I don't know what it is that you've done, not really. And I don't care, I really don't. Except that my father's involved in some way." He glared at her. "And that really pisses me off."

"Yes. I didn't know that would happen…"

"What? Higgs? That *what* would happen?"

"None of us did. I'm sorry."

"All I want is the truth. Do you know where my father is?"

"He's waiting for you. And when the time is right, you'll find each other."

She was moving away, her fret separating from his. He called out, "Higgs, wait! Tell me where he is!"

But her face and form were merging into the darkness all around, as her last strands of mist drifted away. Her voice came out of the gloom, saying, "It's too late now. We have gone too far, and cannot step back into the lighted path."

And then Nyquist was alone. He rushed forward, trying to find her. But his fret never seemed to move in the right direction; the doctor was too skilled in hiding, in the use of the mist as a place of safety, and of secrets.

Well, let it be; he had more important things to consider.

It was coming up on half past eight. He made his way to the outskirts of the village, and carried on across a field. He climbed the gentle hill, and as he did so, he thought about the case, and all that he knew. Two people had died. He couldn't help thinking that he was to blame in some way, for the deaths, as Gerald Sutton had claimed. His arrival in the village had set off a series of unforeseen events. The only hope he had was to find the killer before another poisoning took place. And always at the back of his mind lingered a thought he hadn't dared to consider, until now: that his own father, George Nyquist, was in some way involved in the deaths. Saints forbid, he might even be the killer. Madelyn Arkwright had hinted at such a connection.

If he could prove otherwise, that at least would be a result. Of a kind.

Nyquist reached a borderline of trees. Beyond was Morden Wood, as he now knew it. He entered the arched doorway of the branches, his fret lighting the way a little, enough that he could make his way forward, one careful step at a time. He brought to mind the directions Professor Bryars had given him at their meeting: *Walk through Morden Wood and take the left-hand path at Sylvia's Glade. And then keep on walking.* Yes, he would follow that route, perfectly contained inside his globe of light. The trees came into sight, one by one, each branch momentarily illuminated, each tangle of twigs, each cluster of white berries. And so he moved on in this manner, taking his own body lamp with him, and leaving darkness in his wake.

Soon he was in the myre wood, at the center of the forest. He saw a first label hanging from a branch, and then another, and then many of them, the further he went along. Sylvia's calling cards. The names were lit by the fret and easily read, even as they turned and fluttered in the night breeze: *Black Hearted, Collector of Cuckoo Spit, Home to Squirrels, Beetle Bath, Eye of Skull, Mr Hollow, Mystery Twig*. His face and hair brushed against them as he passed along. The hoot of an owl shivered at Nyquist's fret and set it trembling – the sound moved across the haze as a streak of color, and then faded from sight.

A few more steps brought him to a wooden hut in a clearing. Sylvia's Glade. He rapped on the door of the hut and called out, "Sylvia, it's John Nyquist. Are you in?" He tried again, using a different name: "It's me, Written in Blood." But even this brought no response. He pushed at the door and it swung open, and he stepped inside. There was no sign of any occupant. Hundreds of labels hung down on pieces of cotton and string from the low ceiling. He read a few as he moved further inside: *Read Me Slowly, Spell of Speech, Message for a Ghost, Silent Name, Sylvia's Favorite, White Wing, Cocoon Poem*. The room was sparsely furnished. There was a table and chair, and an iron grate and chimney breast, where pieces of wood were stacked in readiness of a fire. It was all very neat and tidy, every surface spotless. He examined the table where a set of boxes held her supplies of string, blank cards and wax crayons. Even the table and chair, and the boxes had their own labels attached: *Waiting for Words, Midnight's Ink, Sit Down Here*. A series of ledgers were slotted together on a small shelf. He took up the latest one – *Sylvia Keepsake's Record of Taxonomy, Volume 4* – and he opened it to find an entry for every branch and tree, with its new name. Also named were birds and animals, and people. Nyquist leafed back through the pages. He saw Edward Fairclough: *Born to Follow.* He saw Gladys Coombes: *Lady of the Lake.* And so on. A few other villagers he didn't recognize. He found his own entry from last Thursday: *I met a stranger in the woods. A lost soul. I called him Written in Blood.* And this, from just two days ago: *Mrs Agnes Dunne gathering berries. She was rude to me. I called her Twig Stealer.* That was enough: one more clue to add to his collection.

He made his way back outside. Contained within his very own bubble of moonlight, he felt he might be the only thing of flesh and blood for miles around: flesh, blood, mist and light, an intermingled creature, courtesy of Saint Athelstan. But as he left the glade, a strange and disturbing thing happened: his fret started to falter, to flicker and die around him, the sparkles of light popping out and the mist dissipating. So then: here at the glade, the power of the saints ran out, and the ordinary world took over. This was the borderzone. Nyquist was now unprotected, and he felt naked, exposed, and terribly cold. He checked the time on his wristwatch: well past nine o'clock. Shivering, banging his hands at his sides, he wondered about making his way back to the village? But no, he had to keep on, he had come too far. Too much was at stake.

He took the left-hand path from the clearing, as directed.

This deep into the wood, at this time of night, silence and darkness reigned. The trees grew closer together. He had to squeeze between their trunks. Here and there, ripe clusters of moonsilver brightened the branches with their promises of stillness, and sleep. Eternal sleep. But he kept on, and soon enough the woods thinned out and he came to a stretch of open land, where a low hill rose up from the wood's edge.

And there on the hill's summit stood his destination.

Clud Tower.

The clouds drifted away across the sky, leaving the moon to look over the land. Only one sliver of darkness remained at the moon's edge; it was almost full, and he could see the building clearly. And he understood Sadler's fear, for this was the one place that villagers could never name, or even admit to knowing about.

Nyquist walked the overgrown path that led to it. He stood in contemplation, looking at the tall structure. It wasn't circular, as he'd imagined from the blurred photograph he'd been sent. Rather it was made of a series of flat walls, perhaps a pentagon, or a hexagon in cross-section. He would have to walk round to make sure. It was made of old stone, long darkened by age and the weather and moss and damp. There was a heavy wooden door, painted green, and padlocked shut.

Why had he been sent a photograph of this place?

From the crest of this hill Nyquist could look down into a further valley and across to the other side, faraway, where a few lights were seen, evidence of dwellings, farmhouses perhaps, or the homes of another village or town. Perhaps Bligh, or Lockhampton?

He set off around the tower, moving rapidly. He counted five walls, and then he came back to the green door. There was no sign of any other way in. He walked around it again, to check for details, this time going anticlockwise. He passed one wall, another, the third, a fourth, the fifth wall. But there was no sign of the door. He must have miscounted. He carried on around in the same direction, counting walls as he did so, and he reached twelve walls before he stopped, trembling with a sudden fear, that he might be lost and never find his way back again. A cloud covered the moon. It was pitch black. Something was rustling close by, an animal, or a spirit. It breathed. Quickly, Nyquist set off in the opposite direction and found the green doorway, after just five walls. He gasped with relief. By now, his face was damp with sweat and his hands shook, he couldn't control them. It took him a good minute to regain a degree of calm.

The tower was pentagonal in shape, he had to keep that in mind.

Five sides. Five sides only!

He set off once more, widdershins, and quickly became lost again, for one wall after another passed by, and the doorway did not appear. Now he stopped. He was out of breath, as though he'd been on a long journey. He took a few more paces, still counting. Sixteen walls. Seventeen. He looked out over the valley and saw the same pattern of lights down below. After a moment's rest he retraced his steps and counted the walls – one, two, three, four, five – and he came to the green door. He felt like he'd come home, that he was safe once more.

Here was the truth: walking around it in a clockwise direction, Clud Tower had five sides only. Walking around it anticlockwise, the tower had more than five sides. Many sides, Nyquist didn't know how many. Perhaps they went on forever, never repeating, and he felt dizzy thinking about such a thing. But he knew this: he would never find what he was looking for in a tower of five sides only. He had to walk the other way around, and keep on walking until he found another door, or some object. Or a person.

Nyquist's journey began. He gave himself a limit by noting

the time on his watch: half an hour of circling around, and then he would call it quits, and set off once more through the woods, back into Hoxley, and his room above The Swan With Two Necks. The thought of his bed filled him with yearning; he imagined himself under the sheets, warm and secure. Instead he was walking around Clud Tower, endlessly walking, counting the walls as he passed, and then miscounting them, and then giving up on keeping score. Only the thought that all he had to do was turn around, walk past five walls, and the door would be there for him: only this kept him sane. And so he carried on.

By his wristwatch he had been on the go now for twelve minutes.

And then he came across a feature he hadn't seen before, a piece of chalked graffiti depicting a complex knotted shape. Opposite this was a small circle of stones and bricks set in the ground, forming a hearth with the remains of a campfire inside. Nyquist bent down. The ashes were cold. He should have felt glad at this, for now he had a sense that he was actually moving on, passing into new territories. But his whole body was shivering as he continued on his way. *Widdershins, widdershins!* He remembered what Doctor Higgs had told him, about never taking a left-hand path around a church, otherwise you might meet the devil. It certainly felt possible right now, in the dark, in the bitter cold. Every new wall that he reached, he expected to see someone waiting for him, a dark-eyed stranger holding a knife, or a wild beast, or a demon clinging halfway up the tower on hooked claws. His mind raced ahead, into fear and trepidation. One wall, another. One more. Around and around. Eighteen minutes on the dial. He reached the stone fireplace again; he knew it was the same one because of the graffiti on the wall opposite. But there was a difference; this time the ashes of the fire were smoking, and a few cinders were glowing red in the gray dust. He bent down and felt the warmth of a low heat on his palms. It made him wonder: perhaps he was traveling backwards in time, or forwards even? He felt nauseous. Could he even trust his wristwatch? He put it to his ear and listened. The ticks came at irregular intervals, like those of a damaged heart. Where the hell was he? What day was it? What was making that noise, that low soft whispering sound from the next corner? It sounded like a creature slithering along. Nyquist shivered with fright. *Keep moving, keep moving!* But as he got to his feet he stopped and looked down again. There was glint of bright silver in the embers. He picked up a stick and shifted the ashes around until the object was revealed. It was a coin, an old coin by the look of it. He moved it to the side of the stone hearth and then tried to flick it onto the ground, but something was holding it back. He shifted the ashes a little more to uncover a green thread attached to the coin. It was a tendril, of the kind he was now used to. Here was a fourth object of consequence. Nyquist flipped it onto the ground around the stones. The coin was warm to the touch. It was marked with the date 1666, and the portrait of a king, one of the Charleses, it looked like. A bewigged individual. The tendril emerged from the coin's edge, and straightaway it made its way to his fingers, wrapping itself around one of them. He felt the series of tiny burrs hook themselves into his flesh, and a tiny dot of blood was formed, like that around a pinprick. But he forced himself not to panic, to stay true, even as his body flinched, even as the hooks cut deeper into his flesh. Having had the other three objects stolen, he had to be glad of this attachment, he had to welcome it. There was no other way.

He turned the next corner. The slithering sound stopped. He was still alone. Twenty-five minutes had passed since the commencement of his journey. One wall and then another, and another. One more! His mind was weakening, and his body was growing tired. His eyes blurred over. He focused on every last bit of damage to the stones as a marker of life, to know that he was moving on – and every scratch and mark of graffiti in the same way, the chalked names of long-forgotten loves serving as a compass. On, and on. Without thinking he was counting the walls, starting again from zero: one, two, three, four, five, six, seven, eight, nine… Now he stopped, for he could hear the Tolly song from around the next corner of the tower.

Sing along a Sally, O
The moon is in the valley, O

Nyquist walked around the corner, and stopped again. His entire body was bound to that moment, and not a further step could be taken.

Here was the mask, the living mask.

The mask of knotted twigs, bound with barbed wire.

The mask that hung suspended in the dark, just a few feet away.

The twigs that creaked and rustled together.

He knew a woman was wearing the mask, for her song continued a while longer, high and sweet in the night air.

Nyquist didn't know what to do. His eyes blinked away sweat, and tried their best to see clearly through the gloom. He was frozen to the spot.

And then, at last, the song came to an end.

He could move forward.

There was a hissing sound, from deep inside the bound twigs. Her voice.

Nyquist was close enough now to see the wearer's eyes staring out from the darkness within, glistening. Those were human eyes, he told himself. Nothing more! He had to force himself forward. He tried to speak, but couldn't, his mouth was still sealed with fright.

He reached out...

But the Tolly Woman turned from him and moved away around the next corner of the tower. Nyquist followed, doing his best to keep up with her, but every corner, every wall, seemed to take her further away, until at last he rounded one more corner and she was gone. But he could not stop, not now. He moved on. One wall, another. So many walls. He was rushing ahead, uncaring, almost stumbling in the dark.

And then he stopped, out of breath, his body protesting.

But around the next corner and he could see flickers of light and trails of smoke. The smoke caught in his nostrils. He took another few steps, slowly now, painfully, and found himself once more at the campfire. This time the fire was fully alight, roaring away in the night. And sitting on a small wooden stool by the fire, warming her hands, was a woman.

He stood before her.

"Agnes Dunne?"

His voice croaked on the words, as though long out of use. But he had to ask because of the changes she'd made to her appearance.

"That's right. I've been waiting for you."

She gestured to a second stool. Nyquist sat down opposite her, across the fire.

Agnes took a bite out of a cracker.

The Tolly mask was resting on the ground, just by her side.

For as good long moment they sat in silence, the two of them, allowing Nyquist to get his breath back. And then Agnes said: "It's been a while since I posted the photographs to you."

And still he couldn't speak.

Agnes pulled a twig from the Tolly mask and added it to the fire. She was burning it, piece by piece by piece. Nyquist saw that a lot of the twigs had already been taken for firewood and kindling. Only the barbed wire held the effigy together.

She asked, "Did you have your fortune read?"

He nodded, and he took his Madame Fontaine card from his inner pocket and handed it to her. She read this and smiled to herself, and then asked, "You've followed a pathway through the woods?"

"I have."

"Very well then… ask a question of the fire."

His lips moved awkwardly. The words were trapped in his mouth and would not spill over into sound. He thought that if he spoke them, they would surely float away, unheard, and be wasted.

Agnes was looking at him calmly, waiting for his response.

At last Nyquist said what he needed to say, staring into the flames.

"Can you tell me where my father is?"

The twigs crackled in the fire and smoke and ash took to the air, a marriage of ghosts bound for the night sky.

PART 4
THE PENNY BLOODS

A SEVENFOLD KNOT

Agnes Dunne spoke softly, summoning a spirit. "If Creeping Jenny permits, I will draw your story together from its various strands, filaments, roots and offshoots." She took out a cigarette and used a burning twig from the Tolly mask to light it. This act of sacrilege gave her some pleasure for a smile played on her lips. It was soon gone.

"Two people of the village have died. Another is lost to madness. The reasons for these acts are varied, but they all come from a single idea: that blood always returns home, in the end."

Nyquist didn't respond. Her eyes sought his over the flames.

"Really, I believe that to be the case. It's the reason why you came to Hoxley, John Nyquist. And why your father made the same journey."

"And your part in all this?"

"I wish to take revenge on those who brought harm, both physical and mental, to my husband, Mr Thomas Dunne of this parish."

She spoke carefully, weighing each remark as though defending herself in court.

Nyquist let her proceed at her own rate.

He'd first seen Agnes Dunne in a series of portraits, photographed and processed by her husband. He next saw her image carved in wood as the face of Madame Fontaine, this time created by Len Sadler. Both men in their own ways had idealized her. In lighting and mood, Thomas presented her as a glamorous tousled-haired Hollywood actress in a cover shot, while Sadler made her out to be a pagan goddess. But the woman sitting by the fire – now talking, now in silence, now putting another twig to the flames – looked very different from either presentation. The long curling locks of the portraits had been severely chopped down into a more functional style. Her skin was wind-chafed. Her facial features were defined entirely by the bone beneath, not by muscle and fat. Her eyes held darkness. Many tiny scratches marked her cheeks and brow, some of them scabbed over, others still fresh. The thorns had dug in.

Nyquist asked her, "Did you steal the Tolly mask from the museum?"

"I removed it from captivity, yes." That smile again.

"And you've taken to wearing it?"

"Now and then." She nodded. "I know people will frown, for it's only meant to be taken up on Saint Algreave's Day, but I needed to feel as my husband did."

"So Thomas played the Tolly Man this year?"

"He did. It was a dream of his for so long, but the committee turned him down a good many times." She smiled faintly at a memory. "So he was very excited this year, as you might imagine." The smile faded. "I guess that's where it all started."

She looked at him. "I don't suppose you know much of our traditions?"

"I've had a crash course."

"During Saint Algreave's Day, the Tolly Man parades about the village, frightening the children, dancing with maidens, offering mock duels to the young men. And so on. It means very little these days, an empty custom. But towards the end of the day, the volunteer is taken out of the village for the grand unmasking, witnessed by a few of the elders only."

She took one last drag of her cigarette and then threw it into the fire.

"I waited until they had set off, and then took the same road. I gave them ten minutes' start. Mr Sadler drove me in his van."

"You followed them?"

"There was no need to *follow* them, for we all knew where the unmasking takes place. A place called Birdbeck Tarn."

"Where the airplane crashed?"

"That's right. Leonard wanted to come with me across the fields, but I insisted that I did this alone."

"Why, Agnes? What were you hoping to find?"

"The unmasking was a great secret in the village. As children we learned a little of its mysteries, the way it affected the wearer of the mask so much, for instance, or how some people never recovered from the extreme nature of the ritual. So, I was worried. Worried for my husband's welfare, but also... I wanted to *know*. The truth. And the thought of Thomas going through this ritual without my knowing, well, it upset me."

She plucked another twig from the mask and set it to the flames.

"Ours was a volatile marriage, often fraught. On other occasions, yes, quite passionate."

Sparks flew up into the air. Snow was falling, but a brief

flurry only, thank the saints. The fire roared on and Nyquist warmed his hands at it and leaned forward to feel the heat on his face. With a shiver he realized that he missed his fret. But when he looked up again, he felt that all the known and unknown stars were visible, to the last pinprick of distant light – and here he was, sitting at the center of it all, listening to a tale being told.

"It was a high summer's day," Agnes said. "A warm and bright early evening. From the top of Hawley Ridge I could see everything that happened, as they gathered around the tarn. We were always warned off going there, when we were kids, because it's said to be the place of ghosts, and a site of worship for the demon, Creeping Jenny."

"I've been there," Nyquist told her. "It's an eerie place."

"Yes. The Tolly Man ceremony was designed to keep the ghosts away from the village, at least that was the story we learned at school. I now believe the opposite."

She took a moment to gather her words.

"There were five people in attendance, each standing at the pool's edge. Thomas, with the mask of twigs still in place. Nigel Coombes, Ian Bainbridge, Jane Sutton, and Doctor Irene Higgs. Every year those four would take the Tolly Man out to the tarn, to perform the unmasking. And this year, I was a witness, an unseen spectator."

Agnes paused. Nyquist was worried that she might not continue.

He asked her quietly, "Do you want to go on?"

"I do. Your question, about your father, must be answered, as best I can manage it."

He nodded his thanks for this.

"The Tolly mask was removed. Nigel and Ian helped with

this, and Doctor Higgs examined Thomas's face. He'd been wearing the mask for many, many hours and he must have been very badly cut up from the thorns. But the doctor made no attempt to heal him. She left the wounds open, so the blood would flow freely. And then he had to kneel at the side of the tarn and look down into the water, at his own reflection. The other four watched him as he did this. I don't know what was being said, if anything, I was too far away. Perhaps they were chanting. After a while, Thomas stood up and he paused for a moment on the bank, and then he walked forward into the water, towards the propeller at the pool's center. He ducked down and lowered himself below the surface. He did this quite willingly, I could see that. But it still worried me. And I waited, and waited, hoping to see him come up again. But he didn't appear, not for some minutes. I thought surely he was drowning, but then at last I saw him. His head broke the surface and he took a great gasping breath. I could see the distress on his face. His hands were flailing around, splashing at the water, and he struggled to get to the bank. The others helped him to climb out. They looked to be delighted. I had the sense that their ritual, whatever it might be, had worked."

Here Agnes stopped, her story interrupted by a loud screeching sound. The noise was made by a raven that flew down and entered the glow of the firelight. *Scraw, scraw.* It landed on the soil near the fire. Sparkles of light caught at the tips of each wing. The sound of its call was loud and insistent until she calmed it with a gentle pat on its beak. Nyquist saw the silver mark on its brow and knew it be the same bird that had stolen his naming card, and that turned up in the budgerigar's cage at the Bainbridge house. Agnes spoke to it, as she would to a household pet.

"There, there, Mr Peck. Have you been hunting for trinkets?"

The bird answered her in a series of softer screeches.

"Nothing doing, eh? Nothing on offer? You poor thing."

"You own a raven?" Nyquist asked.

"I don't *own* him. You can't own a raven. But his spirit was linked with mine, on Saint Malachi's Day last year, when all animals and villagers join as one. It is the same power that Leonard uses, to train his pigeons." She smiled. "I have, over my life, gained some little knowledge of the earth, the trees and the air. And how the various elements might be turned to use."

"He stole my naming card."

"Yes, Mr Peck showed me that. *Written in Blood*. A difficult name to live up to."

"You think so?"

"I hope you have enough left in your veins once the writing is done."

Agnes fed the raven half a Sutton's cracker, which he gobbled down in one go. This was enough to get Mr Peck flight-worthy again, and the bird took off, a darkness of feathers gathered by darkness of sky. A silence settled between the two people.

The bird had broken a spell.

Agnes sighed. She pointed over her shoulder to the knotted shape painted on the wall and said, "This is a witch's knot of seven folds. Likewise, there are seven people involved in the story, at its heart: Thomas and the four elders. You, John Nyquist. And your father."

"How many sides are there to the tower?"

She laughed gently. "Five, Of course."

"And widdershins?"

"Four hundred… and sixty… nine. All told. And then the traveler will come back to the main doorway. At last. Oh, at long last! But there is another entrance along the way. Move on seventeen walls from this one, leftwards of course, and you will pass the fire once more." She smiled into the flames. "The fire will be out this time, stone cold. But keep walking on from there, and twenty-five walls afterwards you will reach the second, smaller doorway. This one is unlocked. I've been staying there, inside Clud Tower. There's a fireplace, and a chimney. A bed of straw. It's cozy enough, if you wrap up warm. No ghosts, or none that have any interest in me. Cracker?" She had an entire packet open at her side.

Nyquist refused the offer. "Will you tell the rest of it, if you can?"

Agnes looked despairing. "It's not easy."

"I understand that, but–"

"Too much has been lost."

"Tell me. You have to." For the first time since he'd met with Agnes Dunne, he felt his anger rising. "Tell me, goddamn it, Agnes. By all the saints, I need to know."

She narrowed her eyes. The colors of the flames danced on her face. She said in a monotone, "I find it disturbing that the left-hand number of sides on the tower isn't divisible by five, to correspond in some way to the right-hand path. Yes, very strange indeed."

Hearing this, Nyquist was aware that he might be talking to a murderer. There might be limits to what she allowed herself to say. Or she might be mad, completely so, and therefore unbound by the limits of meaning and logic.

He asked, "Did you come here as a child?"

"No, later on. When we were teenagers. Leonard and I. It was a place you were never supposed to visit, because of the curse of the Clud family. Leonard really didn't want to come, I had to persuade him. We were sweethearts, I guess. He followed me. But he would never walk round it widdershins." She gave a little laugh.

"How many times have you walked all the way around?"

"Twice. Just to confirm the number of sides."

Nyquist leaned over and took a twig from the Tolly Man mask, and he placed it on the fire. Agnes had closed her eyes, but his action must have moved her in some way, for when he leaned back in his chair, she took up her tale again, quite freely.

"I got up from my hiding place and walked quickly across the fields to Leonard's car. He was waiting for me. We drove back into Hoxley. All the way he wanted to know what I'd seen, and in the end I lied and told him that the elders had removed the mask from Thomas, and said a few prayers to Saint Algreave, and that was it. I'm not sure if I convinced him or not. Well, it matters little now. For I had no real conception of what I'd seen, exactly. Such knowledge came later."

"I still don't understand what this has to do with my father."

Agnes nodded. "I am coming to that. For the first month, nothing happened, and I put all thoughts of Saint Algreave's Day from my mind. And then Thomas started to change. He lost weight. His face was gray, his eyes drawn. He was looking out on other worlds, that's the only way I can describe it. I knew he'd been going to see Doctor Higgs a fair few times, and these visits increased now. I thought he was ill, and it worried me. But whenever I asked him for news of his ailment, whenever I pleaded with him, he wouldn't answer, only saying it was nothing, that he would soon be well again. And indeed, he did seem to get a little better."

She put another twig on the fire. The mask was starting to look fragile by now; a few more sticks removed and it might collapse entirely.

"There were times when he went out alone, for hours on end, and I never found out where he was going. I suspected he was having an affair. But it was more than that, much more, for whenever Thomas returned, he would look worse than before. And his illness really started to eat into him now. He looked drained, his hands would shake, his skin was peeling in places and his face caved in at the cheekbones. It looked ghastly. He'd stopped taking photographs, as far as I knew. I had to fulfill our existing orders myself. And yet he was driven by some other purpose." She thought for a moment and then continued, "At one point I walked into the darkroom unexpectedly, and I saw him pouring something into the developing tray. It wasn't the usual chemicals, I knew that. But when I confronted him, Thomas lost his temper and told me to get out. He effectively banned me from the room, locking himself inside. Saints preserve me, it was a terrible time."

Agnes's face showed her discomfort; memories were infecting her, spreading through her body like a fever.

"Never, in all our years of marriage, had I seen him like this. And then, one day..."

She stopped and drew in a breath. She reached for a cigarette, only to find the packet empty. This made her frown. Nyquist offered one of his own, but she refused, and drew herself taller in her seat.

"Thomas began to age," she said. "His hair grew thinner,

and he was very distressed by that. The skin sagged around his neck. He seemed to put on years, *years*, in a few weeks, and there was nothing I could do but watch, and worry. I knew that something had gone wrong in that pool, in the tarn, with the open cuts on his face. He'd become infected by something in the water, that filthy water. A bacteria or germ of some kind. I really believed this, and I went to the doctor's surgery, demanding that she tell me everything, all about Thomas's illness. But of course she muttered away about the patient's right to confidentiality. It was pitiful! I felt like telling her that I'd witnessed the unmasking, and all that followed. But I didn't, I kept it to myself."

The marks of the thorns on her face glowed bright red, inflamed by her anger.

"The thing is, John, another truth worried at me."

"Which was?"

"Have you heard of Adam Clud, and his part in the village's history?"

"Maude Bryars told me a little about him. He was the very first Tolly Man. And viewed as a villain, an evil man from an evil family."

"Yes, that's how he's perceived. Well, Adam's wife was named Guinevere. She was by all accounts as bad and as crazed as he was, and met with an untimely end. Stories and legends have grown up around her. And ever since I was a child, I have heard tales of how the demon of Guinevere Clud might be summoned up, under the correct circumstances. Over the centuries her first name was modernized to Jennifer."

"Creeping Jenny?"

"Herself. Her spirit."

"You think this is what they were doing, the elders? Summoning a demon?"

"I do. I do. And I saw the process take place before my eyes, as an act of possession. For within a few days I barely recognized the man who stood before me, my husband. He was thirty-nine years old. But he looked ten years older than that, easily. He wouldn't even talk to me anymore. Thomas retreated into himself, and I barely existed as a person in his world. I was no longer his wife, except for one aspect alone: that I cared for him, and cared deeply. But I could do little that was good, or useful. He would often not even respond when I said his name. And then he told me one day – quite calmly, with no trace of madness – that he was no longer to be called Thomas Dunne, that he would prefer to take up a surname from his family tree, his great-great-grandmother's maiden name."

"Which was?"

"Your own surname. *Nyquist*."

The flames flickered in the circle of stones. Far off an owl hooted, a lonely sound in the night.

"You may find her grave in the churchyard, if you wish. Myrtle Winifred Nyquist–"

"Stop. Please." Nyquist stood up. He began to pace about, agitated. The air grew darker about him. He said, "I won't let this story happen," without really knowing what he meant. "I won't let it happen." He stood with his back to her, facing the wall of Clud Tower, staring at the sevenfold knot. "I won't let it happen." Whispering now, over and over.

Agnes waited a moment. "I know it's difficult."

He turned to her. "You don't understand. I've never had anybody, not since I was a child. I was abandoned twice over, by my mother's death, and then by my father. I've been alone ever since. But I have lived! I have lived in a city half in darkness, half in light, and been happy within that world. I have at times drank myself into oblivion. But always, always knowing I would be the one in charge. That I would fight! Fight on." He drew a deep breath and he gazed at Agnes and he said, "But now… to know of a family, of a line, a bloodline… I cannot grasp it."

"Sit down. Sit down, please, John."

He stayed on his feet, but he kept himself still, and he waited.

She said, "The photographs drew you here, didn't they?" He nodded. "So then, let me tell you how they were taken."

This settled him a little. "Yes, I'd like to know."

"As I said, Thomas had given up on photography. But he was still going into the darkroom on a regular basis, at least once a day. One evening I joined him there. He was no longer locking the door and he made no protest. By now, only his work mattered to him, and I don't think he cared if I knew his secret or not. He took a clean piece of photographic paper from a box, and set it adrift in the tray of developing fluid. I stood there and watched as he lowered his hands, his two bare hands, into the tray." She licked a flake of tobacco away from her lip. "I didn't understand, but I made no attempt to stop him. I needed to witness the full extent of his illness, or his madness, whichever it was."

Nyquist said, "He'd taken the fluid from the tarn?"

"Yes, yes. I know that now. But all I could do was watch as he kept his hands in the tray. Minutes went by. Not a word was spoken. He was concentrating deeply, forcibly. His eyes were gently closed. I believe he was forming an image in his mind. And then he drew his hands from the tray. I stepped closer. The piece of photographic paper floated in the liquid, alongside dead insects, seeds, a leaf, bits of silver stone. And I looked on in wonder, I really did. It was astonishing."

Nyquist took his seat at the fire. "You mean an image formed on the paper?"

Agnes nodded, grateful for the confirmation. "Yes. Oh, it was a blur, that's all, a dark fuzzy shape with a few smoky dots of light in it, showing the bare traces of a human face, nothing more. And Thomas was disappointed, I could tell that. But he placed it in the fixing tray and then he hung it on a line to dry, alongside other images, earlier efforts, all of them showing the same blurring, and the darkness. He was… he was trying to create something from the depths of his mind, trying to bring it alive, and it just wouldn't come out properly, not yet."

"He didn't need a camera?"

"It was a kind of direct exposure, that's all I could think. But he could not yet control it. It took him a few days to get it right. I helped him, I had to, because I didn't want him to be alone. And all the time he was changing further, and becoming in my sight a different man – or rather, another man was taking control of him. Only the photographic project gave him any kind of hope. He was no longer going outside, so I had to do all the work as well, to support us, and the shopping and everything. He couldn't show himself to anyone, because he'd changed so much. One time Doctor Higgs knocked on the door, but he refused to let her in. It was shame, or anger, I don't know which. God knows how he felt when he looked in a mirror." She frowned, and found a little strength. "This is when I grew closer than ever to Leonard Sadler. He was my truest companion."

Nyquist leaned forward. "Agnes, you said that your husband produced photographs, using this new method. Were they the ones sent to me?"

"They were. But that came a little later. The first successful image was rather different. Here, I can show you."

She had a duffle bag next to the stool and she rummaged around in it for a moment, and then drew out a single photograph. "He created this by the same technique, the laying of his hands in the tray, in the waters of the tarn that he'd carried here, and then closing his eyes, his whole being concentrated in the process. I saw it all happen, the image slowly forming on the paper, right before me."

She handed the photograph to Nyquist and he looked at it. The image was grainy, and still blurred, and dark around the edges, but enough light had gathered in the center of the picture for a shape to be seen, clearly seen, conjured into view as from a dream. His eyes were drawn to the figure revealed. He found himself shaking.

"Do you know what you're looking at?"

He nodded. "I do. It's a young boy, he's holding a toy gun. He's five or six years old. I remember this back yard." He looked at her. "My father chalked those goal posts on the back wall for me. And this washing line, the dustbin, everything… I remember it all."

"Now do you see, why you had to come here?"

Agnes pulled another stick from the Tolly Man, causing it to fall into pieces, a face collapsing into nothingness.

PORTRAIT OF WOMAN WITH TWIGS

"I asked Thomas who the boy was, and he said, 'My son. It's my son, John.'"

Nyquist continued to stare at the photograph, as Agnes Dunne talked on. He was barely listening.

"He said it over and over again, like a spell that had taken him over. It hurt me to hear him talk in this way, for we were a childless couple. And always would be."

Now he looked at her.

"My mind raced, trying to understand what my husband was saying. I asked him, 'You mean you have a child already, by another woman?' It was all I could think. But he gazed at me blindly, without speaking. He was as confused as I was, about what was happening. He was in pain, as well. Physical pain. His brows were knitted, his teeth set hard in his mouth, exposed, red raw at the gums, and I saw a tiny trickle of blood coming from one nostril. He'd been through hell. Just to produce this one, grainy, blurred image of a child. And for what purpose?"

"He... he made... he made this happen..."

Nyquist was searching for words. Agnes reached over the fire to take his hand in hers. "Everything changed at that point," she said, "after that photograph. I knew I was dealing with something I could never understand, or control. I pledged only to look after Thomas as I could, because I know for certain he would've done the same for me."

He pulled away from her.

"Anger was growing in me. Anger at the people who did this to my husband, the so-called elders, the committee in charge of the Tolly Man festivities, self-appointed one and all, serving only themselves – Sutton, Bainbridge, Coombes, Higgs." Disgust flavored every name. "They knew precisely what they were doing. And Thomas was their victim, their chosen sacrifice."

Nyquist took another look at the photograph. "I will keep this. Please."

She nodded. "I tried to get Thomas to explain, but my questions only riled him, and he started to shout at me. He was turning violent. I left and he slammed the door behind me. I heard him turn the lock."

Nyquist felt cold, he could hardly feel his hands, his fingertips, he was shivering. Stray thoughts tumbled one upon the next.

Agnes continued, "A few hours later Thomas came into the living room. He apologized to me for losing his temper. I looked him fully in the eyes for the first time in weeks; usually he turned away from me, as though ashamed of what I might find."

"What did you see?"

"A face not unlike yours, John." She took in each of his features in turn. "Of the same lineage, the same blood. But aged. One man halfway to being someone else. He would no longer answer to the name *Thomas*." She paused, and then said, "You do know, you know what name he wanted to be called by?"

"I know."

Almost in dread, almost in hope, he said his father's name out loud. Almost in pain. He felt that all his adult life was leading to this place, this one moment, these words.

George Oliver Nyquist...

"Of course," Agnes continued, "part of me still thought Thomas was being delusional. That the physical changes were in some way psychosomatic."

"What did he do next?"

"He had with him another seven photographs, the ones I sent to you."

"He asked you to post them?"

She nodded. "I had to find your address. It was a hell of a business. The only clue he gave me was the name of a city, Dayzone, and his son's full name."

"He didn't know anything else about me?"

"I don't think so. I had to drive into Lockhampton, to visit the library there. I looked up *John Henry Nyquist* in the telephone directory for Dayzone. There were two listings, and a further seven *John or J. Nyquists*. I rang each in turn and made my enquiries. Only one person could help me, saying that John Henry Nyquist no longer lived at this address, but he had a forwarding address, in Storyville."

Nyquist told her, "Yes, I moved there a few months back."

"They had an old directory for Storyville, but you weren't listed there. So I gave in. I was all set to send them to the forwarding address, but for some reason my hand would not drop the envelope into the postbox."

"You were worried? Of sending them to the wrong address?"

"No, not that. But I suddenly imagined you looking at the photographs, especially at the one of your father's face, distorted in that way. I knew it would be a shock to you, and that it might well ruin your life, whatever… whatever your life might be." Agnes glanced away. "I lied to my husband. I told him I'd sent them. But it was only much later, about two weeks ago this was, that I found the envelope again and decided to send it on. Guilt, I suppose. And the thought had already entered my head, of what my next course of action must be. Perhaps sending them to you was one last attempt at stopping myself?"

"Well, they found me. Eventually. Thank you."

"I didn't know what else to do."

"Why did he want me to see the photographs? There was no letter, or explanation."

"He did try to write a letter. He took some time over it, could never get it right. And he ripped up one sheet of paper after another. In the end he told me to send the photographs on their own. He said that they were enough, and that you'd understand."

"I'm trying to."

"Thomas was existing at that moment on a kind of borderline. An internal border where one person crosses over into another: we all have those, even if we don't like to think about it."

"We are never one person only?"

"Exactly. And for Thomas this border had now been made real. Your father's spirit was crossing over, taking charge. The photographs came out of that period of confusion, when one side of him was still fighting the other, in every moment that went by. One of them wanted to remain as he was, the other wanted to change completely."

"Which was which?"

"I truly don't know." Agnes shrugged. "But I think the plea for help, calling you to the village – that too was born from the same confusion."

Nyquist struggled to take it all in.

Agnes was speaking more to herself by now. "When I got back home from the library, I could see that Thomas had changed yet again. And I'll continue to call him by that name, for as long as I live. Thomas Dunne."

"How did he look?"

"Distant. Like he was standing a mile away from me, just across the room. It was almost impossible to talk to him. We grew even further apart."

"He left you? Agnes, is that it?"

She nodded. "We were barely speaking to each other. We were no longer husband and wife, but two strangers in the same house. He kept to his rooms, never venturing outside." She laughed bitterly. "I remember people asking about Thomas, how they hadn't seen him in a while, and I made an excuse, saying that he'd gone away, that he was looking for a new place of business, in a new town. And then one morning I woke to hear him screaming. Oh, it was a terrible noise, it pained me to my heart, it did. I rushed out of bed and found him lying on the floor of the darkroom, clawing at his face with his hands, trying to tear his skin off. There was... there was blood. Blood on his fingernails."

Agnes breathed in deeply. She wiped at the corner of one eye with her hand. And her fingers continued on, to the cuts the Tolly mask had made on her.

"I see it now as one last attempt to gather back what was his. His own face, his features and memories, and his life,

Thomas Dunne's life. His rightful life! But when, later on, I cleaned his face, I could see that the change was complete. I searched his eyes desperately for a sign, an inkling, that I might yet spy the man that I loved." Frustration crossed her face. "In vain. For another man now lived in his body, and upon his face. Another man."

Nyquist clung on to what she was saying.

"And that night he left, in the early hours. Creeping away. I don't know where he went. But I knew, I just *knew*, that he was gone for good."

"He went to live in a cottage outside the village, near King's Grave."

"I didn't know that."

"And then, a while later, I believe he was kidnapped. Taken away."

"Yes, that makes sense. They would have to wait for the opportune moment, for the ritual to work properly. Thomas would have to be changed utterly, with every last vestige of his old self removed."

Nyquist could see the sense in this. But he had to ask, "But what were they trying to do, with this ritual?"

"To bring Creeping Jenny into the world. Each of them with their own purpose."

"What about Len? Leonard Sadler?"

"Oh, he was kind. He was glad, in a way, I'm sure… that Thomas and I were growing apart. Of course, I could never tell him the truth. But he could sense my anger, my rage, and he took it for something else. He gathered an amount of hope from it. And myself in turn, I could have done with a loving hand in those times. But in truth…" She stared deep into Nyquist's eyes. "In truth, I was alone. And have been so, ever since."

She stirred the embers with a stick. A tiny red glow was uncovered.

"I put a sign out-front, saying that we were closed for business, and I refused to open the door for any customer. Or even for my friends and neighbors. And in the darkness of my house, I nurtured my pain, and gave it sustenance, and fed it daily on bitterness and I cursed the saints, aye, all three hundred and sixty of them, and I blasphemed against the old gods. Only Creeping Jenny escaped my curses, for I hoped she would see my story concluded as it should be, in blood and justice."

The depths of hurt were evident in every mark on her face, every line, the cropped hair, the ash-smeared fingers.

"Until, the urge to take some… *recompense* came upon me. Yes, that was the word. To take some payment for the loss of my husband, and for all they had done to him. For how they had used him, and submitted him to this trial."

"Are you saying… Agnes, look at me." She did so, reluctantly. "Are you saying that you killed Ian Bainbridge, and Jane Sutton? Is that what you did?"

"I came to Ian's house on the night of Saint Meade, when the entire village lay silent around me. There would be no argument from him, because of the ruling, when I showed him exactly what I thought of his part in this. I swear, that was all that was in my mind. And his poor wife, why, she hasn't uttered a word in a good long while."

Nyquist thrust his hands into the pockets of his overcoat. He asked, "What did you do?"

"At most, I thought I might spit in his face. I brought Mr Peck with me, to wreck havoc in the household, and to shit on the furniture. But when I got there, Ian let me in willingly.

His face showed a kind of relief, as though he welcomed my visit. He gestured for me to follow him, into the kitchen, and there we both took a seat. Before him on the table was the bowl with the moonsilver already in it, each berry ripe for the eating. A twig from the myre tree lay close by."

"He'd picked the berries himself?"

"That is the case. That very day." Agnes reached into her duffle bag and drew out some papers. "There was no sign of Ian's wife, although I once heard a noise from upstairs. So the two of us sat there in silence. And then Ian picked up the branch and he pressed its sharpened thorns into his face, first here, then here, and then again here, pressing the thorns deep until the blood flowed. Like a penitent monk he was using a scourge on himself, hoping to cleanse his soul of sin. But his face held little expression, and there was no sign of pain, only a cold determination. He lay the branch down and then wrote a few lines on a sheet of paper, even now keeping his silence. I have it here."

She handed the paper over to Nyquist. He read the words:

Together, we have summoned the spirit of Creeping Jenny. Once known as Guinevere of the Tangled Woods, wife and true companion of Adam Clud. Our Lady with the Knotted Hair, whose hands spin and weave the threads of green that connect all things together. I have committed a crime against nature in so doing, and will be punished for it. I wish to take back all I have done. Alas, I cannot.

She gave Nyquist a second sheet of paper. "Now this." It read:

I wanted only to rescue Hilda's voice from silence. For that purpose, I made a bargain. All to no avail. And now my story is coming to an end.

Nyquist thought of Bainbridge's reaction to the tendril in the teacup, on that first night. He surely believed that he was looking at part of the body of Creeping Jenny, and the sight of it must have tipped him out of balance. He had overstepped the mark, and fully expected to pay for it with his soul.

"You saw him die?"

Agnes nodded. "I did. I watched as he made a sign of blessing with his hands. Then he took the berries one by one into his mouth. I sat there, and did nothing at all until his body stilled, until only his eyes held any semblance of life, and then they too were empty."

She was speaking now in a flat, dispassionate manner, reporting an incident.

"I let the budgerigar go, and left Mr Peck behind in the bird cage as a warning to the other three, that they might know that a similar fate awaited them."

Nyquist didn't say anything. He looked on as Agnes rubbed a careful, tentative finger in the ash that covered the ring of firestones. She smeared this onto her face, darkening her skin in daubs and stipples. She explained, "They say the ash of the burned mask is the best cure for the thorn bites."

"Who says that?"

"The old gods of this land, and the martyrs long dead. It can be studied in the ancient books kept in the museum. Professor Bryars says it as well. And Mrs Sutton, the head mistress. The saints grant her rest. There are tales aplenty."

Her face suitably marked with ash, she continued: "Ian Bainbridge had given me an appropriate means of revenge. I went out in the myre wood and gathered berries and branches for myself. I had to laugh when Mad Sylvia called me *Twig Stealer*. For I had other, far more serious crimes in mind."

"You would kill Jane Sutton?"

"No, not yet. My first victim would be Nigel Coombes. I worked with each saint, as it was chosen, improvising within the rules. And so that day I wore the mask of Alice Grey, as did all the women of the village. I was everybody, and nobody, and such disguise allowed me to sup ale with the clientele of the pub. Afterwards, I hid in the cellar and waited until all the doors were locked. For many hours I sat there, nursing my hatred. And I waited still longer after the lights went out, to be sure. I crept up the stairs. I stood over Coombes, listening to his wheezing and snoring. His sleeping face sickened me, red with drink as it was. I had with me two myre twigs, their berries still unplucked. They are at their most potent when first taken from the tree. I would pop the moonsilver into the landlord's mouth, that was my plan, a whole handful of them, and clamp his lips shut and hold myself there as best I could as he struggled and the juice did its work on him, slowing his breath and the strength, until he gave in to me."

Agnes's facial muscles were tight with rage as she brought that night back to life.

"But I could not commit the act. I thought of his good wife, some few months dead, and his daughter, Mavis, and their grief. I remembered the family portraits Thomas had taken of them, just a few years before, all smiling in their Sunday best. And I knew that, like Mr Bainbridge, Nigel Coombes had good reason to summon an old spirit. He had a story that sorely needed mending, as only the good hands of Creeping Jenny might. So I walked out of his bedroom and

I paused at your door, John, for I was curious, most curious. I had heard tell of you, of your arrival in the village, so I opened the door and stood over you with the two branches of the myre tree crossed over my face, like this, and I gazed at you through the tangled twigs and the berries ripe and moon-dusted. I felt at that moment that I actually might be the Tolly Woman, fully embodied. And I saw in your face the face that Thomas had become. The story he had told me was a true one: you were the son of George Nyquist."

"How did that make you feel?"

She thought for a moment and then answered, "I knew that Thomas was gone from me, probably forever."

Nyquist was tired. But he had to gain all the knowledge he could.

"What about Jane Sutton?"

"That was an easy task, for really that woman had no excuse. She desired power only, for herself and that measly, puffed up husband of hers. And do you really think a demon – ancient, real, dead, alive, or otherwise – would have any part for such things? No. Not at all." Agnes smiled. "The saints blessed me again that day, allowing me to wear the fret as a disguise. I crept about the village at my ease, entering the school without trouble. Mrs Sutton had been teaching a class all about Creeping Jenny. I had to laugh, seeing that. Her story unfolded, and all I had to do was show her the berries, and she practically begged me to feed her. There was a little struggle, granted, but I treated her as I wanted, twisting her body into a hideous position as she succumbed to the poison. I wanted the village to see her in pain, this woman of so-called breeding. Lastly, I pressed the thorns of the myre tree against her face, in payment for Thomas's wounds." Agnes grimaced. "The guilt in these people runs close to the surface, as does the fear. All four of them knew by now: they had conjured a demon beyond their control." She looked at Nyquist. "Your presence here indicates such."

Nyquist stood up. He took the half crown coin from his pocket. The tendril uncurled, reaching out into the air, searching for his flesh. Agnes was intrigued by the sight. She said, "I never realized the elders had gotten so far in their task."

"You think this coin is connected to Creeping Jenny?"

"I have sung the songs at school and read the poems and played the skipping games. As a woman, I have prayed to her on several occasions, that she might bring a good conclusion to my story. But I've never seen a portion of her before. May I?"

She took the coin from his hand and turned it this way and that.

"I trust you know the rhyme? *Mr Brown likes half a crown, but the devil takes a penny.* Well you are playing Mr Brown in this drama, who represents I think the commoner."

"I've been called worse."

Agnes watched with intrigue as the tendril tried its very best to reach out towards its owner. "It wants to get back to you, look! Oh. You are a part of this ritual, Mr Nyquist, a vital part. No doubt the elders were surprised at this. They would have expected the demon to reach out for one or all of them, not a stranger to the village. Your father did well, drawing you here."

"How does the ritual end?"

"I don't know." She handed back the half crown.

"I have to leave you now," he said. "I need to get back to the village."

Agnes gave him a gentle smile. "I believe there's another person involved, beyond the four who gathered at the hill pool with Thomas. But I don't know who it is."

"I'll find out."

"Good. And if you find my husband, will you bring him back to me?"

"If I can."

"I would like to show him the juice of the berry on my hands, the same color as blood. The blood I poisoned."

Nyquist set off, taking a clockwise route around Clud Tower, until after passing only five walls he came to the locked door. He walked down the pathway back into Morden Wood. He passed through the forest of naming labels, which spun and fluttered and shone in patterns of moonlight among the trees. And here his fret returned to him, a little weaker than before, but welcome. He was warmed by it, and felt safe within its comfort and glow. They would only have a short time together, man and mist, before the day ended. He made his way quickly to Hoxley-on-the-Hale. Midnight chimed softly on the church clock as he entered the village and his fret faded once more, seeping into his body, treating each and every pore as a doorway. It had served him well. Back in his room at the public house, he turned on the gas fire and poured himself a glass of whiskey from the bottle at his bedside. He remembered for the first time in hours the wound he had taken. The bandage was still clean but he could feel the dull ache of his injury. He thought about tomorrow and what it might bring, that he might at last find his father, or the man who had taken on his image at the least. His other self moved in the mirror. Half known, half unknown. But no eye contact was made.

Instead, Nyquist stood at the sink and washed a pair of socks and the neck and armpits of his favorite shirt, the one with the embroidered collar and cuffs. He'd worn it on his first day here. How long ago that seemed! And now here he was, his hands warm from the soap and water, scrubbing away. Life in exile. He hung the shirt and socks in front of the fire and sat up a while longer, smoking a cigarette and sipping at the Scotch. The alcohol calmed him. His left hand played with the half crown, allowing the green tendril to tickle and cling at his fingers. *Two steps forward, one step back, widdershins, widdershins, turn and clap.* The tendril dug into his flesh. He sang with a low voice, in a whisper: *Call for Jimmy and call for Jack, Creeping Jenny is at my back.* The story was pulling him closer. He turned off the fire and switched off the light and crawled into bed. His eyes had barely closed before he was taken away by a deep fathomless sleep.

A SONG IN THE NIGHT SKULL

It was two hours before dawn on the next day, Tuesday. Not a single light was seen in any of the houses. The only movement on the high street was a cat slinking along, the world her own to enjoy. Inside the silent church two people, a brother and sister, were conducting a simple ceremony. A third person, their great-grandmother, lay prone on a stone table. Her name was Ethel Clegg. She was very old, ages old, with not one portion of her skin left unwrinkled. Her eyes were rheumy, stained black beneath, and her breath wheezed in her lungs. She was thin to the point of being sunken into herself so that very little was left of her body. Her clothes were rags and her fingernails were two inches long, with enamel the exact same color as her hair: piss yellow. Her great-grandchildren stood near, waiting for her to speak. At last she did so. The man bent down closely to hear the whisper of her voice. Ethel's breath was not unpleasant, holding the scent of juniper and earth and cat fur.

A saint's name was spoken.

A few minutes later the two people exited the church and walked the pathway between the gravestones, the beams of their torches guiding them, until they split at the bridge, the woman taking the road to Lower Hoxley, the man continuing onto the high street. Gordon Clegg wore a long gray overcoat and a bowler hat, and he carried in his shoulder bag a number of envelopes, all identical, one for each household in Hoxley-on-the-Hale. His sister Maureen was performing a similar task for the village further down the valley. And so between them, the siblings made sure that every letterbox received its due delivery.

At half past six in the morning an alarm clock went off in the master bedroom of The Swan With Two Necks, waking Nigel Coombes. Yawning, he pulled on his dressing gown and went downstairs to the hall, where he stooped, groaning a little, to pick up the envelope from the doormat. He read the name of the saint written on the card inside, and wondered how the choice would affect his day, and his plans. The ritual would be delayed. He thought of his late wife, the lovely Gladys, as he made his way down to the cellar where he kept his collection of homemade icons, an identical pair for each of the 360 saints. Coombes arranged them by the date of their martyrdom, an order he knew as well as the price of a pint of beer. He picked up the two icons for Saint Yorick. One of these he gave pride of place on a shelf above the main bar, and the other he placed in the guest room. The icon was lying prone, his finely modelled hands folded over his chest in a gesture of repose. Likewise, John Nyquist was still asleep. Coombes looked down at him for a few seconds, considering the bountiful pleasure it would give to strangle the intruder, just because of all the questions the detective had been asking, and the trouble caused, and Ian and Jane dead by their own hands. *Damn it.* Everything was going wrong, and yet he'd been promised so much, so very much! But it seemed that Mr

Nyquist was important to their plans, so the landlord turned away from the bed. His eye passed over the bedside cabinet where a half crown lay. Coombes took note of the coiled green tendril that covered the profile of the king, and he sighed deeply. Another bloody job to do! With careful fingers he lifted up the coin and carried it downstairs. The tendril waved about, angry at being taken away. It made the landlord shudder, even to think that Creeping Jenny might touch his skin. Ruddy hell, but he'd be glad when this was over! In the back garden of the pub he used a trowel to dig into a flower bed, unearthing the metal box he had buried there yesterday. Usually he kept the night's takings in the box, but at the moment it held a more precious commodity. He placed the half crown alongside the other three objects – the book of birds, the teacup, and the Enfield revolver – and he locked the box once more and reburied it, hearing all the time the noise of the four tendrils as they clawed at the dark interior, struggling to reach their only goal: John Nyquist. It was not to be. Not yet, at least. Coombes made his way back to his own bedroom. He climbed back into bed, and was quickly asleep. He had a lot of dreaming to do.

Over the next hour, more and more Hoxleyites woke up and found the envelope on their doormats. They too placed the icon of Yorick on window ledges, sideboards or on special display stands. Many people went straight back to bed after doing this, while others stayed up for as long as they could. Some villagers had been asleep the whole morning, being retired or alone, with no early commitments: they would fall under the saint's authority without knowing it, blissfully ignorant of what was about to happen.

The milkman delivered the milk, the postman delivered

the mail. Some of the letters and bills were read; others lay on the doormats untouched. People had their breakfasts and chatted idly as though this were an entirely ordinary day. Nobody got ready for work.

In Yew Tree Cottage, Hilda Bainbridge sat at her kitchen table, drinking a cup of tea and eating a slice of toast. A photograph of her husband Ian was propped up in front of her. Tomorrow she would bury him. Gerald Sutton took a different approach to grief: he had been up and about since a quarter past six that morning, planning a full day's work, hoping to lose himself in labor. So the opening of the envelope had saddened him at first, but after a minute or so he welcomed the news. A different kind of escape awaited him.

In her surgery on the high street, Doctor Higgs was making telephone calls, canceling all her appointments. Her patients would have to wait; and anyway, no one ever grew ill on Saint Yorick's Day. In the Fairclough household on Hawkshead Lane, young Becca and Teddy slept on in their respective bedrooms. Teddy was out of work, and school had been canceled for the day, after the death of the headmistress, and so neither brother nor sister had any reason to get up early. In contrast, Professor Bryars had been awake since seven o'clock. She knew precisely what the day entailed, and was happily turning the pages of an old ledger, studying the names of the villagers of yesteryear and imagining their lives, the good and bad days they must've suffered as one saint after another took charge of them. *How blessed we are*, she thought, *to live in such a place, and to never be satisfied with the everyday. To never know what tomorrow might bring. It makes each waking a new adventure!* The corner shop had opened at eight in the morning as normal, but Mrs Featherstonehaugh was now locking the door and putting the *CLOSED* sign in the window. The shop had been open for just fifty-five minutes. It was almost nine o'clock. She made her way back up to her little bedroom and started to get undressed. In the cold of the church, the vicar lit the votive candle that stood in front of the Saint Yorick's icon.

In his room above The Swan With Two Necks, John Nyquist slept on.

As the top of the hour approached, a hush fell over the streets and lanes of Hoxley-on-the-Hale. Here and there a straggler was seen, an unfortunate person who had been caught out by events, or who did not for some reason know of Yorick's reign over the day. Maybe they saw an icon in a window and hurried to get home, panicking. By now nearly everybody was either in bed, or sitting in an easy chair, awaiting the first chime of the clock. Most were asleep, but some were still awake, enjoying these last few seconds of conscious thought. Doctor Higgs was one such. She had dismissed her maid for the day and was now settling into her favorite armchair in the living room. She arranged her limbs comfortably, her hands in her lap. Her face expressed an amount of worry. She thought of the argument she'd had with John Nyquist, and wondered for not the first time whether she had made a mistake with this undertaking. But no matter now, events were on their course. Her eyelids were growing heavy.

The church clock called out the hour.

On the ninth chime the doctor fell asleep.

Simultaneously, all the other villagers fell into sleep.

In Puzzle Lane an old man didn't quite make it to his front door and he collapsed to the roadside and remained there, curled up in a ball. The same thing happened to a young woman in Lower Hoxley, her body folding to the ground in the comparative safety of her garden. All the cats and dogs of both villages were also in slumber, wherever nine o'clock happened to find them, inside or out. In bowls and aquaria goldfish were hanging in midwater, unmoving. In his birdcage in Yew Tree Cottage, Bertie slept peacefully, clinging to his perch, his head tucked into the feathers of a wing.

The whole village of Hoxley was now in slumber.

Saint Yorick had them in his thrall.

The hours passed. Nothing happened. The streets remained empty. There was very little noise. The wild birds chattered in the trees, for they were not bound by the village's rules; likewise the insects in the soil continued to dig and hunt.

Babies in their cots, boys and girls, young and old, men and women: all slept on.

Nyquist lay in his bed. He was breathing easily, his eyelids fluttering slightly: evidence of a dream. Every so often his body shifted to a new position.

The sun reached its highest point and started slowly to descend. Shadows shortened and lengthened. At half past two in the afternoon a little rain fell, wetting the hair and faces of those few villagers caught outside, but not waking them. The shower didn't last long, and the skies cleared once more.

The afternoon came and went, and twilight arrived in its place.

It was a quarter past four.

Nyquist slept on.

The village slept on.

The sky darkened further. Time passed.

The church clock chimed six times.

The final chime seemed to act as a signal. In one house after another, in one bedroom after another, in living rooms, gardens, wherever people and pets were sleeping, a movement was seen. It might be the tapping of a finger or the twitch of a cheekbone, the slow wagging of a cat's tail. The quiver of an eyelash. One by one the villagers stretched and moaned, and then sat up in their beds or wherever they were resting. They all rose up at the same time and started to get dressed, if they needed to. Their eyes were almost fully closed, with only a narrow slit to admit the barest amount of light. It was enough. They moved at a steady even pace, making hardly any sound. Mothers bent down at cots to pick up their babies, wrapping them in extra blankets for warmth. Old men groaned and rubbed at their joints, and then braced themselves for the task ahead. One or two remembered the battlefields of their youth, and this emboldened them. In step with everyone else, they made their way outside and started to walk along lanes and alleyways. They greeted each other with nods and hand gestures only: no words. In this way, the village of Hoxley-on-the-Hale gathered itself for an evening's stroll. In Lower Hoxley, they did the same, bound by the same spell. Saint Yorick guided them all. In the lower village they made their way to the small central square with its war memorial and dried-up fountain. Whereas in Hoxley-on-the-Hale they congregated on the village green. It was half past six by the time they were all in place: Young boys and girls hanging on to their parents' hands, babies in prams, teenagers and the newly married, the middle-aged and the elderly, all were there. And all of them still asleep inside their heads; only their bodies moved, following orders that had nothing at all to do with the individual mind. These were the members of the Hoxley Somnambulist Society and Saint Yorick was their guide, and their leader. *We are one. One village. Here we stand in waiting.* Nyquist was but a single villager among many, his overcoat pulled around him, his face without any expression, his eyes set to a soft focus. Not a thought disturbed him, not even when Dolly Copple started up a tune called *Barefoot Maiden* on her concertina and Fred Oswaldtwistle, butcher, joined in on his homemade three string fiddle. They played it at half the customary speed, giving it a languid, spectral air. But nobody danced; the beat was too slow and the people too bound by sleep. The skies were clear, the night crisp. Blade of Moon held her branches high and a soft breeze ruffled the waters of the pond. And then it began, as the clock chimed seven.

The music continued and a young woman started to sing.

A barefoot maiden
Across the moors did seek
her sailor boy so bold,
Who died upon the silver sea
Aboard the Ivanhoe.

It was Becca Fairclough singing, her voice piercingly clear in the evening air. She sang it as June Holler would sing it – simply and cleanly, without artifice – and the melody cut to the heart directly. A few other people joined in, not many; a fragile harmony. Nyquist found himself mouthing the words, even though he had never heard the song before.

Across the moors
She heard her sailor cry
And spied his shape so fine,

His uniform in tatters
His blood all mixed with brine.

And then a hush fell over the congregation. Another four people had arrived on the green, each from a different direction. It wasn't obvious at first, for these newcomers moved as the village sleepwalkers did, slowly, drowsily. But a faint glow came off them, enough to bring attention, and a murmur ran through the crowd. Some people stepped back in wonder at what they saw. The first to arrive was Mr Brian Holroyd. He moved unsteadily on his feet for he had been seventy-two years old when he died earlier this year, from various ailments. His present body had a translucent, shimmery quality to it, like a cloud pinned together in human shape. His only remaining family member was his nephew, Neil: they met each other awkwardly, neither of them knowing quite how to act.

The next to arrive was Gladys Coombes, thirty-eight years old. Her wrists held the twin scars from which her blood had flowed into the village pond. She stood at the pond's edge now, calmly staring into the water. Not everyone saw her, but her widower, Nigel, walked to her, with their daughter Mavis close behind. They both smiled, weakly at first, in disbelief, and then more freely. The third of the dead to arrive was Ian Bainbridge, who had passed away four nights ago, age forty-two. His body showed all the symptoms of moonsilver poisoning. But his face showed no pain, none at all. His wife, Hilda, came to him with open arms and they embraced. It was not quite a firm embrace: flesh did not quite meet flesh. The fourth to arrive was Jane Sutton, thirty-nine years old, showing the same deathly symptoms as Mr Bainbridge. She had died yesterday. Like all the other visitors, her body was a nebulous, drifting shape. Again, there was no evident pain, but Gerald Sutton watched his wife from a few steps away, his face wet with tears that flowed slowly, as from a dream. In Lower Hoxley they had only one new arrival, for only a single person had died in the ten months since Saint Yorick had last been chosen. But this person was seven years old, a boy taken by measles, and the cries of his parents and his two sisters rang out across the village square. The family dog, a terrier called Nelson, bounded to meet his lost playmate.

Nyquist walked through the crowd. Like many others gathered there, he could not see the dead clearly. Only their families and close friends could do that. But he saw enough to know that scenes of great tenderness and love were being enacted. He kept his distance, for the moments between the returned and the living were too personal. But he took joy from it, and hope. An hour went by in this way. The church clock sounded eight o'clock and the dead returned to their own world, disappearing from ours as smoke from an extinguished fire, drifting away into the air. The ghosts of Jane Sutton and Ian Bainbridge seemed to mingle as they vanished, their bodies of dust and moonlight entwined.

They might have been real, these spirits, or the products of a shared vision, but either way the villagers felt no grief at their passing. The green was hushed for a moment, nobody spoke, for a single word would break the spell. And then the people made their way back to their homes, to their beds, Nyquist included. He was quickly asleep and remained so until the morning, when he awoke with the traces of a dream in his mind. This was true of all the villagers, Upper and Lower; to all intents and purposes they had slept for the last thirty hours or more. It was the same every year on the morning after Saint Yorick's Day. Strangely, both Gerald Sutton and Hilda Bainbridge woke up with the exact same phrase on their lips: *I'm sorry*. Their loved ones had spoken to them.

OBJECT NO. 5

Nyquist was still half awake when he woke up half asleep, half dressed in last night's clothes, with his bed half in disarray and half tidy. He got up and washed his face in tepid water and shaved but left a few bristles showing, he didn't know why. Carelessness. On the shelf the new day's icon was waiting for his inspection, Saint Hetta from her label. She was made from the pieces of a child's doll, matchsticks and balsawood, string and glue, the tiny bones of a bird, or a combination of birds, of sparrow and rook: the mathematics of flight reaching zero. All these various components were only partially assembled, as though her body might fall to pieces at any moment. Her hair was tufts of fur and wool: a bizarre concoction, three quarters ragged, one quarter neatly styled.

At breakfast Nyquist's streaky bacon wasn't quite cooked and his eggs were runny. He had words with the waitress about it. The conversation went like this.

"Mavis, my eggs are–"

"I know…"

"Do you think I can eat…"

"No. Probably…"

"Probably? What do you…"

"Probably…"

"Not?"

"Yes!"

He gave up, pushed his plate aside and drank his lukewarm tea. He could hear Nigel in the lounge bar and he went through to speak with him. The publican was talking to himself in broken sentences, muttering about the troublesome wholesalers and the clogging of the beer pumps and how he had no one to help him change the barrels. Nyquist interrupted the flow.

"What's the story with Saint…"

"Oh, it's you…"

"With Saint Hetta? What's the…"

"The story?"

"Yes."

"You will never understand…"

His words drifted away, unfinished. Coombes looked worried. He was a strong man, bred for hard work – but right now he wouldn't even look Nyquist in the eye. He took out a handkerchief and wiped his brow.

Nyquist said to him, "I know what's going on, here in…"

But the sentence would not complete itself. The name of the village lingered, unsaid. He frowned and held his concentration to the one task, and one only, to speak. To speak!

"I know… I know… I know what's going on…"

But still the words would not fall freely.

Coombes took courage from this. He said, or nearly said, "You can still get… you can still get away… from… from here, if you…"

"I'm not… not going…"

"Then there's nothing to…"

"Nothing to…"

"Nothing to say!"

Nyquist faced the other man down. He spoke as best he could and he kept on speaking even though the words were stuttered. "I think… you're in… you're in trouble, Coombes. And you… you know you've… you've taken a… a bad step."

His mouth felt like a knife had been at it.

"Christ…"

A smile came to the face of Coombes, and he leaned in very close and whispered, "I have taken your precious objects from you. One, two, three… and four."

Every hushed word was clear now, finely spoken.

"I have hidden them away for safekeeping. Because you… Nyquist, you're not worthy of their possession."

Nyquist matched the tone, speaking low and close, and found that he could speak more freely in this way.

"Where is Thomas Dunne?"

The two men were less than an inch apart: on any other day of the liturgical year this would have been unthinkable… but needs must.

"How the hell would I know? Now piss off."

Even the swearword was said in a whisper. Nyquist moved back slightly.

Coombes sneered at this. He picked up a clutch of receipts from a table and headed for a doorway behind the bar. But then he stopped. And he stood there with his back to Nyquist, his hands at his sides, the fingers curling into fists. His whole body was tense, every muscle. Nyquist found himself responding in kind. But the landlord didn't turn around. His hands tightened further until the knuckles were red. He was speaking quietly to himself. Nyquist had to step closer to hear.

"Last night, I saw her… on the green… I saw her… I saw my Gladys… she was alive!"

"You were… you were dreaming…"

This was dismissed with a shake. Nyquist felt compassion, for he knew what Coombes had been through this last year. He moved closer still and said in a voice low enough to allow the words to flow, "Nigel, do you honestly think you'll get her back?"

The landlord didn't respond at first. And then he turned to face Nyquist, close up. He spoke softly: "I'll take any chance that's given to me. And if this works, then I'll worship Creeping Jenny until the day I die."

"And if it doesn't work?"

Coombes screwed shut his eyes. He groaned to himself and then whispered, the words hardly more than a collection of sighs. And this time he said something strange:

"The person to blame is working the spell. How can it fail?"

"To blame…"

"To blame for my Gladys passing away."

And with that, he turned and marched off through the doorway.

Nyquist went outside. Everything looked normal, just another day in the village. People went about their ways, and quite a few wore black scarves, and black armbands: in mourning for Sutton and Bainbridge, one or the other or both. Not one person spoke to him, not even by a gesture.

The door of the corner shop was only partially open, and a sign in the window said, "Everything today – half price!"

One man wore half a trench coat, the left side portion only.

A young woman sang one half of a line from a popular song. A passing friend finished the line for her, and they smiled at each other.

A car drove along the high street, its engine stalling.

Nyquist banged on the door of the doctor's house. There was no answer. He tried again, even louder, and eventually it was pulled open a little way by the maid.

"I want to see…"

"The doctor, sir?"

"Yes."

"Cannot."

"Why?"

"Not…

"Not in?"

"Yes."

He concentrated on his words: "Where is she?"

"Gone?"

"Where?"

"Don't… I don't…

"Don't know?"

"No."

And so it went on. The maid set her brows into a frown and held the door firm, her feet braced. For a good second he thought of pushing past her, and searching the place top to bottom. But in the end, he backed down, and instead he forced his lips to work: "Tell her… tell Doctor Higgs that I'll be… I'll be…" He lowered his voice even further, understanding by now that to finish a sentence he needed to whisper. "Tell her I'll be finding out where my father is. Today! With her help, or not!"

That was enough. He made his way to Pyke Road. A car

was badly parked, half inside a garage, half out. A dog barked once and fell silent. In one window after another, the curtains were almost closed, or almost open. And Nyquist himself felt that his mind was only partially working. One step, another, concentrating, moving on. He had to put his thoughts together carefully, to keep himself in key with an out of tune world. *I am, I am, I am.* On and on. Complete. Whole. One thing only!

At least Maude Bryars had a welcome for him. The professor invited him into her kitchen and offered him tea. He turned down the offer, or tried to, but his words were choked off. "Whisper close," she said, drawing him to her. "That way… Saint Hetta cannot hear you. We will fool her! For a time at least. Come on." She closed the gap further. "Don't be shy." He could smell alcohol on her breath, and this close up the look in her eyes – red-lined, fluttery – told him that she was troubled in some way, badly troubled. Her hand was shaking on his arm.

They sat side by side at the table, their chairs pushed up against each other, their upper legs touching, their forearms pressed together.

"There you are. Not too bad, is it?" It was gently spoken.

"No. It's alright. I can speak."

"John, you can say anything you like to me now. And no one will hear."

There was a pamphlet on the tabletop, a few sheets of paper held together with staples. The author was *Professor Maude Bryars*, and the title was *Creeping Jenny and Other Folk Demons*. The cover showed a woman's face made of tangled vines and flowers. Nyquist's head bowed a little seeing this, and his eyes closed, knowing that his fears might well be confirmed. His mind settled in the darkness.

Bryars sang a little wordless song to him.

He looked up and asked, "That bowl of water that you used, with the insects in it, when you removed my mask..."

"Yes, what of it?"

"It was taken from Birdbeck tarn?"

"Yes, it was. And the beetles as well. That is their natural habitat."

He picked up the pamphlet and leafed through it. "How much do you know of what goes on out there, every Saint Algreave's Day, with the four members of the committee, and with the Tolly Man?"

"A little."

Nyquist nodded. He said, "I spoke with someone last night, who told me that a fifth elder was involved, but not present. It was implied that this fifth person might be the leader of the group. Do you know anything about that?"

Now she looked at him. Bryars was shaking badly, but he couldn't tell if this was from anxiety or from drinking too much; perhaps both?

"You're saying this is me?"

He waved the pamphlet in her face. "I'm saying... Maude, it would have to be someone with knowledge of the village's past, and the rituals associated with the past. An expert's knowledge."

"Yes. I agree."

"You seem like the best candidate."

"You surprise me, John. That you would think of me in this way."

He leaned back in his chair. Bryars watched him do it, and smiled. "You are moving... moving away... I will not be able..." Her smile turned crooked.

"So it..."

"Seems."

"It seems…"

"Seems so."

It was hopeless. He stood up, breaking the bond completely, and he walked away until his hand touched the wall in front of him. From here there was no hope of communication. And he waited. He waited until he heard Bryars stand up, her chair scraping on the floor. He heard her footsteps approaching. He listened to her voice, faltering.

"You know… you know I want to…"

"To… to talk?"

"Yes… John, yes! For I am… I am…"

"What is…"

"Help me… help me to…"

Nyquist turned to look at her. "To finish? Yes? Your… words?"

"Yes. On this… this day." She took a deep breath. "We help…"

"Help each other to…"

"To speak?"

"Yes."

"To complete…"

"Yes." She looked at him. "I am… I am… help me… I am…"

"Lonely?"

"Yes. Just so… and scared."

"Talk then." Nyquist held her close to him, too close, face to face. "Talk to me."

It was simple enough, this instruction, and it set the professor going, knowing that only so many minutes might remain in which speech, true speech, was possible. She pushed it all out in one long gasp of air.

"Guinevere Clud was known as a witch, or a wise woman, depending on your point of view. She was a practitioner of plant magic, of poisons and charms made from bloodwort and wolfsbane and moonsilver, and so on. A number of people fell ill, all at the same time, and two of them died. It was in all probability an outbreak of a disease, for the plague was rife that year. It was 1666. But Guinevere was a natural scapegoat and she was punished for her sins. They drowned her in Birdbeck tarn, in full sight of her husband, Adam. I told you the story of Adam Clud being the first Tolly Man?"

"You did."

"Guinevere died shortly after that. Adam must have loved his wife dearly, for her death set him off on a campaign of torment against the villagers. He was caught, and plastered with tar and feathers and locked up for three days in the mocking gate, without food or water."

Nyquist looked at the professor's face, as she looked at him, mere inches apart. He saw every mark and line, every pockmark, and no doubt she could do the same with him: the friction of life, never-ending, eating away.

Bryars narrowed her eyes. "In truth, Adam Clud was a broken man. He killed himself a few weeks later. But not before he had cursed the village of Hoxley and all who lived in it, and all who would live in it, all the generations down."

"What was the curse?"

"That all the dead of the village would join with his beloved Guinevere, in the weeds of Birdbeck. All would be entangled in her clutches, and all their stories would bind themselves with hers. The villagers took to calling her Creeping Jenny, and saw her as a plant that grows only on the borderline between life and death. Once a victim becomes entangled, the vines would drag you to your doom." The professor moved away slightly. "The legend of Creeping Jenny was born... born... from this..." And the further she moved away, the more broken was her speech. "This act of..."

"Of punishment... of murder?"

"Yes. Yes! Both. And now... now she can... can be summoned... yes... and so, by her charms... one story might be changed into another... from bad, to good... yes... by means of... of sacrifice."

This last word was barely spoken at all. Professor Bryars looked exhausted, but she made a great effort.

"I think the elders have tried... each year... and failed. But this year... this year..."

"It worked?"

Bryars nodded. She kept rubbing at her forearm, pressing hard on the sleeve of her cardigan. Nyquist wondered if she'd been injured in some way. "You do know," he said, "that Doctor Higgs is involved in this?"

"I don't wish to know."

"She's ill. Very ill. She's looking for a cure."

Tenderness came to the professor's eyes. "I wish... I wish I could help her..." She sat at the table and her body slumped forward until her head was resting on her arms. Nyquist watched her a moment. He went to the stove and checked the kettle for water. He put a match to the gas ring and spooned tea into the pot. He wanted to put in three spoonsful (one for each person, one for the pot) but Saint Hetta held him by the hand and he could only put in one and a half spoons. He waited in silence for the kettle's whistle to sound. It seemed to take much longer than it should, and he gave up. He poured the half-boiled water into the teapot and gave it a stir. He set cups and saucers and sugar and milk out on the table, and placed the teapot on its stand. And then he sat with Bryars and they waited together for the tea to brew. He poured it into her cup, and then his, and added sugar and milk, as desired. They drank. But the tea was weak, the milk was sour, the sugar was nowhere sweet enough. And the usual feeling a cup of tea might give, that for a moment all things might be well, was not there.

All was not well.

Nothing could be well, not on this day.

But the professor was grateful. She thanked Nyquist for the tea and then she leaned forward across the table, not too close, but close enough for a sentence to make more than halfway sense. Nyquist moved in as well, and between them they tried to find an exact border, where words might find completion.

"John. This is not the day to…"

"Not the day to find my…"

"This is not the day to find your father."

Bryars leaned in further. He copied her. Their teacups clinked.

"Saint Hetta does not allow things to be…"

"To be finished…"

At last their fingers touched on the tabletop, and Bryars could speak freely.

"She does not allow things to blossom, for she could never fully commit to her chosen god or goddess, and was buried while still alive. As the day progresses, her power increases. By nightfall you will be reduced to a word or two at the most, and every action will be curtailed. All your plans will fail, before completion. This is how Hetta feeds. Nothing will work, everything will be in pieces. And it will get worse and worse until midnight chimes."

"I will try, nonetheless. I *have* to."

"Most villagers will be in bed by eight. This is one of the worst saints to deal with."

His face set into a harsh pattern. There was no peace in it.

Bryars pleaded with him: "Wait, at least. At least wait until tomorrow, John." But her voice grew too loud and the words faltered.

Nyquist answered simply: "It happens today." He stood up, but Bryars reached out and grabbed his arm and held him there tightly, as close as she could manage.

"Let me go!"

"Has she visited you?"

He was confused by the question. "How do you mean?"

"Guinevere?"

He nodded. "I think so. She left a different object behind each time."

"Tell them to me, please."

"A teacup, a book, a gun, and a coin. But they were stolen from me, all four–"

Her nails dug into his forearm. "There is a fifth, a fifth object." Her whisper sounded like a scream of pain. "A fifth object calling to you."

"You've seen it?"

"More than that. Much more…"

"You possess it?"

"I am…" Worry took her over. "I am the…" She started to tremble.

Nyquist moved to her. He whispered, "Show me, where is it?"

Her eyes never left his as she rolled up the sleeve of her

cardigan, revealing her bare forearm and the green tendril that grew from the flesh. Bryars looked terrified. She made a croaking sound, and leaned in close, close enough that she managed to say, "I found it this morning, when I woke up. John, what shall I do? I don't know what to do!"

The tendril reached out for Nyquist, wanting one thing only: to bind with him, one story inside another, inside another, inside another...

THE NAMING TREE

At twelve noon that day they buried Ian Bainbridge. About twenty mourners turned up at the church. Nyquist stood at the back of the pews, with Professor Bryars at his side. The villagers were sitting in ones and twos, or small family groups, the women's faces half made-up, the men with loosely knotted ties or with one or two buttons undone. The few children present all had one shoe laced, the other unlaced. The vicar made a valiant attempt at a eulogy, but never quite managed to say who it was that had died, and what he left behind, nor why he should be loved and remembered. Then they all trooped outside to attend the lowering of the coffin into the hard ground. The gravediggers had a task of it, or Saint Hetta had governed their actions, for the grave was a foot short of the required depth. The sky was a low roof of mottled slate. Hilda stood alone, wringing a white handkerchief in her hands, a flag of surrender against her black dress and overcoat. Somehow, against the day's rulings, she had managed to make herself look immaculate. It was bitter cold. Nyquist took up position below the canopy of a tree. He scanned each face in turn, wondering if the fifth member of the committee was present. The one person he really wanted to talk to, Irene Higgs, was conspicuous by her absence. At last the ceremony came to an end and the first clods of earth hit the lid of the coffin. Hilda Bainbridge stood there in silence, perfectly still, her lips trembling.

Nyquist turned to see a lone woman walking along the path.

It was Agnes Dunne.

She made her way toward the grave. By now everyone was looking at her, but she seemed oblivious to this; she simply walked on, keeping her eyes straight ahead. Her face could not be read. She stopped at the graveside and threw an object down into the hole. The sight of this set Hilda to wailing. She was trying to speak, to shout, to cry out, but her curses were trapped inside, expressed only though the lines on her face, and the bitter hatred in her eyes. Len Sadler had to grab hold of her, to stop her from making a physical attack. Agnes flinched a little and then straightened herself, and turned and walked away again. Len took Hilda by the hand and took her to one side. This was a sign for the other villagers to make their own way to the church gate. One alone took a different path, towards Nyquist and Bryars. It as Becca Fairclough. She stepped as close as convention would allow and said to him, "I'm worried."

"Why?"

"It's Teddy."

"Yes?"

"He's... he didn't..." She was struggling, and took another step to make it easier for her to speak. "He didn't come home..."

"Last night?"

"This morning. No sign."

Nyquist frowned. "I don't know…"

"Where is he?"

"I don't know." He leaned in close and took a breath and he pushed on to the end of his thoughts. "I don't know where he is, I swear to you, Becca."

She stared at him in disbelieve. But nothing more was said. Nyquist watched her as she walked away across the bridge.

He stepped forward to the grave. There was a twig of the myre tree lying on the coffin lid, complete with its bunch of white berries, the very thing that had killed Ian Bainbridge. This looked like pure provocation on Agnes Dunne's part. No wonder Hilda had reacted as she did, howling in pain. But Nyquist gave it another meaning: an act of confession.

The gravediggers started on their job, hoping to get it half finished before the rain come down. Saint Hetta deemed it fit that only a few feet of soil should be added; tomorrow the men would return to complete the task, the new day's saint permitting. Nyquist watched them at their work. He couldn't help worrying a little about Teddy, wondering what the young man was up to now: hoping it wasn't anything too stupid. Was he in trouble, in danger?

Was he the fifth person?

No. No, it couldn't be…

Bryars tugged at Nyquist's sleeve, breaking his mood, and he followed her gesture over to the cemetery wall. There was a gnarled and twisted tree there, almost tied in a knot by the pressure of years and the code in the seed. At first he could see nothing of interest, but then a slim dark figure dropped down from the lower branches and started to hurry away. It was Sylvia Keepsake. Moving quickly, he went over to the tree, but Sylvia had already vanished through a side gate and when he tried to follow, he could only see a curving pathway, deserted in both directions. He went back to the tree, where Bryars was standing. Something in the branches had caught her attention. About a dozen naming labels had been attached to twigs. Nyquist read one of them: *Sister Silence*. He reached up to examine each in turn, but they all said the same thing: *Sister Silence, Sister Silence, Sister Silence*. Perhaps Sylvia of the Woods had left the messages here as offerings for the dead and the grieving. He looked at one last label: *Sister Silence*. He pulled it from the twig and handed it to Professor Bryars.

"Who is Sister Silence?"

Bryars explained, or tried to explain: "Hilda's maiden name..."

"Yes... What was it?"

"Keepsake."

"She is Sylvia's...

"Yes."

He stepped close and asked clearly, "Sylvia is Hilda's sister?"

"Yes."

Nyquist looked away, back across the graves of centuries past; and he thought about the case as it lay before him, set out over the last six days, one clue leading to another, or leading away from each other.

Hilda Keepsake. Sylvia Keepsake.

Bryars stepped even closer and said, "On the same day Hilda lost her voice, Sylvia started on her labeling. Words are taken from one person, while the other has a surplus of them, and must expel them into the world, by the renaming of objects. I believe both afflictions are part of the same curse."

"The curse being?"

"Perhaps a first attempt at summoning Creeping Jenny. Now Sylvia is trying to cure her sister, to place words in her mouth, this time asking the demon for forgiveness."

"Of course! Of course…"

"What is it?"

"Something Nigel Coombes said to me before, about the person to blame taking charge of the spell. He was talking about Sylvia."

"Right. Sylvia, who gave his wife a new name, and this led…"

"It led to Gladys Coombes killing herself. Or at least, that's what everyone around here believes!" Now he had it, and his mind turned over and over, as a simple truth struck him. "Because Sylvia started this, Nigel really thinks she can finish it. That she can reverse the spell in some way."

They set off across the bridge to the high street. The funeral party had retired to the pub for the wake. Nyquist looked into the lounge bar. It was a quiet and desolate affair; all words held back by grief and embarrassment and Saint Hetta, combined. He couldn't imagine it would last for very long.

Bryars followed as he went upstairs to his room. He would gather together his few things, his clothes, his suitcase, and transfer them to the professor's house. The two of them would hole up there until this day was done. But his room had been taken over: he saw hundreds of labels hanging down from the ceiling, the lamps, the mirror, the sink, the bed frame. The floor was littered under his feet with the same white cards. They fluttered from the window frame, and they covered his bed, and they were tagged to his shirt and trousers in the wardrobe. His suitcase was filled with them, to the brim. And every label said the same thing.

Exhibit 149. Exhibit 149. Exhibit 149. Exhibit 149. Exhibit 149. Exhibit 149. Exhibit 149. Exhibit 149. Exhibit 149. Exhibit 149. Exhibit 149.

Here was the final proof. Sylvia Keepsake was the fifth member of the committee, perhaps the leader of it. And she was drawing him on, needing Nyquist's involvement – willing or otherwise – to bring the ritual to its culmination.

They walked downstairs. Once they were safely at Bryars's house, it became obvious that the professor was suffering from tiredness or something more. They huddled together at the table. Her eyes were closed, her thoughts far away. He could not reach her. These two people, this room – he felt he was sitting in a dugout in a war, a kitchen battlefield. And then Bryars leaned over, even closer than before, and she brushed his ear with her lips and spoke in a voice that was almost all breath.

"The people involved in this will want to complete their task quickly, I think."

He whispered back, "I agree. The time draws near."

"But today belongs to Saint Hetta. Nothing can be completed."

"Not until midnight."

"And then…"

"And then they will take their chances."

Bryars agreed with him. But her face turned away from his.

He asked her, "What is it?"

She looked back. Her eyes were dark and glistening as she spoke.

"I have seen Creeping Jenny." Whispering, whispering.

"Ever since this thing planted itself in me, I have seen her face in my mind, and felt her breath on my skin."

Bryars rubbed at her forearm, where the tendril was attached.

"She's creeping up on me, just like in the fables I was told, as a child. I am meant to be a part of your story, John, yet I don't want to be. I want only to be alone."

She stopped, and blinked, and wet her lips with her tongue. And then she rolled up her sleeve and revealed the growth on her arm.

"John, will you cut this thing out of me?"

Nyquist didn't reply. There were arguments to be made against the act, but none ruled over the woman's distress and pain. And most of all he didn't want her involved in this, or hurt by it. He found a bottle of whiskey in a cupboard and ordered her to drink, and to drink again, as quickly as she could. It was an easy task for her. Meanwhile, he turned on the gas stove and held a steak knife in the flame for a few minutes. Nothing was said; nothing could be said. He could hear Bryars slurping at her glass. He took the bottle of whiskey off her and poured a generous amount over the tendril and the patch of skin from which it emerged. At the last moment Saint Hetta came into his mind and tried her best to make him only half complete the task. But he dismissed her with the last of his resolve. And then without any warning, he dug the blade into the flesh. The alcohol burned away with a hiss.

Blood flowed. Creeping Jenny screamed.

Professor Bryars passed out.

Half an hour later he had cleansed the wound with hot water, bound the arm with a bandage and tended to her as best he could, putting her to bed. The severed tendril writhed around on the kitchen table. He picked it up with a pair of tongs and held it over the gas flame until it shriveled away into a blackened shred. The smoke stank to high heaven and made him want to gag, but he kept on until every last particle had burned away.

She will not have me, nor anyone alongside me.

He set off from the house. It was difficult making progress, for as the day progressed, his body and mind were being controlled more and more. He felt that Hetta was angry with him, because of his denial. It took all of his will power to keep the task in mind.

The door to the community center was open and he went inside, expecting to see a welcoming party. But the hallway was empty. He went to the door in the side of the stage and made his way through the storage area below, into the Hoxley Museum and Art Gallery. Along the corridors, past the display cases, the exhibits, all in darkness, no lights working, his hands reaching out on each side to seek guidance. In this way he reached the room of masks, and beyond that the door with its painted sign. *Exhibit 149*. Here he had met Madelyn Arkwright. Another woman waited for him now. Sylvia of the Woods stepped close and she tested his expression for weakness, saw a little, enough to allow her to grin and to lean forward, her voice kept low: "Mr Half Written in Blood. You're still alive. Good." She was close enough for the words to form and be heard clearly. He could smell her breath, the stench of forest and wood smoke, and glue and crayon wax. He was sickened by it, but he had to press on.

"Sylvia..." And suddenly he didn't know what to say. His thoughts were broken, his words also. His tongue moved aimlessly. Saint Hetta held him bound, but he tried again with a great effort. "I am looking for my… father. I believe you know where…"

"He's nearby. Very close."

"Show me…"

"First, you must partake. Are you willing?"

Sylvia held in her hand a twig of the myre tree. She plucked a white berry from it, and then a second. "One, two. Just enough. Enough to slow you down, not to kill. Eat! And you will see your father, I promise you."

Trying not to think about the act itself, Nyquist quickly took the berries from her and placed them in his mouth. He saw them as tickets to another land, one way only. His teeth broke the skin of the fruit and the juice burst on his tongue. It had a bitter taste.

He fell forward into darkness, a darkness filled with sleep and dreams and the hours passing, and even his dreams were stunted, incomplete, and the strange visions that passed before his eyes were never quite visions, for he was never quite asleep, never awake, never settled, always moving, stopping, edging along, pulled up short, dragged back by Saint Hetta, and yet he was being pushed forward and manhandled, shoved through a doorway, or led softly through the doorway, he could not tell one from the other, violence from tenderness, he could not distinguish movement from stasis. And yet despite having no hope of moving forward, he did move forward, until the darkness completed itself.

The moonsilver flowed along his veins.

AGENTS OF BODILY HARM

In the endless hours, in the depths of his long sleep, in the cold black pool of his capture, in the fold upon fold upon fold of the void, he lay there and told the story to himself, a story set in a nightmare world of his own creation, himself and the swan with two necks and the tangled embrace of Creeping Jenny and his father's ghost taking over the body of a living man. And then even these dream-formed images were taken from him as the drug worked on his system, slowing him down almost to a standstill until only his voice remained, repeating a few words over and over.

Written in blood is written in blood is written in blood…

And the time moved on without him.

And Saint Hetta sat upon his chest and waited.

And the people gathered in the room around him, waiting, one, two, and three.

And the moonsilver sang its silver song of sleep.

And the village went on with its business outside this room, this building.

And the day went on into dusk into night into quiet into silence.

And the voices called to him, whispering, asking him to wake.

And he listened, he listened from afar.

And he slept, not wanting to respond.

And they called to him.

And he slept, he slept on.

And they called to him endlessly, a chant of loving care, as though they loved him, and cared for him, until he could do nothing more than crawl his way back from the dark pool he had settled in, dragging his body from the depths and reaching up towards the noise, the sound his tormentors made, the whisperers, and so he came crawling forth, dragging himself across concrete to get there, to reach the moment, this moment, this very moment, when he could pull himself at last from the black pull of the drug's embrace.

Moonsilver, Lady Moonsilver, deliver me.

And this time his prayer was answered.

Nyquist woke up.

His eyes were still closed, but he could hear voices, three voices, a conversation. They each spoke one word at a time, at the beck and call of the day's saint, and yet working together they created a new meaning.

He's...

Awake...

See...

He's...

Moving...

Slowly...

Don't...

Not yet...

It's not...

Time...

Not yet...
Wait until...
Midnight...
A few more...
Minutes...
To go...
Until...

Nyquist tried to concentrate, to get himself fixed.

Where was he?

On the floor, curled up.

Yes. Like this, here I am. Arms wrapped around my body, legs tucked in.

He unwound himself from the folded shape, only now daring to open his eyes.

A further darkness.

Concrete floor, dust, a spider moving close to his face, a shard of glass.

A room, dimly lit, a candle or two flickering.

Shadows dancing on the wall.

He twisted around to see the room as a whole, but his movement was halted as a pair of strong hands grabbed him from behind and held him still. Pain shot through him. He was forced into one position only, and from there he could see two women talking, but their faces could not be made out, it was too dark and his eyes were still caught halfway in sleep, in the moonsilver's black dream from which he had barely yet arisen.

Now one of the women came towards him.

It was the doctor.

She bent down and stroked at Nyquist's face gently and he

reacted to her touch in fear but he couldn't move away. His limbs and neck were heavy, carrying great weights. He could not lift himself into the world anymore.

Now his captors were standing in a huddle, talking with their heads bowed close so as to make one creature of their bodies. He could not hear what they were saying, only the hiss of sibilants. But his eyes adjusted and he saw them all as they parted: Doctor Higgs, Nigel Coombes and Sylvia Keepsake.

The doctor was working at a table. Nyquist could not see what she was doing. It scared him. He tried to stand up, to reach forward, but it was hopeless, his arms and legs flailed helplessly, and he heard glass breaking, and a hollow knocking sound. He was surrounded by objects. He saw them now: small bottles, hundreds of them on the floor of the cellar. They clattered against each other, giving off a hollow sound. He recognized them.

The Penny Bloods from the museum.

The doctor came forward once more and this time she was holding something in her hand, a syringe. Seeing this, Nyquist tried to cry out. But his lips were slack, his tongue too slow to move.

Coombes held him firmly from behind.

The doctor bent down and whispered, "In order to attract Guinevere from her slumber we have to entice her. And it seems that you, John, you are the thing she desires, your crazy messed up life. We did not expect such an outcome, not at all. But how sweet it must be. How sweet. To be capable of such enchantment."

Her breath warmed his face, her mouth pressed against his ear. It was sickening, such a close wet contact, but only by this method could she speak.

"I have extracted samples from all three-hundred and sixty saints, from blood and dust and sludge, whatever might be found in the bottles, no matter how old or how rotten, and all for your pleasure, John. Yours alone." Higgs's voice was a soft hush. "Surely, surely now Guinevere will call upon us, tempted by such a thing – a body in which all the saints are contained. All of their stories, all at once."

And with that, she pressed the point of the needle against the soft skin of his neck and pressed forward.

He felt no immediate effect, only a slight twinge. It was quickly numbed.

"My father… where is he?"

"Soon." The doctor held him for a while longer, as the drug took hold. "Guinevere is close, very close, living in the creature we have made for her, from two beings, one alive, one dead, one of flesh and one of spirit."

And then Higgs stood up and moved away, to join the others at the wall. They were all watching him. Watching as Nyquist got to his feet and held his balance, unsteadily, his arms reaching out on both sides, hoping for support. There was none. His eyes were half closed, his body was trembling all over, his brow and palms were covered in sweat. He swayed from side to side. For the first time he saw the circle they had drawn on the floor all around him, and the four objects placed at the cardinal points: the gun, the cup, the coin, the book: from each a green tendril rose and reached over towards him. He wondered which he should step towards first, for all of them were equally tempting. And he wondered about Maude Bryars, and what they would have done with her, if he hadn't cut the tendril from her flesh. It was the last good clear thought he had. His mind started to wander, and the room to blur in his sight. He circled around on the spot, seeking a way out, any direction but onwards, but everything was bound to him, all particles, all dust, the people, the walls of crumbling plaster, the rough floor, the man who sat slumped in the corner of the room. Nyquist stopped moving, he tried to focus. How many people were present? He had to concentrate, to count them off, one by one. Higgs, Coombes, yes, who else? Sylvia Keepsake, yes. Three people in the room… no, no that was wrong, there was himself, he didn't count himself, himself, John Nyquist. Four people in the room, yes. That was right. No, no. Wrong. One more. One more person was here, he was sure of it! He tried to stay still, to hold his sight on a single part of the room, over in the corner where the fifth person waited, sitting against the wall, a face covered by a hood, hands tied before him, a man, an older man, who was it? Nyquist stumbled forward. He dropped to his knees and he read the label that hung around the man's neck on a piece of thread: *Exhibit 149*. He removed the man's hood and he saw the face clearly and recognition passed between them: yes, he knew this man, he knew this person, this face was his father's face, yes, he saw it now, quite clearly and he reached out for him, for his father, and they almost touched, his fingers almost on the skin, the face, the cheeks and brow, almost, and he almost spoke, but something pulled him back, Saint Hetta perhaps, or the moonsilver or the effect of the saints, he could feel them now, growing within him, taking him over all at once, and he was confused, so very confused by what was happening, so many different feelings all at once, pulling this way and that, and he couldn't stop any of them, not one saint, and from every part of his body and soul he felt them calling to him, giving their orders, yes, he could feel them, as one saint made him silent and another

made him long for the outdoors, and one froze him in place for
seven seconds exactly before another made him shudder and
jerk about like a madman, and another saint made him shriek
in terror as the veil of daylight was torn aside and another
made him calm and then one more made him long for
yesterday, to live in peace within his mother's care, but another
saint closed his eyes and would not let him open them and he
now moved about the cellar, blind, blind for a moment of panic
before another saint made his fret come back to life, at last, yes,
of course, the fret of life and knowledge, the perfect map of
mist, the sparkle map of the village showing exactly where he
was beneath the museum and he reached out for the fret in
gratitude and saw his hand wreathed by the mist and then torn
from the mist as another saint took over to make him fall to his
knees and eat the bugs on the floor, the spiders, the lice, he
chewed on them and another saint made him whisper, whisper,
and then he had to shout out loud and then he had to dance
and then to bow his head in supplication, and then to say his
own name over and over and then to fall asleep where he
stood, on his feet, to sleep for a second only and then to wake
just before he fell to the floor and then he did fall to the floor
in pain and his hands reached for his own face to tear the saints
from his body, the penny bloods, he scratched madly at his skin
and at his neck, his bare arms, hoping to reach a vein where he
could suck the poison out, to free himself, but there was no
freedom, not now, not with the saint of moving backwards
taking charge of him, and next he had to sing, to sing out, to
sing out until his throat ran dry, singing of love to a goddess
long dead, long buried, but still he had to sing, to sing in silence,
in darkness, under moonlight, moving sideways, trying to fly,
trying to lose himself, haloed by moths, by ghosts, by words,

alongside wrens and sparrows that landed on his arms and helped him to sing, to cry, to dance alone in the middle of a field, a field he couldn't reach and it pained him so, to not be able to follow the saint's instruction until he was freed from that need by yet another saint and now all he had to do was crawl on his hands and knees and act like a dog snuffling at the dirt, and then he was living inside another person's head and she spoke to him, this person, saying *My name is Madelyn Arkwright, how do you do?* and he spoke back to her and found a moment's respite as she lived for him, and took his pain for him but then he was cast out from there, from Madelyn's head and he was in the cellar once more, alone in his circle, circling, trying to find his father, that huddled shape in the corner, that face, but Saint Hetta still ruled him, he could not get there, and the three hundred and sixty saints ruled him, and the moonsilver ruled him, and he could not reach the thing he hoped for, longed for, the touch of the hand, and he could only yearn to wear a mask and call himself Edmund Grey and to walk along beside his sister Alice and then to tear the imagined mask away and know himself to have no name at all but to be without meaning, to be empty, a void, hollowed out, helpless, and then he had to tell himself jokes, one after the other, oh there was no end to it, he laughed with delight until his sides ached and now the saints were repeating themselves, often operating two or three at a time and so he was silently shouting dancing frozen howling purring flapping his arms birdlike and then reversing shivering masking weeping falling crawling mewling mauling caterwauling over and over all at once and then slowing right down to a barest minimum of human life and then Madelyn spoke to him once more saying, *stay, stay here, stay with me here inside, here, stay here, John, stay with me, stay here don't go, don't leave me*, and he did stay, he found himself alone inside the room inside the head of Madelyn Arkwright, and she said to him, *all you have to do is wait for midnight, that's all, listen, listen, Hetta will let you go then, can you hear the church clock chiming for you*? and he did hear it, the first chime of midnight, and then the second, and he was pulled back into the cellar, into the circle where one tendril after another reached out for him, four of them altogether, each burrowing its way into his flesh, and the cup, the gun, the book and the coin all drifted around him in a vision, with the pages of the book flapping their wings in the air, and his father was there beside him, waiting for him as the fourth and the fifth chimes sounded, and he reached out and saw that his father's face was changing, the skin shifting, his eyes bulging, and Nyquist wanted to scream and he did scream because that moment's saint allowed him to scream, made him scream, urged him to scream, as the bells chimed on, counting, counting, and his father was transformed into another being, a creature made entirely of green tendrils, hundreds of them, thousands of them all tangled together, as the ninth and the tenth chimed out, each tendril reaching out to engulf him, to pull him forward, to drag him down into the soil the deep the seeds the root the trunk, the branches the leaves the buds and the flowers, and the twelfth chime rang out as the dirt and the bark and petals closed over him and for a moment all he saw was darkness.

He could smell the earth.

He could hear a slithering sound.

He didn't know which way to turn, but when he reached out his hands touched at one wall, then another, close to, and a third, each made of closely packed earth with roots and plant fibers. It was suffocating. But the fourth way was open. He squeezed through a narrow passageway and came to a door. There was just enough light here for a sign to be read: *Please knock*. He did so and a voice from within bade him enter. The door opened on a small room with a table and two chairs at the center, below a shaded lamp. The walls were made from the tendrils of green, all writhing about, tightly packed, knotted in coils, and the floor and the ceiling the same. Their movements could only just be seen in the dim light, and their sound was monstrous, a constant slithering and hissing noise.

Sitting at the table was a man. His face was not yet visible, not until Nyquist stepped forward and sat down himself. Now the lamplight fell on the other man's face.

"My son. You got here."

Those few words.

Nyquist started to sob. He couldn't catch his breath. It was entirely unbidden, a simple reaction of the body and the heart. His father handed him a handkerchief and he used this to wipe his face, and in this process, the wiping of tears, he found a voice at last, a weak broken voice.

"I'm sorry. I'm sorry it took me so long."

His father nodded, and smiled. "That's alright. We're here now. I knew you'd make it. I knew you'd find me. Well, I was hoping so."

"I don't... I don't know what to say."

His father laughed gently "No. Neither do I. Not really." But he reached across the table and took his son's hand. Nyquist stared at this exact point of contact. He felt young again, a boy almost.

"Well then, lad, did you bring anything for me?"

"I'm not sure what you mean?"

"Anything? Anything at all?"

"Oh. Oh yes."

He had a bag with him, an old-fashioned shopping bag, the kind his mother used to own. He hadn't noticed until now. Nyquist reached into bag and drew out the objects it contained, one by one, naming them as he did so.

"There's a teacup. A revolver... and a book of birds."

His father was pleased. "*Auberon's Guide*. I passed that on to you, and you brought it back to me. Guinevere follows the strangest pathways, wending her way."

Nyquist took the last item from the bag. "A coin. A half crown."

The four objects lay in a row on the table. Each of them was now clean, free of any tendrils. Unbound.

His father looked at each in turn and then said, "There should be a fifth item."

"Not an item. A person."

"Yes, that makes sense. A sacrifice might be needed."

"That can't happen. I severed the connection."

His father looked at him with a curious expression. "Ah well, we will make do, no doubt. If not that person, some other..." He made an effort and managed to bring a smile to his face. Then he picked up the half crown. "Charles II. An interesting choice."

"Why?"

"The king in exile." He spun the coin on the tabletop and it continued to spin, gathering light from above. "We have until this coin winds down to a stop, one side or the other. And then a decision will be made. Do you understand?"

"No."

His father nodded. "It doesn't matter. Not until it stops spinning."

"Why did you leave me? I was only a child."

It was a sudden question, and it took a while for an answer to come. "I could not bear life. The looks on people's faces, and most of all, on your face. I felt such guilt for your mother's death. It overwhelmed me. And so, I thought I might bring her back. I had heard tales of the land of Dusk…"

"You have to tell me."

His father looked at him with such pain, it was almost unbearable. "There is so little time, John."

"I know. I understand."

Despite saying this, he could feel his fingernails scraping at the tabletop. Nyquist had too many thoughts in his head, all of them playing against each other. Love. Hate. He dug up splinters. The table had many such marks, the signs of despair left by other travelers in other times.

And then his father said, "My son, I died in 1939."

The words brought silence to the room. The two men looked at each other, one in his fifties, the other in his thirties. Between them on the table the half crown was spinning at the same rate, with no sign of slowing down. Some further energy had taken it over. And despite everything he should be feeling, the sight of the coin made Nyquist joyful, a rare and strange emotion: to have these few minutes together, surely that was a good thing!

Nyquist wanted to ask for the truth, but the words were difficult to find and he faltered. He looked on, waiting, and in the end had no need to speak. For his father picked up the book of birds and flipped through the pages idly, one after another, as he told his story.

"I moved through the fields of Dusk, seeking refuge in the mists. It is a desolate stretch of land, but there are some who make their lives on the edgelands, a few, people like myself, who wish to escape from the known world. I fell in with a tribe of fellow strugglers, who had made a camp beside a canal, in an old railway yard. We lived in sheds and old caravans, and hunted rabbits and birds, and the stranger creatures who prefer those parts. In that world of half seen things and mystery, I made my life. But the pain would not go away. Every day I ventured further from the camp, deeper into the Dusk, having heard stories all my life that the mists contain the spirits of the dead. I was seeking your mother's ghost."

He looked up from the book. His face was haggard in the lamplight.

"I will sound foolish to you, I know that. And no doubt cruel, but there it is. Those were my feelings."

"But you failed?"

"Yes."

The coin spun around and around on the tabletop. Was there a slight tremble to it? Nyquist's father saw this and a look of worry came over him. He tore a page from the book. The sound it made was almost painful to the ears, like the book was crying.

He continued, "Not many live long in Dusk. I lasted four years. The perpetual fog got in my lungs and I fell ill. Others had suffered from the same affliction, and I was told that soon I would die, unless I left those parts, and returned to the city." His eyes flickered. "I did try, my son. I made it to the borderline, where Dawn's light fades into the roads of Day, where the fog merges with clean air. But I could not take another step. You would be twelve years old by now, and I had no way of knowing where you were, or how you were doing. And the thought of returning to our house, and finding it unoccupied – or worse still, taken over by another family – well, it filled me with dread."

Nyquist told him, "I did alright, Dad. I made my way."

"Yes, yes, I can see that. You were always strong, and resilient."

"I lived with other families. One of which, the McGregors, were kind to me."

His father nodded and smiled. He looked at the torn out page in his hand and started to read aloud from it: "*Jackdaw. Black plumage with a gray nape... Their song is a squeaky chyak-chyak. A skilled flyer, able to tumble and glide through the air.*" He raised his eyes from the book. "That is useful, yes. A good flyer. That will be needed."

He rolled the page into a tiny ball of paper.

"Do you remember when I used to read to you? At night, before you went to sleep?" Nyquist said that he did. "Good, good. I'm glad you remember."

The coin was drifting from side to side, around its central axis.

His father spoke with difficulty. "We need one more page, I think, for our purposes. But you can choose. Can you think of a bird that flies high, son?"

"I don't know..."

"Think back! You read *Auberon's* over and over, from cover to cover, when you were a child."

The answer came freely. "The lark?"

"The skylark! Yes. A good choice, it flies at the very peak of the heavens. Beautiful. Here, you do it for me."

Nyquist took hold of the book and sought out the correct page: *Alauda arvensis*. He tore it out and scrunched it up and rolled it into a ball.

His father continued with his tale.

"I spent a few hours on the border and then returned into Dusk. I had heard of a certain pool where those about to die might gather, and rest awhile. It was not far from our encampment, a few miles, but I was exhausted by the time I arrived there. I was alone. And I sat down at the side of the pool and I looked over into the water. I was very ill by that point, and could hardly take a breath without feeling a terrible pain. I longed to die. I *longed* for it. And when I saw my reflection, I knew the time was near, for I looked old, far older than I was, as old as I now look to you, my son. And then…"

He shivered, and held his hand to his mouth.

Nyquist waited, without saying a word.

The half crown spun around, slowing now, slowing down.

His father picked up the coronation teacup.

"And then, even as I looked upon myself, I saw myself fading away. *Drifting* away. My reflection moved on the black water and would soon be out of my grasp. And I panicked, thinking I had made a terrible mistake, for I needed to live, I wanted to live! My hand groped in the water trying to keep hold of what I once was, but the face slipped away through my fingers, as water must, as water always does."

He turned the teacup in his hand, and he spoke as from a great distance.

"The pool was empty, moonless, no longer a mirror. And I felt my life flowing away. I collapsed at the side of pool and lay there, half in the water, half out."

He brought the teacup down with a sudden force, smashing it against the tabletop.

Nyquist flinched back in his chair.

The bone-china shards lay scattered about, one containing the handle, another one half of Queen Elizabeth's face. His father picked this one; it had a lethal looking point to it. He said, "It might still be there, my body, rotten to the bone, picked clean by ravens and crows. Or perhaps it has been moved on. Maybe my fellows in the camp buried me, with a few prayers for my deliverance. I know not."

The half crown was no longer a blurred shape. It was waving at an angle back and forth, and both sides could now be seen, heads and tails.

"My spirit drifted home, held within my reflection. Back to the source, from which our family first arose. To this place, this village. I was called here by Guinevere Clud, who reigns over all who are trapped in limbo. Creeping Jenny, as she is known. Her body surrounds us." He gestured to the walls, the ceiling. "All three of us, caught halfway between life and death."

"Three of us?" Nyquist asked.

"Yes, of course. For I am double in nature. Mr Thomas Dunne resides within me. I have possessed him, in order to live again. And for this reason, I will take on the jackdaw's wings. And those of the skylark– uh."

The statement, simple as it was, brought on a vicious reaction in the man's face. His eyes widened in fear and his mouth tightened in an open shape so that his teeth were on view, set hard against each other, top and bottom. His hands clenched into fists. He was struggling against some inner force, that's all Nyquist could think. And his father's expression changed again, and another man's face was briefly seen, taking over the features. This other man screamed out in pain, which made George Nyquist scream in turn. Two mouths screaming, slightly out of sync. It looked like one man was trying to *climb* out of other, and it made Nyquist sick with fear.

"Father…"

The slightest gesture on Nyquist's part, the merest touch, was enough to dispel the other from view, and his father's face returned to normal. He stared ahead, seemingly at his son, but his eyes looked far deeper than that, and further away.

The half crown spun around its course, losing speed with every rotation.

The father looked down at the coin. He struggled to speak. "We don't have long. So please, John… hold out your hand."

Nyquist did so. His father used the sharpest point of the china shard to cut into his own palm, and then into his son's. They rubbed their hands together.

"Our friend will need this blood. For the journey back."

For the first time Nyquist understood what his father was saying, what he was planning. He wanted to speak out, to hold him back, to keep him at the table for a while longer, a minute or so, a few seconds even. But it was not to be. His father picked up the revolver. He checked the cylinder, noting the single cartridge in place. Then he placed the two rolled up balls of paper in the barrel of the Enfield. "One, two. Paper wings. Good. A flight back home." He placed the gun back on the table. "And now we wait."

They both looked at the coin as it spun down and finally settled in place.

"Heads. I'm so glad it came up that way, son. Which means I get to choose. By these wings, by this blood."

Nyquist felt he was eight years old again, asking his father not to leave.

Not yet... don't go... don't leave me...

"Mr Thomas Dunne does not deserve this fate. As for myself, I have been here too long, in this place of shadows. And this borrowed flesh sickens me. It really does."

He handed the revolver over to his son.

"I am sorry, my child."

It was an admittance. And it broke the moment in two. Nyquist tried to reply, to make his own confession, but the words would not come.

Their time here was through.

They looked at each other across the table.

The bulb in the lamp was flickering, stuttering. Soon it would darken.

Nyquist took up the task. He held the gun on target. It was not so different from what he'd done with Maude Bryars, when he'd freed her from Creeping Jenny's control. One slice of the knife. This was the same thing. He kept telling himself that. He kept saying, *This is the same, one quick action, a single movement of my finger. That's all.* But his hand shook terribly, and his body was covered in sweat.

"Is there another way?" he asked.

Nobody answered. Not one person at that table answered.

Nyquist brought his left hand up, to steady his right. He reminded himself that this was a double action gun; he wouldn't need to cock the hammer.

He was all set.

A simple idea came to him, a kind of prayer, a prayer made from tatters and scraps, from the blood itself, the things collected in daily battle, in war, in struggle.

I have found myself here, where I should be lost.

Take aim.

He pressed the muzzle against his father's brow. That spot where thoughts collected before they traveled into the world, and where memories were stored momentarily, before being sent on, to be forgotten.

Just there.

Close your eyes.

FLIGHT OF JACKDAW AND LARK

Through the flesh, through the muscles and the veins, through the bone of the skull. Through the brain. Through the gray matter, the web of nerves.

Through the unknown map of the head.

Through the surface of the looking glass, leaving a hole, flowerlike.

Through the contaminated waters of Birdbeck Tarn. Through the ghosts that dwell in the dark. Through the village of Hoxley-on-the-Hale, along empty streets, lanes, alleyways and cul-de-sacs.

Through the everyday horrors, desires, temptations, moments of love and regret, and all the moments beyond recall.

Through the story as it folds and unfolds, and folds again, and unfolds.

The life left behind, and the life to come.

Through the tangles of the vines and weeds underfoot, and the branches of the oak tree, Blade of Moon. Through the labels in the woodland glade, with their letters and ciphers.

Through moonglow and sunlight.

Through a locked door marked *Paradise*. Across a borderline of mist. Into flesh once more. Into dust. Powder. Blood. Splinters. Across the village green and the pond where the witches were tried and tested. Through the clouded spirits, and the names on the gravestones in the cemetery. Through his father's body: breath, whisper and shadow.

Through the weeping eyes of Creeping Jenny.

Through the words that bring us here to this point, and the words that take us away, these words...

THE POEM OF THE WOODS

There were murmurs and cries of pain in the darkness, but he couldn't tell from where they came. He groped out with a hand and felt his fingers close over the broken remains of a teacup. The edges were sharp to the touch. He was lying on the floor of the cellar, that much he knew. A woman started crying. And then she screamed; it sounded like someone was hitting her. A man spat out words of anger: "You promised me! You promised me! Where is she? You promised me!" over and over. It was chaos. Nyquist got to his hands and knees and he pulled himself along. He was drained of all energy, and each movement took an age. But he made it, he made it out of the circle and he found Thomas Dunne in the corner. A bulb burned into light overhead: it sounded like a creature suddenly finding life. Dunne's eyes held the night within them, and all that had happened. His mouth tried to form a word, a single word, but nothing good was said, nothing could be said. Not yet. There would be time for that. Nyquist helped him to his feet, but in truth they helped each other, for both were weak from the ordeal. Nyquist could see Nigel Coombes and Sylvia close by. Her face was bloody. Coombes raised his hand in a fist to strike her again, but Doctor Higgs stepped between them.

Nyquist pulled Dunne to the doorway and managed to get him into the corridor of masks. The six Tolly Men looked out on their progress, from one year to the next, down through the ages. The penny blood cabinets were empty. They moved on, finding their way to the storage room under the stage and from there to the hall. It was full dark outside. It must've been very early in the morning, but Nyquist had no sense of time at all. The two men made their way down Pyke Road. Every house was quiet, all the lights out, and not a person moved on the street but themselves, these wanderers. Nyquist needed to rest, his legs were failing him, but he had to keep on, to keep on until he reached the house of Maude Bryars. It was the only house with its windows lit up. He fell against the door, with Dunne alongside. It was opened immediately and Bryars welcomed them both inside. In the brightness of the hall Nyquist saw Thomas Dunne's face clearly for the first time and saw that his father had left this body completely, and forever, and he felt his heart break at the thought of such a thing. But then Bryars led them into the living room, where Agnes Dunne was waiting. She rose from her seat and looked at her husband in utter surprise. For a moment she could not move. His face was stricken with hurt. She wept. And then at last she stepped forward and took up Nyquist's burden for herself. Thomas fell into her arms willingly. And Nyquist collapsed.

The village slept with him.

The village dreamed and the village cried in its dreams, and laughed, and the villagers danced in their dreams around the maypole, and the old tree named Blade of Moon hung its branches over them all, in their dreams.

The next day there was no icon to be seen, not in the any window that he passed, nor in The Swan With Two Necks, when he went to pay his bill, and to pick up a few items he'd forgotten. Nigel Coombes refused to take payment. He and his daughter were sitting together in the snug, holding hands. Nyquist left them to it. He walked back to say his goodbyes to Professor Bryars. Agnes and Thomas were still there. Thomas was quiet, withdrawn, not yet fully back in the world. But Agnes and Maude fussed over him. Nyquist smiled at this. He thanked Maude for her hospitality, and the history lessons. She replied in a quiet voice, "Creeping Jenny has given me a little of her power, I think. I might weave stories together in a new way, from the past and the present."

"That's good."

Sorrow touched at him. He drew Agnes into the hallway and said, "The coroner has made his decision, about Jane Sutton, and about Ian Bainbridge. It's suicide."

"I know."

"I would leave it at that."

"I haven't yet made my mind up."

"I'm the only other person who knows the truth. And I assure you… I won't be telling anybody."

She nodded at this. Nyquist picked up his suitcase and slipped away. People were going about their everyday lives, working, shopping, chatting to neighbors, walking the dog. He noticed confusion on quite a few faces. One person was simply standing still, in a daze of indecision. It was Becca Fairclough. And he knew that today was a no saint's day: there was no required behavior. It was a strange feeling, even for him, a visitor. He missed being told what to do and was a little fearful of the choices that lay ahead.

He passed the doctor's surgery and he saw Higgs at the window, looking out. Perhaps the spell had worked for her, perhaps not. He thought of knocking on the door and speaking to her. But no, it was best to move on.

Nyquist took his leave from Hoxley-on-the-Hale.

Within a short while he was approaching Morden Wood. The shadows welcomed him. On occasion, his father's face came to him, as it was when young. A ghost in the trees. It made him think of a dream he'd had, a couple of nights ago. A dream of the dead coming to life, and being with others on the village green, and he wondered for a moment whether his parents might yet find one another.

He walked on. It was a fine winter's morning, and the upper canopy glinted with light as the sun came up. Sylvia Keepsake was taking down the labels from the branches, while her sister stood beside her, helping. Hilda Bainbridge was talking. It was quite a thing to hear. She repeated each word carefully out loud, as Hilda showed her the labels. Each word, each phrase, each name: *Witch's Knot, Scatter Seed, Aerial, Pretty Pattern, Long to Depart.* He watched them for a moment from the safety of a thicket, then he took the pathway that led to the country road, and the bus stop. It was seven minutes to nine. The road stretched away across the moors. He could see the number 16 bus approaching in the far distance, its bright red paintwork stark against the open sky, the endless fields. It dipped into and out of view as it made its progress. A pair of crows joined him on a fence. One of them cawed, the other turned a yellow eye to the sun.

Nyquist looked down at his right hand, at the palm. It was marked with a small scabbed over wound, a single line of dark red. It ached slightly. Here, a sharing had taken place. Here in the flesh, where one world ended and another began, a story had been written: by these wings, with this blood.

EPILOGUE

THE SOMNAMBULIST

Six weeks later, on a Friday afternoon, John Nyquist was getting ready to finish work early when the bell to his office rang. He opened the door and saw Teddy Fairclough standing there. For a good few moments the private eye didn't know what to say, he was so surprised. But he asked the young man inside, and offered him a drink. They drank beer together. It was odd to see Teddy drinking alcohol, but it wasn't the only thing that had changed: despite his ragged clothes and his dirty neck and uncut hair, he looked more confident, his mood entirely suited to the new decade. It was late January, 1960. Things were changing, especially for the young. Nyquist asked to hear his story.

"It all started on Saint Yorick's Day. Do you remember that one?"

"You'll have to remind me."

"It's the day that we all miss, that we sleep through."

"Of course."

Teddy would not keep still. He paced the room. "Well, I woke up. I woke up early. I was standing on the green, and the entire village was there with me, all gathered together. I couldn't believe it."

"I was there?"

"Everybody was." He came to a halt. "It was so strange. People were fully dressed, moving about, but I think I was the only one awake. All the other villagers were sleepwalking."

"The effect of the saint?"

"Yes. But it only lasted a minute or so, my wakefulness. I kept slipping back into sleep, into a dream. And whether awake or otherwise, I decided to walk away. The idea just took me over!" His eyes brightened. "It was twenty past six in the evening: the church clock told me. I took the road that led to the woods. It was a pathway I knew by heart, from years of running wild as a kid. I remember the glade of labeled trees. I walked past *Best Ever Twig* and *Waiting for Springtime* and *Snapped in Two*. And here I must have reached the limits of Saint Yorick's power, for the hypnotic effect fell away. I was now fully awake."

The young man paused. He took a breath. His focus had left Nyquist's office; instead he was staring at the far-off trees of Morden Wood.

"I carried on walking and was soon at the country road, near the bus stop. I knew there would be no bus until the morning, but I waited there, giving myself an hour's leeway. If nothing happened by then, I'd go back home. That was my promise. I tried to thumb a lift. Only three cars went by. The first two ignored me, the third one stopped. I knew the driver. It was Mr Ainsworth, the solicitor from Lockhampton who had taken my father's court case, and he was happy to give me a lift. I had enough money in my pocket to purchase a train ticket, and a little left over. The five pound note you gave me really helped."

"Good. I'm glad."

"Mr Ainsworth helped me out. At Lockhampton station I boarded the first train heading south. Since then I've been wandering, taking on work where I could find it."

Nyquist finished his drink. "What about your family? Becca? She was worried about you."

"I know. But I sent her a letter, telling her I was alright. *Not born to follow*, this is what I told her. Do you understand what I'm saying?"

"I do." Nyquist recalled the name that Sylvia of the Woods had given Teddy.

"But it's so difficult. I never know where to go next. And the saints… they keep calling to me, asking me to obey." His face screwed up in pain.

Nyquist had to wonder: this young man had managed to escape Hoxley, the town of his birth. Not many could say such a thing. And the struggle continued.

"What do you want of me, Teddy?"

"I don't know. A job, maybe?"

Nyquist laughed. "I'm not sure…"

"I'll do anything."

"Well, there's always odds and ends to be done."

"I don't care what it is. I just want to work."

"Sit down."

Teddy did so. He looked at Nyquist with gratitude. And then his eyes downturned. He was on the edge of tears.

"What is it? What's wrong?"

"I can't believe I've made it this far."

"No, neither can I. I didn't think you had it in you."

"Sometimes…" His voice broke.

"Yes?"

"Sometimes I think I'm still back there, in the woods. That I haven't yet woken up from Yorick's spell." Again he paused.

"I know, son. It's difficult to say, to admit to."

Teddy blinked rapidly. "Even now… I feel like I'm still moving on, walking in my own darkness."

Nyquist nodded. He knew the feeling well. And so he spoke kindly.

"Only in the sleepwalker's eyes…"

It was a poem his father had taught him. It rose up from memory.

Only in the sleepwalker's eyes, only in the things he believes he is touching, holding, gathering, when his hands are empty: there is truth.

ACKNOWLEDGEMENTS

First and foremost, thanks to Bridget Penney, who helped with the story from the beginning, and without whose notes and insights, this novel would be far less than it is.

All the good people at Angry Robot Books – Eleanor, Gemma, Sam, Etan, and especially my editor Paul Simpson, for bringing the book into the world.

Michelle Kass, Russell Franklin, and the team at my agent's office, for their advice and support over the years.

As always, I've plagued a number of friends for feedback on ideas in progress: Vana, Steve, Grant, Karen, Paul. Thank you for your input.

Catch up on the Nyquist Mysteries...

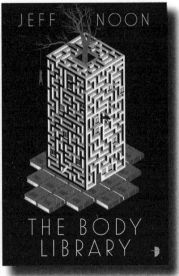